THE NORTH FORK

D1521618

JUDY AND LYNN HANCOCK

All poems in the book are from *A Child's Garden of Verses*
by Robert Louis Stevenson unless otherwise noted.

Cover: U.S. Geological and Geographical Survey
Topography
Colorado, Mt. Jackson Quadrangle
Surveyed in 1907-1909

ISBN -13-9781086651287

We do, however, acknowledge with great fondness the Dearhamer family who owned the Meredith store and operated the post office from the late 1800s until Ruedi Reservoir's construction forced the store's relocation in the 1960s.

TABLE OF CONTENTS

FALL, 1909

As she entered the cavernous station, loud voices announcing trains echoed throughout the chamber. Intimidated by milling crowds, she wished she were with a friend. Immigrant families huddled on benches, cord-wrapped bundles held tightly on their laps, were on their way to destinations and fates unknown. Vague memories of her family coming to Colorado from Canada, her pregnant mother shepherding a sickly husband and five small children flashed in her mind, and her heart went out to these travelers in search of better lives.

While standing on the train platform, she realized how caught up in anticipation of adventure she had been, how little she had considered the distance from home, and how completely alone she would be. Maybe Father had been right.

The ad on the school bulletin board had intrigued her. Several friends were going to small towns on the plains or in the foothills, but none of her classmates were going across the mountains as she was doing. In her imagination she saw herself there, becoming independent and self-reliant, discovering inner strengths without the support or burden of family and friends. Filled with enthusiasm, she sent her application. When the letter offering the position came and she told her father what she had done, he was upset. Why hadn't she talked this over with him? Why would she want to go so far from home? Hadn't the boys' misadventure taught them anything? She had no idea about the kind of people who lived there. If she needed help, who would come to her aid? His questions were pertinent, his concerns legitimate. She hadn't given this enough thought.

They had not discussed it again. Despite his objections she stubbornly determined to live with the consequences, now she was twenty and capable of earning a living.

When the time came to leave, her sisters helped carry her trunk and canvas satchels to the streetcar, kissed her, and waved teary goodbyes. At Union Station, a porter moved her trunk and bags to the train where she would board Denver & Rio Grande Railroad to go, illogically, it seemed to her, south to Colorado

Springs where she would transfer to Colorado Midland Railroad that would carry her north and west to Meredith, Colorado. She was eager to see mountain towns where mining had changed the countryside.

Massive steaming engines pulling into and out of the station, the slow chuffing sounds, rods moving between huge iron wheels awed yet comforted her with their power. Showing her ticket to the conductor, she boarded. She had ridden trains to and from Greeley going to school with three friends and their companionship had insulated her from the anxiety of travel. Slowly leaving the station, the train picked up speed as it entered open country, moving fast, the way trains had gone to Greeley. Being alone and not distracted, she felt how rapidly she was leaving all that was dear to her. She recalled Robert Louis Stevenson's poem she had memorized and recited as quickly as possible as a child, but never understood as now.

> *Faster than fairies, faster than witches,*
> *Bridges and houses, hedges and ditches;*
> *And charging along like troops in a battle,*
> *All through the meadows the horses and cattle:*
> *All of the sights of the hill and the plain*
> *Fly as thick as driving rain;*
> *And ever again, in the wink of an eye,*
> *Painted stations whistle by.*
>
> *Here is a child who clambers and scrambles,*
> *All by himself and gathering brambles;*
> *Here is a tramp who stands and gazes;*
> *And there is the green for stringing the daisies!*
> *Here is a cart run away in the road*
> *Lumping along with man and load;*
> *And here is a mill and there is a river:*
> *Each a glimpse and gone for ever!*

Although she didn't have a window seat, the lady next to her pointed out interesting land features: Castle Rock, Black Forest, and Garden of the Gods' red sandstone formations. Before she expected it, the train pulled into Colorado Springs. For a girl who had never been on her own, the transfer had loomed large, filling her with dread, but the connection was on time, porters transferred her belongings, people were kind, and she soon boarded the Colorado Midland, off on the next segment of her journey.

She found her reserved seat on the aisle next to a middle-aged man who acknowledged her with a nod and crooked smile. She, too, nodded, put the bag she carried under her seat, and sat down. He turned to her, "A good day for a train ride."

"Yes." *Should I be talking to a stranger?*

"Where are you bound?"

Should I tell the truth? "Meredith. It's a small community on the Western Slope."

"You're going home?"

Why does he care? "No. I'm going to teach in their school."

"I see. *She doesn't look over sixteen.* I've been through Meredith. It's quite small."

"They have fifteen pupils." *Did I sound argumentative?*

The conductor came through checking seat assignments. The man asked if she had taught before.

Why does he want to know? "No. This will be my first year."

He nodded, "You've been to normal school?"

"Yes."

"I wish you good pupils. I've taught science in the Leadville schools for many years. We used to have more pupils, but our population keeps dropping since so many silver mines closed. Fortunately, they can still justify a science teacher."

She turned to look at him. He wore a suit, carried a valise. "Oh." Relieved they shared a profession, she relaxed.

"My wife and I are fond of Leadville so we're reluctant to leave. She's a nurse at the hospital and helped deliver most of my pupils. The town is more like family to us than community. In fact, I'm now teaching children of my first pupils."

"How nice." She hesitated before admitting, "I'm looking forward to teaching but I'm anxious about my abilities. I'll have all eight grades. Sometimes this causes me to stay awake."

He chuckled, "Roughly seven grades too many. That's why I wished you good pupils. Even more, I wish you good parents who'll support you. The kids will survive, and I reckon you will too, but you'll have moments when you aren't sure you want to.

It comes with the territory. By mid-year you'll be more comfortable."

The train pulled out of the station heading uphill toward Manitou Springs. She could hear the engine working hard as it climbed the grade. Pointing out the window as they neared Manitou, the man said, "Can you see funicular cars going up the incline?"

She leaned to look out the window, but the train entered a thicket of evergreens that obscured her view. He grimaced. "Let's trade seats when the train stops in Manitou. I've done this trip many times. You should have the window seat." The train pulled into the station, people departed, others boarded.

"Are you sure?" she asked.

"I'm sure. You need to know where you're going and where you've been."

Grateful for the window seat she thanked him. The train started and within minutes the mountain enclosed them as they went through a short tunnel. They entered and left another tunnel and began to cross a trestle that traversed a deep ravine. "Oh, my," she exclaimed, her eyes wide, "we're on a high, narrow bridge."

"Right," he winked, "roughly wide enough for a single train and not an inch wider."

The trestle crossed, she nervously watched their progress: another bridge, then another. She admitted, "I've never felt afraid of heights because I haven't been very high. It gives one a funny feeling."

"It surely does. In a couple of years you can go to the top of Daniels and Fisher tower and see how you feel about being twenty floors up," the crooked smile again.

"I imagine I won't want to lean out a window too far."

They went through six more tunnels in quick succession. "We're finished with tunnels for a while."

She frowned, "It's hard to believe this was the best way into the mountains."

"Well, the Rocky Mountains are formidable. There aren't many ways available given what a train can climb. The Denver & Rio Grande already had their route and the Colorado & Southern had another. Back in the seventies it was a building frenzy. There are three railroads that come into Leadville."

4

"So many? Have you ridden the other two?"

"Yes, but I prefer this one. It's the newest. And for you, it's the only one that goes to Meredith."

"Still, it seems like a lot of trains."

"Perhaps. The mountains are vast and the demand for resources so great, how could one imagine the day would come when there wouldn't be a need for many railroads."

"Did that change?"

"In a way. It turns out that although the mountains are vast, most don't have valuable minerals, which I imagine came as a shock to many of the railroad investors."

"Oh," she waited for him to continue.

He obliged. "Many of the silver mines closed when gold became the principal monetary standard so most of the ore shipments from this area are gone. Silver drove much of the railroad-building in this state."

"But trains are still running."

"Not as profitably."

"Will they all survive?"

"Who knows? This one is struggling in spite of the coal mines it serves. The D&RG will probably do better. It's main owner, General Palmer, worked diligently to make towns he went to desirable to tourists."

"Was he a real general?"

A skeptic. Good. "He was. Even though he was a Quaker he was a Civil War hero. He was also a strong abolitionist and felt compelled to fight, and he fought well. He was a brilliant young man who attended school only until he was fifteen, lest we teachers think we make all the difference. General Palmer died this year."

"Oh." She was thoughtful. "So many don't go beyond eighth grade."

"Alas, unfortunately true, if they get that far."

"He didn't stay a soldier?"

"No. Palmer had bigger plans. Besides the railroad, he started Colorado Springs and Manitou Springs that we just went through. The hot springs there were supposedly healing waters used by the Ute Indians."

She was quiet, thinking of how lives twist and turn, frequently not by any plan. After travelling a few miles up from Manitou, she exclaimed, "Look at that!"

"Oh, yes," the wry, crooked smile, "the Ramona Hotel. Undoubtedly the first Byzantine onion dome you've seen. Quite a spectacle out here in the wilderness, isn't it?"

"Yes, it's so large and strange."

Watching the country pass, she observed, "It seems we're climbing steeply. Will it be like this the whole way?"

"Oh, no. The trip has many ups and downs, but this is the steepest part. A relentless climb. It's called Ute Pass."

"The Ute Indians?"

"Indeed. According to early explorers, it's the pass bison used to access South Park in summers. Utes used it to bring salt out of South Park to trade in Santa Fe and Taos. Then it became a wagon road to get ore out of Leadville until they built the railroads."

They were quiet as they watched the country and small depots pass.

"See the bald mountain to your left? That's Pikes Peak."

"Really?" She was surprised it wasn't rugged, the way she imagined a peak would be. "I've read about Zebulon Pike and his expedition. Thank you for pointing it out. Do people climb to the top?"

"You don't need to. You can ride the cog railroad out of Manitou to the top or take a toll road out of Cascade where the Ramona Hotel is."

"Oh," she was disappointed. The mystery of it was gone if it were so easy to get there.

She watched rolling, grassy land dotted with evergreen trees and aspens giving way to forests in the distance. Before long they went through the small town of Divide, the end of the long climb up Ute Pass and the location of the Midland Terminal spur to Cripple Creek's gold fields.

Sounds of the working engine quieted. "It will be downhill for a while now and the fireman can rest."

She looked at him confused, "Are there firemen on the train?"

He responded to her frown, "A fireman on a train doesn't fight fires, he makes them. He's been shoveling coal all the way uphill to make steam. It's a hard job."

She thought about what that would be like, not to be able to rest when tired. "Teaching is preferable to being a fireman, I'm thinking."

He raised his eyebrows and nodded his head.

They stopped briefly at Florissant. "There are fossil beds here. It would be instructive to bring our students over." He then pointed in a general direction, "The ponderosa pines are nice."

"Which are they?"

"The tall trees. They have long needles and widely spaced branches. See? You'll probably have more spruce, Douglas fir and lodgepole pine in your area."

I thought they were all just evergreens. She started watching the shapes of trees. *They are different from each other.*

"We'll be going up the South Platte to its headwaters in South Park soon. Headwaters is a confusing term because usually a river doesn't spring from the ground in one place. In this case it becomes the South Platte after three small streams come together."

"Do you know why it's called the Platte?"

Nodding, "I do. Nebraska was its original name, an Indian word meaning 'flat water'. Frenchmen translated that to plat. The North Platte and South Platte join in Nebraska becoming the Platte River which flows into the Missouri River. You'll learn many rivers have forks describing the compass point they tend to come from."

Soon they were going uphill again. She could tell because the engine was working harder but not as hard as climbing to Divide. The South Platte flowed alongside the tracks. It wasn't the river she knew from Denver. This was much smaller. They wended their way through three tunnels in Eleven-mile Canyon on to Lake George where the canyon gave way to the openness of South Park, the river becoming smaller as they climbed.

She was surprised when they reached South Park. She wasn't sure what she expected, perhaps something more like Denver's City Park. This was wide-open space, grassland, scant trees, meander lands with little streams flowing into the river. She saw a few homesteads with cattle. She couldn't imagine the loneliness of the families living there. *Where do they buy groceries? How do they manage in winter? Where do children go to school? Is this what Meredith looks like?*

She turned to the man, "Do families live here?"

"Probably from late spring to fall. Then they gather their cattle and leave in winter because wind can be fierce here with nothing to stop it. Snowdrifts pile up against anything in the way."

She put her arms around herself without thinking, to protect against the imagined weather, "It's almost like a big bowl the way the mountains surround it."

Nodding, "A very large bowl, a thousand square miles of it. It has a sad history. Ute Indians lived here. Then the Arapaho Indians, whose culture depended on bison, left the plains following the devastation of the herds by white buffalo hunters. They came here and fought with Utes for territory. The Indians and game all lost out to the gold and silver booms followed by homesteaders and their herds of cattle."

"I think I detect sympathy for Indians."

"You do. We rode roughshod over them and their land. I have great respect for how they survived before we came."

She nodded without responding because she knew so little about what had happened, except history credited settlers for taming the West. She gazed out the window wondering if it were a better place now.

On the train rolled through Spinney, Hartzell and over Trout Creek Pass, which was higher than they had been at Divide, then back down again.

He leaned over to look out the window. "We'll be coming to Buena Vista soon. Can you see the Collegiate peaks?"

She saw a range of mountains across the wide valley, "Oh! They're dramatic. You said they're called Collegiate?"

"I've read geologists named them for their alma maters. Regardless, there is Harvard, Yale, Princeton, Columbia, and Oxford. Nine of the peaks are over 14,000' high and another ten are over 13,000'. If you like tall mountains, it's hard to beat this group."

Feeling overwhelmed with information, she sighed.

Observing her consternation, he chuckled, the wry crooked grin flashing, "I think I can feel Jessie giving me The Look." She instinctively peered over her shoulder to see whom he was talking about. He shook his head, "Jessie's my wife and she has a look she gives me when she thinks I'm being professorial.

Professorial being her way of saying I'm talking too much. If she were here, she would protect you. But alas, you're at my mercy." He winked a comical squint.

Leaving the Buena Vista station, the train descended to the Arkansas River valley then followed the river up toward Leadville, through four tunnels at Wild Horse. After trying to be quiet, Mr. Wallace pointed out Mt. Elbert, Colorado's highest peak, and its near neighbor, Mt. Massive, showing her where timberline began.

"Are we as high as we're going to get?" she asked.

"Oh, no. We'll climb steadily to Leadville and after it you'll go higher yet to get through the Divide."

"Another town named Divide?"

He shook his head, "The Continental Divide. Another tunnel at almost 11,000' in elevation."

"Oh," she sighed, weary and anxious about where Meredith might be in this wilderness.

"Then one more to go, Mallon tunnel."

Trying to be cheerful, "I've gotten fond of tunnels since we always come out the other end."

"A nice perspective. May we always come out the other end of life's tunnels, eh?"

"Yes." *Oh, please, yes.*

"Do you want me to tell you a little about Leadville or are you familiar with it?"

"I'd love to know. I appreciate your telling me."

Gratifying. I'm pleased she's more at ease. "Leadville was the second largest city in Colorado at one point with almost fifteen thousand residents. It wanted to be the capital of Colorado but lost out to Denver. It started with a gold rush but evolved into a silver and lead mining town. It was one of the largest and richest silver mining areas in the world. We had many productive mines and many miners to work them. We also had people who prospered here who weren't miners. You know of the May Company in Denver, no doubt."

"Yes. I go there to dream what it would be like to buy some of those things."

"David May got his start in Leadville as did Meyer Guggenheim," he saw that meant nothing to her, "one of the wealthiest families in America now. In its day it was a sophisticated town with two opera houses, three hospitals and a school for over one thousand pupils. I'll be leaving you at Leadville. My wife will be at the station. I hope you'll get off the train so she can meet you. She always wonders whom I've been boring." He checked to see if she were amused.

When they arrived she saw abandoned structures. "You said many people left?"

"Yes. We have about half the population we once had."

She was amazed at the elaborate train station, much the nicest she'd seen outside Denver. Mr. Wallace gathered his belongings and turned to her, "Maybe you'll tell me your name so I can introduce you."

Is this okay to do? "Josephine Carter. I'm called Josie."

"I'm Charles Wallace. I'm glad to know you." He extended his hand. She hesitated, then took it. He gave her a crooked grin.

They went into the station where Mrs. Wallace greeted him affectionately. He introduced the ladies. Mrs. Wallace seemed glad to meet her, surprising Josie with her genuine warmth. Taking Josie by the hand she asked her questions about her trip, her destination, if she were excited to teach. Josie couldn't remember meeting a stranger who was as interested in her. The conductor announced boarding. "Sometimes we make fall trips to Aspen. If we go this year maybe you'll come with us," Mrs. Wallace said.

"Aspen? The trees?"

"No, no. A town named for them." Mr. Wallace interjected. "It was called Ute City, not that Utes called it that."

Josie asked, "Did Utes live there as well as in South Park?"

"Up until around thirty years ago this was all their land. Then the discovery of silver made the land too desirable to the white man, meaning us, and they were removed."

Mrs. Wallace cleared her throat. "You're right, Jessie. Back to the trip. After Meredith the train continues down the Frying Pan River to Basalt. A spur train goes up the Roaring Fork to Aspen. It's a pretty trip when leaves turn. Aspen was a major silver mining town, much quieter now."

Mrs. Wallace peered at him from beneath her eyebrows and he acknowledged The Look with a sheepish grin. The three parted, the older ones expressing hope she would keep in touch.

"We're only over the mountain, you know. If you need help, we're just a few hours away."

Having travelled over two hundred miles from Denver, Josie had thirty miles remaining to Meredith. The train steadily ascended the valley to the west, then began to climb in earnest, the engine working hard as the grade increased. Past a pretty lake, into dense evergreens giving way to rough-hewn rock walls so close had she put her hand out the window, she felt she could touch them.

Hues of red and yellow creeping into the green foliage beneath trees delighted her. Tall flowers, bright pink against their maroon leaves crowded the tracks, shrubby green bushes bore bright yellow flowers, grasses nodded their seed-laden heads in the draft from the passing train, quaking aspens were clustered in stands among a variety of evergreens, surely some of the ones Mr. Wallace had mentioned. All the while, smoke, cinders, iron wheels clicking on track joints, made the train ever present. The constantly changing scenery was exciting with dark forests, looming mountains and sudden deep valleys below. As they neared the Busk-Ivanhoe tunnel the height, immensity, wide-open vistas, and starkness of surrounding timberline peaks thrilled her.

They would soon be entering the nearly two-mile long tunnel. Windows were to be shut and doors to the car were to remain closed to prevent smoke from infiltrating. Suddenly darkness surrounded them, engine noise filled the air as they continued to climb through the Continental Divide. Then suddenly, light again.

As soon as allowed, windows were opened to let in fresh air. The hush that fell when they entered the tunnel turned to chatter and laughter. No longer pulling up hill, the engine was quieter as it drifted its way down past Loch Ivanhoe. It was dusk when the train traversed Hell Gate, a narrow shelf of rock so high above the valley floor she felt dizzy. Descending mountains in endless curves she was aware of the immensity of the area. As darkness fell she watched for lights and rarely saw any.

On the Colorado map she kept in her lap, she tried to follow their route, but it showed a flat world. She soon lost track of where she was. The map made things look tiny compared to the country she was going through. When in Leadville, she knew she was on the Eastern Slope of the Rockies. Going through the Busk-Ivanhoe Tunnel put her on the Western Slope. Then she was lost again.

When the conductor announced the approach to Meredith she searched for the town. There were only a few lights coming from small windows and what looked like a boarding house. It was dark when the train stopped at a building, a freight-handler jumped from the train onto the platform, unloaded freight, her trunk and bag. She stepped off the train and stood alone, confused, and frightened. She looked helplessly about not knowing what to do. Bewildered by what lay before her compared to what she had pictured, she felt vulnerable. She fought her desperate urge to get back on the train. *No. I've made a promise. The train must turn around and return to Denver. I can catch it then, if this proves too awful.* Never so alone or unsure, she tried to take in where she was and what she should do. The whistle blew and the train headed down the tracks, leaving her and her baggage. Suddenly, a large, cheerful woman appeared, lantern in hand. "I'm Zona, the postmistress. You must be Josephine Carter."

Grateful, Josie took the woman's rough hand in hers, "Yes," she said, "I'm Josie," relieved someone knew who she was, and that person was a friendly woman.

"I'll finish with the freight. Come on into the store. I'll be right with you." She disappeared into the building.

Wiping her hands on a dirty apron, Zona reappeared, the same cheerful smile. "Bet you're wondering what you've gotten yourself into, huh?"

There would be no use denying it. Josie knew it must show. "Yes. I don't know what I was expecting, but it wasn't quite this." She feigned amusement so the lady wouldn't think she was being critical.

Zona laughed heartily. "Bet not. It wasn't what I was expecting either when Ott brought me here in '98."

Josie asked incredulously, "There must have been no one else here. It must have been even more primitive then." She instantly regretted saying primitive.

"Ya. The kids were one, two, and three and I was pregnant. Worst winter anyone could remember. It started snowing hard in November and didn't let up until late February. Snow so deep at the tunnel trains didn't get through from Denver for months. We had over six feet of snow around the house. It was hard going in those days, I'll tell you, but it's passable now. We've got water to the door and the house is kinda' finished and the kids are old enough to help. I feel I'm in the lap of luxury compared to what it used to be." Her outrageous laugh erupted as she slapped Josie on the back.

Josie looked at her in amazement. "Your children. They survived that winter?"

"Ya, thank God, and Ott calmed down because he was working so hard that the last one didn't come for another couple of years." She seemed so cheerful about her lot in life, Josie took heart.

Pointing out the door, into the dark, she said, "There's a little cabin for you next door to the schoolhouse. Wish you could see it."

Josie stared into the pitch blackness. *It's all by itself. There aren't any lights.* "Oh," she said, trying to be cheerful, without much conviction, "I had hoped to be in a boarding house for women."

"Well, there isn't such a thing and you wouldn't want to be in the one for the bachelors, although they might like it." Her jolly laugh wasn't shared. "The cabin's where you belong. It's a heap better than what they had when we got here. The few kids got schooled at home, if their folks could read, write, and cipher, which some of them couldn't. The women eventually got the schoolhouse built and those of us who were comfortable in English besides German, Swedish, or Italian took turns teaching the lot of them. Wasn't any more trouble than teaching our own and it was better for the kids. We put up the first teachers in our houses, a week at each then started all over again. That didn't work too well for anybody, so the men folk built the cabin for the teacher."

"I'm sure both were improvements," Josie tried to sound positive; this wasn't what she had expected. She hadn't realized things could be so backward in her state. There were telephones and even some automobiles in Denver.

"The cabin's small but gets cold in winter. Wind can come through those cracks between the logs. The men fixed it up a bit this summer, but it'll still blow through because no chink's perfect." Her laugh was disarming. "The last teacher complained about snow drifts on the floor after a storm. That got the men's attention, but she quit anyway. Said she was tired of cold feet all the time. That's when we got a new stove. The kids are supposed to keep you in wood and coal. It's part of their job. You tell me if they aren't bringing enough. I'll have Henry help get your stuff moved. Come on back to have supper with us. You can buy groceries tomorrow after you're settled." Zona yelled out the back door.

A tall, thin boy came into the store and Josie took an instant liking to him. He had Zona's friendly eyes, but he carried an oldest child's seriousness.

"This is your new teacher, Miss Carter. Grab a lantern, take her things over to her place and show her where the outhouse is. And mind your manners."

"I always mind my manners when you're around," he stated matter-of-factly. Josie hoped it was a family joke.

He grabbed one end of her trunk and tucked one bag under his lantern arm. She grabbed the other end and a satchel and they lurched down the path past the schoolhouse and around to the cabin.

"Your mother didn't tell me your name," she gasped. The exertion at this altitude took her breath away.

"Otto Heinrich, junior. I'm called Henry to keep me straight from Pa. I'm number one. Wilhelm is number two; he's called Willy. The little kids are Katharina, Hans, and Gertrude. The dog is Hairy." He looked at her quickly to see if she got the family joke.

"Is spelling your strong subject, Henry?"

"Not really. Why?"

"I was wondering how you spell the dog's name."

His eyes danced but he didn't crack a smile. "Any way you want. He doesn't care."

"Maybe Hairy Harry will have to come to school." She could be stoic too.

Inside the cabin he found a kerosene lamp and pulling the match smartly across his raised thigh, lit it, casting a warm glow

14

over the small space. She looked around. He dragged the trunk into the middle of the room, taking up most of the empty space. "Do you like it?" he asked, hopeful. "We really fixed it up."

"Well, yes. It's charming. Very efficient."

"The women made it pretty."

"I can see. How nice of them."

A narrow bed was against one wall, shelves hung on the opposite wall holding a cup, a saucer, a plate, a bowl. None matched. Outfitted with a small table, one chair and a kerosene lamp, a wood- and coal-burning stove, a dresser, a peg with two crude wooden clothes hangers on it, a bench with a wash pail, a bucket, a coal scuttle, and a wood box, it was complete. *Does everything I need for living fit in a room this small?* "Really quite nice. Whom should I thank for the quilt, dishes, and pans?"

"Oh, everyone gave a few things when we knew we were getting a new teacher right out of school. The old one had her own things, but she took them with her. The women were afraid a new teacher might not think to bring all this stuff." He looked down and shuffled his feet. "I made the coat hangers. Someone drew a picture of one for me."

Touched, she said, "That was thoughtful, Henry. Thank you."

She could sense his pride in the hangers and what the community had accomplished. "They were right. I didn't think about dishes...or a lot of things. They've been generous. I'll thank them at our first meeting."

Henry grabbed the cabin's lantern, "Let's go back for supper. I'll show you how to get water in the morning. I've got your lantern so you can get home."

You mean I'll have to come by myself? How will I find the way? What kind of creatures are out there? Oh, please, don't make me come home alone.

Outside he showed her the path to the outhouse. As they headed toward the store it didn't seem as dark as she remembered. "Look at that, will you, Miss Carter?" She followed his pointing arm to see a sliver of moon coming over the hills at the head of the valley.

Josie was spell-bound as it rose. In the darkness, the moon's deep-yellow arc widened until half, then all the golden moon, rose above the hill. The sky glowed, the full moon illuminating the valley. "Oh, my, Heinrich. I can't say I've ever seen anything quite like it." The moon lit the path, their long shadows following them across the meadow. It was almost magical to her.

Supper, too, was like nothing she had experienced: cacophony, chaos, yelling and laughing. Zona's husband, Otto, was a bellowing, good-natured presence whom everyone ignored but who acted as if he were in charge. Zona, the matriarch, let him believe his delusion. Josie sat in wonder. She had expected a disciplined, almost military, atmosphere from the Germanic father. Suppers at home had been quietly informative affairs following a prayer her father sat stonily through. Her mother reported on the good conduct of his sons and daughters. He questioned them, as he felt appropriate, approving their good behavior, and thanking them for helping their mother. They responded. It was not a conversation. On Saturday evenings, he listened to them recite a poem, handed each a penny, then talked to the boys about topics they would find interesting. The girls escaped to their mother's care in the kitchen.

After she helped Zona with the dishes, much to the girls' delight, Josie took the lantern Henry lit and headed out alone with all the courage she could muster. The moon made her journey, certainly not pleasant, but less fearsome than it might have been. Nevertheless, she constantly checked in front of, behind, and beside herself.

When she entered the little cabin, she noticed a simple lock on the door. Panic surged through her. After a frightening trip to the outhouse she dragged her trunk in front of the door. It wouldn't stop anyone intent on entering, but it would alarm her. In the strange bed she slept poorly with troubled dreams.

Awake at the sound of a bell, she pushed curtains from two windows and looked critically at her home. The iron bedstead needed paint. The mattress sagged. The patchwork quilt was nicely done, its bright colors made the room cheerful. It was obvious several women had made squares then combined their efforts. The cupboard held dishes, a skillet, knife, fork, spoon, turner, and wooden spoon. Hanging on a nail, a wash basin. *They thought of everything and I thought of nothing. How could I have been so naive? If Mother were alive, she would have suggested I inquire about a boarding house instead of assuming one was here. When we learned I would live in a little cabin and fend for myself, she would have helped me plan what I would need. She would have sent me off prepared for this silly adventure, not with only a large canister of Earl Grey tea. Oh, Mother, how I miss you. But I'll have to make do. I can buy groceries with money saved for the first month in the boarding house.* She dressed, distracted by thoughts of home. Scolding herself for a lack of fortitude, she dragged the trunk from the door.

A knock startled her. She opened the door and found a lanky, grinning boy with milk, water, and oatmeal. His cheerfulness delighted her. "You're Wilhelm, is that right?"

"Yes'm. I'm called Willy, though."

"Of course. Thank you for bringing these, Willy."

"After breakfast, I'll show you where to get water."

"I'll appreciate that. Will you come back or should I come to the store?"

"Come on up. That's where the water is."

Oh, my. Water a walk away.

After breakfast, she found Zona and the kids working in the store: Henry stocking shelves, Willy sweeping, Katharina filling candy jars, Hans sweeping the platform, and little Gertie dusting cans on shelves.

"Very industrious here," Josie observed when she entered. "I hope this will transfer to schoolwork."

"It will." Zona assured everyone present.

"Can I take her to see where she gets water?" Henry asked.

"No. I said I would," Willy objected.

"Go." She pointed to Willy. "Get Miss Carter a cream can from the porch and don't fill it so full she can't handle it, then come back and get to work."

Josie noted Zona's no-nonsense manner of parenting. *It won't be my style as a teacher. Do kids respond better to firmness? I'll have to find out.*

Small sunflowers blooming near the water pipe caught her eye. "Do you know what these flowers are called, Willy?"

"Don't know. Ask Ma. She might know." *That's something I can do. Help kids learn names of flowers and trees if I can learn them myself.* Willy bent over a pipe discharging water continuously into a gravel basin before making its way to the river. He held the cream can under the pipe until it was half-filled. "This here water is piped from a spring across the river.

17

It's warm enough it doesn't freeze most winters. It's good drinking water. When you want plain water, take your bucket to the river; it's closer."

They carried the cream can together to the cabin where he showed her how to build a fire. She didn't have the heart to tell him she knew how. They had a cookstove in Denver, but he was so pleased to display his skills she let him show her. "There's a wash tub and wash board hanging on the back of the cabin by the clothesline."

"You've helped me so much, Willy. Thank you."

"That's okay. Maybe someday when I haven't done my homework, you'll have a chance to pay me back." A mischievous grin crossed his face.

I imagine I might have that chance. "I certainly hope that will never be the case, don't you?" She watched him watch her expression.

She unpacked her trunk, putting her two blouses and skirts on Henry's hangers. She had brought teachers' guides for eight grades although she wouldn't have a child in every grade, art supplies, maps, penmanship charts, and her pitch pipe. Tools she had learned to use in normal school. As she unpacked, her heart began beating faster, fear rising that she didn't know what she was doing. Kids would figure it out immediately and make her life miserable. She would lose her job, go home a complete failure. *I should go check the school, take some books, see what I've inherited. Keep my mind occupied.*

At the schoolhouse she tried the door and found it had no lock. Desks were in rows with seats upended, fifteen in all. *Not that many kids. Not really. Not if they're good kids. Not if they're mostly little kids.* At the side of the room was a blackboard. She could pull it to the front when needed. Reading, arithmetic, and history books, very used, were stacked on shelves. She opened one and saw it had belonged to Grand Junction Public Schools, next to Glenwood Springs Schools, then Basalt's: hand-me-downs from larger towns working their way to remote areas. On the north wall hung a map of the world, its oceans tattered, but land intact. *Good. Top of the map is always north so they'll learn the world the right direction.* She walked to the east window and looked up the valley. *Morning light will fill the room. The south windows will help warm and light it in winter. If the room had a window to the west, we could watch the sun get low in the sky and we'd know it was time to end the day. Besides, it would make the room brighter. I wonder if they could put a window in the door.* She could see evergreen trees along the valley bottom bordering the river. Sculpted near hills obscured mountains to the north and south. To the east she knew the Continental Divide touched the sky. She had come through that country yesterday and was still feeling overwhelmed by its beauty and extent. She had not known mountains were barren of trees above timberline, nor had she known how the world spread out below when you were on them. Although she had grown up in Denver and seen mountains in the distance for years, she had no idea they were so enormous, so deep, so high.

In the back of the room was a small pot-bellied stove. *I wonder how cold it gets. Will it be able to keep us warm? I guess if it can't we'll have to go over to my cabin, it's smaller. No. Where would they all sit? I guess we'll have to bundle up, but I suppose they know that.* She ran her hand across the top of her desk, smooth and polished by years of wear, undoubtedly another hand-me-down, or were they hand-me-ups, given the altitude? A bell sat waiting for someone to bring it to life. When she picked it up the clapper fell against the side, ringing loudly. She grabbed it so it wouldn't make more noise and looked around quickly to see if anyone heard, as if children would suddenly appear at the sound. Carefully holding the clapper, she examined its tarnished brass bell and worn wooden handle. It looked as if it had called in generations of school children. She would find out soon enough if it still held summoning power.

Studying the surrounding area, she questioned what had brought people here, what had kept them, and would it keep her. She had learned from Zona that besides the post office, grocery store, and boarding house, there was a limestone quarry, a lime kiln, workers' cabins, a few ranch houses scattered across the land, and up the hill, a sawmill.

Walking slowly to the cabin she considered what to do until supper. She couldn't remember being solitary before. The third child in a family of five children, off to State Normal School in Greeley with a group of friends and into a boarding house full of girls, then back home until she left for this job, now she was alone. Completely alone. *What will I do evenings? On weekends? Is there a church I can attend on Sundays so I can see another...am I an adult now? Shouldn't I have asked these questions before I got here?* These thoughts fueled her panic. She had not considered loneliness. She had pictured a town with lively gatherings of young people she could share experiences with. Group outings, picnics, hayrides, all things she had read about in rural communities. Idealized rural farm communities, she realized now. This was not a farm community. This was harsh country, rough people, and not many of those. Even if she met a beau, where would she entertain him? She couldn't invite him into her bedroom. Nine months of isolation. Could she stand it? The mountains seemed too close, making her feel claustrophobic. She couldn't see. In Denver she could see east across the plains forever and to the west, mountains were so far away they didn't limit her view. They were the view.

She collapsed onto the bed, curling into a ball around her pillow. *Whatever possessed me to come so far from home, so far from people I love and who love me and would take care of me? Now I know what Father was talking about. Why didn't I listen? Well, I can be my own person here. No one will be inclined to interfere. Oh, you stubborn, willful, ninny, you've really done it this time.*

She got up, left the cabin, and wandered down the path to the river. The field to the east, filled with purple flowers mixed with small sunflowers, resembled an unkempt garden. A few cabins up stream and the truss bridge for the train barely down the river were her near views. It was a delightful spot to be alone. She sat on a rock at water's edge and watched the river flow. It wasn't a large river, rather one she could imagine wading across if she had a stick for balance and no one to see her holding up her skirts. Looking around to see if anyone were watching she took off her shoes and socks and put her feet into the water. Cold! Icy cold! She tentatively put her feet back in. Not so cold this time. The water was deeper than it looked. Slippery rocks made her unsteady when she stood up. Pulling up her skirt and petticoat she headed into the river. A trout darted upstream from her. She couldn't remember wading since she was a little girl. Thrilled with the feeling of rushing water on her legs she thought being in the mountains might be all right. *Maybe it will be good to be alone and not have to try to be a lady all the time.*

School began. Little children, timid at first, greeted her formally, some using English tentatively. Older kids, more familiar with both school and English, met her with apprehension and wariness, holdovers from the previous year's disagreeable teacher. Josie, nervous, unsure of herself, welcomed them politely, with all the composure she could bring to bear. Having worked with Zona she was prepared with a seating chart. They sat, all eyes on her, waiting for what came next. She froze. She opened her mouth, but words didn't come. It wasn't what she planned, but at last she said, "Let's look at the map and you can tell me where your families came from." She started with Henry who went to the map and pointed to Germany, then changed his mind and pointed to Russia.

"We speak German, but we're called Roosians. Ma says Germans were invited to Russia a long time ago and were called Volga Germans, but I don't know what Volga means."

"We'll have to find out, won't we?"

She helped the next child find Sweden. One found Italy. One found Norway. One found Ireland and England. Regardless of their family's native land, the exercise broke the ice and gave them something to talk about. She moved into her planned day. She would survive.

Friday, completely exhausted from her first week of teaching, she closed her book and said, "The week's over children. Thank you for being so helpful. You are dismissed." The kids' eyes lit up. They jumped from their desks and began to drag them to the edge of the room. "Stop. What are you doing?" she cried. They looked at her with puzzled expressions.

"Saturday night supper," they yelled back and continued to push desks around. She called Henry to her and asked him to explain.

"We have Saturday night supper here every week. It's the only place in town big enough to hold us. It's a lot of fun. You'll like it."

In my classroom? A bunch of people eating? How horrible. What a mess!

The five families with kids came. A few bachelors joined them. Mothers carried food. Kids carried babies and dishes.

Fathers brought chairs. Kids sat on desks or the floor. Covered dishes were adequate and representative of various countries. They played games, kids recited poetry, and Mr. Miller, the old guitarist came, so they sang. Some said they wished they had room to dance. Others said no, it was good the way it was. Dancing leads to mischief. Young and old shared a lively, amusing evening. They cleaned the school and went home.

So busy was she with lesson plans, conquering her fear of not knowing answers to questions, and learning each child's name and capabilities, days passed without her being aware of the change in season. She had established a routine making her days bearable: After school she would make a pan of Earl Grey tea and take it to the post office to share with Zona while they talked.

Around the middle of the month, Zona handed her a letter. "Good news, I hope."

Josie was surprised at the return address: Jessie Wallace, Leadville. She had forgotten about the couple. They invited her to go to Aspen with them as their guest on September 25th. They would be on an early train and come back the next evening. They looked forward to her company.

She read the letter to Zona and explained who they were. "Do you think I should go?"

"Of course, you should go. It'll be a pretty trip and you need to be with someone besides the kids and me."

"Have you ever been to Aspen?"

"No. No need. Go and tell me about it."

Josie wrote to the Wallaces accepting their invitation. By return mail she received tickets and their delight she would accompany them.

The crush of school, the need to keep ahead of her pupils on so many fronts, not to mention the constant lesson plans, preoccupied her. On September 24th, Zona reminded her she was going to Aspen the next day.

"I don't have time to go," she whined, "why did I say I would?"

"You have time. Go."

The next morning, she was at the station when the train pulled in. She quickly boarded, then saw the Wallaces waving. They seemed so glad to see her she was surprised. "Sit here. We're anxious to hear how you're surviving. Do you have good kids?"

She assured them they couldn't be better.

"Then you have good parents," Mr. Wallace put in. "They want you to succeed and they're making sure their kid isn't the reason you don't."

"We can talk about school at lunch, I want her to see the country," Mrs. Wallace said. "Will you tell her about it, Charles? You know so much better than I what's going on with nature here."

He chided his wife, "You've heard it so many times, you could tell it perfectly well, but I do love to lecture." That crooked grin Josie had forgotten. She enjoyed their loving good humor.

"You see, Josie, there is a road between here and Ruedi where there's a gypsum quarry and plant, and after that the connection with the lower valley is by rail or trail. The roads here are spotty. People depend upon the railroad for supplies and travel. Without a railroad the commerce in the valley would be difficult. The railroad has been crucial to western expansion, for good or ill."

"What did they do before the railroad?"

"There were few people here then. No need to cut timber if you couldn't get it to market. Same with lime and gypsum. Railroads and commerce went hand in glove."

"I don't know what gypsum is."

"Technically, it's calcium sulfate dihydrate. No one will expect you to remember that. It's a curious mineral because after it's processed you can add water and it makes a paste that hardens. It's referred to as plaster of Paris by artists who use it for casting and sculpting. Gypsum is widely used for fertilizer and to make many products, including the chalk we all use on slates and blackboards. It comes from that hill over there. It's processed in the large building."

They were soon in a tight, red rock canyon. "This is sandstone, Josie." Mrs. Wallace chimed in, pleased with herself. She looked at Mr. Wallace. "Go ahead. I wanted to show I learned something but lest we forget why we chose this weekend, please notice the color of the leaves and other foliage, Josie."

"Oh, yes. I am noticing. In Denver the leaves turn yellow. Here, with the sun coming through such stands of them, they seem golden and the red ones are splendid. Teaching has so preoccupied me I haven't taken time to appreciate my surroundings. I can't thank you enough for giving me a chance to appreciate autumn."

Mrs. Wallace patted her knee. "We hoped you'd enjoy an outing. We were sure you deserve one."

Through the canyon, past a large ranch and they were at Peachblow quarry across the river. A large hoisting boom was loading a freight car on a siding. Horses pulled the rock across a bridge. Mr. Wallace couldn't resist. "Sandstone is very small grains of sand usually made of quartz or feldspar, bound together with other particles like silicon or clay. Sand deposited by wind or water, with a bonding material, hardens over time. This sandstone has some iron oxide in it which makes it rosy pink. I guess it reminded someone of falling peach blossoms or peachblow as it's called some places. It's the structure stone of a great many buildings in this area, such as the Wheeler Opera House and county courthouse in Aspen, the D&RG train station, and Hotel Colorado in Glenwood Springs. But now notice the high sandstone cliffs to your right. Those are called the Castles." He stopped abruptly. "Josie, I can't see it, but I'm getting The Look." He laughed heartily as did Jessie. Josie rubbed her nose to hide a grin.

Soaring, angular red formations of sandstone formed a backdrop for the flat lands below. Five miles later, they pulled into Basalt, a false-fronted main street, depot, hotel, church with a steeple, and engine house. It was the first real town she'd seen since Leadville. It had about two hundred residents, Mr. Wallace guessed.

"I suppose you know Basalt's name is taken from the volcanic lava."

"I didn't know that. I'm learning so much to share with my pupils. How do you know all this?"

"My father was a geologist. He taught at the School of Mines. He hoped I'd follow in his footsteps but I wanted to teach younger kids."

They wandered around Basalt waiting for the train to leave for Aspen. She liked the town. It was unpretentious.

The ride up the valley to Aspen was beautiful. Fields were flaxen-colored stubble, shorn of their crops. Cottonwoods lining the Roaring Fork River were a delightful blend of greens and yellows. Hillsides covered with oak were a patchwork-quilt of greens, rusts, and amber glowing in the morning sun.

Josie could see the higher hills surrounding the valley and the brilliant patches of aspen nestled among the deep greens of evergreens. Sandstone outcroppings were in this valley too. "Is silver found in sandstone?" she asked.

"Oh, no. Silver is in what they call hard rock. It usually occurs with other minerals, such as lead, as it did in Leadville, copper, zinc, and gold, to name some. Aspen had good veins of silver. I suppose it still may have. At one point it surpassed Leadville in silver output. Aspen was a rich town in its heyday."

She was enjoying the scenery as Mrs. Wallace pointed out spots of color when suddenly they were on a high trestle. "Look down, Josie, that's Maroon Creek, it comes down from Maroon Bells. I've only seen pictures. I understand it's a pretty place."

Josie didn't care where the creek originated, she hoped she would live to see the other side. When they were over the trestle, she breathed. Mrs. Wallace laughed. "It's an experience, isn't it? They've not lost anyone off of it, but sometimes I wonder why not, it's so narrow." Again, they were on a trestle, a short one and although high, not breath-taking. After passing huge smelting buildings and enormous smokestacks, they pulled into the Midland depot.

As there had been in Leadville, Aspen had a deserted feeling, but some of the grandeur lingered. It had gone from the third largest city in Colorado to a couple thousand residents, yet the newspaper told of ongoing silver-mining speculation. After checking into the all-but-empty Hotel Jerome and taking their bags to their rooms, they walked the streets. Josie loved the small-town atmosphere and the cheerfulness of people who greeted them. Returning to the Jerome, they had lunch in the bar. The bartender told them with a chuckle it remained a popular place in town because it had the only public bathrooms.

Josie had never been a sightseer. It was fun, especially with knowledgeable guides. Mr. Wallace was fascinated with Colorado's history, even the recent past, and happy to share what he knew, pointing out the Peachblow stone used in the opera house, courthouse, and Presbyterian Church. Mrs. Wallace tempered facts with window-shopping and people-watching.

Weary of strolling and exploring, they drifted back to the hotel for supper. Josie didn't really know how to behave in a hotel dining room half-full of loud-talking men smoking cigars and gaily dressed women but it was the same jolly bartender, and maybe the same folks eating and drinking, but with new manners and attire to wonder about. Her manners didn't cause alarm. It was a good time.

Over supper Josie learned the Wallaces had no children, though they had dreamed of a large family. To compensate for this disappointment they had taken in children of all ages over the years whose parents either couldn't cope with another child or who had neglected or orphaned them. There had, unfortunately for the children, but fortunately for them, been many of these children to love. At their ages now, they were reluctant to accept young children. The county was pressing them to take in a few who were in miserable situations. They watched each other's face as they told her this, and she could see they both wanted what they had resolved not to do. Feeling she was a surrogate child this day, she tried to make sure their time and money were appreciated.

The next day, Mr. Wallace treated them to a hired buggy to see the Maroon Bells. The valley was dazzling with fall colors contrasting with sandstone cliffs of wine-red high above them. The road was rough but well-travelled and the trip passed so pleasantly they were surprised when they reached their destination. Josie caught her breath at the sight. Not only did the Bells stand at the head of a valley like majestic maroon pyramids, a crystal-clear lake reflected their magnificence as well as the clear blue sky. Surrounded by the dark greens of spruce and brilliant aspen, the palette in the lake was stunning. How Josie wished for her sketch pad. She tried to memorize the scene, but mostly she wanted to remember the cathedral-like feeling of awe the setting inspired.

The return trip to Meredith was in twilight. Small glimmers of light scattered in a country of such unimaginable proportions made her marvel at people's quest for finding a place they could call their own.

Their parting was tender. She was fond of these generous, kind people. They vowed to stay in touch.

Resuming her routine she was surprised one day after school when Mr. Miller, the old guitarist, approached her, said he had quit working full-time at the kiln, and nervously asked if he could come to class when work allowed, sit quietly in back, and listen? He had never gone to school and he would like to hear what the children learned. He said he had requested permission from the school board members. They said it was up to Josie. She asked him if he had not learned to read and write. He shook his head sadly.

"You can also come in after school and we'll get you caught up with the children," she happily offered. He agreed to come. For an hour after each school day they worked on the alphabet and sounds until she felt he was ready to sit with her Aebecedarians and follow along. He was a faithful pupil. She could see him begin to understand.

Besides being her pupil, she found a friend in him. After school, they would talk about the kids. He offered helpful suggestions on dealing with boys. Although he tended to be silent in class, she could see him giving hints to the youngest children to help them through tough passages in their reading or in adding columns. He was an avid learner.

As snow began to cover the ground, she took the children out to see animal tracks and asked them to draw creatures they imagined had made them. Many of the children recognized the larger animals' prints because they helped their fathers run trap lines or hunted with them in the fall. There were many small tracks that didn't merit hunters' interest. These allowed for imaginations to soar. This world, so new to her, captivated her imagination. Taking their slates into falling snow to study hexagonal flakes landing on them, putting chalk marks on the wall to chart the movement of the sun, comparing different shapes of leaves and seeds, studying the structure of various pinecones, helped kids to see relationships between beauty and science. Watching eyes light up as children made discoveries was rewarding, inspiring, and fun.

Living among people who were neither family nor, in the beginning, friends, opened her eyes to ways individuals choose to live and relate to others. She gained confidence with strangers and comfort with older people. She came to see children as distinct individuals. Despite frustrations in tailoring classes to serve so many different grades, she managed. Vexations with her ineptness as a teacher plagued her. But kids were helpful and kind, and, most of the time, willing to do things her way. She learned it was all right to admit she didn't know something because it gave kids permission to do the same. There were times of unexpected companionship when they took hikes together to study a part of nature pertaining to their lessons or to listen to the birds' songs when they studied music. Genuine friendship developed with mothers who took part in outside activities and her relationship with Mr. Miller was surprisingly rewarding.

When she asked children to bring their lunch on Wednesdays if they would like to hear her read a book, she found them engaged and eager to enter unfamiliar worlds. They shared this enthusiasm with their mothers who started dropping in on Wednesdays to hear the stories, at first using an excuse of a forgotten lunch or sweater. Soon she was asked if she would read three days a week. Babies and little ones napped on a blanket by the stove while older kids and mothers sat transfixed. Librarians in Denver agreed to mail books if she paid the postage and they selected ones for boys, girls, young and old that pertained to early American history. They read *The Legend of Sleepy Hollow, Benjamin Franklin's Autobiography,* and *The Last of the Mohicans.* She was surprised how kids seemed to enjoy whatever she read. At Saturday night suppers, fathers would often talk about the stories. People were hungry for entertainment and knowledge about the world outside the valley.

One day she asked the pupils where they would go if they could travel to any place in the world. Many answered they wanted to go to the countries their parents came from. A few chose places they considered exotic. One wanted to see Denver. This inspired her to ask where they would go if they could explore the country around them. She was surprised to learn about near places she'd never heard mentioned.

Early in November she received another letter from the Wallaces, this time inviting her for Thanksgiving weekend. They were happy to tell her it would be a large gathering because they had three children living with them and a few grown ones returning. Delighted by their decision to again open their home to luckless kids she happily accepted their invitation providing she could be useful. Assured her help would be welcome, she joined them for an enlightening weekend.

On her return trip she pondered the difference their kindness made in children's lives and what exposure to education meant to them. She saw how Mr. Wallace's sharing of information in such a casual manner and Mrs. Wallace's dispensing of kindness and expecting it to be shared, had bent these twigs upward and outward. She learned so much more that weekend than she had realized while she was living it. *Yes. There's more to know about teaching than what's in the books.*

As Christmas approached, she began to feel uncomfortable not to be returning home for the holidays but she determined it would be better to remain in Meredith, lest her father persuade her to stay home. She wrote to her family and told them the truth: She was going to stay in Meredith because some people wouldn't have a Christmas dinner if she didn't organize one. Christmas fell on Saturday and the women agreed to make Saturday night supper very special. She particularly wanted Mr. Miller to be with friends and to share in a holiday meal. She asked him to sit with her and bring his guitar to make the party lively. He shyly told her he could never remember a Christmas supper, though he would be happy to sit with her. She spent Christmas day making treats she remembered from childhood. It was the happiest Christmas she'd had in years.

SUMMER, 1910

Although she had never seen fireworks, Josie couldn't help but think of them when she announced school was out for summer. Exuberant children leaped from the schoolhouse stoop onto the bare patch of dirt that was their playground, the youngest singing: "School's out, school's out, Teacher wore her bloomers out." Big kids too old for such nonsense, were teasing and pushing each other around. Before they were far, little ones turned and waved, a chorus: "Bye, Miss Carter." Heading straight to the general store, a penny in each of their pockets for good grades, good behavior, good something, so everyone would have a reward, they were happy kids. Clothes, bright and new that fall, were now patched, outgrown, threadbare. Clothes and kids were ready for summer.

Standing with her back against the door jamb, the bell she had rung in celebration of the last day of school silent in her hand, Josie watched them leave. She went down the step and collapsed onto the stoop, feeling as empty as a dry stream bed. She had grown to love these children, marvel at their aptitudes, cherish their innocence, learn their vulnerabilities, and worry over their weaknesses. Were they now gone from her life, these young friends she cared for and who, she believed, cared for her?

Heavy sobs nearly surfaced. She took a few deep breaths to subdue them as she leaned against the warm building and felt the healing noon sun on her face. The valley, so peaceful it mirrored the calm that comes at the end of a major effort.

Scattered memories of the year cascaded in her mind. At the beginning there had been times of such loneliness and homesickness she cried herself to sleep at night. But once folks got to know and accept her, they folded her into their lives. Winter had passed quickly measured by days in the classroom and slowly measured by long dark evenings. There were times the cold, never-ending snow, gray skies, and short days almost overwhelmed her cheerful disposition. Then the sky would crack open and the brilliant blue of mountain skies would dispel her melancholy. Early spring mud on sixteen pairs of shoes, mud on her skirt hem, mud everywhere, had tested her good nature. Then warm spring arrived: birds returned, pussy willow and aspen catkins decked branches, river ice broke up, tiny spring beauty and delicate pasque flowers poked through last year's dried foliage, the sun moved north over the valley lengthening mornings and afternoons, thawing her winter-weary heart. Everyone's spirit reflected spring's exuberance.

To her surprise, she learned to live with, then cherish, the quiet solitude that came with evening and she no longer felt lonely. Preparing dinner, brewing tea, then sketching from memory on a slate were respites from the noise and confusion of the day and a necessary touch of tranquility before she headed into lesson plans. She became attuned to sounds of nature swirling around the cabin: pelting snow, dripping icicles, violent spring winds, birds' songs, coyotes' yips, the river's roar with spring runoff. Sounds conveying the natural world stirred her curiosity. Animal tracks in new snow revealed a bustling nocturnal realm while she slept. Its mystery intrigued her.

Most important, though, she felt kids had learned. She had honestly earned her pay. Despite her father's misgivings, she had proved to herself coming to Meredith had been right for her. She was stronger now. She had made it on her own. She would return come fall if he agreed.

The playground was as quiet as on the day she arrived. She went into the classroom where kids had helped her stack books on shelves and lifted seats on their desks the way she had found them. She swept the floor, took penmanship charts off walls, and left her desk clean and neat with no traces of herself. Though the school board had offered her a contract for next year and she had tentatively accepted, it was safer to leave as if she would not return.

Satisfied, she picked up her own books and closed the door gently behind her. She stopped to look. It was familiar to her now. Doe Mountain rising to the south, the long narrow valley running almost due east and west, the Continental Divide somewhere high up to the east, Frying Pan River flowing west, meeting other valleys with their rivers until at some point the water from these mountains reached the Gulf of California as the Grand River.

She gathered her strength and went to the cabin. Tomorrow she would return to Denver to reassure her father she survived and being in the mountains had been the right decision. True to her agreement with him, she had faithfully sent half her pay every month to repay him for sending her to normal school. In one more year she would be free from her obligation although it had not been onerous. There was nowhere near to spend money though she and Zona had taken a day off and gone shopping in Basalt. She had bought warmer everything: long-johns, stockings, mittens, scarf, heavy shawl, and overshoes to keep her feet dry. Snow had come in late September. It was still snowing in May.

Along with payments to her father she sent cheerful reports of whatever she thought might convince him and her sisters she was safe and doing her job. She told of community gatherings and how kind people were. She did not mention the bachelors who were mostly older men and who treated her as a little sister because even at twenty she still looked like a kid. She also suspected Zona had had a word with them. Ever the mother hen, she had been a concerned, protective friend.

She entered the cabin reluctantly, not wanting to face the trunk and bags. The feeling she might never see this room again felt like a final farewell. She had taken the precaution of packing into shipping crates belongings she would not need in summer so if she couldn't return for some reason, Zona could send them to her without much effort. She had packed her trunk lightly to have room to bring back some comforts she missed, things her mother would have sent with her. She had her own money and would enjoy shopping for them in Denver. She also had put aside money to buy art supplies for the children and some inexpensive musical instruments for ones who showed aptitude. She would visit friends her age and spend leisurely hours with her dear sisters. The train would leave in the morning and she would be on it.

Girding herself for an emotional experience, she said goodbye to mothers who had become friends. She knew it would be easier if she could be cheerful and positive about returning in the fall even though she knew she might not return. She thanked them for their help, laughed with them about mistakes she'd made knitting and quilting, and told them again they had special children.

Mr. Miller was a particular concern. If she didn't return, he might not continue his education. She couldn't be lighthearted with him because he was too perceptive. Taking his hand in hers she asked him to please keep studying. She would write to him and she hoped he would write to her someday. He asked her to please come back. She was his friend. She handed him the second and third grade readers. "Willy is going to help you," she assured him. She had given Willy twenty-five cents to be a tutor. "Please keep reading and writing. I want us to stay in touch." He looked away to hide his emotion.

Zona would have none of the goodbye. "You'll come back. Maybe not to teach, but you'll come back. We'll say goodbye next time."

Waiting for the train the following morning, she was surprised to find Mr. Miller there to send her off. He handed her a small sleek wooden letter opener. "Did you make this, Mr. Miller?" she inquired, rubbing its polished surface.

"Yes'm."

"It's a sculpture. What is the wood?"

"Rock maple."

"Beautiful. It must have taken hours to make it so smooth."

He nodded.

"I'll cherish it and when you write me a letter, I promise I'll open it with this."

His eyes twinkled. "If you'll come back next year, I may learn to write well enough to write you a letter." She kissed his wrinkled cheek and boarded the train.

As Josie went through the Continental Divide for the fourth time she resolved if circumstances at home permitted, she would return a few weeks early so she could explore the country around Meredith. She didn't know exactly how she would do this but Zona would.

Josie had written to the Wallaces telling them she would be going through Leadville on her way home. She received a letter by return mail. They would be at the train station to say hello, if even for a few minutes. She felt she had given them no option, but she had no idea when she might be through Leadville again. It was a joyful reunion. School was out for Mr. Wallace and Mrs. Wallace was working the evening shift. They caught up with news. Mr. Wallace congratulated her for receiving a contract to return. They told her of an additional child they had taken in: a girl from miles up the valley who wanted to go to high school but didn't have one in her area. Josie was curious about the arrangement which they said was satisfying for them and helpful to the girl. They hugged her and put her on the train.

Friends. She had made many good ones this past year away from the protection of home, away from school mates. A variety of people she would never have dreamed of befriending had invited her into their lives. *I'm lucky to have met such generous people. I hope I'll remember to extend friendship to people who would benefit from kindness as I have.*

What a surprise Denver was to her: noisy, crowded, dusty. She felt closed in by buildings and people. She could find some of the peacefulness of nature she craved in the park near their house and she walked in it alone whenever she could find an excuse. It was good to be with family, just not all the time. Mourning doves' sad coos seemed to call to her. Sometimes she forgot to look before she crossed the street and once a car honked at her. She couldn't believe how rude that felt. A stranger honking at her! Nowhere did she come across children she could talk with. She missed the sounds of their laughter.

Her household duties resumed as if she had never left but she found reasons to escape. She went to the public library to find books identifying wildflowers, birds, animals, and trees of the Rocky Mountains. She sketched some she had seen and copied their names and descriptions so she could teach the children about the flora and fauna, as the librarian called them. She asked if maps existed of the mountains around Meredith. The librarians helped her decipher a copy of the Hayden survey's <u>Geological and Geographical Atlas of Colorado</u> from 1877. For hours she studied the map trying to remember where her students said they'd like to explore. There was something intriguing to her about the North Fork of the Frying Pan because the kids said there were some pretty lakes up there. She couldn't locate them on the map, but she could find the North Fork.

She tried to convince her father this job suited her. She regaled her sisters with anecdotes about each child, about Zona and Otto who had taken her in as one of their own, and about the women who had taught her to knit and quilt.

She amused them with her first week of teaching. How Friday had at long last arrived and at the end of the school day she felt she would collapse. Dramatically raising her eyebrows to show horror, she told what happened next with Saturday night supper. Her sisters were delighted with the story and intrigued by the guitarist. Had he been a musician? Why was he there? She could tell them what she knew about Mr. Miller, which was little.

Her sisters listened with boundless curiosity. Her father tended to be silent and left the table as soon as supper was over. He didn't suggest she not return. "You've made a deal. We keep our word," was all he said when she told him they asked her to return and she accepted. But she felt he could see she was happy, she was growing up, and she was paying him back for the tuition.

Hoping to encourage Mr. Miller's reading skills and to make reading feel personal she sent him and Zona letters telling of her time in Denver. She included a note to Zona asking her to read them to him. She suggested he write over her printing to help him with his writing. She got a post card back from Zona saying he enjoyed the letters but she didn't think he was writing on them. At the end of summer, she received a letter with Mr. Miller's return address. It was brief, thanking her for the letters. His printing was precise. He signed it "Mr. Miller." She quickly wrote to tell him she loved receiving it. His letter opener worked perfectly!

LATE SUMMER, 1910

When August came, she began to pack her trunk with treasures she had amassed over summer: school supplies, teapot, tea kettle, mixing bowls, drinking glass, towel, vase, mirror, yarn and knitting needles, fabric for a quilt, and more warm clothes. She splurged on a bottle of lilac perfume for Zona. The instruments in their cases would be baggage. She was better prepared this time and anxious to go.

When she arrived in Meredith, Zona treated her like a long-lost child.

"It's great to be home, Zona. I missed you all."

Zona laughed her wonderful laugh. "We should be able to change your mind about that!"

Josie asked if Willy would help her with her trunk. Zona yelled and he showed up. "Now, I think I'll go home." Josie and Willy hauled the stuffed trunk and instruments down to the cabin. Entering, she was surprised at its size. It was so small. She hadn't remembered it that way. The crates she'd left behind cluttered the space; the trunk nearly took up what was left. But it was home. She and Willy returned to the store where she bought groceries and filled her cream can. "I'll see you in the morning, Zona." Her walk home in the near dark with no full moon rising this year, was not fearsome. She knew her way.

The next morning, perched on her usual seat on the windowsill, Josie was happy to be back with her dear friend. "So, what are you going to do until school starts?" Zona inquired. "You've got two weeks."

"You mean what I'd like to do or what I probably will do?"

"Start with the 'like to do.'"

"What I'd like to do is go camping but a girl can't go without a man, so I guess I'll have to settle on 'probably.'"

"Why can't you go without a man?"

"Oh, Zona, you know why."

"No. I guess I don't."

"Well, you know." She couldn't believe her practical friend could say such a silly thing. "I mean, how can a woman hike in a long skirt for instance?"

"What does that have to do with a man?"

"A man could take me on a horse. I can't go on a horse alone because I can't ride and I don't know anything about horses."

"Go on."

"There are so many reasons, I don't know where to start."

"Give me more."

"How could I carry all that stuff myself?"

"Some others."

"Maybe I'd be afraid all alone."

"Now that's a real one."

"What do you mean?"

"You've finally come up with one good reason why you couldn't go camping alone. The others I think we can deal with."

"Do you mean you would actually consider sending me out there all by myself?"

"Wait a minute, Josie. I never said I was going to 'send' you out there. I'm going to help you go, if you want. This is your idea not mine."

"It was only a dream."

"Then you don't want to go?"

"Yes, I want to go. It seems impossible. That's all."

"You want to go? Think about it."

Josie looked out the window down the valley full of August's dark greens. Flowers filled the meadows. Barn swallows that had been babies in nests under the eaves when she left carved arabesques in the sky.

"Yes," she said impulsively, "I want to go."

"Then I'll help. I always dreamed of going myself. If you do it, you can tell me about it. Now, where do you think you'd like to go."

"Up the North Fork to some lakes. Have you ever been there?"

"With five kids? Cooking over a fire? It's rough enough here I don't need to walk to work. But someday I'd like to go with just Ott."

"But do you know about it?"

"No. Willy might know a kid who's been there, I'll ask him."

"It would be good to find out about it. Do you think he'd mind helping me get the trunk and crates up to the school?"

"Doesn't matter what he minds. He'll be there in a few minutes."

After they were through moving the school things, Willy said, "Ma said you might hike up the North Fork and I'm going to be the one to help you if you go and to keep my mouth shut about it."

She laughed. "It's probably just a silly dream, Willy. Your mom said you might know a kid who's been up the North Fork. Is it a difficult hike?"

"Don't know. Haven't been there. Matteo has."

"Could you please ask what he remembers? I'm curious about how far it is and if there's a trail."

"Sure," he laughed, "hard to do with my mouth shut, though."

After he left, she went around the schoolroom, surprised and delighted by the new window in the door. She lovingly touched desks, folded seats down, arranged the room in a different configuration than she had found it. Then she had been afraid to change it. Now, she knew what she wanted. She put books, maps, and art supplies on shelves. She was excited to share the instruments. She hoped at least one had a gift for music because it would be fun to sing to a banjo and guitar even if they were cheap instruments she bought at a pawn shop. Maybe Mr. Miller would be willing to help, if asked nicely.

"You got them where?" her father had exclaimed in horror about the pawn shop purchases. "What were you doing in that part of town?" She explained the music store sent her there when she told them how much she could afford to spend.

"I didn't feel intimidated by the derelicts. I ignored them. They seemed harmless." Her father shook his head. What had she become?

Her trunk and crates emptied of school supplies, the room rearranged, she picked up the bell on her desk and rang it loudly. She had learned the powers of the venerable instrument. A smaller school bell at the pawn shop had caught her eye and she had bought it on a whim. She wanted one of her own to have as a souvenir of teaching in Meredith. She rang it with the other hand. It was a different tone but melodious. She rang them both together and laughed. She was an orchestra by herself.

"Did you want me?" Willy was at the door.

How embarrassing: caught playing. "Oh, yes, I am ready, Willy. I wasn't ringing for you, though, I was comparing the old bell with the new one I bought." She hurriedly shut the trunk and they carried it to the cabin.

For the rest of the afternoon Josie arranged her purchases, tidied the cabin, and went to the river for water. Remembering her first day there she went wading. She hugged herself with happiness.

The next morning Willy knocked on her door and told her Matteo said they made it to the lakes in one day and there is a trail. She thanked him for good information.

She went to the store, wandered around, looking in the candy case, at rows of canned goods, boxes of soap, bins full of potatoes and onions. The aroma from the cabinet containing tobacco and cigarette papers was sweet and reminded her of her father before he became ill. *Oh, heavens, he would disown me if he knew what I'm cooking up now.*

Zona finished the morning mail and joined Josie. "Did Willy find out what you needed to know?"

"I think so. Matteo reached the lakes in one day. There's a trail. Do you think I'd be safe?"

"Safe? Well, yes, I think you'd be safe most anywhere hereabouts."

Josie looked at her, incredulous. "Do you really think I can do it?"

"Ya. We'll work on it. Now about the skirt. There's something I think we ought to try."

I've done it again, haven't I? "Tell me what to do."

"Decide how many days you want to be gone and see if you have shoes that could take hard hiking. Then tell me if you still want to go and I'll help you make a list of stuff you'll need."

Josie thanked her and went home to consider not only the shoes but her courage.

Later in the afternoon Willy was at her door again. "Ma wants to talk to you when you have a minute."

"Please tell her I'll be right up."

The reality of what she may have gotten herself into with Zona struck her. *I can't believe I blurted out this impossible desire to go camping. Can't I say I didn't really mean it? Why can't I admit a mistake? My stubborn streak has always gotten me into trouble. I'll tell Zona it was an unreasonable dream. I'll keep it and someday I may be married and my husband will take me camping in an acceptable manner. Maybe Zona can't put anything together and I won't have to admit I'm afraid to go.*

Walking slowly, clutching her small gift, she realized Zona was a person who never saw an obstacle she couldn't overcome. Josie loved her spirit and had learned about courage from her. It was this mettle that had taken her to the pawn shop. It was this attitude that let her buy instruments she couldn't play herself but felt a musical child could make them work. Zona's enthusiasm affected everyone. *Maybe I've gone too far this time. Maybe I need to learn how to back down.*

Zona came out of the back room with her arms full of clothes that she dumped on the counter, grinning like a 'possum, as she would say. "Here. Take these home and try them on. I'll come down in a few minutes to look at you. Don't come up here or you'll give away our secret." She acted as if she were playing a great joke on someone. She was as animated and happy as Josie could remember.

"What are these?"

"Go. Find out."

Josie could see they were worn shoes, shirts, and jeans. One of the shirts she recognized as Henry's from last year. She shook her head and picked up the bundle and headed out the door.

Trying to suppress her delight, Zona called out, "See you in a few minutes."

Josie remembered the perfume in her hand. It felt inappropriate for this strong, resilient woman. She had wanted to give Zona a gift she would never buy for herself, but this seemed silly. She tucked it into the pile of clothes.

The bundle, spilled onto the bed, revealed two pairs of worn Levi's, two old shirts—one Henry's, one Willy's, an engineer's cap with a puffy top, and a heavy jacket. Did Zona really expect her to put on these boys' clothes? She turned them over in her hands. *No. I can't fit them. I'm not shaped like a fourteen-year-*

old boy. What is she thinking? But I'm going to have to prove it to her. She slipped off her blouse, skirt and petticoat, leaving her in chemise and drawers. Picking up the shirts, she thought how ugly boys' clothes were, almost as ugly, she thought, as women's drab white blouses and dark skirts. Girls wore pretty-colored ginghams and calicoes; boys got muddy brown plaids or dull blue stripes. She selected the striped one and put it on. She chose the larger pair of jeans and pulled them on. *How do I fasten these crazy metal buttons?* She tucked in the shirt, pulled the fly closed and buttoned it clumsily. She looked in the new mirror. The jeans fit perfectly. She filled out the seat more than Henry had, but they closed and weren't too long. Her heart ached they fit so well. *No wonder men won't take me seriously. I look just like them.* She knew she didn't have a proper bosom, nothing like her younger sister's. She had hoped, otherwise, she looked like a woman. This confirmed she didn't. *I look like a boy up and down and everyone knows it or else Zona wouldn't have suggested I could fit into these.* Dejected, she sat on the bed. *No wonder. No wonder!*

Zona knocked as she came in. "Let's see." She was full of cheer and fun. Then she saw Josie sitting with her head down. "What's this?"

"Oh, Zona," and she started to pucker up.

"What? What's this all about?"

"I look like a boy." She patted her chest.

"They're fine. They'll make milk just like the big ones and that's all they're good for."

Josie sighed. Zona had an answer for all her objections. She tried again. "I can't wear pants. A lady doesn't do that."

"Says who?"

"Well, everyone knows."

"Then everyone doesn't want to go camping. Stand up. Let me see you."

Josie stood obediently. Nodding, Zona said, "You're skinnier than I thought. But don't worry, someday you'll get fat like all women do, then you'll worry about that." She turned Josie around to examine her. "Perfect fit."

She wound Josie's long hair up in a knot and piled it on top of her head, pulling the engineer's cap snugly over it. "Look."

There, in the mirror was a fourteen-year-old boy looking back at her, leggy, thin-shouldered, wide-eyed.

Her shoulders sagged. "I'm not pretty."

"No, but you're all right. What's important is, you'll pass for a boy, don't you think?"

Josie stared sadly into the mirror. "Yes. I guess I will." *But what kind of victory is it, to look like a boy?*

"Great." Zona slapped her on the back. "Here, try on these shoes. I think Henry's will be too big. Wait, you need heavy socks. Get out those you knitted last winter."

Josie couldn't believe what fun Zona was having. Didn't she understand how much this was bothering her to be so easily stripped of her femininity? If she hadn't known better, she would have thought Zona was mean-spirited, but she had never known her to do one hurtful thing. Josie pulled on socks, then the scuffed high-top boots. They were a little big. One more pair of socks would take care of the problem; better than too small. Her hands lacing the boots were feminine. *But who cares about pretty hands?* She could feel tears coming so she swallowed hard. Zona didn't have patience for tears.

"Oh, look, Josie. You almost spilled your bottle of perfume." She picked it up and held it to her nose. "Ah. Flieder. Reminds me of my childhood." She set it down gently.

"I bought it for you, Zona. It got lost in the shuffle."

"Me?" She picked up the bottle, almost caressing it, and smelled it again. "No, child. Those times are gone. I'm too rough. You keep it and let me smell it sometime." Her eyes were soft as if she remembered a time when she might have loved a bottle of lilac perfume. Her manner changed abruptly as if she were ashamed of her softness. "Let's get back to business."

She took Josie by the shoulders and turned her around. "Look at you. You can hike to your heart's content and no one will guess you're a girl. Now, I'll line up a pack animal for you and you can be off." She was triumphant. "Ain't it great how it's all working out?"

"I suppose so. It's happening so fast." She forced a cheerful face.

"Shucks, child. I hate it when people have dreams they can't make come true."

"Did you have dreams, Zona?"

"I suppose, a long time ago. But the kids are my dreams now. Living here is Ott's dream. You borrow other people's dreams and let them be your own. It's part of being a woman. But when you're young and have your own dreams, you need to make them happen." She patted Josie on her bottom, "You look so pert in those," and headed out the door. "I've got to get. Now, don't let anybody know but Willy. We've got to include him so he can help us pull it off. When you decide when you're going, let me know." She was gone as quickly as she had come.

Josie looked in the mirror. It confirmed everything Zona said. She was not a beauty. She knew that. Her father had told her as much when he caught her looking in the mirror once. "There isn't a one of you girls who can hold a candle to your mother when it comes to looks."

Afterwards she studied her sisters' faces. He was right. They took after his side of the family and those women weren't known for beauty. She did look like a boy, maybe one with a feminine face, but who would guess, if they saw her, she was a twenty-one year-old woman, independent, employed in a responsible position?

She sighed and sat down. The jeans were remarkably comfortable. She felt unencumbered. She had been in a long skirt for several years. There were no options. All ladies wore them. But in jeans, she could sit the way she had always wanted to sit but couldn't and be ladylike. She pulled one foot up onto the chair and put her arm around her knee. Very comfortable. She crossed one leg over the other with the ankle resting on her knee. That felt good. She put it down and slouched. That was okay. She stood and put the chair facing the wrong direction and straddled the seat, the way she had seen men do when they wanted to talk to someone. She squatted in front of an imaginary fire and didn't have to worry if her skirt were getting dirty or in the embers. That was an advantage. She looked at the boots. What difference would it make if she scuffed them or got them muddy? Who would care? She could clean them when she got back. All winter the hem of her skirt had been wet from snow. What an advantage it would have been to wear pants instead. *I really should have been born a boy. It would have been easier and besides I have the shape of one.* She sighed. *It's not fair. Why do I have to go through life as a woman, looking like a boy, so no man will love me, but I don't get the advantages of being a boy–or a man. It's just not fair.*

She undressed, put on her skirt and blouse, and folded the clothes that would take her into the back country. *I'm going to go. I am going to go. If I look like a boy, then I might as well act like one.*

Willy became an important resource. He told her what Matteo could remember about the trail, the distance, and the terrain. What Willy could remember Matteo said and what she would remember of what Willy told her didn't inspire her confidence she would make it to Savage Lakes. "Just remember, when the stream splits you go left. There isn't a trail on the right one. Stay on the trail." *Well, I'll go for as long as I'm able and get as high as I can, then I'll come home. Why do I have to have a destination?* She considered how long she could be out before she would get lonely. She decided on four days and three nights. If Zona would help her plan food, she would do the rest. What rest? She had no idea what she would need. Matches. She would certainly need matches. Something to sleep on and wrap up in. She looked at the beautiful quilt. *No, absolutely not. I can't sleep on the ground with that lovely quilt. Oh, what has come over me? I feel like I'm running away from something. This has no joy in it. I wanted a little adventure, not some expedition in costume. It's like a theatrical show: me on stage, making a fool of myself.*

Surrounded by gunny sacks filled with canned goods, oatmeal, prunes, cheese, bread, salami, a potato, and tea, a wire grate for the fire, skillet, heavy spatula, pan, fork and spoon, her sleeping roll–an old wool quilt of Zona's–one tarp to make a tent, another to sleep on and to cover the pack, a warm but heavy water-proof canvas coat, a long rope, and extra sets of clothes, Josie felt she was off to the end of the world. She included her sketchbook with drawings she had made of flora and fauna. Zona sneered at the number of things Josie thought she would need but had herself packed enough food "for an army", as Willy derided. Reassessing, she and Zona agreed to cut the rations by half and eliminate one change of underclothes. But they didn't admit it to Willy. Going over everything with her several times, Zona and Willy instructed her how to build a fire ring and fire. How to string rope between two trees and put the tarp over it. How to stake its corners so it wouldn't flap in the wind. And to keep her food tucked into a pannier away from the tent.

Because of their friendship, Josie confided in Mr. Miller about her camping trip. Did he feel she would be safe? Was it too risky for a woman? Did he think she could be a convincing boy?

As they weighed these questions, she could tell the trip made him nervous. The day before she left he knocked on the cabin door. She was surprised to see him as he'd never been there before. She invited him in.

"No'm, t'wouldn't be proper. I haven't come to visit. I have something for you." He handed her a miner's lamp. "You might need to get around in the dark." He unscrewed the bottom to show her the rocks then put it back together. He asked her for some water. "You put a little water in the top part." He removed the lid, added water, then replaced the lid. "Take this lever and move it to here. It drips water on the rocks and makes a gas. Can you smell it?"

"Yes!"

"Good. When you smell that you're ready to light it. Strike a match, hold it here."

"That's a bright light!"

He nodded. "When you're through, move the lever back which turns it off then dump out the water. This many rocks will last quite a while and should be plenty, but don't use it when you don't have to."

"This is so much better than the candle I was taking. Thank you."

He nodded and pulled something wrapped in cloth from his coat pocket. "I also want you to take this gun with you."

"Oh, Mr. Miller. I don't think I want a gun. I couldn't shoot anything."

"Yes, you could. You might have to. All you do is point it and pull the trigger." He unwrapped the pistol, took the bullets out and showed her how to point it, where the trigger was, and how to pull it. "Here, you do it." Reluctantly, she took the gun and pointed it at the floor and pulled the trigger. "Again." He nodded his head for her to do it again. "Okay." He put the bullets in and gave it back to her. "You have five bullets. That should scare anything. Promise me you'll take it with you, in case."

"In case of what?" she asked, horrified.

"In case the donkey breaks a leg and you have to kill it. In case a bear comes around."

"A bear!" Josie was alarmed.

"Yes'm, they live here too. They won't hurt you if you don't threaten them, but they will eat your food. Noise would frighten one. Or in case you need to signal for help."

"Signal for help? Why will I need help?"

"If you break a leg."

"But who will be up there to help me?"

"Well, someone will be, if you don't come back." He seemed so concerned, she agreed and thanked him for taking care of her.

I don't have to take it out of the pack. He'll never know. She wrapped it as he had and again in a shirt and buried it at the bottom of a gunny sack.

The panic she experienced when she got off the train the first time again welled up in her. It was small comfort to know Willy would accompany her to Biglow's where they would rent the donkey. He would walk with her for about three miles up the North Fork road, past the two houses to the trailhead. Then he would go back to catch the train heading down the valley. After she went a bit farther on her own, she would go into the forest, change her clothes, and be off on her exploit, or whatever this was. She hated to contemplate what it might end up being. Her misgivings were so numerous she couldn't count them, not the least of which was the pistol in the bottom of the pack. She could get lost. Not really. You can't get lost in these mountains; come down hill, they assured her. It all comes down hill. *A smart person would back out. An intelligent person wouldn't have gotten herself into this position. A lady would not be dressing up in boys' clothes to do something women aren't supposed to do in the first place. Oh, Mother, please don't watch. No! Please watch over me.* Sleepless nights. Troubled days.

She stood waiting for the train to take her to her fate. She tried to smile bravely as Zona, buoyed by the excitement of adventure, clapped her on the back and wished her "safe journey." *Oh, indeed. Safe, stupid, journey.* True to form, Zona enthusiastically waved goodbye to Josie, a reluctant camper, and to Willy, her skeptical companion.

After wavering about the duration of the trip, they had talked her into two days in, one day there, and two days out. This seemed reasonable to Zona and Willy when planning the trip. It became reasonable to her too, given where she wanted to go and considering the infrequently used trail might be difficult to follow. As she waved goodbye to a beaming Zona, Josie almost wished they could trade places for five days. *Let her have this adventure. She, who started having children at sixteen. She, who is only thirty-one now and would love to get away from the post office, grocery store, kids, Otto too probably, for five days of peace and quiet. But no, it's me, who has nothing to run from who's running away. This makes no sense.*

The train stopped briefly at Thomasville, then headed up the valley. A quick stop at Biglow to let her and Willy off. Leaving her beside the tracks with her gunny sacks, Willy climbed the hill to Biglow's and was soon back with a donkey wearing a pack saddle with panniers. She knew what saddles looked like, but she had never seen one like this. It had wood where a person usually sat, more wood made two X's over the back of the saddle. Hanging off the X's were two dirty canvas bags with loops at their tops. Willy handed her the donkey's lead rope and put her provisions in these panniers. The donkey rubbed its head against her shoulder and she jumped. It jumped in response.

"Whoa." Willy yelled. "What happened?"

"I think I scared it."

"Hold her steady. Let her know who's boss."

She looked helplessly into big brown eyes. It knew who boss was. There would be no contest. *I might spend five days a hundred yards up the road from where I am right now if it requires me to be boss.*

"If you'll dig out your disguise, I'll pack it with your lunch where you can get at it." She watched closely to see where he put both the clothes and lunch. He carefully weighed the two packs. "If you don't balance them, Miss Carter, the saddle will slide to the heavy side." He hung the panniers on the opposite cross arms and placed the smaller canvas over them. "Now, watch and I'll show you how to throw a diamond hitch."

"A what?"

"A diamond hitch is what you tie over the tarp that covers your pack, see? To keep your stuff dry when it rains."

Please, no rain.

"Then you have to snug it down, so it doesn't flap and scare Daisy. Animals don't like things flapping in the breeze." He started pulling the belt with the hook at one end and a rope at the other end under the donkey. "See? Like this."

He made turns, twists, and fancy loops. She couldn't follow anything he was doing. "Would you mind doing it once more, please? I think you lost me there at the first." She felt hopelessly overwhelmed.

"Here. Take the rope, and I'll show you what to do."

He guided her hands through intricate maneuvers. "See, when you're through, the rope forms a diamond on top. That's where it gets its name." He smiled at their handiwork. "Do you want to try it once more, by yourself?"

No! "Yes, if you think I should."

He undid the rope. She reached under Daisy and grabbed the belly strap with the hook. Daisy raised her hind hoof and Josie jumped back.

"Did you see that? I don't think she likes me."

"She shifted her weight. She doesn't care about you unless you abuse her. Now, try again."

She started over and got the strap under Daisy. She tried to remember what came next but looked at him helplessly. He didn't say anything. She draped the rope across the top then hooked the rope underneath and continued taking the rope around the panniers, brought the rope up, did a couple of loops over the ends of the panniers and tied it off. There was no diamond on top.

"Let's go over it once more."

She tugged at the rope. He guided her slowly through the maneuvers. It was starting to make a little sense to her, but only a little.

"There," he announced. "You're ready."

Ready? She looked at the road ahead and the hills surrounding them: absolute isolation. *Ready? For what?*

They walked about three miles up the road. Her every-day-boots worked well on it, but Zona had been smart to give her some rough ones to wear on the trail. Willy walked ahead of her just as her brothers had distanced themselves from little sisters. Daisy, on a lead rope, followed obediently as if she knew to behave since Willy was there. Josie frowned at the docile animal hoping they could learn to cooperate.

At the end of the road, Willy stopped. "This is as far as I go. I have to catch the train down." He checked the cinch on Daisy. "You know how to put the saddle on, right?"

She looked at him. *Doesn't Daisy wear it?* She shook her head.

His shoulders sagged. "I guess I should have asked earlier. I can't do it now without taking everything off. You undo this strap, here, see?" He put his fingers around the cinch strap. "Pull it through this ring until you have about this much left then pull up hard and finish it with a girth hitch. You should be able to get your two fingers under the leather, see?" He showed her. "She'll take on air to make it looser, so check it after she's all loaded then tighten it. Make sure you get the breeching strap right or it'll make her mad." He lifted Daisy's tail to show where the strap went that kept the pack from slipping forward over her narrow withers. Looking at her face, which showed total confusion and near panic he said, "Golly, Miss Carter, I'm sorry I didn't ask before we loaded her. I don't have time to redo it now."

"I'm the sorry one, Willy, I didn't know I needed to know how to saddle her. I mean, I didn't know I should ever take it off."

He looked defeated. He wanted to make her trip successful. He was flattered she and his mother trusted him, but there was so much she didn't know. If Otto knew what these two ignorant women were up to, he'd have a fit.

Feeling as defeated as Willy looked, Josie apologized. "I'm sorry I'm so ignorant about all this. I think your mom and I didn't appreciate what camping involves. I want you to know, it was my idea, not hers. She just helped me. Do you think I'd better go back with you?" she asked hopefully.

"No. I don't mean to talk you out of your great adventure. By any chance do you know how to hobble her for the night?"

"Do what?"

"Hobble" He looked limp. "You have to put handcuff-like things on her feet, so she can't run away. Otherwise, she'll come home without you. They're in the bottom of the pack. Just turn sideways," he put his shoulder into Daisy's withers, "and pick up a front foot and buckle the hobble around it, then do the other side. She won't give you any trouble. She's a good old donkey. Ma found the best one in the valley. Everyone says she's smarter than their neighbor and sometimes they say which one." He wanted to lighten the mood. It didn't work.

Helplessness was overwhelming her. "Do I need to know any more about her?"

"Who knows? I guess you can always come home early." Weary with the burden of her ignorance, he also knew he would be the one to come find her. That would be easy because she'd probably be half a mile up the trail. "Look. If she comes home without you, we'll come looking for you and if you hear us hollering, holler back so we can find you."

She nodded. *I guess this is when I shoot the gun.* "I'll try to do everything right, so you won't have to come get me. I promise."

"Oh, it's okay. I won't mind if I have to."

"Have you ever seen a bear, Willy?"

"Once. A long time ago. They aren't common. You'll be lucky to see one. I'd love to see one again."

"You don't consider them a problem?"

"No, neither should you." He was sensing a mutiny. His mother had taken him into her confidence because she had no one else she could trust to get Josie started on the trip now that Henry was working at the quarry. If the trip were ruined at the last minute because he scared her with tales of bears, his mother would be furious with him. "Don't worry, Miss Carter. You'll be okay. I don't know anybody who sees bears up there. Promise." He crossed his heart and spit on the ground.

She looked at him steadily. She couldn't tell if were saying there weren't any just to get himself out of a jam. "I hope you're telling the truth, Willy, because if you're not, and a bear eats me, I will never forgive you." *And I mean it!*

Grinning, he shook his head. "Don't worry. Have a good time. See you in four days." He turned, hurrying down the road. He looked back to see if she were following him. They waved to each other. He went around a curve and her contact with civilization disappeared.

Coming up the North Fork road a timberline peak was perfectly framed by lower mountains. The trail where she started was in a chilly, tight valley affording no view of the peak and no sunshine. She knew it would be a long, slow trip, especially if she dallied. To make friends with Daisy, who was contentedly grazing, Josie patted her and noticed her fingernails were dirty from tying the pack. *Well, I guess my hands won't give me away. But give me away to whom?* She looked at her skirt, dusty boots, and smudges on her blouse. *I'm not very feminine even in my girl clothes.*

A short way up the trail she retrieved her boy costume and went behind a clump of trees. When she emerged, she appeared a different person. She tucked her skirt, blouse, and shoes into the pannier so she could return to her feminine self when the trip was over. No one meeting her would guess she was other than a young boy on a camping trip.

The mountains that lay before her reached 11,000'. She was starting was at 9,000'. *Why? Why am I doing this crazy thing? It makes no sense. It's as though some inexplicable force that's once set in motion stays in motion, so I'm going as if I've lost all control over my actions.* The valley floor widened as she climbed and almost leveled out. *I can handle this,* thinking the meadow might go on forever.

The trail ascended the North Fork of the Frying Pan River to two lakes lying below Savage Peak, the stream's headwaters. Although prospectors had explored the area none had found enough precious mineral worth the effort of getting it out. The valley that had once known the indomitable energy of man in search of treasure lay tranquil before her.

The first hour of her journey she spent in wonder: the density of trees; diversity of wildflowers gone to seed; those still blooming; various shades of green, red, and gold in undergrowth; the fragrance of pine, fir, and spruce; the musty smell of bogs. She wanted to preserve it in her memory. Gradually realizing there were no indications of man except the faint trail, she reveled in the pristine forest. Alongside the stream plummeting down the mountain over and around boulders in its bed, the trail came to a steep incline and petered out.

She gingerly crossed the creek on exposed rocks and headed up the steep hill to a gentle slope. She wound around huge boulders, always climbing. Daisy followed, stepping over downed logs, working her way between trees passable for Josie, but tight for the bulging panniers. Stopping occasionally for a refreshing drink, they continued up and eventually came upon the trail.

Weary, she stopped to eat. Had anything ever tasted as good as the hunk of bread, pieces of cheese and salami? After lunch she lay back on the soft grassy mound next to the stream. Overhead the sky was brilliant blue. Huge white clouds billowed like sails on a ship, or so she imagined, her memories of sailing ships on Lake Ontario now dim. A gray bird larger than a robin watched from a spruce branch. A squirrel's chatter filled the air. Perched on a rock, a fat woodchuck whistled. *Glorious, simply glorious, this feeling of space and absence of time and responsibility to others.*

She picked herself up, snugged the pack as best she could and headed uphill. Lavender flowers bloomed alongside the creek in full sunlight. Stately purple stalks hugged the stream. Yellow flowers with heart-shaped leaves, which looked like the arnica in her drawings, preferred evergreen shade. Because her mother had used arnica as medicine, she was fascinated to see it growing here. Occasionally, she came upon a fat toadstool which she hadn't researched because she didn't know mushrooms grew wild. She loosened ropes on the pack, found her sketchbook and pencils and quickly drew one of the beautiful, shaggy brown ones. She would find out if they were edible, because she knew some were poisonous. Trying to keep her boots dry in a boggy area, she walked on downed logs and jumped from one hummock of moss to another, an advantage of wearing pants, while Daisy slogged through, an advantage of not wearing shoes.

The sun was low in the sky and clouds were building in the west. She decided it was time to pick a spot to make camp. She hiked until she came to a peaceful meadow with the North Fork, a small stream now, flowing through it. A high spot felt dry. A nearby rock outcropping would make a good place for a fire. Turning to ask Daisy if she felt this would be a good spot, she realized she was talking to the donkey as if it understood and would answer. *Oh, heavens, and I'm only part of a day out.*

After tying Daisy to a tree, she retrieved her sketchbook. Studying ins and outs of rope on the pack, she began to draw. When she had the correct steps, she untied the rope and took off the panniers. Then she wandered around until she found two trees spaced the right distance apart, but it was rocky underneath them. She searched until she found a place that would do. She looked back to where her packs rested. A fair walk away. *Oh, well, I don't need to sleep by the fire. Wait. I don't need to carry all my stuff to the tent, Daisy can do it.* Feeling proud of this insight, she put the panniers back on Daisy and led her to the trees. After tying the tent rope with an overhand knot, stretching it to the other tree and tying it again, she threw the tarp over and watched it sag almost to the ground. She took it off, pulled harder on the rope and re-tied it. It sagged. She put the rope higher so when it sagged it would still give her room to get under it. This worked in a sloppy way, but it worked. She staked the corners. Pleased with her little shelter, she crawled in and peered around. Not a lot of space for her and her things, but it would do. She spread the ground cloth and put the quilt on top. *What a charming little room with a nice breeze coming up the valley.*

The sun was getting lower. *It would be smart to eat before sunset, so I'm not stumbling around in the dark.* Casting a pleased smile at her tent, she saw it sagging even more. Daisy, standing with her saddle and panniers on, made her heart sink. She had to hurry to get it all done as well as cook dinner before the sun set. *Oh. I need to build a fire ring and gather wood.*

She hurried to Daisy, lifted off the panniers and heard the hobbles rattle. *Oh, no. I need to handcuff her.* In her sketchbook she drew how the leather cinch strap went through the brass ring. Then she sketched how that funny strap went around the donkey's backside, under her tail. She undid the saddle and found the blanket was separate. *Too much, way too much stuff.* She looked at the hobbles: buckles on two belts with a chain in between. "We can do this, can't we, Daisy?" She put her shoulder against the donkey the way Willy had and picked up a foot. "You dear creature, you seem to know what to do." She buckled it and went to the other side. Daisy cooperated. Josie stared at her. "Are you going to take care of me, or are you going to run away?" Daisy didn't move. "All right. I'll trust you once." She laughed out loud. When would the second chance come? She untied Daisy and watched her hop her front feet over to the stream to drink. "Oh, please be a good donkey and stay."

Back at her sacks, she got food, the pan, matches, and stopped by the stream for water. The wilderness exhilarated her. *This is what I wanted. This is exactly where I hoped to be.* Having gathered kindling, she built a fire. When the water boiled, she poured some for a cup of tea then replaced the pan with the skillet into which she dumped a can of pork and beans, her supper. It had sounded okay at home; it looked like a lot of beans now. The bread, cheese, and salami were lunches. She couldn't eat them. She remembered prunes. To break the monotony, she would have one now and a couple for breakfast.

Sitting on a rock, eating supper out of the pan, she looked down the valley and up at the peaks. Those clouds were darker and much nearer and a cool breeze was picking up. She went to her sacks to get the coat. In the bottom lay the fearsome gun. If she took it out, was there a chance she could shoot Daisy? Very carefully, with two fingers she picked it up by what felt like the handle. She breathed deeply. She had not killed the donkey or herself, yet. Wrapped in additional layers of clothing, it seemed less ominous.

As she ate, she observed the north facing slope of the steep valley. Lush with evergreens and bushes it contrasted with the south facing slope which was littered with angular slabs broken off from rocky cliffs high above in winter's freeze-thaws. Sparse, scrubby trees grew among rocks where they could get a toehold. Here, on the valley floor, were stands of aspen and where a water course came off the hills, willows. Reflecting a sunset brilliant with orange, peach, and deep blue shadows, the peak at the head of the valley began to glow until it looked lit from within. *What must it look like in winter when it's snow-covered?* She grabbed her sketchbook and tried to capture the colors and her feeling of elation in words.

After eating she put the remaining food in a pannier and hauled it away from her tent and tucked it under a tree. Washing her skillet and fork in the stream, rinsing the can so it had no smell to attract a bear, she returned to stir the fire until there were no embers. *This is when I should light the lantern, I think, but where is it?* Daisy was standing nearby, head lowered, tail to the wind. Josie undressed, pulled on long-johns and coat hoping to see stars, but clouds had massed overhead.

A raindrop. *Oh, my. I'm not prepared for this.* Taking inventory of what was outside the tent, she gathered pannier, saddle, and blanket and pushed them inside. She climbed in behind, wind beginning to whip the canvas, rain coming down hard. She had barely made it. Lightning shattered the sky. Thunder ricocheted off rock cliffs. Wind-driven rain from the west was coming through the open end of the tent. She struggled to move the pannier to form a barricade at the narrow entrance. The tarp grew heavier on the rope, sagging more, making it difficult to sit upright. *So, go to bed.* Stretching out, rocks poked her which she awkwardly dug out. She put the saddle blanket under her. *Better. Not perfect.* Wind and rain flapping and pounding the tarp, thunder rumbling overhead, had a curiously frightening, thrilling effect on her. Tired from exertion, drained by dread and excitement from the whole undertaking, she lay down and soon was asleep.

When she awoke the sun was beginning to come over the shoulder of the peak. The sky was clear, the air chilly. *Daisy. Where's Daisy?* She grazed not far from where she had been the night before. *You dear creature.* Pushing the pannier out of her way so she could get out from underneath the sagging tent, Josie remembered to pull on her shabby engineer's hat, her ultimate camouflage. Here in the solitude of the wilderness she couldn't imagine needing it. Wincing at her poor excuse for a tent, she knew if it hadn't been for the pannier it would have been on top

55

of her. She pulled the stakes and hauled the tarp to the top of a large boulder, turned the panniers so sun would hit them, spread the saddle blanket to dry before she put it on Daisy. The quilt needed sunshine if it were to keep her warm that night. Busy as a housewife, she straightened her home. She took the hobbles off the donkey, telling her she was a good girl, and led her to the stream to drink, then tied her loosely to a tree. Gathering dry twigs and dead branches under overhanging boughs, she built a fire. The food under the tree had not suffered an invasion. In no time she would be eating oatmeal. *What an exciting world this is. If Father could see me now!* She almost said it out loud.

She guessed she had come halfway and might make it to the lakes by night if everything would dry so she could pack. She flipped tarps, quilt, saddle blanket and everything else she had strewn around. The sun's magic was working.

Estimating it to be ten o'clock by the sun's height, she needed to go. She led Daisy to the campsite and put the blanket on her back. Gingerly lifting the tail, Josie put the strap under it and pulled the saddle forward. *Could someone have thought this was the best way?* It didn't matter. She reached under Daisy and grabbed the cinch strap, threaded it through the ring and pulled it tight. *Is this when she does the air thing?* She couldn't imagine this good-natured creature would pull such a stunt. She would check later. Studying her drawing, she made loops in the leather cinch strap and pulled. She didn't want to make Daisy uncomfortable. Pleased, she stood back to admire her workmanship and saw Daisy let out a big breath, loosening the strap. Josie tightened it. She lifted the semi-dry panniers onto the cross arms of the saddle. She weighed the gunny sacks, determined they were equal and put them in the panniers, leaving her lunch where she could reach it. When she was through loading, she put the tarp over it and began to throw the diamond hitch. By following her diagram, she made a reasonable facsimile of Willy's art.

Leading the donkey through the meadow, she saw the trail ahead of her, a welcome sight as she had lost it several times when they went through bogs and crossed the stream to avoid downed timber. The climb was not steep but constantly up. When she determined by the sun and her stomach it must be about lunchtime they stopped. The meadow was full of tall spikes with tiny purple flowers that curled at their ends. She sketched them for later identification.

When she got up from lunch, she noticed the saddle did not align with Daisy's back. The cinch strap was loose. She wrestled the saddle into place then tightened the cinch again. Ahead she could see mountain sides towering above her, but she could no longer see peaks. *I hope that's a good sign.* Ascending until at last, by late afternoon, she came over a low rise and there lay the lake, shimmering in the sunshine with a beauty like no other. Cradled in a bowl beneath the peak, the tranquility of the setting stopped her. She didn't want to disturb its perfection. Grassy areas surrounded the lake strewn with large boulders from ancient glaciers. Huge fragmented rocks sheared from the mountain cluttered the surroundings. Hardy flowers from summer persisted in blooming even as fall crept down the peaks. Such a spectacular panorama of natural beauty and peacefulness far exceeded her dreams. She was filled with joy.

The trail abruptly ended at a camp site. Although not recently used, the rocks for a fire ring remained, log stools surrounded it, and a make-shift corral in the trees awaited Daisy. *I wonder who was here and why?* She looked around for some sign or tell-tale trash to give her a clue. There was nothing. She tied Daisy to a tree and hurried to the lake. Standing at its edge she threw her arms out, her head back and shouted, "Thank you, World." Her voice echoed off the rock cliffs. She hugged herself in happiness. She had made it. Turning around, she froze. A man leading a mule was coming toward her.

He's seen me! She panicked.

"Hello," he said and stuck his hand out, chuckling to himself that the display he'd just witnessed was not a man's weird behavior but that of an exuberant kid.

"*Shake hands like a man,*" she remembered a teacher telling the boys. She held her hand out and the man gripped her hand hard. She winced but squeezed back, like a man.

"My name's Andrew Allan." She stared at the ground. He had to ask, "And yours?"

My name? She couldn't look at him. Remembering to drop her voice a few notes, she answered. "Joe?"

"Well, glad to meet you, Joe. Mind if I share the lake with you?"

Share the lake with me? With a man? She was horrified. She couldn't move. Andrew looked at her expectantly. Her silence confused him and he awkwardly said, "I can move on if you'd like. I don't mean to intrude."

Without looking at him she answered, "It's. . . okay." *What did I say? That he could stay when he offered to leave? What's the matter with me?*

"Great. This is one of my favorite places."

Deep voice, "Oh?"

"Yup. Came through with the survey crew last year. Thought it was beautiful."

"Yes."

"I've been following your tracks. Guess you just got here."

Startled, her voice rising. "Yes." *He's been following me.*

"Picked up the trail below Henderson Park. I spent last night at Tellurium Lake, looking around."

"Oh."

"Picked your campsite yet?"

"No." *But I'd like to be as far away from you as I can be.*

"I suggest that spot over in those firs where the lead surveyor was last summer."

"Is that where you'll be?" her voice as low as she could make it.

"No. I'll be down by the lake again."

"Oh." *Good, get as far away as you can.*

"We could share a campfire, though."

How can Joe possibly object to that? "Okay."

"Good. I'll go set up my camp. See you in a while for supper."

She nodded and he left.

Andrew shook his head. *Never had such a warm welcome. Like asking a girl for a date. Either he's painfully shy or scared of strangers.*

Josie watched him go to make sure he left. *Now's the time to escape. We can slip through the trees and head back down the trail.* She started to lead Daisy out and saw Andrew at the lake. He looked up. *He's seen me. He'll follow me again. Maybe I'm safer here with the gun.* She studied the forest and decided if she were back in the trees she could hear him coming in the night because he would step on downed branches. It would also afford more privacy, not that privacy would matter if he were up to no good. She led Daisy into the densest part, undid the sloppy diamond hitch and pulled the tarp to the ground trying to figure out which trees it would fit between. Knowing the sagging problem, she made her first knot very high, stretched the rope and tied it high around another tree. Remembering the rocks under her back, she kicked the dry needles to find hidden lumps. The story of the princess and the pea a Danish teacher had told her class came to mind and she reminded herself she was no princess but there was nothing wrong with avoiding pain. Satisfied, she draped the tarp over the rope and saw it sag pitifully. *That's just what happens.* Pulling out the corners she pounded in the stakes. She unloaded the panniers and began putting her gear into the tent. In the bottom of the sack lay the gun. She unwrapped it cautiously and held it in her hand the way Mr. Miller had shown her, but she didn't put her finger on the trigger. *In an emergency, I'm to point and shoot. I can do that. If I have to, I'll shoot him.* She put it in her coat pocket. *I hope he'll wait until I fish it out of my pocket before he does anything bad.* She grimaced at how hopeless protecting herself would be.

She was taking her grate, pans, and utensils to the fire pit when she saw Andrew coming from the lake with his cooking equipment. *Please, please don't guess I'm not a boy. Maybe Zona wasn't the best judge I look convincing but if I keep my head down, my voice low when I'm forced to speak, maybe he'll be on his way in the morning and I'll survive. I hope he can be quiet and enjoy the scenery and not try to make conversation. Why did I have to do this stupid adventure that could turn out so badly? Mother, are you watching over me?*

Andrew put down his gear and looked around for her tent, locating it in the trees. "You're back in there."

"Yes." *I was hoping you wouldn't see it in daylight.*

"Ready to cook?"

"Yes."

He lit the fire then busied himself poking in sticks they had gathered, all the while watching her and wondering why she was wearing a heavy coat.

A four-word vocabulary. This could be a long evening. Why did I suggest sharing the campfire?

"You go first, Joe. I have some mushrooms to clean before I start."

She began to peel the potato.

"A potato. Interesting. Never tried a potato up here. Does it take long to cook?"

She had no idea. She shrugged. "No." His watching made her nervous and she cut the potato into larger chunks than she and Zona had discussed. It would take a while to cook those even at lower altitudes. She opened the can of corned beef hash, skimmed fat from the top to fry the potatoes.

Andrew could see he was making Joe uncomfortable by watching and he had been watching closely. There was something strange about Joe's hands: they were what? Fine boned? Long tapering fingers? Peeled the potato like he'd peeled lots of them? Something about them didn't seem right, even though the fingernails were dirty. He shook it off. "I'm going to the lake to clean mushrooms."

She nodded. *Get rid of him.*

He walked slowly. He couldn't imagine the potato would cook through. He took his time getting the water, washed his hands and the mushrooms, messed around and slowly came back to camp. His mind was struggling with who this curious kid might be. Was he a runaway because he was different? He seemed ill-prepared for a camping trip, not the way a father would typically send a boy out alone.

At the campfire the potato was still frying. Seeing him sit, Josie quickly dumped in the corned beef and stirred it until it was warm then pulled her skillet from the grate and nodded to him.

"No hurry," he said, "I'm happy sitting here looking at the view."

She shook her head and took a bite of potato. It was hard but she chewed anyway, hoping he couldn't hear it crunch.

He ducked his head so she couldn't see his grin. He put some butter from a jar into his skillet and sliced mushrooms into it to fry. He pulled a large loaf of bread from his sack, cut off a hunk and put some deviled ham on it. "Care for bread with your dinner, Joe?"

She looked at the tempting piece of bread extended toward her. "Thank you." Her deep voice wasn't predictable, and this made her nervous. She reached for the bread.

I think this is how you tame wild animals. "Got it in Leadville a few days ago before I took the train to Thomasville. It's been knocking around on the mule but I think it still tastes good."

"Yes." She nodded. *Oh, yes. It tastes good with that delicious deviled ham. So much better than a can of beans or raw potatoes and barely warmed corned beef.*

Andrew stirred his mushrooms which were giving off a delectable odor. Josie, frowning, watched him carefully. He saw her concern. "Boletus edulis. We ate them last summer and never got sick. Usually little worms in them, but they're food too. Lots of cultures would relish them. Here. I'll give you a taste."

"Oh, no." She forgot her deep voice. She might like mushrooms; she was sure she wouldn't like little worms.

He hid his grin by bending over his cooking. After the mushrooms browned to a caramel color, he put them on his plate, dumped a can of corn into the pan and spread the remainder of the deviled ham on a hefty piece of bread. When the corn was hot, he offered her some.

She couldn't accept his food without offering him some of hers and her raw potatoes would reveal her incompetence which would be embarrassing. She shook her head. "No, thank you." Her deep voice faltered.

He nodded, guessing what the problem might be and sat back on his log to eat.

"Rugged up here, isn't it?" he asked.

"Yes." Trying to hide the crunch of her potatoes, she continued to eat.

He didn't ask any more questions during dinner but caught quick glimpses of Joe as he could. The way he held his fork: not like most country folks who grabbed the handle with their whole fist. And small bites. Not the way a kid typically ate. This boy mystified him. He guessed Joe was having trouble fitting in with other boys his age and this trip by himself was an excuse to get away from teasing and ridicule. Memories of a misfit boy he'd known troubled him. That boy's life had not ended well.

While they were quietly eating their dinners, Josie glanced at Andrew. He was blonde, not handsome but had a pleasant face, several days' growth of beard and large hands. She knew he was tall. He had on denim pants and sturdy, well-worn boots. Quick peeks were all she dared.

After she had eaten supper, she went to the lake to get water for tea. She wanted to offer to get Andrew water as well but didn't trust her voice. Filling her pan very full so he could have some of hers she carefully carried it back to the fire. She put the pan on the grate and sat back to watch it heat. He was looking at the volume of water. "Tea," she said, and with her eyes down, "For you too."

"Thanks, Joe. Tea'll feel good as the temperature drops."

Nodding, "Yes."

"Where'd you start your hike?" he asked.

Oh, no. He wants to talk. Why can't we be quiet? "Biglow."

"Is that where you live?"

"No."

"You're from around here, then?"

"Meredith." *Why did I tell him?*

"Lived there a long time?"

"No. Yes."

Guess it hinges on the definition of 'long'. "Do you have a school there?"

"Yes."

"What grade are you in?"

"Finished eighth." *How old does that make me?*

"About fourteen?"

"Yes."

This is too much work. Either I do a monologue or I'm going to my tent. "We should have stars tonight. Moon was full a few nights ago, so it won't be up for a couple of hours. Last night I got a glimpse of it through the clouds. Beautiful the way it turned them gold. Were you out last night in that rain?"

"Yes."

"Get a little wet?" He pictured her tent and how effective it would have been in a rainstorm.

"Yes." She gathered their cooking gear to wash. *Got to get out of here.* He watched her with surprise.

"You don't have to wash my stuff."

"My job." She headed resolutely to the little stream that drained the lake. *What is he thinking?* She'd never seen a man do dishes. Her father had never so much as carried a dirty cup to the kitchen. Otto would never consider helping with dishes. That was woman's work. When she returned, Andrew was putting more wood on the fire and the water was starting to boil. She put the cleaned items on the grass and rinsed them with hot water. Then she put tea leaves in to steep. Andrew watched all her busyness with interest without saying anything. She watched him carefully. It was getting dark!

"Cup?" she asked.

He pulled a metal cup from his sack and handed it to her. She scooped out some tea and handed it back to him then did the same for herself. They sat back on their stools and watched the fire, each sneaking glimpses of the other one.

"I have some Hershey bars at my tent. I'm going to get us one." He asked her if they had Hershey bars in Meredith.

She nodded although she'd never bought one there. She'd had a Hershey bar a couple of times at school when she'd splurged. She couldn't imagine having one at Savage Lake.

"It'll taste good after your big supper." He ducked his head to hide a mischievous grin.

When he returned, he handed half to her. Her eyes widened. Shaking her head, "They're yours," in a deep voice.

"I've got more. I keep them wrapped in damp rags so they don't melt. They look kind of tough, but they taste good."

She didn't put her hand out to take it, "Too much."

"Nonsense. I have more." He continued to hold it out.

She looked up at him, then dropped her eyes, reaching out for the gift. "Thank you."

"You're welcome." *A little tamer with each bite.*

Eating it slowly to savor the luxury, she finished it and said, "Good."

"Glad you liked it. I'm enjoying the tea. It tastes like lemon?"

It was her one indulgence on her teacher's salary. It had been her mother's favorite and something Father had given Mother for presents. She nodded, "Earl Grey."

Unusual for Andrew, he didn't know what to say. Why would a kid from Meredith know about Earl Grey tea let alone bring it on a pack trip? He studied Joe's face as best he could. It was the way he walked and moved his hands that seemed unusual: a little feminine? *I think we may have a troubled kid. Maybe if I don't push too hard he can relax and be friendly.* "Stars are starting to come out."

She looked up. "Yes."

"Know any up there, now?"

"No."

He pointed overhead. "The big W? That's Cassiopeia." Joe shook his head without looking up. *Joe doesn't care. Know when to quit.* "Mind if I play my harmonica? Campfires make me feel like music."

"Okay." *Then you won't be asking so many questions.* She was tired of being cautious. She wanted to relax and enjoy the quiet of the evening and to quit patting the gun in her pocket. Andrew began to play a soft, plaintive tune she hadn't heard before. She was entranced by the sweet coarseness of the sounds. When he finished the song, he knocked the harmonica on his knee and began again, this time with a song she knew, "Oh Susanna", then a rousing "Clementine." Back to a quiet song with "Old Folks at Home." Thinking there was nothing more to do, he lit his miner's lamp and said, "Guess I'll be going to bed. Sleep well."

Deep voice. "You too." *Now can I relax? Does he really believe I'm Joe or is he playing along with me?*

She stirred embers into the dirt and worked her way carefully to her tent. She lay awake for a while thinking about the man who had disrupted her tranquility. She gave him high marks for his patience with Joe, a boring boy who bordered on rude with his unwillingness to talk. She wasn't sure she'd have been so tolerant. She hoped he would leave in the morning, maybe even be gone by the time she was up, but he hadn't said goodbye. She listened for footsteps, a broken twig, a rustling of the low branches. Weary from her hike, fearful of the man, exhausted from being on guard, listening and hearing nothing but wind in trees, Josie finally fell asleep. She didn't sleep soundly. The raw potatoes made her stomach ache.

Andrew didn't go to sleep quickly either. Troubled by observations and behavior that conflicted with Joe's appearance, confused by strange hints of civility that clashed with uncivil behavior, he struggled with impatience with Joe and a desire to befriend who he thought was a friendless kid. Was he being raised by an over-protective mother who was making him a momma's-boy and was he trying to escape those tendrils? Was his family hostile to his strangeness? At last he slept. It had been a long day.

Rising early, Andrew surveyed the unspoiled, peaceful world surrounding him and saw a magnificent buck drinking at the end of the lake. Without thinking of the previous night's awkwardness, he slipped quietly to the campfire to see if Joe were up so he could share the sight of the deer. Joe was not about. Andrew went to the tent. Joe was still asleep. He stopped. There was a long braid behind Joe's head. *A braid? Joe has a braid?*

He stood. *Is he a girl? Joe's a girl?* He left as quickly and quietly as he could.

Why didn't she tell me when I first met her? Well, of course she couldn't. She was completely vulnerable. She didn't know me. No wonder she was so dumb struck when I appeared out of nowhere. That explains the scene at the lake. No wonder she made up a name for herself. What is her name? That's why she kept that ridiculous hat on all the time. And those clothes must be cast-offs from someone. Those pants. She wears pants! Never seen a woman in pants before. Her hands. I knew there was something wrong with those hands and why she automatically thought she should do the dishes. He's a girl. How dumb could I be?

He sat on a rock by the lake's edge, hidden by his tent, and tried to come to grips with the new reality. *A girl who wanted to know the wilderness and could only know it as a man. What does that say about us? She had to fake being a boy to do something that's all right for boys but not for girls. It's what Mom harps about. She took a chance on not meeting anyone, of having her experience and getting away with it. She has gumption. Of course, she wore pants. Women can't hike in long skirts. I've ruined it for her. Absolutely ruined her experience. I can't imagine how terrified she feels. She doesn't know me. Bet she was going to leave after she saw me and was afraid I'd follow her. Of course. I'd already told her I'd been following her. She felt trapped. Had to hope her disguise would work and I'd leave this morning. I need to apologize to her. No. Can't do that. She mustn't ever know I know. It'd frighten her. I need to protect her, take care of her, honor her secret. Oh, yes. Her honor. She can't be here with me without a chaperone. What am I thinking? One of us has to leave.*

Of course, I have to leave this morning. What if she needs help and there's no one to help her? I'm rationalizing staying with her because I'd like to know her better. She intrigues me. Well, she is intriguing. I haven't met a girl like her. I'm calling her a girl when maybe she's a woman. Which is she? Which am I? Boy or man? In-between, I guess. Maybe she's in-between too. Maybe my age. Maybe someone I'd like to know better. I don't even know her name. What difference does a name make? I admire her spirit. I'm not thinking clearly. Not going about this systematically. Systematically, I have these options: One, continue to play along with her being a boy and stay here another day as planned. Two, tell her I'm packing after breakfast and leave without telling her I know. Three, tell her I know she's a girl and see if she wants me to leave. He threw some rocks into the water then noticed the smell of smoke. *She's up. I have to choose an option. One, I can't continue to play along because she's not that good at it and I don't want to. Two, if I pack and leave, I'll never know who she is and I'd like to know her. Three, if I tell her I know, that's the honest thing to do, and maybe she'll say I can stay, we can hike together and enjoy each other's company for a day or two.*

He realized he was talking to himself, he hoped not out loud. He looked up to see if "Joe" were watching him and was relieved to see she was not standing there. *What to do now? How am I supposed to act? No different. Just be me.* He was throwing more rocks into the lake. He stopped. *Calm down. Be natural.* He took a deep breath. *We make everything so complicated. Why can't Joe and I be friends just because he's a she? It makes a difference. It just does. I'm going to be honest, it's the best option.* He grabbed his food sack, a coffee pot full of water and headed toward the fire.

Josie was sitting on a log stump, poking sticks into the fire when he showed up. She didn't look at him. Without looking at her, he put his coffee pot on the grate and said, "Good morning, Joe," and sat down.

She nodded.

"Joe, I have to talk to you." He hesitated, not certain this was how he should proceed. "There was a beautiful buck at the lake this morning. I wanted to show it to you. When I couldn't find you I looked in your tent. You were still asleep. You didn't have your hat on and I saw your braid." His head dipped down. He was feeling this option may not have been the best one. He blurted out, "I have to be honest with you. I know you're a girl. I didn't come to your tent to spy on you. I wanted to share something with you." His hands fidgeted nervously.

He looked up to see her reaction. She was staring at him with frightened eyes, her hands in the coat pockets. She didn't say a word.

He continued without watching her but jammed his hands into his pockets to hide his nervousness. "I understand you might be alarmed because you don't know me, but I want you to know I'm honorable. I won't hurt you. I won't ever tell anyone about camping near you last night. I know I have to leave." He knew he was talking too much and too fast but he was so nervous he didn't know how to stop.

She didn't reply. He tried again. "I want to tell you about myself. For the past two summers I worked on the U.S. Geological Survey. I was in my sophomore and junior years at Mines. That's Colorado School of Mines, a college in Golden. Golden's west of Denver and where my family lives. Classes I take at Mines are about mining and things related to it. Anyway, I got this great job working on the crew. I learned a lot from the surveyors and geologists. I didn't have much free time, so I wanted to come back to get to know this country better, besides, it's beautiful up here. I've been going to some of the lakes this side of the Continental Divide and doing some scratching in the dirt, as we say. I have a draft of a map they've done of this area. I can show it to you."

Still she didn't respond but her eyes weren't as wide open and frightened looking. He took a deep breath. "Be all right if we have breakfast together?"

She didn't look at him or move. Finally, she nodded.

"After breakfast if you want, I'll pack and leave." *Now just be quiet and let her think this through.*

The coffee water was making boiling sounds. Josie picked up her pan and went to the lake for water, returning without saying anything, simply putting it on to heat. Andrew went to the lake for water with his pan, returned and put it on the ground. The coffee water was boiling. He took the pot off the grate, put coffee into the water, put his pan on the grate, then moved out of the way. Josie dumped her oatmeal into her water with some salt and stood back. He scooped oatmeal into his pan, added salt, and sat back down. He stirred the coffee and after a few minutes, he poured himself a cup, tasted it, then asked, "Coffee, Joe?"

Without looking at him, she said, "Yes, thank you," in her normal voice.

He smiled slightly and poured her a cup without saying more.

They took turns stirring their own oatmeal. When Josie's finished cooking, she removed it from the fire, sugared it, and began to eat. "Wait," he said, and offered her raisins and a jar with condensed milk in it.

She looked at him, not knowing if she should accept his food. He nodded to her, "It'll taste better." His voice sounded apologetic.

She nodded and accepted the treats. He took his oatmeal from the fire, put the embellishments on it and sat quietly eating.

Not knowing what to do next, he offered her more coffee which she accepted then thanked him.

She dug in her food sack and produced six prunes which she put in her skillet as a serving dish and handed them to Andrew. He looked at her. She looked at him. He smiled nervously. "Thank you. Sure you won't want them?"

She nodded her head. "We share."

"Okay. We'll share what we have." He took three.

She swirled the grounds in the bottom of her cup, shuffled her feet, then began gathering the dirty pans and cups.

"I'll do the dishes," he jumped to his feet.

"My job."

"Don't be silly. Men can do dishes. Be right back." He bolted for the lake.

Glad for the chance to think, her thoughts began to tumble. *What am I supposed to do? If I ask him to go, I'm ruining a part of his trip, yet he's ruined mine. But he didn't mean to. He's been honest with me. If he were up to no good would he have left when he saw I'm a girl? He was nice to me when he thought I was a boy and he must have thought I was strange and rude. He wanted to show me the stars last night and I could have learned something. But is he the kind of man who'll go to Thomasville and brag about being alone in the woods with a girl? And if he does and it gets to Meredith and they figure out it was me, will the strict parents demand I go because I'm unfit to teach their children? Will they be right? How could I explain to my father why they dismissed me? But if I'd always done what I'm supposed to do, I wouldn't be here. I wouldn't be in Meredith. I wouldn't have gone to normal school. When can a person think for herself? Why can't a person trust another one? Am I ready for the consequences?* She put her head in her hands, wanting to avoid a decision. But also feeling her stubborn nature rebelling against people she didn't know or care much about dictating her behavior.

Andrew returned hoping they'd reached an understanding until he saw she didn't want to look at him. He set her pans on her side of the fire and put his on his side. She watched him, realizing he hadn't left his where he could pack them. She looked at him with a mixture of fright and anger. He read the expression.

His nerves rattled by her silent observation, he began to talk compulsively again, "Look, I know I said I'd leave if that's what you want but I was going to take a hike today, using this as base camp. There's some country I'd like explore. When I thought you were a boy, I was hopeful you'd let me show you the area and explain something about rocks and geology. I don't know if you'd be interested in those things, but if you can trust me, I'd love to share them with you." He felt a desperate need to communicate his good intentions but didn't know how.

She looked up, silently studying his face as if she could read in it what "trust" meant to him. She had to admit he looked pathetically earnest.

He couldn't keep quiet. "Can we hike together, or should I leave?"

After a long pause, she said, "I'm confused, Andrew. It's all coming at me so fast I don't know what I should do."

He nodded. "I'm trying to understand. It's so different for a woman. I wish my mom were here to interpret your concerns. I know you have to guard your reputation. I promise I'll never tell anyone about being here with you, if that's what's bothering you."

"Partly. There's so much at stake if I make the wrong decision."

For what seemed to him a long time, she struggled with her options. Despite resolving to keep quiet, he offered, "Can we compromise? I know you're a girl. You know I know. I'll keep calling you Joe and you can keep wearing that awful hat." He ducked his head to hide a grin.

With that, she gave him a reluctant smile. "I'm not too practiced at compromise but if I can be Joe I think I can go on the hike with you. Will we be back in time for you to pack and leave if I decide I can't do this?"

"Yes. We'll make sure to be back in time. I'll leave then if you want me to go." He was emphatic regarding his intent.

She watched his face. His serious frowns couldn't mask his kindness. She simply nodded and drew patterns in the dirt with a stick.

He gave it another try. "I'd enjoy your company on the hike."

"I think I want to trust you." She looked up. "I'd enjoy going."

He wasn't sure he'd heard her correctly. "You'll trust me?"

"Yes." She stood, straightened her back, and said, "So, let's go."

"Okay." He jumped to his feet. "Get your lunch ready, and we'll be off. Take a coat."

Don't worry. She patted her pocket. "I will."

Andrew called to her from the lake. "Ready to go?"

"Almost." Her bread, cheese, salami, and tin cup were on a rock. She didn't know how to carry them. She folded her coat over her arm, careful not to let the gun slip out of the pocket.

He came up, wearing a wooden-frame pack and offered to carry her food. "This your only coat?"

"Yes."

"Well, it's bulky. Let's go to my camp." He went to his tent, a real tent, and came out with a short piece of rope. "Here, tie this around your coat like a belt. It should stay on that way. Let's go." He took off in long strides across the tundra. As they hiked, Josie found she could almost match Andrew stride for stride. How glorious it was to walk so freely, unfettered by a skirt and petticoat wrapping around her legs or a rope pulling a donkey. Thrilled by the freedom, she stretched her legs out even more. How good it felt to be really hiking. Andrew caught himself. He turned to see where Josie was and found her right on his heels. "Sorry to be walking so fast. I have long legs and forget."

She patted her legs, grinning, "Mine are long too." *Would a lady have said that? It wasn't that long ago they were putting skirts on piano legs because they were indecent. Now I'm wearing pants and asking him to look at my legs.*

He grinned in response. "I have my map. I can show you where we're going." He unfolded the map on the ground. The North Fork was very different from the Hayden map. It was now the left creek and less steep terrain. *Isn't that interesting they would change their minds? And there are the lakes! They weren't on the old one.*

She studied it, looked from the map into his eyes and smiled. *Oh, my word. What a smile. And she looked at me!* He realized he was grinning stupidly and ducked his head. Trying to regain his composure, he pointed to shallow contours above the lake. She was glad because she felt she could keep up.

When they came to a little spring they stopped. Josie untied her cup and dipped it into the clear water. Longing for her sketchbook so she could draw an unusual flower she saw growing in a rock crevice, she gently lifted its petals to examine it.

The tender expression on her face and the intensity of her observation charmed him. "You probably know it's a columbine," he offered. "They made it the state flower a few years ago. I don't know its Latin name. It blooms earlier at lower elevations; flowers are later up here. Still, I'm surprised to see one."

Intrigued, she looked at him because he understood what she wanted to ask.

As they walked, he handed rocks to her. "See these? They're feldspar crystals." Or, "Quartz." Or, "These seams are what miners were looking for because cracks might be filled with deposits containing valuable minerals such as lead, gold, silver or all of them combined." Josie always looked, held the rocks, and nodded.

Forgetting herself she said, "Mr. Wallace said …."

Startled by the outburst, he said, "Yes? Who's Mr. Wallace?"

"A teacher. From Leadville."

Leadville? Is she from Leadville? "So, you know about rocks?"

"No."

Curious. Andrew was afraid he was boring her with constant explanations, yet she seemed interested. He couldn't tell until she picked up a rock and showed it to him. Delighted, he gave forth a long explanation on the formation of mica. She listened patiently as he talked over her head, but she was fascinated with how much he knew.

She could feel they were gaining altitude faster than widely spaced contour lines indicated. He had changed his mind because he was anxious to reach the crest. As they climbed, they came to a steep rock face. Andrew reached a ledge then extended his hand to Josie. It was a natural gesture any considerate man would offer a woman. She hesitated to touch him then took his hand. On the ledge shy smiles confirmed they had reached a tentative truce. One more ledge, a helping hand, and they were on the ridge.

"Oh, Andrew!" The view was immense and beyond anything she had seen before.

Pleased she was impressed enough to say his name, he explained, "You're looking at the Continental Divide. Some people think it's a straight line running north and south when in fact it follows mountain chains, or merely higher elevations in land as in Wyoming and New Mexico. It wanders all over the states it goes through."

"Oh." *So much I don't know.*

They moved steadily up the ridge until they reached the crest. From there they saw a whole range of mountains.

"Breathtaking," Josie sighed. Nothing was between her and the rest of the world.

"Glad you like it." Sharing the view with someone who appreciated it made him happier than he had imagined. "That's Mt. Massive. It's so close, it's hiding Mt. Elbert, our highest mountain. Sorry you can't see it."

"I've seen it. From the Leadville side."

Another Leadville clue? He took off his pack and pulled out his binoculars. "Want to look?"

"I don't know how." She was uneasy using something expensive she could break.

"Here. Look through them and move this knob, like this, until everything's in focus." He paused. "Focus means till it isn't fuzzy."

She nodded and peered through them. Things were blurred till she turned the knob. "Oh. It's so close." She quickly handed them back to him. "You look." To see the vastness of the terrain, the primeval, jagged beauty stretching in every direction, and be aware this was but a small part of the map of Colorado, was disconcerting, their insignificance humbling.

Scanning the mountains with binoculars he spotted a mine dump in the next range he would love to investigate. Getting there from here with a mule would be impossible because of the distance. "See those mine tailings? That's what I like to explore. Try to figure out what miners were chasing. It took a lot of work to move that much rock. It means they thought they were on to something; maybe the vein ran out. Some veins go a long way and others don't amount to much, but a fellow doesn't know until he digs."

"Very uncertain, isn't it?"

"It's a gamble. Mining seems to attract gamblers. H.A.W. Tabor was a gambler." He waited for her to say she knew about him. But she didn't respond. "He was a prospector in Leadville who also owned a supply store along with his wife. He took a gamble and traded a couple of miners equipment for a third-interest in their mine. Turned out to be a good investment and H.A.W. went on to own some valuable mines but in the end he and his beautiful second wife lost everything. His first wife of twenty-five years, though, who just steadily took in boarders and laundry as well as running the store and post office, ended up being one of the richest women in Denver. It's one of my mother's favorite jilted-wife-revenge tales." He was tickled with his story.

She grinned. "Women don't seem to be the gamblers men are."

"They aren't all men, you know?" His eyes twinkled.

"Some miners are women?"

"I don't know about that. One of the most famous gamblers is Poker Alice. She's moved from mining camp to mining camp, always dressed in the latest fashion, and smoking a cigar. She's rumored to have done well."

Sounds like she's a woman who won't let the men always win. Must confuse them. That's probably why she's good at it.

Andrew watched as she considered Poker Alice. She seemed mischievous before she turned serious.

"Do you gamble?"

"I suppose we all gamble on some things. *Like you're gambling on me.* Risking hard-earned money doesn't appeal to me, though. I don't think the gold-bug will bite me, either. I'm interested in the science of mining, not the possibility of riches. I like rocks and their chemical make-up and how their components behaved over the eons. You know, like how limestone turns to marble under intense pressure."

She was slightly startled. She'd heard of the quarry in Marble but didn't know what marble was. Shouldn't she know this, living at a limestone quarry? She couldn't believe he was talking to her as if she were intelligent.

"I've been to Marble," he continued, "a remarkable bed. A train goes to Marble. You can go there someday if this is your home." He hoped she would confirm this as her country.

Her mind drifted. *If I were really Joe from Meredith I would work at the quarry as Henry does. I wouldn't be riding a train to Marble for an outing.* She changed the subject. "You're studying this?"

"Rocks, yes, and if someone finds valuable mineral, how to mine it."

"Oh."

"Limestone deposits are interesting geologically."

"Oh?"

"Science says there was a large sea here and some creatures who lived in it made their bones or shells from calcium carbonate in the water. When those creatures died their remains fell to the ocean floor and after eons turned into limestone. That's what they're mining in your area. They turn the limestone to lime in the kilns."

She was ashamed of herself for not knowing this. She should have asked Otto or Mr. Wallace about it. One of them would know and be happy to expound on it. "What use is lime?"

"To make plaster for walls and other stuff."

"Limestone is dead sea creatures?"

"Well, that and calcium carbonate from the water."

She looked puzzled. "Were miners geologists?"

"They probably found out as much as they could because it would make or break them. I'd guess they traded information."

She was finding Andrew very much to her liking: How kind he was, how he wanted to share what he knew. The sort of man she would like to know better. A man who knew how to do the dishes! A man who would talk to her about interesting things. ·

They sat on the mountaintop to eat their lunches, sharing bits of what they had. She had so many questions now she had someone to ask. "Why lakes?"

He shook his head. "Why lakes." he repeated. "You've heard about the Ice Ages?"

She nodded. "A little."

"Well, as you may know, Earth has gone through many periods of very cold weather. During those times glaciers formed heavy masses of ice that slowly moved, scouring the land with the rocks and debris they carried. They also pushed a lot of this stuff ahead of them. When things got warmer and the glaciers melted, the stuff they were pushing often formed a dam that made a lake. As for the alpine lakes, maybe it was the same thing but I really don't know. But thank you for asking. I was glad for an excuse to talk." He found this funny, dipping his head to hide his amusement.

He has a sense of humor about himself. I like that. "Thank you for telling me these things." *I hope I can remember so I can tell the kids without too many mistakes.* She was relaxing.

Lunch over, they began their hike back to camp. As they approached the lake, he stopped. Without watching her, he shoved his hands in his pockets and said, "I don't know if you've decided if you want me to leave. Maybe you'll let me know when you have." *Please let me stay. I want to know you better.*

Without responding, she started walking again. *He's been so nice, why would he change? Wouldn't it be selfish to make him leave at this time of day? Where would he go? Haven't I already put my reputation at risk? Wouldn't it be interesting to talk to him tonight when I can be me?* She said softly, "I'd like you to stay and have supper."

Don't act silly now because you're nervous. "Thank you, Joe. I was hoping we could have more time together. I don't often find someone I can talk so freely with."

Not knowing what more needed to be said, they hiked on.

He broke the silence. "I need to do some laundry. I imagine you'd like time to yourself." He didn't watch to see her reaction to his manufactured task for letting her be alone. She'd come here by herself and perhaps she wanted solitude.

"I do have some things I'd like to do." It was easier talking to him, now that she'd given up the deep voice.

Back at camp, she quickly grabbed the sketchbook and headed to the upper lake. She found a seat on a rockslide behind the lake where small flowers were growing in tufts of grass between boulders. She sat peacefully drawing exquisite, dainty flowers, as if miniaturized because short summers at this elevation didn't give them time to be exuberant. She looked at the tiny flowers and the seeds they were making with a new appreciation for their hardiness.

A chirping whistle surprised her. Looking for a large animal she saw the noisemaker: a small furry creature with no tail and little round ears. It looked like a toy. Before she captured its image, it disappeared into the rockslide. She waited. It reappeared on top of another rock and chirped again. She drew quickly. If Andrew could see the sketch, he could identify it. So taken with the small animal, she didn't see Andrew coming over the grass between the lakes.

He called a hello and proceeded to walk towards her. "Thought I might find you here. What're you drawing?"

"A little fellow," she answered.

"May I see?"

She handed the book to him without thinking. He glanced at the drawing. "You've met a rock coney or pika. Appealing, aren't they? They don't hibernate. They harvest grass, dry it, put it under rocks and live on it all winter. See stacks of grass around? That's their labor."

Entranced by a creature small enough to fit on the palm of her hand, she said, "I wish I could have one as a pet but I suppose they're perfectly happy to be wild."

Pleased she was so friendly, he said, "I imagine you're right. Most animals would probably prefer a natural life, but we want companions, work animals, or whatever, so we tame them. What we really want is someone to talk to who won't tell us we aren't making any sense." They laughed. He looked at her with surprise. It was such a merry laugh.

Holding the sketchbook, he asked. "Mind if I look at what you've drawn?"

She recoiled. Flowers drawings from the Denver library with their Latin names were in it. How would she have done those in Meredith? What would they reveal about her? "I...I don't think you'd be interested," and she reached for the book.

He was taken aback. They were only drawings of flowers, weren't they? He wasn't going to judge her artistic ability. He handed back her book without saying anything, but he felt awkward. Had he violated her privacy somehow? What had she drawn she didn't want him to see?

Josie avoided looking at him, embarrassed how she'd acted. It was obvious she'd made him feel bad. She handed the book back to him. "I'm sorry how I behaved. You may look. You need to know I borrowed a book that had flora and fauna drawings and I copied them."

Flora and fauna? He took the book; he didn't know if he wanted to look in it or not. Reluctantly, so he wouldn't seem petty, he opened it, turned the pages and saw what she had drawn: flowers and the pika that day, a lone mushroom, a mountain with a description of the sun glowing on it and the emotions she experienced, sketches of a cinch and a diamond hitch with lots of arrows showing the direction of the rope, and little elephant heads. He hid a smile. These were followed by careful, precise drawings of flowers with Latin and common names along with notes on their colors. Trees, showing their leaves and needles, and small animals followed.

"These drawings are beautifully done, Joe." He looked at her and studied her face as he handed the book back to her. *Who in the world is this sensitive, strong girl?*

"The librarian said these were the deciduous and evergreen trees I need to know and some of the flowers and animals."

They have a librarian in Meredith? "You've taught me something, Joe. I learned about trees in a kid's book but didn't learn about needles. Maybe someday you'll make a copy of those for me."

She glanced up. *Someday? Would they have a someday?*

"Some fellows on the survey crew did terrific drawings. Botanists were an important part of the team. We were doing more than surveying and analyzing rocks and strata."

"What did they do with their drawings?" She was curious because she would love to draw wildflowers and make a book for children.

"They hope to publish them after doing a lot of research. They pressed flowers so they had details they may have missed in the field. You know, whether leaves are opposite or alternate, those kinds of things. There are books for lower altitude flowers but not many good ones for the high country, they said."

I guess my pictures will be for the children at school.

"There are good books on botany in Denver. I'll try to find the one we had on the crew. Guys who were interested in flora and fauna can tell me what to get. I'll send you one."

She bowed her head to hide her blush. *I can't accept gifts from a stranger.* "I'll read it, draw the flowers and send it back to you." She was anxious to change the subject. "Your laundry went well?"

"Quickly. Wasn't as dirty as I thought. Ever done laundry in one of these barely melted chunks of ice?"

"No, but I've waded in the Frying Pan and I believe you." They laughed and the tension was broken.

"I'll leave you to your sketching. I'm reading a book about this area. I'll be at camp." He tried to sort out the clues she'd given him: she knew a teacher in Leadville, a librarian was typically found in cities, she'd waded in the Frying Pan. He shook his head. *Where does she come from?*

When she returned to camp, he came up, full of good intentions. "I noticed your tent this morning," realizing he shouldn't remind her of that, he blushed, looked away, and nervously went on, "if we work on it together, I think we can give you a little more room." He jammed his hands in his pockets.

"I thought there may be better ways to do it; I haven't figured them out, though." It was her turn to hide a smile, seeing how uncomfortable he made himself. He reminded her of the big boys hiding their sensitivity.

They walked into the trees and Andrew shook his head. The rope, tied with granny knots, was so high the tent was a couple of feet wide inside. "Let's untie the knots and put in some that work better." He pulled off the tarp, took out her knots, tied one end of the rope to the tree at a reasonable height with a bowline and went to the other tree. "Here, Joe. We'll pull, take a couple of wraps around the tree to hold it. I'll give it a couple half-hitches. That should keep it up."

She didn't want to get close to him to pull on the rope, but she had no choice. Together they pulled, he held the rope taut while she passed it around the tree. When he finished tying it, they put the tarp on. "Much better, Andrew. Thank you."

He shrugged, "Yup. Lots to learn about camping. It's handy to have someone's help."

As they started to leave she said, "Oh, let me get my lamp. I have one too. I forgot it last night."

"They're really something, aren't they?"

"I don't know. I haven't used mine yet."

As they sat eating supper, she asked, "Do you suppose the Indians ever came here?"

"It's probably a little high for good hunting." he said.

"Oh. It's hard to realize if we'd been here around thirty years ago we would have been trespassing. I've been told this was Ute land then."

"Yup." There had been strong opinions on the survey crew about Indians.

"How do you feel about the Indians, Andrew?"

"I don't know how I feel. It's complicated. When one group of people moves onto land already occupied by another group it seems to mean trouble."

"Don't you think we'd do it differently now?"

"With hind-sight? Probably not." Her questions made him uneasy. He wasn't comfortable sharing many of his thoughts. He'd prefer to know her mind better before he shocked her with some of his unconventional ideas. He began nervously breaking a stick into pieces and throwing them into the fire.

"I'd like to think we get kinder as we understand more," she said.

If I say what I think, will that end my chances of knowing her better? He sighed and forged ahead. "I agree that understanding is important. History, though, doesn't tell us that people change their behavior much to go along with available facts. I think people mostly want to do what they believe is right. I think more important factors may be hardships like hunger, fear, pain and so on. It seems to me that people get kinder as hardships decrease and happiness increases. What I'm saying, Joe, is that I don't think people change. It's the situations they find themselves in that change their behavior."

"You don't think we'd do it any differently now?"

"If you have a conversation with old Denver folks, you know that Colorado proudly did its share in killing the Indians out on the plains. John Chivington, the good Methodist minister who helped found the University of Denver, was infamous for leading the Sand Creek Massacre. He ordered the killing of all women and children who, up until the massacre, thought the Union protected them because the Arapaho and Cheyenne were peaceful. That was just fifty years ago."

Josie drew circles in the dirt with lines through them, then added, "Maybe you're right. When I read about that I thought it wasn't only the Indians who suffered. How could you live with yourself knowing you'd done that? It made me sad, how awful people can be."

He nodded. *I'll bet she was sad.* He tried to see her face in the firelight. He was quiet. "I hope I never have to go to war and am told to kill people I don't even know."

"No. Men are asked to do terrible things to honor their country. Do you ever wonder, Andrew, what life's about? Sometimes I'm so confused." She drew new circles in the dirt.

He nodded, sighed, and broke more sticks. Guessing she had been raised a good Christian, she might be offended if he challenged those teachings. *This could be too much. But I'm being honest and if this offends her then maybe I don't want to know her better.* "I've thought about it some. Last summer when we up here with nothing to do at night, I'd study stars and wonder about religion, fate, souls, and predestination." He watched to see her reaction, but her face was in shadow. "Here's what I came up with, which is simple: I doubt if anyone really knows and I think it's okay not to know."

"But, Andrew, people do say they know. The Bible tell us what to believe."

Bad choice. I may have just lost her. "Yup. People wrote the Bible. Just like people wrote other holy books. Lots of folks will tell you they know why we're here or what we're supposed to do. I don't think they really do know. When you consider all the religions saying so many different things, it makes you doubt any of them have the truth. If there is a God, I think he'll approve of our not being too gullible and if there isn't a God, well…"

"You do know that's heresy?"

"Umm hmm."

"You may find this shocking, but it's difficult for me to admire a deity who requires worship. And what kind of being asks a man to kill his son and then says he doesn't have to, but

81

then he sacrifices a ram. What kind of being would find that satisfying?"

"You're asking rational questions about an irrational subject that I can't answer. It seems to me we need to live our lives using the best rational information we have: Be kind, honest, and do more than our share. Then not worry too much."

"I've always wished I knew what was right. I like what Jesus said. What bothers me are Christians who claim to love him yet who seem to be very selective about practicing what he preached. I would be happier if people lived the way they say they should or else quit talking about it so much."

She's still with me. "Love your enemy. Turn the other cheek. Give away your money. Judge not." He threw some sticks into the fire. "Getting people to live a life at odds with human nature would make a kinder world and we'd all benefit, but are people capable of doing this? It seems not. So, was Jesus wise to ask us to behave in ways we find nearly impossible, so we feel guilty all the time? Or were these goals we should strive for and understand if we have trouble with them? I think if we do our best to be decent, kind people and don't judge others too much since we can't know their lives' circumstances, we should be content."

Josie, scratching through the circles, said, "Maybe you're right."

She's questioning dogma. He broke more sticks and they sat silent for a while. Then Andrew, trying to relieve the solemnity, asked her when she intended to leave.

"I'll be going in the morning. I figured two days in, one day here, and two days out."

"You won't need two days out; it's all downhill."

"I have to meet the train on the second day, so I need to be there early."

She's taking the train; is it to Meredith, Leadville, or a city with a librarian? "Great. I planned to leave tomorrow as well. If you don't mind, I'll go the first day with you. I have some exploration I want to do for a few days up a creek to another lake."

Does this mean he wants to be with me? Don't look at him, he'll see I'm happy. Hesitating, she said, "That would be nice."

Very nice. "Good. We'll get an early start." Light was leaving the sky. With a feeling of evening's chill and the anticipation of night coming, Josie buttoned her coat and felt the gun bang against her leg. She smiled at the thought of it while she watched twilight soften the edges of this rough, wild world. She stirred the fire and dipped another cup of tea for them.

"I'll go wash our dishes." She picked up his plate and their skillets.

"You don't need to wash my dishes."

"It's my turn." *Think of that, taking turns doing dishes with a man.*

When she returned, Andrew was stirring the fire, adding wood to it. Pulling the harmonica from his pocket he began to play. It was peaceful. She waited for a break and asked, "You played a song last night I didn't recognize. It was the first one. Remember?"

"Wildwood Flower. An old English tune about unrequited love."

"Will you please play it again? I enjoyed it."

Darkness gradually wrapped them in mystery.

After he finished the song, she thanked him, and sat quietly looking at the sky. "I've enjoyed the stars as a magnificent display of lights. You seem to know about them. Can you explain them to me?"

"I know practically nothing about them. I had a book as a kid that told me names of some constellations and bright stars and gave me a basic understanding of the universe, but it was written for a child, so that's the depth of my knowledge. I'd study the star book, run outside to try to find them, run back inside and read it again. Last summer I did try to figure out the movement of the stars because we were up here where you can see them so well. I came up with something that helped me. That was only a couple of months of observation, though."

"Is it complicated, what you figured out?"

"Oh, no. A simple concept. First, you need to realize there are so many stars they can be intimidating. I know a few bright ones and some constellations and that's enough for me. It helps to know that besides the stars, the planets move through the night sky and look like a star and can confuse you. I call them tricksters because I never know which planet I'm seeing except Venus. It's the morning star and the evening star. It's always close to the sun and it can be bright. You can't always see it. Anyway, the first and most important thing, is to find the North Star and tonight that's easy because we can see the Big Dipper. Where the land's flat you can always see it; up here in the mountains that can be a problem. Anyway, let's look for the Big Dipper. See those seven stars up there that resemble a dipper like you drink out of?" He pointed to the northern sky.

"Yes, I can see a dipper. I've never noticed it before."

"Good. Go to the two stars on the outside edge of the bowl. They're called the pointer stars. Imagine a line from those two stars going to the right about four times the distance between those dipper stars and you'll see a fairly bright star."

"I think I see it. Are there some stars making an arc going up from it?"

"Yup. Those make the handle of the Little Dipper. The brightest, and the last star in the handle, is the North Star."

"Then I've found it for sure."

"You've found home base. That's important. Wherever you are, if you look up and find that star, you're looking exactly north. It's what's been guiding people for centuries. Think of the North Star as the hub of a wheel that extends to the edges of the sky. As you can see, there is a lot of the wheel we can't see right now if the North Star is at the center. At various distances on the wheel away from the hub are the twenty or so constellations and stars whose names I know. The stars appear to move around the North Star as if the wheel were turning ever so slowly. They seem to move across the sky at night, and they also advance throughout the year going from east to west. It's interesting to watch a particular bright star. You'll notice it moves a little more to the west every night."

"If stars move a little west every night, won't we lose them eventually?"

"Yup. The summer sky is the other half of the rotating wheel we see in winter. Do remember, though, we're the ones turning and not the stars. But it really is easier to visualize, I think, if you forget about our turning. The stars seem to move, the way the sun seems to move." He tried to see her face so he'd know if she were following this explanation, but it was dark. "I think I've talked enough and it's getting late."

She laughed, "Leaving me with stars spinning around in my head. Before you leave, will you please show me a few constellations?"

"Sure. Find the North Star?"

"I have it."

"On the east side of it, across from the Dipper is a big W called Cassiopeia. See it?" She nodded. "If you go a little south of it you might see a large square with a point, like the roof on a house, aimed at the North Star. It's called Cepheus. Can you find it in that mess of stars?"

"I can see the W. I haven't found the house. Oh, wait. It's big. I was looking for something smaller."

"Great. Due south from the North Star, you'll see a very bright star: Vega. It's the second brightest star. West of it is Arcturus. To find it, go to the Big Dipper and 'follow the arc to Arcturus'. It's the third brightest star."

"Where's the brightest star?"

"It's Sirius but we can't see it now. It's a winter star."

She studied the sky, following his pointing finger. "I do believe I see them too. Do you know the mythology about Cassiopeia and Cepheus?"

"Nope. Do you?"

"I do. Cepheus and Cassiopeia, the king and queen of Ethiopia, were the parents of a girl named Andromeda."

He interrupted her, "Andromeda's a constellation too."

"Interesting. Well, Cassiopeia bragged that Andromeda was more beautiful than the sea nymphs, which irritated them, so they asked Poseidon, god of the sea, to do something. He sent a sea monster to capture Andromeda and to chain her to a rock. Perseus saw her, fell in love, and killed the monster. Andromeda and Perseus married and had many children. The first one was Perses who named the Persians. You know, a normal, happy family's history."

"A little adversity strengthens ties. Perseus is another constellation in the same sky as Andromeda and her parents. Probably won't see him tonight because the peak is in our way."

"I don't know what happened to the kids." *I wonder why we never heard about them.*

"Do you read a lot of mythology?" He considered it akin to fairy tales which he didn't like.

"Never. My younger sister went through a mythology period and told us stories every night. We heard the same ones many times with different elaborations."

"The dippers are also called Ursa Major and Ursa Minor. Ursa means bear."

"I don't have a story about them. Can I say I've seen two bears tonight, though?"

"Yup."

She laughed. "So, I'll tell them I did see a bear or rather two bears!"

Them? "You can, but they probably won't get your joke."

"It's not a joke. It's a different kind of bear. Kids will love it."

Kids? Does she come from a large family? Does she have kids of her own? She can't have!

He was shocked at the thought and quickly put it out of his mind. He looked toward the peak. "Moon won't be up for a while. The stars will get brighter as the west gets darker. I hope you'll get to know the stars. It's fun to see the sky at various times of the year. Nowhere to see them better than up here in the mountains where you live." *If this is where you live.*

She didn't respond. Distracted by the fire burning down, she realized it was time to go to bed. "Thank you for a nice day, Andrew. I wouldn't have done that hike on my own."

"Thank you, Joe. Sharing made it a special day for me."

"I think I'll turn in early because I didn't sleep too well last night. Those raw potatoes gave me a tummy ache."

He grinned at her honesty. "I'm going to bed now too. See you in the morning." He lit his lamp and headed to the lake.

In the dim light, she tried to sketch the stars and the few names she thought she remembered. Josie could hear his harmonica. The soft music was almost a lullaby. She lit her lamp, wandered through the trees, and went to bed.

Although tired from lack of sleep the two nights before as well as from their hike, she couldn't sleep. She lay awake thinking about how safe she felt with Andrew. She realized she didn't know men at all. Her father, a reserved man, was not conversational. She had gone to school with boys but didn't know them well. There had been her brothers, but brothers and men are not the same thing. Zona's Otto was boisterous, opinionated, and funny, but she couldn't say she knew him. Mr. Miller was a good friend and a man, but he was more like a grandfather or father to her and really, she knew nothing about him. She liked what she'd seen of Andrew. He was kind, at first to her Joe, and now to a girl whose name he didn't know.

The morning, crisp and brilliant, woke Josie with a start to the smell of smoke and cracks of breaking wood. Peering through the end of her tent she saw Andrew. When she appeared, he asked, "Sleep well?"

"Yes, thank you. And you?

"Yup, thanks. Ready for breakfast?"

Then she smelled the coffee.

"Coffee?" he asked.

"Yes, please."

"Having oatmeal for breakfast again?"

She looked impish. "Yup! Shall we cook in one pot?"

He chuckled that she teased him. "Sure," pleased with the change twenty-four hours had made.

She tried to hide her happiness by keeping her head down to stir the oatmeal. He saw it and thought what a cheerful face; it made him happy. He offered her raisins again after the oatmeal cooked. "I don't like my raisins cooked so they get soft like little swollen bodies," he grimaced.

"Oh, neither do I. I want them to fight back." They exchanged happy glances.

After they finished eating, Andrew said with a touch of sadness, "Guess it's time to pack."

"I think so. It shouldn't take me long. It may take Daisy a while to get dressed though."

"I can help with that. Remember, I was a wrangler last summer. Your trusty beast of burden is waiting in the trees."

She looked where he was looking and saw he had brought Daisy to her. "Thank you."

She gathered up their breakfast things and started down to the lake with them. He stopped her. "My turn."

"I don't mind doing dishes."

"Rules of camp. We take turns."

"Oh, well then, I want to follow the rules."

He got quickly to his feet, gathered the equipment, went to the lake, washed them, and brought hers back.

"Thanks. I have my stuff ready for the panniers except for lunch. I learned the first day to keep food handy. I don't think I know how to untie your knots in the tent rope, though."

"I'll get them, then saddle Daisy."

She nodded. He must have seen how she had Daisy packed when he came in. It was probably all wrong.

He picked up her thoughts. "Not that you don't know how. I thought maybe I could be helpful."

"I'm glad for your help and so is Daisy. I don't know much about animals...or saddles."

He cleaned Daisy's pad, brushed her, and put on the pad. He unbuckled the breeching strap and put on the saddle. "Oh," she said, "is that how you do the strap? I scooted the saddle forward after I put the strap under her tail. I didn't see the buckle." She felt embarrassed she hadn't seen such an obvious thing.

"Whatever works. I don't imagine the animals care." He was grinning to himself. He tightened the cinch and did the fancy looping with the strap as if he'd always done it.

"Did you grow up with horses?"

"A couple of horses. Now it's Prince. A gentle, patient old fellow. Family pet, you could say. They taught us three how to hitch up a buggy, pitch hay and clean a stall. I learned about horses and mules in general the past summers and they're not all as cooperative as Prince and Daisy. Our crew was a couple of other college guys and me. We oversaw the pack animals, cooking, cleaning campsites, and other things. Those summers taught me about life in a way I never learned at home. They were a good experience."

"Is mule another name for a donkey? I know they're also called burros, jackasses, and Rocky Mountain Canaries because of the noise they make."

"Umm. A mule is a cross between a horse and a donkey."

Andrew could guess what she was thinking and didn't want to discuss how horses mate with donkeys, but she persisted. "Why would they do that? Why wouldn't they let mules make their own babies?"

He took a deep breath, "Mules can't make babies. I don't know why. The only way you can get a mule is by a donkey and a horse being the colt's parents." He quickly changed the subject. "Help you fold the tarp? It's easier with two people." They folded it and he put the panniers on the cross arms. Since her gear was in gunny sacks it made quick work of loading. He draped the ground tarp across the pack. "Looked like you did a diamond hitch. Right?"

"I tried. I have a sketch if you need it."

He cheerfully answered, "That's okay. I got it down the first summer. Tough one, though, isn't it?"

"It gave me a bit of trouble." She winced at the memory of his seeing her drawing.

"It occurred to me," he said, "if we get to our campsite early enough maybe you'll hike with me to a little lake. It's steep, but if we're not leading the animals, we should be able to make it." *I'd love to share it with you. It's another special place.* He finished throwing the hitch. "There you go. If you want to start, I'll load the mule and be right behind."

She turned, looked at him and smiled. He smiled. They both blushed and quickly looked away.

The trip to the next campsite was uneventful. They stopped a few times for water and to look at wildflowers. He showed her the stream he would go up the next day. When they reached a meadow below the stream they would climb to the lake, he said, "Do you think this is a beautiful spot?"

"I do, it's lovely."

"Where would you like to put your tent?"

She pointed to some close trees. He nodded. "I'll leave you here, unload the mule and come back to help with it."

She unpacked Daisy, noticing Andrew's pretty diamond and how tight it was on the pack. She dragged out the rope and tarp for her tent, took Daisy to the stream and hobbled her. She saw

Andrew across the little meadow. He'd selected a spot a discreet distance away.

He was cheerful when he came up. "Are you ready? I'll teach you how to tie a bowline. It may come in handy someday. It's a good one because it's so easy to untie."

He tied the rope on the first tree, again wrapping the second with her help. *Don't get too near.* The thought was in both their minds. He tied the half hitches, then realized he hadn't taught her how to tie a bowline.

"Sorry. I forgot to show you how to tie the knot."

"That's okay. I probably won't have much need of it."

It was late morning, plenty of time for a hike and lunch. "My tent is ready. Do you care to go in a bit?" *Care to go? In a bit? I've never used those words before.* He was so embarrassed he didn't wait for her answer. He hurried to his camp, grabbed his pack and lunch.

When he returned, they looked briefly at his map and decided the stream was the best route to reach the lake.

"I'll carry your drawing things and lunch in my pack, if you'd like." She quickly retrieved them from the panniers. They struck out, Josie letting her long legs go free, keeping close behind Andrew. Walking as she was capable of walking she almost wished she'd been born a boy. *No, I don't want to be a boy. I want to be a wife and mother someday.*

Would her mother approve of what she was doing, she wondered. Fun was her mother's guiding principle when they were little. Until Father came home, of course, then children were to be seen, maybe, but not heard. They all understood. When her mother got sick and died all joy went out of the house. Father had turned into a silent, grieving presence they tried to please. When her brothers died in Panama, grief overwhelmed them.

She escaped to normal school with her father's begrudging support. He didn't want to lose another child, he said. But he let her go. She earned her teacher's certificate and was paying him back. She said she hoped for the same for her little sisters. He said he'd see. She loved her remote father, but his sadness was oppressive and though she sympathized with him she couldn't help him overcome it. She had to leave that sad household.

"Penny for your thoughts." Andrew had stopped at a lookout.

Startled by his comment, she said, "Not worth a penny."

"You seem unhappy."

"I was thinking of my mother and father."

"Care to tell me about them?"

"My mother died five years ago. I was very close to her. I'm her oldest girl."

"I'm sorry. Your father, are you close to him?"

Close to my father? "Can one be close in a distant way? I believe I challenged his patience after our mother died. He expected silent obedience and I wanted to negotiate."

I'm thinking you and Mom have a lot in common. "He was open to negotiation?"

"He'd met his match in stubbornness and grew weary of my arguments. It wouldn't be correct to say he was open, but I did get my way."

Shaking his head. *Poor devil.* "Someday I'd love to hear what your way entailed." *I doubt it was this trip alone in boys' clothes. He'd never have given in on this. And rightly so. Or maybe not. How else would I have met her? But that's what he'd have been afraid of.*

The hike grew steeper and they quit talking. Andrew wended his way up the hill, drifting from the stream when it cascaded down rock faces, staying close to it when there was open terrain. When they reached the meadow, the lake lay peaceful and luminous in the sun. It was a special place. "Andrew, let's see if we can come up with how this lake makes us think about people."

He looked at her quizzically. It sounded like something a teacher would say to a class. He chuckled. "Okay, Joe. I'll work on it."

They spread their lunch on the backpack and quietly contemplated the lake. When finished eating, Andrew announced, "My assignment comparing the lake to people: As quickly changeable as a girl's lively face." Josie blushed. He watched her reaction. "Let's hear yours."

Trying to put into words feelings she was having about him, she offered, "Calm or sparkling, peacefully reflective or rippling with energy, this lake, like an interesting person, fascinates." She studied his face.

His look was gentle. "Thanks. I'll think about that. Could you repeat it, please?"

She wrinkled her nose. "I don't think I can. It doesn't bear inspection. Just try to remember how it made you feel." They exchanged awkward looks.

Andrew offered the sketchbook. She found a rock to sit on at lake's edge and looked around for what she wanted to sketch. Gazing pensively across the water, Andrew leaned against a tree. She turned to the last page and tried to catch his look. She would love to have a picture to remember him by. When she saw him rise, she turned the page to a flower she had sketched the day before that he hadn't seen. He looked over her shoulder.

"Where do you see that?"

"Oh. It's one I saw yesterday and wanted to remember." *That was weak.*

He nodded. "I suppose we ought to be going if you're through sketching. Would you have time to copy one of your drawings before we leave tomorrow? I'd like to have one to remember the trip." *Sounds false. Seems like a keepsake. Yup. I want a keepsake.*

"I'd love to give you a sketch. I'll try to make a good one for you in the morning if I have time." *I'm too willing. I want him to have something to remind him of me, don't I? Yes. Yes, I want him to remember me.*

The descent went quickly. When they reached camp, they gathered food for supper, sharing, as had become their pattern. It made for more interesting meals, especially his contributions. They enjoyed stars again and the harmonica. After a while Andrew stared quietly over the landscape.

"A penny for your thoughts," Josie said.

He nodded. "You'll probably be surprised what I was thinking."

"Will you tell me?"

"Sure. Mom and my aunt."

She was surprised. "Really?"

"Well, Mom's been our cross to bear."

"Your <u>mother</u>?"

"A family joke, but she has been, in a good way. She'd have none of that woman's-work thinking in our home. We boys, which is all she had, knew how to sweep, dust, and do dishes at an early age. When neighborhood boys wanted to play, we lied about our work so we wouldn't get teased. She's very independent, a suffragist. When we were little, we marched with her until we reached an age when we refused to go. Many suffragists don't have husbands, or if they do, husbands who lend support, but Dad respects what she does. When Colorado passed Women's Suffrage–the first state in the Union to do it, I can sort of remember we celebrated. She freely admits Wyoming voted for it earlier but it was only a territory, so Coloradans conveniently don't count it. She keeps marching, hoping the nation will catch up." *I'd love for her to meet you. She'd find a kindred spirit.*

I'd love to meet her and your father. They may explain you. "She sounds interesting but intimidating."

"She's both. She has a lively, logical mind and is willing to say what she thinks and usually says it well. Sometimes in a shrill voice." He grinned.

Josie reflected. How differently her family behaved, where the man was king of his castle, provider, and protector, except her father wasn't. Denied those roles because of his illness, her father maintained his authority because her mother accorded it to him. Josie wondered about her mother's ability, and her father's, to maintain what was obviously incongruous. It had preserved his dignity. At what cost to her mother, she would never know. Did her mother long to offer her opinion or tell her father he was wrong, even once? Or did she, in private? *Curious. It never occurred to me they may have had a different relationship away from us.*

She answered Andrew, "We come from very different households."

"I suppose we are who we are. I think a person's family makes a difference, though."

She didn't respond for a while. "You mentioned your aunt. Whose sister is she?"

"Mom's older sister. They're very close. Aunt Janet had girls, Mom, boys. Aunt Janet is my great friend, almost like a mother. A no-nonsense woman who sort of raised her brothers and sister in a truly loving way because Grandma was too busy being the breadwinner."

"Too busy to raise her own children?"

"She ran a boarding house while Grandpa read. The kids all worked there. Maybe Mom's concern with child labor came from that. Near as I can tell, those kids didn't have much of a childhood. Mom and Aunt Janet are remarkable. Both made loving homes that respect their kids' differences."

"Would the home you want to create someday be like your parents'?" *That was too obvious!*

He hesitated. *I need to say this right.* "I would like a home where each person is valued for who he or she is. Everyone comes to life with different attributes. It's a shame when a person doesn't get to develop them, don't you think?"

"I hadn't thought of it in such a way. Perhaps my mother did. She was a gifted artist. I've always wondered what she'd have produced if she'd studied art and had time and proper supplies. I don't think anyone ever encouraged her. But she found our strengths. My Christmas present, even when I was quite young, were pencils and a sketchbook. My next sister, story books and sewing materials. The youngest received notebooks for her writing and flower seed packets. Mother got to keep her egg money which she spent on us kids."

"I would have liked your mother. I need to know more about your father," he said.

"He came from a home where men and women had distinct roles. His sister came to visit once and she told us about their home life. Very strict Scot-Presbyterian. Even though he left the church, I do believe he struggled to rid himself of the strict part. He trusted my mother to soften our world. I try to remember his kindness to us as little children when we recited poetry to him. Before he got sick, he was a cheerful man."

To change the subject Josie brought up another author she'd suggested the pupils read. "Since you're part Scot, have you read any of Robert Louis Stevenson's books?"

"Mom read to us when we were little. She could use the Scots dialect a wee bit." He ducked his head, grinning. "Both my grandfathers were Scots and Mom's dad, who loved to read to us, was quite good at the dialect since he was born in Scotland. He made it a lot of fun. They read all of Stevenson's kids' books to us. Did your mother read to you?" he asked.

"Most nights. We had Stevenson's *A Child's Garden of Verses* as soon as it was available, I think."

"'*Dark brown is the river,*'" he intoned solemnly.

Dramatically, she added, "'*Golden is the sand.*'"

With affected seriousness, "'*It flows along forever.*'"

"'*With trees on either hand.*'" they said together, laughing.

"Counterpane and Leerie. Did you love those too?" he asked.

"'*I have a little shadow that goes in and out with me.*' Yes. We loved them and could recite them to my father. His only request of us was that we recite a poem to him every Saturday. The boys learned silly ones. I tried to learn a new one each week. Our middle sister had a modest repertoire. But my youngest sister recited the same one, always, and he let her get away with it. She was his favorite. She never was stubborn."

"Och. Not a good Scot, methinks. What else did you read as a child?"

"My favorite book was *Heidi.* It made me want to live in the mountains and now I do."

"You haven't lived in Meredith all your life?" *I'm prying. I didn't mean to do that.*

"No," hesitating, "we came down from Canada."

"Oh." *Interesting.*

"I have some questions about stars. Would you mind talking about them again?"

Putting his hand over his eyes like a sailor, he said, "Remember this one?

'*And high overhead and all moving about
There were thousands of millions of stars.*'"

"Sort of. Wasn't there something about a dog?"

"Yup.

'*The Dog, and the Plough, and the Hunter, and all,
And the star of the sailor and Mars.*'

I learned that part when I was studying the stars."

She nodded. "Didn't it end something like '*stars going round in my head*?' That's exactly how I feel."

"I imagine anyone who tries to understand the stars feels that way. In the poem the Dog, Plough, and Hunter are all names of constellations and '*star of the sailor*' is the North Star. He mentions Mars, a planet, is in there making it all more confusing. Even though it's written as if a child were observing the stars, he wrote this as a man who had spent time at sea."

"Do you know those stars?"

"By different names. You know the Plough. It's the Big Dipper. The other two are winter stars."

"It's not confusing enough with one name; they have several?"

"I suppose many because every sea-faring culture gave them names."

"Oh."

"What helps me is to find the North Star, then turn and face due south. That gives you a big sky and you can watch the stars move through it–on that big wheel we talked about. If you're always facing the same way, the movement of the stars makes better sense. See the really bright star to the south of the North Star?" He pointed almost overhead. "That's Vega. We saw it last night."

"Umm hmm. Do you know what the Milky Way is?" she asked.

"It's that long band of stars across the sky," pointing overhead. "It's so many stars it looks like milk, I guess."

She scanned the sky. "Oh, I see it," she said enthusiastically. "I thought it was a cloud."

"You won't always see it going this direction. It moves on the wheel like everything else."

"It's hard to visualize the center of the wheel when you can only see part of the wheel."

"It was difficult and disturbing for man to realize he's not the center of the universe."

"It's still difficult, I believe."

"Indeed." Reluctantly, he said, "Guess it's bedtime." He lit his lamp.

Light from the fading fire didn't illuminate his face well but she watched him as she recited:

"*And O! before you hurry by with ladder and with light,*
O Leerie, see a little child and nod to him to-night!"

He looked at her, sitting on a log in her jeans, that awful hat pulled over her hair, a playful smile on her face, the firelight flickering. It was all he could do to leave. He nodded, he hoped Leerie-like. His voice was soft with wistfulness, "See you in the morning, Joe."

"Good night, Andrew." She watched him disappear into the darkness, waited for the harmonica, and soon heard him playing "Red River Valley", a song her mother had sung to them about the Red River in Canada. She sang quietly:

"*From this valley they say you are going.*
We will miss your bright eyes and sweet smile,
For they say you are taking the sunshine
That has brightened our pathway a while.

So come and sit by my side if you love me.
Do not hasten to bid me adieu.
Just remember the Red River Valley,
And the man that has loved you so true."

After the song, he quit playing. Feeling melancholy from the words and mournful melody, she sat by the fire, mindlessly stirring coals, wondering why he had chosen that song when he hadn't played it before. She hoped he knew the words.

As she lay wrapped in her quilt, she tried to reconstruct their conversations. *Do I have to keep my name a secret? I want him to know who I am. Maybe it's better the way it is, but it's hard to see what harm it could be to tell him.*

When she came to breakfast the next morning, he greeted her with a cheerless, "Morning."

Drinking his coffee he argued with himself. *Can't I just ask what her name is? No.* He shook his head.

"Is something wrong?"

"No. Why?"

"You were shaking your head."

"Oh," flustered, "just thinking this is our last morning together, and I wish I were going with you. You know, to make sure you make it to the train all right."

"That would be so nice of you. I'll be okay. I made it in by myself."

"I know. Of course, you did. I only meant I would enjoy your company and now I won't have it, that's all."

After she dished up the oatmeal and they sat quietly eating, she wanted to lighten the mood. "I saw a little pinkish bird with a gray head. It chirped."

"Sounds like a brown-capped rosy finch. We saw them last summer. They like high altitudes. You can hear them in early summer when they're establishing territories. I'm glad you saw one."

"How do you know so much about everything?"

"Maybe I'm making it up." He ducked his head so he wouldn't appear to enjoy his own joke. This made her laugh.

"I don't think you are, but if you are, I'm fooled." She hid her face. *That was obviously a flirty thing to say.*

Quietly drinking coffee, both were solemn. It was their last morning together and he didn't know if she lived in Meredith or somewhere else. How would he ever find her?

Her thoughts were similar. *Why will he ever look for me? If he does find me, will he like me as a girl? Will I ever see Andrew again?*

Breaking the silence he asked hopefully, "Were you able to make a copy of a drawing for me?"

"I was. I woke early." She pulled the sketchbook from behind her and opened it, careful to conceal the drawing of him. She had meticulously copied the columbine he had identified, then cut the page neatly with her pen knife. She handed it to him.

"Columbine." He felt sentimental. "We found it together."

"Yes. You knew what it was."

He frowned. "You didn't sign your art."

"I never do."

"Will you, please?" *And please use your real name so I can find you.*

She wrote very small at the bottom: J. Carter.

He read the signature. "Not Joe?"

"I don't usually go by Joe."

"You didn't write another name instead."

"J. seemed enough."

After glancing at each other, they dropped their eyes. *Why 'Joe?'*

Was I too obscure? I hope not.

I've got to ask. "Will you be going to Meredith?"

"Yes." *Yes. I'll be in Meredith, I promise.*

I think she's telling the truth. I have nothing else to go on.

"I'll help you get packed. Guess you'd better be on your way." *To Meredith. Please go to Meredith.*

"Thank you. I'd love your help."

After packing Daisy and watching him throw the diamond hitch, Josie turned to Andrew and put her hand out. "Goodbye, Andrew. Thank you for all you've done for me and for teaching me so much. I've enjoyed knowing you." She felt tears sting her eyes. She looked away quickly.

He took her hand but didn't give it a hearty shake. "Goodbye, Joe. I can't remember being as comfortable or talking as freely with anyone as I have been with you. I hope we'll meet again but no matter what, I'll never forget this time." He looked down and dropped her hand.

She led Daisy down the trail. When she turned around, Andrew was watching. They waved goodbye.

What a stupid thing I've done. I've met the nicest man in the world, and he doesn't know my name. I'll never see him again and I didn't have the courage to tell him who I am. How could he love a girl in boys' pants who'd camp out with a man she doesn't know? It's unthinkable he could. I've completely debased myself.

Covering four miles to the trailhead faster than she expected, she reached the spot to resume her feminine self. She hid to change into the rumpled skirt and blouse, took off the ugly cap, undid the braid, combed her hair, tied it back with a ribbon, and changed her shoes. *Now I'm a muddle of a woman in this ridiculous long skirt and white high-necked blouse with mutton sleeves all wrinkled and dirty from dealing with Daisy, but who cares?* She headed down the three miles to meet Willy, hoping she wouldn't meet him too soon. She stopped. The perfect diamond hitch would be a dead give-away. She undid the hitch and tied it haphazardly. Downhearted, she continued.

Meanwhile, Andrew returned to the stream south of the North Fork trail and headed up. After a hard climb, he and the mule reached a lake. He pitched his tent, made a fire, then sat, looking west the way Joe had gone, wondering how she had fared and how he would find his J. Carter.

Reaching the rail siding, she found a spot along the North Fork to sit in the shade and rest. She couldn't return Daisy to Biglow's because they didn't know she had her. They had rented her to Willy and Willy would have to take her home. The train pulled in shortly and Willy jumped out of the caboose and it was off again. She stood, waved to him.

"Hey," he said, "have a good trip?"

"Oh, I did. Savage Lakes are beautiful."

Happy she'd made it, he took Daisy and undid the diamond hitch, smirking. Josie unloaded the sacks of equipment and thanked Daisy for being such a good girl. Willy groaned and led the donkey home. The train going down would arrive in an hour.

"I was sure hoping you'd be here," he said when he returned.

"I took two days to come out, as we planned. But I had time to climb to another lake north of the trail yesterday."

He looked at her skeptically, "How did you know there would be a lake up there?"

She blushed. "I guess it seemed logical the stream came from something."

"Yeah, I guess." He was puzzled why she would take that on when she had a long walk out.

After what seemed an interminable wait, the train came. Since there was no passenger car, they boarded the caboose and soon were in Meredith.

Zona was on the platform to greet her. Giving her a big hug, she looked expectantly into her face. "You survived!"

"I survived. I had a wonderful time." She almost burst into tears but smiled broadly to overcome them. "Thank you so much for everything you did. I hope you'll get to go sometime. It's beautiful up there with the stars, wildflowers, and views of the whole world. I loved it and I couldn't have done it without you." She hugged Zona again who was also almost in tears. Josie grabbed her sacks minus the tarps and left as quickly as she could.

In the cabin, she collapsed on the bed and cried. *This is what broken-hearted means. I didn't know it hurt so much.* Through crying, she went to the river for a bucket of water for washing. She built a fire, got the wash tub and scrub board from the outside wall, then waited for the water to boil. Retrieving her sketchbook she studied the drawing of Andrew. He had a nice face, not a rugged or rough face as some men have; it was a pleasant, kind face. She wished the likeness were better. She wanted to remember his face exactly as it was: lively with inquisitive eyes, an intelligent look, a quick smile, laugh lines when something amused him, his lips pulled tight to play the harmonica. She wanted a living face, not a static drawing, but it was what she had. Very carefully she cut it from the book and propped it on the dresser.

Looking at the sketches of wildflowers she realized she hadn't given Andrew an address where he could send a flower book. *Well, of course I didn't give him an address, what name would I use? Besides, he probably didn't mean it.* She stifled an upwelling of tears. *I must remember it for the precious time it was and not bemoan it's over.* The water was taking so long to heat she went to the post office to take her mind off Andrew.

Zona wanted to know all about it. Josie was brief. She told her about the camps, the rain the first night, Daisy, the lake. Then she was less than honest. "I met a nice man coming out who walked with me a while. I told him my name was Joe. He seemed okay with me as a boy." She felt her face grow hot.

Zona tilted her head and raised her eyebrows. Josie looked away. "I'd better get back to my water. I'm anxious for a bath." She made a quick departure.

The water was boiling. She dumped it in the tub, got another bucket of cold water, tempered the hot with it and set the remainder on the stove. She washed her hair then stood in the tub and washed her body. After dressing she attacked the camp clothes. She would wash them again because they would need several scrubbings. She threw out the dirty water, put fresh water in the tub and went for more. *This is good to take my mind off him.*

When she had done what she could to erase the grime and smell of smoke, she made a cup of tea and took it outside. *Now. Now I can think. I will never want to leave here lest he come looking for me. Why, oh, why didn't I tell him the truth when I could have?*

After her tea, she knew she had to talk to Mr. Miller. She returned the miner's lamp and gun, thanked him, and said she hadn't needed the gun. "But it did give me a sense of comfort that I wouldn't have had otherwise. You were very thoughtful to want to protect me."

He was relieved, both because she hadn't needed it and she hadn't hurt herself with it. "You had a good trip?"

"Yes. A very good trip. It's an experience I'll always remember." But she didn't seem happy.

He cocked his head. "Tell me about it."

"To start, I'd never been around an animal like the donkey, didn't know anything about camping, I got rained on one night and stuff got wet because I didn't make a good tent. I reached the lakes, which is what I wanted to do and they were more beautiful than I could have imagined." She looked at that wrinkled, caring face and couldn't pretend with him. "There's more to tell you but I need some time to sort my feelings. I promise I'll share it with you, I just can't now. I hope you'll be patient with me. I'll need your help understanding what happened."

"Important thoughts can take time. I can wait till you're ready. I'm proud of you for being brave. Sometimes we need to do things that make us uncomfortable so we learn we're tough enough to take it."

"Yes. You're right. I think I need to be toughened up." She stood, thanked him for being her friend and went home.

For two days she worked obsessively in the school, cleaning desks, washing windows, and scrubbing the floor, trying not to think of Andrew. She loved the window in the door. They would now have afternoon light. She wanted the room to look inviting, inspiring, not intimidating. Finally, she had it right.

She avoided the post office. She didn't want to talk to Zona for fear she could read her mind. *It will help if I can have a few days to regain my composure.* She looked up and saw little Gertie running down the path, Hairy following close behind.

"Hello, Gertie."

"Hi, Miss Carter. Mamma wants you to come to supper tonight. She said you won't have to talk. Whatever that means."

You dear woman. "Please tell her I'd love to come to supper. I'll bring a jar of raspberry jam." She had brought back six jars she and her sisters had put up. They were a precious treat.

"Oh, goody." And she was off, running to tell the news, Hairy in hot pursuit.

Look at that little girl run. She won't be free much longer. She'll have to become lady-like and what an awful burden womanhood can be.

The west-bound train would be coming at 4:10. Thinking she might have mail from her sisters, she went to the post office. Zona sensed Josie wasn't ready to share details of the trip; intuition told her they would eventually come. At the post office Josie perched on the wide windowsill to wait for the train. Zona took the mail sack to meet it and returned followed by a man. "Josie, would you mind helping him while I do the mail?" she asked. His back was to Josie.

Josie asked, "May I help you find something?"

It's her! I've found her! He turned around, "I believe you may."

Her hand flew to her mouth. "Andrew," was all she could whisper.

He beamed with joy. "I'm looking for Miss Carter." His eyes danced. "Can you help me find her?"

Completely unsettled, she looked frantically around the room searching for a private space. "Will you go for a walk?"

"I'd like that." He was surprised how she looked dressed as a woman, her hair neatly combed, draped softly around her face, and tied back with a ribbon.

Zona was taking it in from the post office window. It was as she suspected. There was more than "a man on the trail."

Josie led him toward the schoolhouse. Part way there she turned to look at him. He looked different without his beard. She could hardly contain her happiness and nervousness. "This is where I teach."

"I see."

She led on. They climbed the step to the schoolhouse. He asked, "May we go in?"

"I probably shouldn't go in with you, but you're welcome to look around."

Standing in the middle of the room he nodded, his laugh lines deepening. The puzzle pieces were fitting together. Looking over the room, he observed maps, pictures, penmanship charts, arrangement of the desks, clean windows, bells on her desk, banjo and guitar on shelves, and rocks: the feldspar crystal, quartz, and mica. He didn't know she had kept them. He touched them lightly. He rubbed his hand across the top of her desk, then saw the chalk board with Big Dipper, North Star, Little Dipper, Seephius, Casiopia, and a smudge of chalk for the Milky Way. *I didn't know she sketched those. I don't know how to spell those Greek names either. I'll have to send them to her.* He stood in the room until he felt he could remember it, could place her in it in his thoughts, then he came out.

"I would have brought an apple if I'd known. Would that make me the teacher's pet?"

"Most likely."

She sat down on the stoop and he sat beside her. "May I know your real name now?"

"It's Josephine. I'm called Josie."

"Therefore, Joe."

"It was all I could think to say. I hadn't planned on needing a boy's name."

"No. The Carter part. Is that correct?"

"Yes. I didn't want to lie to you anymore."

"Thank you, Josephine Carter, called Josie." His eyes had such a soft look she had to look away before she cried with happiness.

"I don't remember your full name," she confessed. "I was so afraid, I didn't pay attention to the last part."

"I'm sorry you were afraid. If I'd known you're a woman I'd have behaved differently."

"That's what I was afraid of."

"Right. I didn't mean to frighten you." Shaking his head, "You must have felt defenseless."

"Not really. I had a gun; I'd never shot it."

Alarmed, "You had a gun?"

"Yes. Mr. Miller lent me his."

"Well, thanks for not shooting me."

"You're welcome. Think what I would have missed."

"I hope you would've missed me since you'd never shot it."

"Point and pull the trigger. That's all I was supposed to do. I had five chances."

"It could have changed our relationship. It would have helped me decide to move on."

"Then I would never know your name, like I don't know it now." She grinned.

He nodded. "Andrew Allan. A good Scottish name. Funny you have Scottish ancestry too."

"A sterner variety, I'm afraid. But my mother was a gentle, kind, English-Scot. I take comfort in her legacy."

His eyes didn't leave her face. "I think I see traces of that side. Your mother, did she die or was that part of the story?"

She couldn't answer for a moment. "I could never lie about my mother. She was the most compassionate, loving person I've ever known. I miss her every day. If you'd known her, I think you'd understand."

"I'm glad you had a kind, loving mother. It makes a world of difference." He watched her face. "Your father sounds severe."

"Yes. And no. We left Canada when I was five. My father had been a successful carriage-maker, but consumption weakened him so he couldn't do heavy work. He needed a dry climate to recover. We were dependent on his sisters' husbands to help support us until he got better. It was difficult for a proud man. To help him maintain his self-respect my mother treated him as if he were strong and still protected us. When Mother became ill, he was gentle and caring with her. I saw him in a completely different light, how much he loved her. I'm sorry to say he can bring out the Scottish stubbornness in me. It's nothing

I'm proud of." She looked at Andrew to see if he understood she could be difficult. He was laughing.

"A side I haven't seen. I'm forewarned. Thank you. From Canada, though," he looked confused, "to here?"

"I'm from Denver. Last year was my first year here."

"Denver! The library!"

"Did you wonder about Meredith's library?"

"It puzzled me. We're almost from the same town, you know. I might have met you there, but how could I find you among 200,000 people? I had to find you in the mountains and get to know you without all the clutter of a big city."

She agreed, then asked, "Why were you nice to me when I was such an odd boy?"

"Why wouldn't I be nice to an odd boy?" He stared into space. "Some people aren't kind to folks they don't understand." He seemed sad to her. "I grew up with a boy as a friend who was remarkable but unusual. A gentle, creative kid who never fit in. As we grew older, it became obvious he was different. His father thought he could beat it out of him. Other kids were mean and teased him. I didn't come to his defense as I should have. The poor kid committed suicide. I've always regretted my part in that. Who knows what he might have given us with his creativity? The world needs more gentle souls, not fewer. You, as boy Joe, reminded me of him. I thought you were running away from life and needed a friend. In a way, I suppose, I was making it up to him."

"Thank you for wanting to befriend a child who may have needed a kind companion." She tipped her head to look at his sincere face. *He's a very nice man.*

Looking earnest he said, "And to renew my pledge, I'll never tell anyone about being there with you."

"Thank you. I believe you." She needed to ask a question. "Can you forgive me for being the kind of girl who would dress like that? In pants?"

"Work well, don't they?"

She frowned. "But can you forgive me for being that kind of girl?"

"There's nothing to forgive. Society's at fault, not you. What kind of girl does that make you? An adventuresome, courageous girl." His head tilted slightly. "You are still a girl in many ways, good ways, also a woman and now I see, a lady."

She felt herself blush. "You flatter me."

"Flattery's false praise. This isn't even a compliment. It's the truth."

Without looking at him she said. "Thank you. I've come to expect the truth from you."

He put his hand over hers. "And I've come to expect an open, inquisitive, and creative mind from you. A mind I'd like to know better. Will you let me?"

She nodded. "I'd like to know your mind better as well."

He stood, gave her his hand to help her up, but didn't drop it. "I have to walk back to Thomasville now, where I'm staying. I catch the train tomorrow morning and there's a lot to do before I leave. If I write to Miss Josie Carter, will she answer my letters?"

"I will write to you, Andrew Allan, happily."

He lifted her hand and gently pressed it. "Till we can be together again, I will think of you. Please remember me."

She nodded; tears gathered in her eyes. "I will."

He bent, and quickly, lightly kissed her hair, and was gone.

Supper at Zona's that night was a blur: a swirl of talk, laughter, kids squealing, Otto barking orders. Zona ignored the confusion and put a delicious meal on the table of venison with mushrooms in cream on spaetzle. Everyone seemed to enjoy themselves. Josie floated through the evening in a daze. Alone in her cabin afterward, she stared into space. Had he really held onto her hand after he helped her up or did he forget to let go? Had he really kissed her hair, or did she imagine it? Maybe he bumped into her accidentally, but he didn't apologize. He said he would write. He asked her to write. She studied the drawing that was not his face, not nearly enough like him, not so tender, not so strong. She wanted to hold it to her heart, but she couldn't wrinkle that precious reminder.

Undressing slowly, dreamily, she climbed into bed, then abruptly went outside to look at stars. His stars. They would be above him too. Was he looking at them, remembering her? She saw the Big Dipper among a profusion of stars, more than she remembered. Grinning when she found his favorite, the North Star, and two constellations she had found with him, she said their names. He taught her those. They shared that memory. She looked east toward Thomasville, "Good night, Andrew. Thank you."

Labor Day came and went. School started the next morning. Josie had gone over lesson plans for fall during summer and found she wanted to change many things now she knew her pupils. Since they all heard what other grades were learning she wanted to vary some topics. Others were set in stone. Reading is reading; what they read could be chosen if they got the basics. This year she felt ready. They could have more fun with every subject. Two older kids had graduated. There were two new pupils in first grade. Four younger boys who had been manageable last year were now twelve and thirteen. They might present challenges.

Uncertainty over Andrew tempered her excitement, but when children and Mr. Miller arrived, their eager faces and happy dispositions took control of her emotions and the day quickly passed. Then, concern returned. As busy as she was, her mind flitted to Andrew when there was a moment of quiet.

As soon as school was over, she calmly walked to the post office lest Zona were watching. Zona was watching. Her wise eyes followed Josie as she went absent-mindedly through her days getting school materials ready, the classroom organized.

Josie knew there could be no letter from Andrew for four days because of Labor Day. Maybe he forgot her and there would never be a letter. She tried not to think of this possibility, yet it crept into her mind. Acting casual about being at the post office when the mail train was due, she perched on the window ledge and studied the scenery. Zona bustled about the store. Not one word had Zona uttered about Andrew. She waited, watched, and kept her fingers crossed this inexperienced girl would not have her heart broken.

The sound of the train, barely perceptible to those not anxiously awaiting it, roared in Josie's ears, bringing either elation or disappointment. She gave him every possible excuse for not writing. She rationalized all the reasons why there would be no letter, still, her heart was set on one.

The train pulled in, a man dumped freight and a mail bag on the planks, Zona handed him her bag, the train was off. Josie watched it go, feigning indifference. Busy in the post office, Zona sorted mail.

"Looks like you have a letter, Josie."

How could she appear not to care, that it might be from a sister or friend? She flew to the window with her hand outstretched. She couldn't even say "thank you" to Zona. She took the letter, ran to her cabin, and opened the envelope.

September 2, 1910

Hello,

I hope that didn't startle you the way it did the first time I said it. In fact, I hope you're more comfortable with me now than you were a week ago, now that I know your name and you can remember mine.

Have you had a chance to look at stars? These moonless nights the constellations seem lost in the clutter, don't they? My last night in your country I went outside to look at them and they seemed unusually clear and bright. It reminded me of sitting around a campfire with you–as if Cassiopeia, Cepheus, and the rest were our friends. (I had to look up how to spell them.)

"Miss Carter, Miss Carter?" Little Gertie's voice was excited and shrill.

Josie quickly tucked the letter under the pillow and called for Gertie to come in. "Is something the matter?"

"No. Momma said for you to come up and get your package and I was to high-tail it."

"A package?"

"Yes. Wrapped in brown paper." Her eyes were wide with excitement.

Gertie led the way, skipping, thrilled to be the messenger with such important news. Josie's mind raced over who might send a package. Surely not her father, nor her sisters, either. She hadn't gone off without anything.

The package was not large. Gertie easily could have carried it, but Zona was curious. Josie's heart raced. It was from Andrew. "Want a pair of scissors to cut that string?"

Josie blushed. "That would be nice." She didn't want to open it here; she couldn't not open it now. Inside lay two illustrated books, one for wildflowers and one for birds, and a new sketchbook. The note on top said, "To help you get acquainted with your neighbors, Andrew." Josie hugged them to her then looked helplessly at Zona. "He's very nice." Zona nodded and put an arm around Josie. "I hope so, child. I do hope so."

"Can I see them, Miss Carter?"

"Not with your dirty hands, you little rascal," said her mother. "Josie'll let you see them later. She wants to look at her presents by herself first."

"Come down in a little while, Gertie, and we'll look at them together." *Now I need to finish his letter.*

In the cabin, she was torn. She wanted to see the books he had chosen for her, but his words were more important. She put the books carefully on the table and retrieved the letter.

It feels strange to be in a city after wandering the hills. Noise, confusion, people, demands on my time. That makes me sound important, don't you think? Demands on my time are to register for school, pick up books, and get new clothes. Not all that demanding. What's frustrating is I've lost the abandon of a wanderer, an appealing freedom. Providing one has food, shelter, and a home to go to when one is tired of wandering. A nice life if one's parents will afford it!

Please write, Josie. I would love to hear about your year teaching and what goes on in a small mountain community in winter. What you're thinking is important too.

I enjoyed getting to know you, both of you.

Sincerely,
Andrew

Oh, Andrew. I enjoy knowing you too. She ran her fingers over his letter, studied the penmanship, his signature, reread the words slowly and carefully out loud, wondering if he wrote it as it came to mind or struggled with how and what to say before he penned it. She knew her response would require drafting it on a slate until it was right, then with her best penmanship, try to make it look spontaneous.

She tucked the letter beneath the pillow. Inside the flower book he wrote: "For a wildflower." In the bird book: "May you be as free." Beautifully precise illustrations with detailed descriptions filled the books. What treasures these would be, for the information as well as for the craftsmanship. She would spend hours studying them.

A small voice, "Miss Carter?"

"Come in, Gertie. You're going to love these. Let's sit on the stoop to look at them where we have good light." Together they pored over the pictures, trying to decide if they'd ever seen such a flower or bird. Gertie sighed, "There are so many things to know, aren't there, Miss Carter?"

"Yes, and so many things to enjoy if you know to look for them. Before you go, Gertie, I want you to take something to your mother. Wait here, please."

Josie returned with the lilac perfume in her hand. She put a drop on her finger and rubbed it behind Gertie's ear, then smears on her wrists. Gertie watched, fascinated. "What is that smell, Miss Carter?"

"It's lilac, but your mother may call it something else. It's made from a flower. When you get home, give your mother a hug. She'll understand." Gertie lifted a wrist to smell the perfume.

"It's pretty. Do all flowers smell like this?"

"No. Some don't smell much, others do. Each flower has its own fragrance, like each child has his or her own way of behaving."

Gertie nodded and said she'd better go. As she slowly walked Josie could see her looking at flowers as she'd never slowed to look before, all the while smelling her wrists.

Josie reread Andrew's letter. He'd been light-hearted, said he wanted to know her thoughts, was interested in her life at school, implied they would be writing all winter. Could her answer be as light and cheerful and still say as much? She took out a slate and began to scribble. It was hours before she felt it was right.

September 6, 1910

Hello, Andrew,

You didn't startle me–again. I return your friendly greeting this time, although I may not give as firm a handshake and my voice may not be deep.

Given the demands on your time, I feel fortunate to have received your letter. I am happy to know you arrived home safely and are preparing to go to school. If purchasing texts is an indication, you intend to study, providing wanderlust doesn't overcome you. Your parents may have something to say about that proclivity.

The stars <u>have</u> been beautiful. I, too, looked at them the night you mentioned and was able to identify two constellations you showed me and thank you for so kindly sending me their correct spelling. Fortunately, no one here caught the mistakes, so I didn't get a check mark beside them. It is different looking at stars in such darkness instead of when the moon is about to rise. I'm anxious to watch them as seasons change and to ask you what I'm seeing.

The beautiful books you sent are already treasures even though I have been through them only three times–twice by myself and once with little Gertie who was immensely curious about what I received. We went through them page by page and were entranced–by the art and number of specimens. Thank you for choosing such elegant editions and for inscribing touching, kind words. I will begin to document birds and flowers and hope to show you my efforts someday. You chose a sketchbook for real artists. The paper is much nicer than I have ever drawn on. I hope to do it justice.

I was walking with Zona yesterday and we saw branches broken off chokecherries by a bear and oak leaves stripped from trees where it gathered acorns. Such tiny morsels for a creature heading into winter and trying to build a layer of fat.

And no, I did not have a gun with me, but I was not afraid. I had Zona!

Thank you, again, Andrew, for teaching me so much about this country and now for giving me the chance to know it better. I will always cherish this knowledge from you.

Sincerely,
Josie

She wanted to add, please write again. No, she hoped she didn't need to. She reread the letter several times before she copied it to stationery. Then it occurred to her she could personalize it with a tiny drawing of chokecherries. She had brought a small branch home with her to study. She took great care to capture it.

Josie's letter had not been completely accurate. She and Zona had not gone for a walk but to pick chokecherries for jelly Zona made every fall. When they had a bucketful they took it home and Zona taught her how to prepare the fruit. Josie kept a jar as a gift for Andrew and didn't want to ruin the surprise. There had been no confidences shared that day, which Zona had hoped for.

As Zona expected, Josie's letter went by return mail.

After supper Josie took the flower book from the shelf and studied the first drawing, the Oregon grape. The text included its Latin name then described its appearance, where found, when in bloom, and any practical uses. She had seen this small yellow flower in spring on its holly leaf bed. Then when she and Zona had been out picking chokecherries, she had seen blue berries above the leaves. She would try to eat a berry next time she saw one. For now she would sketch it as the book's artist had so she would know what to look for. Pleased with her sketch she decided to take it to class and open their day with a lesson on the flowers in their valley. The children should know their neighbors too.

School went well. The big boys were behaving as well as she hoped they might. She was pleased children had not forgotten everything they learned last year. Mr. Miller looked over the musical instruments and said they'd do for kids and agreed to help whoever showed an interest. The instruments were a success and she was fascinated by which children seemed most inclined to want to play them and how quickly they managed to make chords.

At night she did her schoolwork before allowing herself the luxury of rereading Andrew's letter then sketching a flower or bird and reading about it.

After waiting impatiently for three days, Zona handed her a letter when she went to the post office after school. Josie accepted it with more grace, even though her emotions were rattling her composure, and walked to her cabin.

September 9, 1910

Good Morning, Miss Carter. Good Morning, Miss Carter. Good Morning, Miss Carter.

Is this how your day starts? May I add my Good Morning, Miss Carter, to the chorus? Would I get special treatment with a bouquet of wildflowers? May the student decide what special treatment includes?

Thank you for your letter and delicate drawing of chokecherries. A bear should feel lucky it avoided you two out on the loose. I'm jealous I wasn't on that walk with you even if Zona were there. Have you tried a chokecherry? Choose one that's not too ripe to get the full effect.

Well, I've purchased the texts, registered, and am decked out in new clothes–a pair of pants with cuffs, no less, and two new shirts. Fortunately, clothes are casual at Mines because we often play in dirt. We even have our own mine.

I trust you celebrated Labor Day. I did, though I've done precious little labor in my life. Next year I may be more qualified to be honored, which is by way of telling you I'm going to be working for Dad on weekends to clean job sites and do some estimating. Charity on his part because sites get cleaned without my help and estimates get done. He appreciates I would like to earn money this year. (Yes, I have worked for him summers for years, however, I'm no longer an apprentice sweeper; I'm now a journeyman and accordingly he's given me a raise in pay.)

I can't remember your words exactly when you expressed a desire to learn about mining. Something like, "Really?" Regardless, I've decided a friend would share his knowledge or at least what the books say. Would you prefer metallurgy or mining engineering? Or are you like my mother who says to bring her a pretty rock and not spoil it by talking about it so much?

I'm wondering if you come home for Christmas and hope you do. Said mother would like to meet my friend Joe. (We must determine what you'll wear. Cuffs are fashionable this year, you know, and we're a stylish family.)

Sincerely,
Andrew

Oh, Andrew, I didn't know you were a tease. You were so nice to Joe. You remind me of boys on the playground who pull girls' braids. I like it. You may pull mine.

She reread the letter, smiling because she knew what was coming. She was also reading between the lines. Did he want her to come home so he could be with her? Had he told his mother she wore pants and an engineer's battered old hat? What would she think of such a girl? Would he have told her if she wouldn't approve? And if he had told his mother, was it time to confide in Zona?

After reading it she tucked it in with the other one.

Tidying the classroom, concentrating on lesson plans, and grading slates took time she would rather have spent thinking about Andrew. Drawing a bird or flower for the next day was a joy. *If I discipline myself to think about him only after my work is done, I'll make more progress on all my tasks and have time for a longer supper.* It required more discipline than she could muster. Her thoughts flew to him: *Did you see that bird? It may have been a wren. Feel the freshness in the air? Do you think it's getting cooler in the evenings? See service berry leaves turning the color of a ripe peach? Would a walk to the river interest you?* She longed to share this delightful world and to have him make it richer. She missed him.

When she finished her schoolwork, completed the drawing, and quieted her mind so she could write, she answered his letter, trying to keep it lighthearted as he had done, yet filled with subtle hints of her affection.

September 13, 1910

My Dapper Friend,

I hope to see you in your new clothes someday. Fashionable isn't a word we use in Meredith and I fear if you appeared in cuffed pants they would guess you're growing into them. Since you have alerted me, I will note your smart style, given the chance.

School began as you suspected Sept. 6. As I suspected the big boys are rowdy but in fear of their mothers who tend to be of a rougher variety, I imagine, than what lives in Golden. Since I knit and quilt with their moms, I could tattle on them. Which I won't do, unless they're truly dreadful. They're good boys, though, and we'll survive each other.

What has been surprising to me is their enthusiasm for learning about flowers and birds, "their neighbors", as if they had no idea they were here. I have been copying a drawing from your beautiful books each night then sharing it with the kids. It's giving me a chance to explain some of the scientific words the books use, if I understand them myself. Thank you so much for making this a friendlier neighborhood.

Other surprises are a couple of the older kids' musical aptitude and some of the little ones' pretty voices. I wish you were here to play your harmonica for them. They would love its mournful tunes. We would have to do it around a campfire to truly appreciate it, though.

I didn't come home for Christmas last year because I thought my father might ask me not to return. If I come home this Christmas and your mother would like to meet a young person who has no idea who she is, I would be happy to borrow "Joe's clothes" and amuse her with my changing voice. But no cuffs! Joe wears cuffs only when his pants are too long and by Christmas they should be about right.

There was a little fox in the meadow tonight. His tail has such a fluffy white tip it looks like a thistle gone to seed. He's very secretive and yet he watched me closely, from a safe distance, as if to determine if I'm friend or foe. I hope he can see I'm the former.

Sincerely,
Josie

Did she strike the right balance between friendship and affection? She was unsure of his feelings. It would be improper, and unladylike, to assume he wanted more than a correspondent, but he hinted he did. She had never had a boy for a friend. Never had a beau. Maybe this teasing was what boys did with friends. She feared reading too much into his letters, yet her heart would not make light of his intimations.

The children applied themselves to their lessons. Older ones helped the next younger ones as she worked her way up the age groups. Some lessons were appropriate for all students: science, on a basic level, when she discussed her drawings; and geography. Music was a communal activity and she was pleased to have Mr. Miller in the classroom because children had grown fond of him and the guitar.

A week after Andrew's last letter, she received another.

September 16, 1910

Good morning, Josie,

Is the sun beaming in your window and waking you to sounds of rushing water? I like to imagine it is. It's so nice to have a gentle alarm clock, not a bossy one like mine. I'm up early this morning because I have an eight o'clock class and it's a good walk to get there. I usually ride my bicycle but it has a flat tire and I'd rather write to you than fix it. I wanted to have a few minutes with you before I leave because I have something to share. Last evening coming home, I saw the first sign of fall. On North Table Mountain—are you familiar with it and its twin, South Table Mountain? Large flat buttes standing east of Golden, divided by Clear Creek. I'll spare you the geologic details, which, I'm sure, you'd find fascinating. Well, up there, some bushes have turned bright red. I'm not sure what they are. Could be sumac or perhaps chokecherry. I didn't care. They were brilliant in late afternoon sun and I thought of you. I knew they would make you happy and that made me happy. Someday I'll take you up one of those buttes, if you'd like. I'll go first to kick rattlers out of the path unless you'd prefer to do it. They really mean no harm unless you take venom personally. Yes, I've seen some. No, they've never bitten me, or even tried. I sound brave, though, don't you think? Got to go. Be back when I'm smarter. Correction. When I'm more educated, maybe.

After supper

The leaves are still there. Still making us happy. I'm home and not much more educated. I find my mind wanders in class. I know I should be paying attention and I mean to because I enjoy the subject and will find the information useful at some point, besides, he's going to test us on it. But I drift. I hope you don't have any students staring out windows with vacant looks in their eyes. A sure sign they're distracted. Better jerk their chains. Please don't jerk mine; I'm enjoying my memories.

An interesting thing happened on my way to class. A guy came by on a bicycle-looking thing that had a motor. He made a terrible racket. It sure looked like fun.

Thank you for telling me about your drawings for class. I'm sure the kids have seen those flowers and birds but didn't know them. Boys, especially, have trouble admitting they don't know everything, as you may remember from a recent encounter. Do girls share that crippling trait?

Please tell me what else you're teaching. Perhaps if Mines can't educate me, you can. I may go look at stars now. They won't be as bright as in your dark valley, especially tonight because we have a full moon in two nights. If you want to look at nine o'clock, we can watch them together. I'll play my harmonica if you'd like.

Sincerely,
Andrew

She sat on the cabin's stoop and read and reread his letter. *Why is he distracted? I am. Is it for the same reason? He wants to share beautiful things with me. I want to share with him. What is there about that? Why does sharing something with someone, whether it's the children or Andrew, make it richer?* She mused on this for a while then studied the letter again. *He's teasing me about snakes. He must know girls typically don't like them. Has he known many girls? Maybe he even has a girlfriend now. No, I can't think that. It would make me too sad. He'll tell me if he does, one way or another.*

Her evening proceeded as usual. At nine o'clock she promptly went to watch stars and listen for the harmonica. Soft breezes gently ruffled oak and cottonwood leaves near her. She imagined she could hear "Red River Valley" again. It brought both a smile and a sigh. She answered Andrew's letter.

September 20, 1910

Andrew,

Were you a naughty child? For some reason I think I see an impish, mischievous boy hiding between the lines of your letters. Tell Teacher the truth.

Here's my truth. I do not like snakes! Sometimes boys bring one to school to terrify girls and I would rather faint than let them know I'm afraid, so I ask them to show it to all of us. We admire it even though it may be a drab gray, still a marvel how fast it slithers along. One boy brought in a brilliant green snake. Even I thought it had that one redeeming feature. Occasionally I have seen a snake basking in the sun where I get water and I have shuddered and encouraged it to leave. There are no poisonous snakes here, I'm assured, but that's not all I'm afraid of. This will make you wonder at my good sense. I'm afraid of simply seeing one. Do you know Emily Dickinson's poem about the '*narrow fellow in the grass?*' She said a snake gives her '*Zero at the bone.*' I agree.

Here's something that <u>will</u> delight a naughty boy. Zona fixed a delicious dinner and I asked how she made it. I'm trying to learn about cooking from these kind women from such diverse backgrounds. She said it was venison with onions and wild mushrooms in cream on spaetzle. I did not behave badly. I thought you would get a good laugh at my discomfort at having eaten all those little worms. Be honest. Did you grin and duck your head the way you do?

Yes. I have a nice alarm clock but it's not the sun. To get men to work on time the foreman rings an old locomotive bell. It's quite pleasant and necessary because I don't have a clock, only my mother's pendant watch.

You asked what I'm teaching now. To the Aebecedarians, I'm trying to get the alphabet across as well as English. The three R's to the next batch. Is there anything sillier than the English language? Take *do* and *so*. How does one explain those *o* sounds to a child? And what happens to the *o* in *do* when it becomes *does* or *don't*? Then there are their homonyms *dew* and *sew*. Why don't *dew* and *sew* rhyme? Try to explain the *ough* sound in *bough*, *though*, *cough,* and *slough* to a third grader who's struggling with English. Let's face it, English is a mess! Older boys are doing geography, grammar, math, and rhetoric. Interestingly, a girl a grade below them is doing better in math than two of them.

The past two teachers didn't teach much history, I'm told. Probably because our pitiful history text is so simplified and boring as to be useless. There may be better ones. If so, they haven't made their way here yet. So, the curriculum is up to me. Last year we started with American history: pilgrims, founding fathers, a little about the Constitution. During lunch I read several books to them relative to that era: Washington Irving tales, Benjamin Franklin's autobiography, a book about the Revolutionary War, although war is so glorified it seemed more fiction than history.

Over summer, I researched causes and effects of the Industrial Revolution and how it affected slavery here. One of the books made the connection between the popularity of machine-made cotton cloth and the slave plantations of the South. We are working our way to the Civil War. I need to make this interesting to grades four–eight. I made a timeline this summer showing the inventions of the late 1700s and 1800s. I had to wonder if we could see the future, would we see such dramatic forces coming as people experienced then?

How I would love to sit by a fire and discuss this with you. I would value your insights plus suggestions for books boys might enjoy. I know some for girls. (I am a girl, you will remember?) Will you think about this, please? But not in class! If it doesn't take too long to write down your thoughts, I will be grateful and so will the children, depending on how advanced those thoughts are.

I, too, must get busy. There was a Black-capped Chickadee in the oaks tonight. Most of them seem to leave in summer and return come fall. I've also learned their cousin, the Mountain Chickadee, has a white eyebrow. They sing their name, DeeDee, and are cheerful little neighbors. Thanks to your book, I call them by name. We barely nodded to each other last year.

Sincerely,
Josie

P. S. Wave to me from the top of the mountain and bring me back a branch, please. Yes, the leaves and you make me happy. I was looking at stars tonight at nine o'clock and listening for your song.

As she stood on the stoop looking at stars, she remembered that first night at Savage Lake and how terrified she had been of this man who intruded on her outing and proceeded to make it her most memorable four days. *How does one know when something so unexpected will pop into one's life and change it forever? I think there will always be a "before Andrew"; will there be an "after Andrew?" I hope not.* She reread his letter and fell asleep.

After school, the room tidied, slates and blackboard washed, she wandered to the post office. "You've got a letter, Josie." Zona looked concerned. This was all moving too fast for her comfort. Josie was surprised it was from Andrew. She had a letter yesterday.

September 17, 1910

Dear Josie,

I apologize for the silly letter I wrote yesterday. In my mind I see us hiking together as we did. You, free as a bird, climbing over boulders and up rocky trails without a care. I think of you, certainly not as Joe, but as Josie, uncaged. Last night I realized that asking you to hike up Table Mountain with me would be impossible in clothes society forces you to wear. It was almost a cruel joke to tease you with it. I'm sorry. Really sorry it must be so, because I enjoyed myself in the wild with you and I think you enjoyed your freedom. Let's hope soon fashion will let you dress so you can go exploring comfortably–with me. In the meantime, I'll propose sensible walks long skirts can survive.

I hope I didn't make you sad. I never want to give you a reason for sadness.

Sincerely,
Andrew

She read his letter quickly, Zona watching from behind the counter. Josie folded it and turned to her dear friend. "He was afraid he'd said something that might make me sad, Zona. He'd invited me to hike up a mountain in Golden then realized I couldn't go in a skirt and he was sorry."

Zona studied Josie's young face and felt relieved the letter hadn't brought unwelcome news. "I'm glad he didn't want to make you sad, and he understood it could and apologized. Some men have trouble figuring us out." Her laugh held a world of experience.

"Zona, I don't believe I told you how we met. Do you care?"

"I care he doesn't break your heart. When you're ready to share the rest, I'll find it interesting. You seem to have made quite an impression on the 'man on the trail.'" She smiled with quiet understanding of the fine line between nosiness and concern.

"I'll tell you about it." It was a time of understanding and optimism on Zona's part. She didn't criticize one thing Josie had done. She, too, would have wanted to know that young man better when she was younger.

"We'll hope for the best, Josie. That's all a body can do. Don't let romance blind you though. Don't make excuses for him if you find things you don't admire. The more you know him, the more he knows you, the better." This wisdom from a woman who married at fifteen.

Since she had told Zona about meeting Andrew and Zona hadn't been scandalized by their camping together, it gave her courage to tell Mr. Miller. She trusted his good sense and if he didn't disapprove of what she had done he could give her good advice about men. The opportunity presented itself when they crossed paths out walking and they decided to rest on a grassy spot.

They sat quietly enjoying the view. "Mr. Miller?"

He cocked his head. "Yes?"

"I'm ready to tell you more about my camping trip. It may take a few minutes."

"I have time."

"I had an experience I haven't told you about."

"You mentioned it. I've been waiting to hear it."

She studied her hands. *I hope he's not too strict.* "Well, everything went as Zona and I had planned until I got to the lakes. I had just arrived and when I turned around there was a man coming toward me. He stuck out his hand and introduced himself as Andrew Allan. I tried to talk low like a boy and said my name was Joe. He asked if we could share a campfire and I didn't know what to say so I said yes in a deep voice. I was very frightened and wanted to escape but he could see the trail from where he put his tent. I put the coat on with the gun in my pocket and set up my tent. He came to the campfire for dinner and tried to talk to me. I would only say yes or no. It was awkward and I felt vulnerable except I had your gun and five bullets."

She looked up from her hands to see if he understood what he had done for her. He gave his slight nod. She pulled some grass to twine. "We cooked our own food and I was so nervous I didn't finish cooking my potatoes and when I ate them, they crunched." She could see the creases around his mouth deepen although he tried not to smile. "He grew tired of talking to himself and started playing his harmonica. Finally, he went to bed. I lay awake a long time with the gun near listening for footsteps. I didn't sleep well because I was frightened and there were the raw potatoes." She looked at him and they shared grins.

"The next morning he saw a buck at the lake and came to get Joe to show it to him. I was still in my tent asleep and he saw my braid. He hurried away but at breakfast he told me he knew I'm a girl and would leave if I wanted him to." She paused.

Mr. Miller nodded for her to continue. "He told me he's a college student in Golden, learning to be a mining engineer and will graduate this coming spring. We had breakfast and he said he had planned to hike that day and come back to his tent that night and he invited me to go with him. He would leave when we got back if I wanted him to. I didn't know what to do. He'd been nice to Joe who was almost rude to him and Andrew had been so nervous and uncomfortable telling me he knew I'm a girl that I felt he was okay. He was on the government survey crew last year and was knowledgeable about the area and I could learn about it. Maybe I was wrong, but I took a chance and decided to go with him providing he would leave if I asked him to. We agreed I would continue to wear my hat to hide my hair and he would call me Joe." She looked up. He nodded.

"We had a nice hike and he talked to me about geology, flowers, mining, and philosophical things. It was interesting and when I asked him questions he would answer in a way that made me comfortable asking more. It felt right talking to him. I didn't ask him to leave and we had a good conversation at dinner and he told me about stars. I kept the gun with me even though I wasn't frightened anymore." She had been braiding and unbraiding grass strands. She looked at him.

"Is there more you want to tell me?"

"Yes. He told me he would guard my honor by never telling anyone we were together unchaperoned. The next day we left those lakes together and when we reached where we were going to spend the night, we set up our separate camps away from each other like before. That night we talked more and it was as if we'd been friends for a long time. Our last day he went back up the trail to go to another lake and I came home." She looked up to see if he were angry or disappointed.

He looked at her with great tenderness. He had never known the kind of companionship she described. To hear about this awakening of affection as she expressed it, was as near to love as he had ever been. Never had anyone shared with him a confidence as she had just done. He coughed to hide his emotion. "Is that the end, Miss Carter?"

"No. I hadn't told him my real name, although I had told him I live in Meredith that first awful day and he came to find me after I got home. We've been writing since. He's been thoughtful and kind."

Mr. Miller rocked a little, regaining his composure, thinking, staring into space. "You didn't shoot him. That's good." His weathered face showed traces of humor.

"Yes. I did think about it though. After that second day, I became more comfortable. But I kept the gun in my pocket."

"Good. Lots of men are nice, Miss Carter. Not all of them are safe for a woman. I'm glad he behaved. Will you tell me from time to time, if you still think he's a good man?"

He doesn't seem disappointed in me. He didn't scold. She assured him she would talk to him about Andrew. When they parted, she reached out and touched his arm. "Thank you for listening."

His rough, speckled hand patted hers. "Thank you for telling me. I've had no one like you, you know."

FALL, 1910

Josie answered Andrew's apology about climbing Table Mountain. It didn't escape her notice he called her "Dear" for the first time. She would try it on her letter to him.

September 21, 1910

Dear Andrew,

You did not make me sad. Your letters fill me with joy. It isn't your fault we behave in such a silly manner by letting someone decide for us what is proper and improper. It takes more courage than I have, though, to challenge such conventions–at least in public. I couldn't have done as I did if I hadn't gotten myself into an absurd situation with Zona who was determined to help me realize a dream and I didn't have the gumption to back down. So, there I was, pretending to be a boy.

I noticed today how quiet the world is in fall. I didn't appreciate it last year because it was all so new to me. When I left in June it was noisy with high water crashing down the river, songbirds singing, coyotes yipping, and flickers pecking on anything standing still. Now, it's silent as if getting ready for winter even though it's only September. It feels like story hour before bedtime when children quiet down from a busy day. I did notice bluebirds flocking though they're not noisy about it. And have you noticed how spring announces itself with the bright yellow of dandelions, arrow leaf and mules' ears then exits with another burst of yellow in the turning leaves and goldenrod?

Have a pleasant day, Andrew, and please don't think I'm fragile. If you upset me, I'll try to be grown up enough to tell you nicely. You've let me know it would not be your intention.

I look forward to exploring with you, regardless of my attire.

Sincerely,
Josie

P.S. My friend Mr. Miller asked about you today. I told him you are thoughtful and kind, however you didn't bring me an apple.

Tuesday she hoped for a letter. She hurried to the post office where Zona greeted her with a letter in her hand. Even Zona had started looking for them on Tuesdays, hoping he wouldn't forget her friend.

September 23, 1910

Dear Josie,

Both your letters came today and were gratefully received. They were as usual a bright reflection of you. Thank you for accepting my apology. Your letters fill me with questions. What was your dream? Did you realize it? Please tell me about Zona. Also, I know you aren't fragile because you were camping by yourself. You do seem tender and strong at the same time and women confuse me.

Josie, I have another question. I'm just going to blurt it out. Do you have a boyfriend? I will tell you now I don't have a girlfriend. I have dated a few girls and somehow it just didn't work. The girls were perfectly fine yet there was something missing. They were some of the longest evenings I have ever spent. I'm not good at telling jokes or small talk, or probably big talk for that matter, still there was no connection. Do you remember when we left each other the last day on the North Fork, I told you I could talk with you and share things with you and how wonderful that was? I'd never known that before. Now I'm nervous and probably saying too much so I'll change the subject.

Josie put the letter in her lap. *He doesn't have a girlfriend. He wants to know if I have a boyfriend. Does he care? Does talking to me, sharing with me mean he feels we have something special between us? Is he asking because he doesn't want to get his hopes up either?* She tried to follow the change of subject.

You talked in one of your last letters about history. You'll be surprised to learn I have a jaded thought about that. Humans seem remarkably uninstructable when it comes to learning from history. Often I have found that history books give an unbalanced account of what happened. There's more to life than war and politics yet those are what seem interesting to historians. More interesting than when someone discovered anesthesia. I'm fascinated with what man's creativity produces and will add there seems to be a great disconnect between his dysfunctional social behavior and his remarkable technical ability

Jaded! I warned you. Jaded can mean cynical, which I hope I'm not. Skeptical, I try to be. You may know jade is a beautiful green stone, relatively hard, not the hardest but tough, and when polished has luster. My rock metaphor means I may not be as hard as some. Tough, maybe. I hope you'll find me polishable. You'll become more familiar with jaded as you get to know me.

You mentioned sitting around a campfire and discussing things and I think, could there be anything nicer in the world? Then I think there may be; it would always be something with you.

You mentioned the Industrial Revolution and Civil War. On the North Fork I told you about my mom being a suffragist. Well, after Colorado passed women's suffrage, she took on child labor and animal welfare. She's something else. If you are up for a real discussion about the bad effects of the Industrial Revolution, she's the one to talk to. She might suggest you read *Oliver Twist* if you haven't. It tells of poor children's lives, not especially dreadful factory lives, but survival. Charles Dickens' intent was to open the eyes of the English about children born into poverty, she says.

On to the Civil War or the Great Un-civil War. More questions than answers. What real harm would have been done if the South had been allowed to peacefully separate-from the North? Would the South have soon followed the many countries that had already abandoned slavery? What if

128

the money spent on the Civil War had been used to purchase the slaves' freedom? About your comment regarding cotton cloth and slavery, another question. Do you think another crop would have had a different effect? Many Africans were taken to countries to work on plantations other than cotton, such as sugar and coffee.

Now, briefly about snakes. I will protect you. I'll always go first and tell you not to look and them to leave. You may trust me.

Must study, alas. I'm anxious to have your answers.

Sincerely,
Andrew

P. S. I enjoy hearing about your natural world. Thank you for inviting me into it and for drawing a delightful picture of chickadees.

P.P. S. I asked Mom if I "grin and duck my head." She stared in disbelief. Said I'd done that since I was three.

Josie sat reading, smiles playing on her face. She turned to Zona and said, "He writes a good letter. I feel I'm getting to know him better all the time. How long did it take you to know Otto?"

Surprised at the question, she answered, "Know Otto? Not long, I guess." She considered, "He has a good heart, a big bluster, he's a hard worker and a steady man, but know him? I see him sitting and staring out the window in the evening and I have no idea what's on his mind. Never says what he thinks about, if he'd like a different life, where he'd rather be, or if I'm the woman he wants to be with. We go through life as if it's what we're supposed to do. Don't think about it too much, at least I don't. We don't need to know more about each other. I think maybe you do need to know more about your Andrew. The letters are good, Josie. Keep him writing."

She thanked Zona for the advice and headed home.

What would it mean to be someone's girlfriend? He wants me to get to know him and I feel I already do. I wonder if he feels he knows me. How do you know when you "know" someone? What do we say or do that reveals us to others and do we give a true picture or a flattering portrait that makes us appear the way we want but isn't really ourselves? And when a person sees the real us what happens? I want him to know me. Who am I?

She felt disquieted during supper, thoughts tripping over themselves as she read his letter again. She kept to her schedule because if she didn't, she would neglect her job and besides, looking forward to answering his letter gave her time to think about what to say.

September 27, 1910

Dear Andrew,

I want to answer your letter paragraph by paragraph but that is so perfunctory. Let me say your thoughts fascinate me. They seem so fully formed. When did you think these things? I can't imagine tiring of asking you questions. Will you mind?

Now to your questions. After Mother died and Father was responsible for raising us, he became strict about our whereabouts. Also, the management of the house fell to us girls, especially me since I was the oldest. This didn't leave much time for socializing. You will recognize this as a way to make me feel better about not having a boyfriend or ever having had one. I have wondered if you have a girlfriend. Thank you for offering that information.

Now to your other questions. When I returned from Denver in August, I told Zona I would love to go camping but I couldn't go without a man. She said why not? I explained to her and she said nonsense. Then I said I couldn't hike in a skirt. She fixed that with Henry's clothes. I couldn't come up with more excuses, so I went. She's like a strong wind. You want to be going her way. That wind can also carry you along with her enthusiasm. I love her spirit and it brought me your friendship.

Now, about the Industrial Revolution. I will read *Oliver Twist*. If we can see history from a child's point of view it will make it more believable. Some mothers and Mr. Miller, when he can, join us for the readings. They're hungry for something besides their daily lives and they enjoy stories, no matter what they are. For some, it's a chance to improve their English.

My friend Mr. Miller, who lent me the gun I didn't shoot you with, worked railroads. I'll ask him what he knows. Although he's very quiet, maybe shy, he may talk to the children. He's been with them now for a year and they regard him as a grandfather.

Regarding the Civil War questions you posed: I try to imagine the difference it would have made if the North had purchased the slaves' freedom and not destroyed the Southerners' homelands. I've read giving former slaves the vote caused troubles in the South too. Emancipation solved and created problems, it seems.

Do we share the same weather? If so, perhaps you've been having brilliant sunsets as well. The colors take my breath away: golds, oranges, deep roses, dark blue shadows. Words elude me. How to describe radiance? We need to see them together, then you'd know.

The deer's color has turned. How quickly they lose their beautiful summer's russet to winter's gray.

Sincerely,
Josie

She requested *Oliver Twist* from the Denver library. The cruelty of it appalled her. She knew she couldn't read it aloud. Dickens' language was too complicated for the pupils to understand and her voice would crack in the heart-breaking parts. She decided to tell the story, at least to begin.

Realizing she couldn't finish it in two weeks, she wrote to her sisters asking them to find a used copy for her.

Tuesday a letter came.

September 30, 1910

Dear Josie,

Thank you for your answers, especially one. It was not my intent to pry into your private life but if you have a boyfriend then some of the things I was saying–and thinking–were inappropriate. I will say that if you had let little boys, or big ones, get to know you, you would have had many boyfriends by now. I'll look forward to hearing more about Zona. I have much to thank her for.

Yesterday, we had an excursion to Clear Creek Canyon and it made me think of you, more than usual. Aspen leaves are turning shades of yellow and red there, so I imagine you're having a brilliant display as well.

Ever been up Clear Creek? It's a narrow valley accessible by Colorado & Southern Railroad. Although Denver lays claim to the first gold, miners traced it to Clear Creek (probably where Golden got its name) and followed the gold to Idaho Springs, Blackhawk, and Central City where intense mining now takes place. We made a grand day of it, riding the train to the gold fields, going into Argo Tunnel that will eventually be about four miles long and connect mines underground. We've been there before; it's always an adventure and a look at what we're heading into. We used our little picks to poke around in tailings as if we knew what we were doing. I'm glad you weren't there to watch because you may have laughed at how pompous and self-important we were, trying to show off our knowledge and hoping we were guessing correctly. Did your mother warn you men can be ridiculous sometimes? My mother has mentioned it on occasion–not subtly, I might add.

You asked about my thoughts. I spend time alone because I'm not very sociable, meaning I prefer a few friends and not great gatherings. I do enjoy trying to understand people and I'm ashamed to admit, for a self-described student of human nature, I didn't figure you out until I saw your braid. After that, I especially wanted to figure you out. Still do.

Back to thoughts. (Have you noticed I drift when I think of you?) On the survey crew we usually did jobs independently and spent a lot of time hiking, working with mules, setting up and breaking down campsites, also bothering the geologists. This gave me time to think about things like people and religion, how we seem to need to form into groups and how often those groups become competitive even to the point of hostility, and about other troubling traits of mankind. You said in your letter that my thoughts seem fully formed, well, maybe, but fully formed is not the same as well formed. At school if you offer a thought the first thing the guys do is look for weaknesses. Then they attack. It's rigorous and on some level productive. It doesn't make you want to share ideas much. Can we do it differently? Could we first look at the value in our thoughts then move on together to look at the problems, gently? Wouldn't it be better to complete than compete?

Josie, Josie. This has gone on for pages. You'll learn not to get me started on Questions of Great Importance.

Please have a pleasant day. Enjoy a warm and glowing fall. You drew perfect leaves.

Sincerely,
Andy

Taking his letter up the tracks until she found a grove of aspens, she settled into soft grass. A patch of aspens across the river glowed red, most were a luminous lemon in the sun.

Who is he? I don't know many men, yet I've never met anyone quite like him. He writes as if we're going to be together someday. I'm not sure he knows me as well as he thinks he does. When he does get to know me, will he be disappointed? She folded the letter carefully after reading it a third time and lay back to gaze up into a canopy of shimmering leaves turning yellow.

She heard rustling in grass behind her. Mr. Miller was going home from a walk. "Good afternoon, Mr. Miller."

"Good afternoon, Miss Carter. Are you out for a walk too?"

"I am. Mr. Miller? When we're not in class, I'd like you to call me Josie."

"You're my teacher."

"I hope I'm also your friend. Will you join me in this beautiful spot and tell me where you've been walking?"

He slowly lowered his old body into the grass. "I've been up Miller Creek. I go there to remember my family. I had older brothers and little sisters. I'm not sure of their names. It calms me when I recollect one."

"What were you called?"

"Llewellyn. I don't know how to write it. I'm called Miller, mostly. When I mustered out of the army, my pay was in an envelope with my whole name on it. I kept it so I'd know who I am. When the paper got wet the ink ran and I lost my name."

"We can find how to spell your name. I'll write to the library. They'll know. Then you can learn how to write it. Would you like that?"

Staring into the distance, he nodded. "I would like to write my name before I die."

"I'll write to the library tonight so you'll have lots of time to practice."

She saw him looking at the envelope in her lap which had been neatly opened. She beamed. "You can see your letter opener is fulfilling its purpose, and I think of you every time I use it. It's a beautiful tool."

His eyes were moist; he looked pleased. They walked to the store together where he picked up a few groceries and went home.

"You like Mr. Miller, Josie?" Zona asked.

"He has a sadness I don't understand, but, yes, I like him very much. He's been a good student and an inspiration for the kids. He seems gentle, also a little wary of the world."

"He takes a special interest in you. You've been kind. I get the feeling he hasn't known a lot of that in his life. He treasured your letters this summer. I doubt he wrote on top of them, regardless of what you suggested. Wonder where he comes from."

When Josie answered Andrew's letter that evening, she struggled how to respond. He was still being lighthearted in places, then would veer into seriousness and a future together. Could she respond in kind or would that be presumptuous if he didn't intend that interpretation?

October 4, 1910

Andy?

I didn't know you go by Andy. I like it. It's a friendly name. I like Andrew too.

Your trip to the gold fields sounds appropriate for students at Mines. Have you ever worked in a mine or do you want to? I don't know why you're studying metallurgy. Perhaps you told me when I was someone else.

Mother did not tell us men can be ridiculous. She should have thought it occasionally, if for no other reason than reading the newspaper. However, she was a charitable soul and uncritical of others. I did not inherit those traits. I see faults. Don't be nervous, I haven't seen any in you. And ridiculous is not exclusively a masculine trait. Consider women's clothes.

It is, as you say, a glowing world. I read your letter in a grove of aspens and felt warmed by the leaves and your words, except I fear you are imagining me as someone you would like me to be. You are a thoughtful person. I am not. I react. I read or hear something, and think it's true or false, kind or cruel. I don't come up with original thoughts. I am, however, skeptical of many things people take for truth. What I'm trying to say, Andrew, is I'm afraid you will find me boring after a short while and when you do, I will understand.

She stopped. *Could I really understand? It would break my heart but, yes, I could understand I'm not the person he thinks I am.* She drifted into memories of their time together and his trusting her with his thoughts and believing she understood. *If I had listened critically, would I have asked him to explain himself better? Will I tire of his thoughts and being put in the position of questioning his reason and could I do it gently if I disagree? And with questions, yes, even gently put, will he change his mind? Will I be obstinate?* She pushed her letter aside and went outside to look at stars; they lay behind a cloudy sky. *Like answers to my questions. Andrew, are you looking too? Is it all misty and veiled from you as well? How will we know, before we break each other's heart, if we complement each other? Will we grow weary of our differences? I need to talk to you, see your face again, have you touch my hand, assure me.* Inside, she picked up her pen.

The stars hide from view tonight and the clear message I sought is not there. I feel a need to see your face, to hear your voice.

To less ponderous subjects: *Oliver Twist* is slow going. I have written to my sisters and asked them to find a used copy and to send it to me. So far my listeners have found the story engrossing, and dreadful. Wait until we get to the despicable characters in London.

Oh, Andrew! Lightning! Such a sudden rending of the night. All that brightness, as if it were a peak into something awesome behind a ripped black cloth. Then darkness just as quickly repaired the tear. I stepped outside. The rain smells as fresh as I remember it on my trip, but with less dire consequences. A roof is a luxury.

Good night, Andy-Andrew. Sleep dry.

Sincerely,
Josie-Josephine-Joe. Take your pick.

Days passed slowly. She wanted Andrew's reply to her concerns. On Tuesday, regular as the train in summer, she had his answer.

October 7, 1910

My Dear Josie,

I'm having a time not scolding you. First, for not asking me to find a copy of Dickens for you. I would welcome an opportunity to be helpful. No. I want you to need me. I want to take care of you. It's important to me to be important to you. Do you understand?

Then, for thinking, even for an instance, you could ever bore me. You are like sunshine. Your open mind, curiosity, and creativity are refreshing and fill me with joy. I don't want a duplicate of myself. One of me is often too many. I've never known anyone like you. I will not grow tired of you. You may find me tiresome. Let's find out.

What do I intend to do with a mining engineer degree? Who knows? My parents also wonder. Mom explains to people who inquire, I like pretty rocks. I'll be qualified to be an assayer, maybe a mine inspector. I could work in mines and learn more about mining and someday amount to something. My real interest, though, is the chemistry of rocks, strata and what we can learn from them. I don't know if one can make a living looking at rocks. Who would pay for that? A question my father poses. The dean of the chemistry department has offered me a job teaching freshman chemistry after graduation. That may be what I do until I find myself, as if I've been looking. It would afford my parents a new set of questions. We would all welcome those. I realize this will not be reassuring. It doesn't make me sound like a good bet, as I'm sure your father would be happy to point out. Please don't despair. I don't mind working hard, I like problem-solving, and someday I'll mature, we hope.

Jobs are going well. Dad says I seem happier in my work so it's worth the extra five cents. He says estimating is essentially correct. Things I miss I make up for in items I double count. He said I'm distracted, but he understands.

Josie, I am distracted. I think of you all the time. Thank you for including your drawings on the stationery. They make me smile and remember happy times together. Wish I had known sooner you were you, because we would have had another evening. I wouldn't change a thing about our time together, though. It gave me you.

Fondly,
Andrew

P. S. For your information by way of Mom: in 1900 one-third of our Southern mill workers were children.

There's so much heartache in the world and I'm wondering what "fondly" means? My values are questionable. I can't solve those problems. Now I need to think about what I can solve. If I read between the lines, no, he says it outright, he says he wants to be important to me. He's distracted. He wants me to need him. He says, "Let's find out." Oh, Andrew, I want to find out too. She put the letter with the others.

School was going well. Children, especially boys, were interested in her chart of inventions during the Industrial Revolution. They were fascinated to learn that iron hadn't always been available. She was reading to the children, their mothers, and Mr. Miller, a biography of James Watt and his frustrations in creating a successful steam engine because craftsmen hadn't acquired the tools or skills necessary to build his concept. Girls and mothers weren't as interested in steam engines as boys but it was a story and they listened.

They were intrigued with cotton gins, spinning jennies, and flying shuttles though they had never done the tedious job of separating cotton from its seeds, spun fiber, or worked a loom. They also talked about the root of the word engine. People considered the new inventions products of "ingenuity" giving rise to the word "engine." Both gin and jenny were short for "engine."

Children knew concrete and were surprised to learn that lime, like their lime, combined with clay, baked and ground to a powder made cement. Cement powder mixed with sand, gravel, and water hardened into concrete.

Many of the inventions mentioned affected their lives: their clothes were woven by a factory using spun fiber; iron rails and steam trains hauled their lime, lumber and cattle to market giving their parents jobs. Their eyes opened to a larger, complex world, deeper history, and a little economics.

October 11, 1910

Dear Andrew,

Thank you for explaining so clearly your ambitions. I will convey them to my father should I mention you to him. I confess I haven't had the courage to do that yet because I don't know how to explain our meeting without having him disown me.

I need to tell you about an eye-opening experience with Mr. Miller. I was talking in class about the economics of the Industrial Revolution, explaining families had spun linen and wool in their homes in rural England and sold it to families that wove the thread into fabric. When they couldn't compete with the new industries, they moved to cities to work in factories in order to survive. Coal mines were necessary to provide fuel for the machines and this coal was being mined by children as well as women and men.

It was when I began to talk of coal mines that Mr. Miller became agitated. I waited until the children left and asked him to stay a minute and I tried to discern if something I said had made him uncomfortable. Was I misrepresenting what took place?

He shook his head. He couldn't look at me.

I said the children enjoy having him in class. I asked if one of them said something to upset him.

He shook his head and started to cry.

I asked him to please forgive me if I said something to hurt his feelings.

He wiped his eyes and said he worked those mines when he was a wee lad. It brought back bad thoughts. He said he's an old man and cries easily now.

When he could talk comfortably he told of working in coal mines starting when he was six years old. When he was about nine, he came down with typhus along with his mother and two younger sisters. His father and three older brothers were in the mine when a fire broke out, killing them. The company gave his mother money to pay for their deaths. His mother and sisters didn't survive typhus and he spent the money on debts and burials. Since that time, he's been on his own. They were Welsh. He made his way to Newport and found work at the dock running errands. He eventually signed on to a ship taking coal to London and it was there he was shanghaied and taken to sea. He was still young. The sailors were either former prisoners or captured as he had been and were locked on board until it sailed. It was a brutal ship that went from Africa to Brazil, illegally carrying slaves. The voyage was the worst thing he ever experienced, and the mines had been horrific. Sailors were violent, floggings frequent, disease rampant. Their lot was better than the slaves' who were chained to the lower decks. They had little to eat or drink and the sailors treated them cruelly. His life on board was constant abuse, overwork, and thoughts of throwing himself into the sea. When he reached shore, he escaped. He has never forgotten the nightmare of that voyage. He found work on a ship carrying coffee to America, then worked in New England shipyards and factories until the Civil War broke out. He felt he owed a debt to slaves he had helped transport, even though they had been taken to Brazil. After the war he worked for railroads laying track. That's how he ended up in

Meredith working at the kilns. He heard about a place called Miller Creek. He wanted to live there. It was as close as he would come to being with family. It's where he wants to die.

He said he'd never told this to anyone. It makes him ashamed, how poor they were, how ignorant. He never wanted a family because he didn't make enough money to support one and didn't want a child of his to know what he'd known.

It made me cry, Andrew. He apologized. As if he needed forgiveness for making me hear about a life that has been so harsh and unrelentingly lonely. What confuses me is England and America are both Christian countries. How can people reconcile their actions with their beliefs when any thinking person can see they conflict? Help me, please. I'm at a loss to understand.

I asked Mr. Miller if he could tell his story to the children. He will try.

I apologize for such a sad letter. I need you to comfort me. Me! I've had a life of ease with loving parents who shielded me from this kind of ugliness. But I feel wounded. After his story, I was so angry with people I went for a long walk.

I wished you were with me. Beneath bare aspens is a carpet of gold. A few leaves linger in the trees signaling fall's end. You would remind me to see the beauty in this world.

> Needing your steady mind,
> Josie

She put the letter into the mail slot and later realized she had failed to put a drawing on it. Already depressed by Mr. Miller's story, she curled up on her bed. *I've shared misery. He deserves better. I was wrapped in such sadness I couldn't remember to give him a little token of beauty. If I never hear from him again, I deserve it.*

The next day Mr. Miller came to class and sat quietly listening to the reading group, following along in his reader. When it came time for history Josie asked him if he would share his story with them and he sat, looked the children over, and began.

"When I was about the age of this one," he chose a little boy of six, "I went to work in a coal mine in Wales. I hadn't gone in the year before because I stayed home to take care of my little sisters so my mother could work in the mine. She made more money than I would have. When she was with child again, I went in." He proceeded to tell his story, slowly, without emotion. He told of being on the docks in Wales and how little he earned, of sleeping under stairs, eating from garbage piles, begging for food from rich houses. Had people turned him in he would have been sent to the workhouse. He told of going to London on a coal ship as a cabin boy and how the slave traders caught him and held him captive. He stopped. "If I may, I will continue another day."

The children were wide-eyed. "Six?" said a child who was eight.

"Yes, some were younger."

They asked questions about his work. He told them little children opened doors when the coal cars came through, or if they were strong, they climbed in narrow tunnels to dig coal or were harnessed to small carts and pulled them like a horse. Soon no more questions arose. Josie thanked Mr. Miller and said she and the children would listen to his story the next time he was willing to share it. She dismissed class early because she could tell no one could focus on lessons. As the children left, Mr. Miller hung behind. He asked if what he said was all right. She assured him it was. It was difficult for kids to hear, but since America still allowed child labor, they should know about it. He nodded and turned to go. "Mr. Miller," she said, "I hope you've finally found a home here." He nodded.

The next day after school she went to the post office as usual. Zona wanted to discuss Mr. Miller. Kids had not quit talking about it at supper and mothers had come by and said it had been the same at their houses. They wondered if Mr. Miller would tell his story at Saturday night supper because they wanted to hear it first-hand. Could Josie talk him into it? They knew he was quiet.

The following day she told Mr. Miller what had transpired. He nodded. He heard the same at the kiln. Men were curious about his life and how he had survived. Would he talk to them all? He thought he could do it.

October 14, 1910

Dear Josie,

I wish I could be with you. This may be inappropriate, but I want to hold you in my arms to comfort you. I'm trusting this won't offend. If it does, I hope you'll forgive me.

Your Mr. Miller had a truly miserable life. I wish it were unique. I talked to Mom about your letter and she gave me statistics she has been taking to Colorado politicians. One-fifth of children between ten and fifteen are employed, only eight per cent of high school-aged kids are in school. Most children attend school irregularly, meaning they don't receive a decent education. A national bill that was introduced in 1906 to prevent child labor in factories failed. She said every large city has an orphan problem and not enough orphanages to accommodate them. They live on the streets as Mr. Miller described. When they turn to crime, we're shocked.

You and I have had lives of comfort and security. Let's hope someday every child will know what we've known.

You asked about people's actions versus their beliefs. At Savage Lakes we discussed religion being at odds with human nature and human nature often prevailing. It's who we are. I have a question for you: How can people be so analytical in one part of their lives and so gullible in others? I see this repeatedly. I hope we never have to compromise what we think is Truth and never succumb to belief. That word bothers me. It implies we're asked to believe what won't bear scrutiny. I trust scrutiny.

I feel we're compatible in our thoughts and how we view our world. Do you feel this too?

With affection,
Andrew

I missed a drawing but understand.

Yes. I would love for you to hold me and feel you understand what I'm thinking without having to explain.

October 18, 1910

Dear Andrew,

You are kind to offer to comfort me. I would gladly accept if you were here. I'm sorry I wrote such a cheerless letter last week and didn't include a drawing. I wish this week I had better news to report but it will be much the same as last. Please bear with me because I need someone to help me understand what I'm learning.

After the children heard Mr. Miller they went home and told their folks. It seems everyone wants to hear what he has to say and they convinced him to share his story Saturday night.

Have I told you about Saturday night suppers? The families gather in the schoolhouse for a covered dish meal and gossip, sing, tell stories, whatever makes them happy. Sometimes children perform which gives us an opportunity to practice rhetoric or little plays. They're pleasant evenings.

The food is usually representative of countries they've hailed from and interesting. I enjoy the suppers a great deal because I see children's families and that helps me understand them.

This past Saturday night everyone seemed especially talkative. Soon the ruckus calmed in anticipation. I told a little about their history class and how gracious Mr. Miller had been to share his life story with the children and how some in the community had asked him to share it. He sat with his head down and hands clasped. I asked if he were ready to speak. He nodded. Then, without standing, began.

He briefly told what he'd said to the children and continued with the slave ship, his life on docks in America, running errands and working in factories and on construction in the North. By the time he was almost grown he had gained enough strength he could work alongside men. This meant he earned as much as a man and for the first time he could remember, he was able to buy enough to eat and afford a room to sleep in. That was about 1850.

Andrew, I was amazed he could talk with such calm and no sign of bitterness. It was fascinating to watch faces in the room. Children were wide-eyed. Fathers nodded in understanding. Mothers held their babies closer.

He worked as a hod carrier and became a mason. Tiring of that, he worked at a furniture factory for a few years. In '61 he joined the Army of the Republic and went to war against the South. They were four years of hell and he hoped these boys would never have to know war.

He looked at the older boys with such concern it made everyone look at them differently—not as kids—as soldiers. It was an uncomfortable reckoning.

After he mustered out, he worked as a gandy dancer laying track to build the transcontinental railroad Union Pacific was building out of Omaha. Sometimes they worked fifteen-hour days in a race against the Central Pacific across the western states to determine where they would meet. That job ended in 1869. He stayed in the West building other railroads.

I looked at Mr. Miller's stooped old body and thought how it had never known rest. He still works and he must be about seventy-five.

When he heard about the construction of the Colorado Midland he came to Colorado and went to work on it in 1883, staying with it until he felt old. In '95 he quit and settled down as a kiln worker. He didn't ever want to dig rock again.

He said he wants to die in the cabin he built on Miller Creek out of stone left over from the kiln's construction. It's beautiful sandstone from Peachblow quarry. He's proud of his little house. He mentioned the flagstone floor made from stone he had quarried himself, although he didn't enjoy quarrying, he assured them. Shrugging as if to conclude, he stopped.

No one talked. No one had moved or squirmed during the summing up of his life. I thanked him for sharing his story. Suddenly the room erupted in chatter; people started questioning him and telling him how much they enjoyed hearing his story. He sat there with a dazed look on his face, not believing anyone could find such a pitiful life worth hearing about.

Then they all wanted to share their stories until Zona took charge and suggested everyone would get a chance at subsequent suppers. They seemed pleased. I looked at that group and realized only two of us over twenty had been born here.

It snowed again the other day, enough to frost hills and to cover the ground for a while. Enough to make mud. It's very difficult to keep a room clean with all those muddy shoes. Oh, my. That seems so trivial after Mr. Miller's story.

> *Dare I say it?*
> Affectionately,
> Josie

She included a drawing of grasses, their shadows falling across snow.

Josie was surprised at the response to Mr. Miller's story. It was as though a silent and unseen person became real. Not that anyone had been unkind to Mr. Miller, they had not thought about him. After the supper, they treated him differently, deferentially. Families invited him to suppers. Little children wanted to hold his hand when they walked with him. In school, some of the middle ones were more willing to help him with his reading and writing, others, mostly older boys to her surprise, had already befriended him.

October 21, 1910

Gentle Josie,

My suspicion is you've changed Mr. Miller's life and he has fallen a little in love with you. As he should. In a fatherly way, of course. Of course! Or I would be jealous and I'm not. I'm glad he has found friendship.

I imagine those were years to forget. Your sharing this has given me much to think about and some stimulating conversations at dinner. I always read your letters aloud to my folks so we can discuss them critically. (I'm teasing, to make you smile.) Your letters are precious, and Private, trust me. Thanks for your affection. It warmed my heart.

It will be interesting to read about stories from Saturday night suppers which sound like chaos but fun for those who enjoy chaos. I'm trying to imagine you at the first one. Let me know if the folks can resist the temptation to embellish their life stories to make them more dramatic than the fellow's whose came before. It would be characteristic of many men, I think. Maybe you'll see if that's true of women as well.

I struggle to remember how you look and sound. By any chance, do you have a photo of yourself you would share with me? I'll take care of it. I don't think you can send your voice, but which one would you choose?

Lecture! My mother–have I mentioned my mother?–never allows shoes in the house. We, Dad included, take our shoes off at the door. There are rugs at the door to collect dirt, snow, or whatever we drag home. There's no reason for kids' shoes to come into your classroom and make such a mess. Unsolicited advice, but there it is. It works.

Of late, I have given reports of my poor performance. I want you to know I passed a test. As distracted as I've been lately, it's noteworthy. We played in dirt again. This time it was hydraulic mining. You may know what that means. If not, they use high pressure water to wash away a hillside–the placer. The resulting mud flows into a long chute called a sluice box that has ridges in the bottom. The mud flows out and the heavy gold particles get trapped behind the ridges. It sure makes a mess of a hillside.

I love to write to you, Josie, because I feel close to you. I love getting your letters more because they're insights into your mind and character which I'm enjoying knowing.

On a lighter note, the talk around school today was all about airplanes. I'm not sure what prompted it. Isn't it something though, to think about machines up there flying around?

Well, this has gone on too long so I'll say good night, Sweet Josie. I loved the drawing of grass and its shadows. '*I have a little shadow, it goes in and out with me.*'

With affection,
Andrew

Rereading his letter she was ashamed she hadn't asked what he was doing. So absorbed in her world, she had forgotten his, but he kindly told her with humor. She needed to be more fun for him, not so serious. She loved to laugh. He had no way of knowing this, because she had not been carefree when camping with him. The few minutes they had at school had been serious. What would it be like for them to be light-hearted?

October 25, 1910

My Distracted Friend who passed a test
Methinks you've always done your best
No surprise that you've succeeded
Concentration's all you needed.

There. My thoughts on your scholastic achievements. I doubt anyone would offer you a job teaching chemistry at the college level if you suffer from poor performance. I hope, however, I understand your being distracted as I face a similar challenge.

Winter is in the air bringing longer nights, gray skies, and cool ventures outside. Kids have been restless with the changing season. Thank you for your suggestion about muddy shoes. I told the children we were going to try it. Mr. Miller looked concerned and the kids were dumbstruck. We took our shoes off for two days then came Saturday night supper. The kids were protective of the floor but the men were having none of it. If we had done it, I honestly think the smell may have been too much. I understand that some of the women thought it was a good idea and tried it at home. It was a disaster. My credibility in the community has suffered. I'm backing away from the plan with as much grace as I can muster.

Thank you for explaining the hydraulic mining process. I shared it with the class because I thought all mines were tunnels into mountains. Mr. Miller was in class that day and added there are also what they call pit mines. In coal country they are deep, open holes in the ground that may be enormous. You undoubtedly would have much to add.

I'm happy to tell you Mr. Miller wrote his full name this week for the first time: Llewellyn Miller. The Denver librarian sent us how it's typically spelled. I would never have guessed all those L's. Today he was asking children how to spell words. He seems more open now since children have befriended him. I heard him laugh today, which I had never heard before.

I can't remember what your laugh sounds like. I can tell from your letters you have a sense of humor, though much of it has been at my expense. I trust you find other subjects funny.

Here's what happened this week that will make you smile. I knitted a pair of mittens and when finished, I realized I had made two right-hand ones. I am now in the process of making two left-hand mittens. They are gray with snowflakes across the front which is why I can't wear one upside down. This is by way of telling you I frequently don't plan ahead. Some may say I'm impulsive. Less kind people might say I'm scatter-brained. I hope you're a kind person.

I will report on Saturday night supper next letter.

An overcast sky tonight so no stars. I will be out there at nine o'clock regardless. Clouds can be interesting as well.

With fondness,
Josie

She included a drawing of a snow-covered spruce bough.

She read her letter dismayed she had failed at being light-hearted. *Why is it so difficult to be funny in a letter? Perhaps I made him smile once or twice but I wanted to make him laugh. If I could see his face, watch his reaction, maybe I'd know what amuses him. Zona's right: Keep the letters coming. We'll discover each other as well as we can.*

She took her letter and a pot of tea to the post office the next day in time for the train and stayed to visit with Zona.

"You've got a letter, Josie. Don't know what I did with my time before you came."

Pleased, since she hadn't had a letter from her sisters recently, she was anxious to know what was going on at home. Surprised it was from Mrs. Angus Allan at Andrew's address, her heart raced. Was something wrong with Andrew? Was she writing to tell Josie to quit writing to her son? Her hands trembled as she opened the envelope.

October 22, 1910

Dear Miss Carter,

Our family, particularly one of us, would love for you to come to Golden for Thanksgiving weekend. My sister, Andy's Aunt Janet, who lives a few blocks away, has invited you to stay with her during your visit. She is a widow whose three daughters have grown and married. One of their rooms will be perfect for you. She is a lovely woman and you will be in safe company there.

If you can be away from school Wednesday through Sunday, we will send you a round-trip ticket. Andy will meet your train and bring you to Golden.

Hoping you will join us, we look forward to meeting you.

Sincerely,
Margaret Allan
(Mrs. Angus Allan)

She quickly read it again. Her heart had not calmed. "Zona," she whispered, "she's invited me to come for Thanksgiving."

"Who?"

"His mother. She says I can stay with his aunt, but what about my father?"

"The aunt wants him to come too?"

Josie laughed, "No, I don't think he'll approve."

"Your father's not in love."

"Oh, Zona, don't say it like that."

"Not saying won't make it any different."

"We're not in love. We're friends. He hasn't said he loves me."

Zona huffed and muttered under her breath, "None so blind as those who will not see."

"How do you know that proverb?"

"Didn't know it's a whatever. An old woman I knew from England used to say it. And you're changing the subject."

"Would a nice girl go to stay with a boy she admires?"

"A nice girl would stay with an aunt in a different house. His mother is taking care of you. He didn't invite you to come stay with him. His mother knows you're a nice girl. If she didn't, she

149

would discourage his admiring you, as you call it."

"But what <u>will</u> I tell my father?"

"You're asking me? I wouldn't tell him. You're on your own now. Father's never want to let go of daughters. He might find all sorts of reasons why you shouldn't do this and none of them any good."

"What if they don't like me, then Andrew won't either?"

"Better find out now."

"Oh, Zona, you're so practical. Don't you ever worry?"

"Doesn't help. But ya, I worry about the kids, about having enough to eat, about Ott getting hurt. But it doesn't help."

"I guess not. So, you'd go?"

"You bet I would. Nice ones don't come along that often."

Josie shook her head, read the letter again, said goodbye and left.

What if they <u>don't</u> like me? What if they want a pretty girl for Andrew? A lady who wouldn't dress up in boys' clothes and go off in the woods by herself? What do they know about me? What has he told them? Oh, how I wish I were pretty.

She wasted her evening. She tried to plan the next day's activities and kept drifting back to what to say to Mrs. Allan. What if her father found out she was in Denver and hadn't come to see the family? Hadn't asked his permission to do this? What would her sisters think if she didn't tell them? They knew nothing about Andrew and she was going to visit him. That night was not given to sleep.

October 27, 1910

Dear Mrs. Allan,

Thank you for your kind invitation to join your family for Thanksgiving weekend which I happily accept. I look forward to meeting you and Mr. Allan and if your other sons are there, to meeting them as well. Need I say I will be happy to see Andrew again?

Please thank your sister for inviting me to stay at her home. I gratefully accept her generous offer of hospitality.

Sincerely,
Josephine Carter

She had written and crossed out words and rearranged sentences till she couldn't do it anymore. By copying it onto good paper, sealing and stamping the envelope, she felt she had crossed a line in growing up.

October 28, 1910

Dear Josie,

I trust you've received Mom's invitation. I'm anxious for your response. Please, please accept. I want to see you again more than you could know.

Whenever a letter comes from you Mom starts reciting that old folk rhyme:

"A frog he would a-wooing go,
Heigh ho! says Rowley,
A frog he would a-wooing go,
Whether his mother would let him or no,"

then she drifts away. Do you know I'm wooing you, Josie? Do you know I don't see you only as a good friend? As Mom put it, with a smirk, "I think you're smitten, Andy." She's right. If being so forward offends you, please tell me. If friendship is all you want, then I ask to be your friend. I'll be very disappointed but will try to behave and not push my affection on you. Please be honest. I'd rather know now than later. You've made me feel I can be honest. I hope I'm not mistaken. Regardless, <u>please</u> come for Thanksgiving.

With anticipation,
Andrew

P. S. Creativity seems to come spontaneously. I love systems. Predictable, boring, systems. Probably why I enjoy chemistry. Perhaps we'll balance each other, make a good team and be reasonably normal.

November 1, 1910

My Dear Andrew,

You have not been too forward. I want to be your good friend as well as being wooed–but by a frog? I have not known for certain your feelings although you have given hints. I have tried not to read too much into them, yet I have succumbed to wishful thinking. You have made them clear, so now you will know mine. I, too, am anxious to see you and to know if we still share those feelings we had when we were together. Our letters have given us the chance to see into each other's minds. Now we need to see into our hearts. It is my hope that whatever one of us feels the other will feel as well.

In three weeks, we will be together again. That weekend will tell so much.

I will write to you tomorrow about what is happening here. Tonight, I am aglow with your letter and can think of nothing else.

Heigh ho, my Frog,
Josie

November 2, 1910

Dear Andrew,

This morning dawned so brilliantly I feel nature has been reading our letters and is sharing our happiness. It was cold last night. Frost feathers cover the snow, sparkling in the sunshine. It is so dazzling, I can't but think of you.

Saturday night was, as usual, pandemonium until after supper, then everyone quieted down to hear Olaf. He was born on a farm in Sweden, the sixth of twelve children. As soon as he was able to walk he cared for the chickens and weeded the garden so older kids could tend cows, milk, and help make cheese. He worked his entire childhood, never went to school. His mother, who had somehow learned to read Swedish, taught them on spring evenings when calves were suckling and work was lighter. His oldest brother stayed to work the farm that could support only his family and the old folks. Younger ones came to America. He married his wife and they worked their way west. He never wants to milk another cow.

His wife, Olga, told much the same story. Her mother died with the last baby and Olga took over the kitchen and housework as well as taking care of five younger children. She taught me to knit. She sells beautiful sweaters to sportsmen back east. She and two younger sisters came to America to be nannies when their father remarried. They married Swedes they met on the boat. She was nineteen. Neither she nor Olaf has been back home. They would love to see their families again, smell the ocean, taste good cheese, and eat fresh fish.

They were followed by Otto and Zona. Both are Germans who came from the Volga river region of Russia as children with their parents. Otto had no schooling except a little in the winter. His father put him to work when he was six in the sugar beet fields in eastern Colorado. The whole family worked there. They saved enough to buy a farm, but Otto didn't want to farm. Zona was lucky enough to go to school until she was eleven when she started working in a mill. She came west when she was fourteen to help an aunt who had triplets and a bunch of other kids. Then she and Otto got married. They were fifteen and sixteen.

To answer your question: I don't think they embellished their stories. They didn't mention hunger or mistreatment, only hard work. The Swedes miss their families which made them sound loving.

Andrew, I have a school problem. A plain looking girl ten years old is my most disruptive student. She is usually sullen and uncooperative and I find myself getting angry with her. I'm ashamed to say I want to punish her. Then I ask myself, punish her for what? Does she want to be that way? I'm frustrated. I need your thoughts.

I must prepare for tomorrow. I was woefully prepared today. The kids asked what was wrong with me. I didn't explain. They wouldn't understand about your wooing me. But their parents will so I've posted your letter on the bulletin board.

I know it's only November. Days seem short, though, and I prefer to dream in sunshine because it reminds me of being with you. So do star-filled nights, but it's too cold to dream for long.

Fondly,
Josie

November 4, 1910

Dear Sweet Josie,

Your letter today assured me you are coming for Thanksgiving. Mom said you answered in the affirmative but I needed to hear it from you. I'm so happy.

Knowing you welcome my wooing is the most marvelous news I've ever had. I will woo you enthusiastically, constantly, and as long as you'll allow. Notice I did not say romantically. I don't know how to do that. You may find giving me hints will yield more gratifying outcomes, providing they fit within the system.

If you know when you can leave and when you need to return, I'll make reservations and send tickets. I'll happily meet your train. Will you be wearing boys' clothes? If so, I'll greet appropriately.

Josie, I've been distracted all fall. Since your letter I'm hopeless.

I'll try to focus on your letter about Olaf and Olga. We discussed it at dinner and Dad said many people believed idleness in children bred degeneracy. Those families considered children came into the world to produce for the family and to take care of parents in their old age. Dad has no delusions of his sons supporting their parents, which is a sign of his wisdom. It was a Puritan belief that "idle hands are the devil's workshop" and whose hands are apt to be idle? Children's hands, that's whose. Put them to work! It sounds as if your friends' parents understood work. In fairness, parents were no doubt working hard too, and had worked all their lives. Dad says average families like ours with idle, pampered little kids are relatively new to the world. Unless one's family was very wealthy, and those children probably would never know hard work. Aren't we lucky to have had happy childhoods and to know the satisfaction of working?

Was that clear-headed and logical enough to convince you I'm not completely adrift thinking of Thanksgiving?

You ask about Free Will, although you didn't call it that. Oh, boy. Of life's riddles: Where did we come from? Why are we here? Where are we going? What's beyond the end of the universe? What can we take credit for and what do we have to accept blame for? This last question <u>should</u> give us the most trouble. People aren't willing to spend time considering the underlying reasons for human behavior. We put people in prisons and seem to want to endlessly punish them without taking time to consider what factors in life may have brought them to this point. We seem to prefer labels, like good, bad, evil, or hero. In general, it seems to me, in most all areas, except science, people prefer accepting bad answers to asking good questions.

In any event we can't live our lives assuming either total free will or total cause and effect. So how to deal with this? For achievers they should always be aware of how the greatest part of their success is due to the pure good fortune of being born with or benefiting from things like intellect, energy, appearance, education, group support, etc. and they need to be charitable to those less blessed. For those born less fortunate, they need to know they have some control over the single most important element of happiness which is a good attitude. Regarding your disruptive girl, though, I have no idea.

Thank you for questioning life. Thank you for inviting me into your world so we can explore it. If I give you thoughts you don't agree with, please question me. We want honest thoughts.

If you're feeling days are short <u>already</u> in early November, you will surely feel that way by winter solstice in late December. "*In winter I get up at night And dress by yellow candle-light.*" If we're lucky, Thanksgiving weekend will give us some good memories of short days to keep us happy during the rest of winter.

Whoops! Slipped back into "Dream of Josie" and floated away with you. A wonderful thing to do.

Affectionately yours,
Andrew

I enjoyed the drawing of footprints in the snow.

Terror set in. What would she wear? Her shoes! Should she take gifts, then what? Time to talk to good, down-to-Earth Zona.

As she sat in the window watching Zona finish some tasks she wondered how often that woman had ever had a moment to sit quietly with a cup of tea to think about whatever her heart desired, not about what to cook for dinner, nor what she had to accomplish the next day. Idle thoughts, luxurious, random, non-consequential thoughts. Maybe jot a poem or hum a tune. Did her own mother ever have that time? Was that why she loved church? It filled her mind with thoughts outside herself, gave her a peaceful respite from concerns and housework.

"There!" Zona announced. "Done. Now, Josie, what's on your mind? I can tell something's bothering you."

Laughing at her insight, Josie didn't hem and haw. "I'm afraid of his family. First off, I don't have anything pretty to wear. These awful high-top shoes are all I have here. I'm afraid Andrew won't remember I'm so plain-looking and he'll change his mind and I'll be stuck with strangers who don't know what to do with me and I can't go home to my father." She was war-dancing, as Zona called it.

"Stop. He'll remember how you look. I hope not in the engineer's hat. If he doesn't remember, your pretty eyes and big smile will charm him anew. Have a pretty dress at home?"

"Yes. The one I wore to church. It's not too pretty but it's better than this." She held up the black skirt, grimacing.

"Well, have your sisters mail it to you. Explain you have an invitation for Thanksgiving dinner and you'd like to look nice. You don't have to say where dinner is. Have them send you shoes too. What else do you need?"

"I need a present for his mother and one for Aunt Janet."

A mischievous twinkle danced in Zona's eyes. "How would they feel about gray mittens? You're half done." She laughed so heartily Josie had to laugh too.

156

"Perfect. You've solved my worries. I'll go home and dance myself into a stew on something else."

She ran to her cabin and wrote her sisters. She included money for postage and begged them to send the dress and shoes as quickly as they could.

It snowed the next day. Snowed as if it were trying to get winter over with in one storm. Recess had to be indoors and the children, usually better behaved toward one another, were being mean-spirited. Exasperated, she said, "Sit down. I'm going to give you a lecture. You need to know that your teasing and poking fun can be hurtful. For those of you who feel smug about something you can do or how you look, you need to think about how much of that you can take credit for or were you born that way. You should never feel superior about things you had nothing to do with. You need to think about this all your life. How much of who everyone is, and this includes all of you, is mostly just good or bad luck. Now be kind."

Mr. Miller came to her after class. "Can I talk to you?"

"Yes, of course."

"Why did you say that to the kids today?"

She hesitated. "I think children need to understand people aren't all born with the same advantages. Was what I said wrong?"

"No'm. It's important they know that."

"It's something my friend Andrew and I just discussed in our letters."

"Your Andrew, does he write you letters like that often?"

She nodded, happily. "Once a week. I ask a question that troubles me, and he answers what he's thought about it. I usually agree even though I didn't come up with it."

"Someday maybe you'll tell me more what he says."

"I will, Mr. Miller. I'm sure he'd be interested in what you think. You have years of experience we don't have. We're still trying to figure out life. You could bring wisdom to our thoughts."

Shaking his head, he said, "Experience isn't the same as wisdom, Josie." He patted her head and left.

Interesting how curious he is about Andrew.

My Dear Andrew,

I <u>definitely</u> will wear boy's clothes if you'll wear a dress. Appropriate greetings matter. Guess who will be more comfortable? Given my wardrobe options, if I dress as a boy then at least everyone could laugh about me to my face. Oh, Andrew, I am wracked with uncertainties about meeting your family. I wish you were meeting mine instead. You, with cuffs on your pants, would seem such a catch they wouldn't know how I managed. How did I manage? You know I didn't set out to "catch" someone, don't you? It was the furthest thing from my mind. What a horrible concept that "catching" is, as if men were prey. Do you feel preyed upon? Oh, pray, prey, do tell.

Will you please explain to your mother I don't have company clothes with me and since I'm not going home this trip my attire will be plain? I think your mother will understand and men won't notice–I hope. I don't want to make you ashamed of me.

You mentioned we are lucky to have had such useless childhoods and we are. I'm reluctant to concede pampered even though I was. We are also lucky to have lived in a place with good air. It has made all the difference to my father, meaning he's alive, and Mother said he wouldn't have survived another winter in Goderich on the cold, damp shores of Lake Ontario.

Mr. Miller wants to know what answers you have given to my questions. May I share with him what you've said?

I will briefly catch you up on Saturday night suppers. Anders and Elsa Karlsson came from Norway. His father was a lumber man, hers a fisherman. They were married, twenty and twenty-five when they came over. She doesn't miss cutting bait or cleaning fish which she did from the time she was four; she does miss eating them. Anders says he grew up with sawdust in his hair. At first, they settled in Wisconsin so he could work lumber there. He heard the price of mine timbers, so they bundled up the five kids and came west. When mining slowed, he worked the charcoal kilns at Sellar Meadow then found he could make more at the lumber mill here. Their son Lars Karlsson is very bright. I wish he could go on to school but I don't think they understand its value. They have three kids here. Two girls have grown and gone. Two boys work the lumber mill.

I'm wondering what effect these stories have on children. They've heard their own parents' tales, but to learn other kids' folks had rough childhoods may make them appreciate how lucky they are to attend school and not work all the time.

School is going well. I'm still telling and reading *Oliver Twist*. We took a break for James Watt. I think I may be telling it next year as well. We've done the wretched baby farm where Oliver suffers beatings for being hungry. It made my discipline of sitting in the corner seem rather tame. Not that it happens often.

Have I bragged about our musical achievements? We performed at supper. Banjo and guitar accompaniment for our chorus singing "Red River Valley" and "You are My Sunshine." The clapping was prodigious. You played the former the last night we were together. It made me sad, but I hoped you were sending me a message. Not to Joe, to a girl like me. The next supper will be a crafts show by parents. We have some expert quilters, knitters, whittlers, and Mr. Miller, who makes doll furniture and sells it in Denver. I'm looking forward to it. I will display my two right-hand mittens.

There are three stars very close together in the east. Do you know what they are? They are in line, more or less, with the North Star and a very bright star due east. This is at nine o'clock when I star gaze and dream of a fellow stargazer.

Good night, Dear Andrew, sweet dreams,
Your Josie

Wednesday, November 9, 1910
Dear Josie,

There was a terrible explosion at Delagua coal mine near Trinidad last night. A spark undoubtedly ignited dust and gas. Our professors are taking the seniors down by train tomorrow morning so we can learn how to prevent disasters like this in the future. We'll also be available to help if we can.

Please don't worry. The damage has been done. I don't know when I'll be home to write and don't want you to wonder why you're not getting a letter.

Fondly,
Andrew

P. S. You may share with Mr. Miller anything you wish. Maybe he'll add to what we've thought or correct it, if necessary, and we'll be better off for his thoughts.

She read the letter to Mr. Miller asking him questions about coal mines he couldn't answer because when he worked in one, he was only a child. He tried to comfort her. Sensing she was still concerned despite his reassurance, he asked her to play checkers that evening at the store if Zona wouldn't mind.

No letter the next day. She stayed in the post office and fussed with things, asked Zona to let her sweep, then sat dejected. Mr. Miller came for groceries.

"What's the matter, Josie?"

"No letter. I don't know what's happening at that mine."

He patted her head. "You're like a daughter to me, Josie. You hurt, I hurt."

Filled with emotion, she reached for his rough hand. "Thank you, dear friend. You would have been a thoughtful, kind father."

They sat quietly on two chairs, her hand on his, until he asked her to play checkers.

"This time I'll try to win."

He smiled slowly. "You'll have to go some." They played; he won. Again, he tried not to.

She could hardly wait to get her mail each day. A letter. It was not from Andrew. It was from the Wallaces inviting her to Thanksgiving. She felt guilty for wishing their letter had been from Andrew, but it distracted her that night to tell them a little about him and their connection through Golden. She regretted she couldn't be with them, knew they'd understand, and told them when she'd be going through Leadville.

There was no news from Andrew and she became more anxious. The box arrived with her dress, shoes, and a new ribbon matching the dress. The letter inside said their curiosity was all-consuming. Please write to tell them where she was going and with whom.

Thanksgiving! She had forgotten about it.

That night she wrote, knowing if he were home to receive it he would have written to her, but she had to communicate with him.

Monday, November 14, 1910

My Dear Andrew,

I am writing because I must. I don't know where you are or if you are all right, but I need to be with you, if only in my mind.

I read your letter to Mr. Miller and he tried valiantly to comfort me by playing checkers but I'm so distracted, even though he tries to let me win, I still lose.

Please write as soon as you are home and safe. I need to know.

Yours,
Josie

Finally, on November 17, she received a letter.

Sunday, November 13, 1910

My Dear Josie,

We're still in Trinidad and what a nightmare. The Victor-American Mine is in a place called Delagua and they believe there could be as many as seventy-five miners killed. One, Willis Evans, an engineer, went to Mines two years ago. We knew him well. Last month at another coal mine they lost eighty miners. It has made us all very determined to work on safe practices.

The chaos is unbelievable. They are still retrieving bodies from the rubble. It's difficult to coordinate with outside services because there are no phone lines. It's also difficult with rescue workers because there isn't a common language. You can't imagine the number of tongues spoken. Mexican-

Spanish, mostly, Italian, German, Japanese, Slavic, Greek, Scots-English, and finally, our English. I wouldn't know one from another. It's what someone told me. This is the fourth major coal mine disaster in Colorado this year. Coal mines are more dangerous than they need to be. We know how to avoid some of this. I have thought of your friend, Mr. Miller.

The governor has asked colleges in the state to recommend mine experts to investigate the cause of the explosion and the legislature passed a resolution calling for an investigation, though it seems there's no money for one. They will listen to what an expert says. In other words, nothing is going to change the laws to protect miners.

We're trying to be helpful to the rescue crews, also observing what we can. Please be assured we're not going into the mine. They don't want us there. The miners know their work. We don't. We'd get in their way. We're hauling food and water, trying to keep onlookers out of the way, and generally doing what we're told. We aren't in danger. I'll write to you when I have more time. I don't know when we'll be home.

As always,
Your Andrew

She sought out Mr. Miller and they sat on a bench outside the grocery store and she read him the new letter. "I feel much better about him. I was so worried. Thank you for being so nice to me."

"Worry rarely helps."

"It's true. I have a new worry. May I talk to you about it?"

"If you think it would help."

"As you know, Andrew and I met this summer under rather strange circumstances and we've become good friends, but I think he intends more than that." Mr. Miller laughed his almost silent laugh. "Why are you laughing?"

"Because he'd be a fool not to intend more. And you intend more too."

"How do you know?"

He laughed again. "You don't have a poker face, if that's what you're asking."

162

She sighed. "I'm worried because his parents have invited me to come for Thanksgiving. I'm to stay with his Aunt Janet, a few blocks away. Zona says that's acceptable. My problem is when we were together in the mountains, there were interesting things like geology and stars to talk about. What if we can't talk to each other in the city? What if we don't find each other interesting anymore? What if his parents don't approve of me? What if he's forgotten how plain I am? There are so many possibilities for disaster, what will I do if it is a disaster?"

"Come home." He patted her hand. "Josie, Josie. You may not like him as well as you remember, but methinks he remembers you correctly. Aren't your letters to each other interesting? You're not a beauty. A smart man doesn't want a beauty other men envy. It can lead to trouble. What you are is likeable. You are kind, smart, and lively and people enjoy being with you. He will too. Who knows about parents? If he likes you and you make him happy, they will approve of you. If it doesn't work out, come home. Your heart will be a little broken, but hearts heal when you're young. There will be other men who will find you lovable. Guaranteed."

His kind old face gave her such comfort she kissed his wrinkled cheek.

"I could never have talked to my father as I have to you. Every girl needs a kind, wise Mr. Miller in her life."

He rubbed away tears filling his eyes. "Every old man needs someone who thinks he's wise." He stood. "Now go, have a good time, and if it doesn't work the way you want it to, then you've learned something about life. If it does work, you're both lucky." He patted her head, nodded, took his groceries, and said goodbye.

Two more days and no communication. Finally, a postcard.

November 17, 1910

Josie,

I'm sorry about not writing more. We've been busy around the clock. I'll see you in less than a week. I will be home by then. Promise.

Andrew

November 19, 1910

Dear Miss Carter,

Andrew asked me to send you the enclosed round-trip tickets he got for you. He apologizes for not getting them to you sooner. We will expect you to come to Denver on the 23rd. Someone will meet you at the train. We are looking forward to your visit.

Sincerely,
Margaret Allan
(Mrs. Angus Allan)

Another letter at the bottom of the mail sack. Zona sat beside Josie as she read it.

Sunday, November 20, 1910

My Dearest Josie,

We arrived home last night. I have rarely been as glad to be anywhere as I was when I walked through the door of this house. I trust you received my postcard and Mom's letter. When we are together, I will tell you about the nightmare of Delagua. What I must tell you now is how thinking of you sustained me. On night watch your letters came to mind and I went over them again and again. I hiked the mountains with you, sat across the campfire from you, watched you prepare meals, heard your voice–in all its ranges–and laughed and cherished you.

My summers on the survey crew marked a change in my life. Being down there in that horror, clarified much for me. I will tell you my thoughts when we're together later this week. Can it be? We'll be together on Wednesday.

How precious you were to me there in that carnage. By the time we left, miners had recovered seventy-eight bodies. The company says the payroll indicates one or two more. Who will ever know for certain?

Anxiously awaiting you,
Your Andrew

"He's home and safe, Zona." Josie looked into her friend's sturdy, kind face and felt such warmth radiating from it she hugged her. "What would I have done without you?"

"You'd have survived. We always do, we women. It's menfolk we sacrifice. If we make it past the babies we have to watch our boys go to the mines, out to sea, or to war. It's luck, Josie, that any of us lives. I doubt it's our prayers that make the difference. They just help us bear it." She gave Josie a gentle push. "Now, go home and pack. You've got a ticket for that train tomorrow and you'd better not miss it. Someone's looking forward to seeing you."

Josie nodded and ran to her cabin. Mothers who came to story hour had volunteered to cover school on Wednesday and she was free to go. She gathered her clean clothes, the dress, shoes, ribbon and the two pairs of mittens. He heart had never felt so light. She ran to the river, fetched water, heated it for her bath and to wash her hair. She would, indeed, be ready to go.

Waiting for her on the platform were Zona and Mr. Miller. It had snowed all night and was still snowing in the morning. They chatted idly until they heard the train coming up the valley. When they could see the billowing smoke Zona patted her. "You'll have a great time but come back."

Mr. Miller stood aside. Josie went to him and put her arms around him and he put his around her. "I can't wait for you to meet Andrew. He will love you too." The train pulled in; the passenger door opened. She was on her way.

The train chuffed up the valley, past Thomasville where Andrew had stayed, past Biglow where Daisy lived. Immediately, they crossed the North Fork. On it steamed past Norrie, around Horseshoe Bend, then Sellar Meadow, through Mallon tunnel, and sooner than she wanted, the frightening Hell Gate precipice.

It was then thoughts began to flood her mind. *I'm not pretty. My clothes will be an embarrassment to his family. We'll have nothing to say to each other. It's easy to be clever in a letter when I can think about what I'm saying. And it's easy for him to be so loving since he doesn't have to face me. I should have read up on the news so I could sound informed. What if he only talks about rocks? No. He talks about a lot of things. Really, he talks over my head on most of them. He'll think I'm shallow. He'll know I am. When he sees me, will he realize how unsophisticated I am, compared to his college friends? What if it doesn't work the way we hope it will? Why couldn't I have been pretty? It seems to compensate for so many shortcomings.*

Through the Continental Divide, the train glided down the mountains. Scenes passed before her eyes: snow-blanketed peaks, drifts along tracks at higher elevations, darkness of evergreens against white. It was spectacular. Still, she stewed.

At Leadville she got off the train, not knowing if she hoped the Wallaces would be there or not. When they called her name and came hurrying over, their good cheer and delight in seeing her almost overwhelmed her. Mr. Wallace was especially glad to see her because he had written to an old friend of his father's, a professor at Mines, who told him Andrew was one of their finest students. He congratulated her on having found such a nice man. Trying not to feel they had violated her confidence, she thanked them for their concern. They told of their extended family and when the conductor called "All Aboard" she was glad to escape.

Why did I put Andrew's name in the letter? He'll think I'm spying on him. Worse, if he finds me awful, and doesn't want to have a friendship anymore, he'll feel penned in by gossip, and I'm sure there is gossip now among his teachers. She took deep breaths and looked out the window. *I should focus on the beauty of this, not on my pitiful worries. Mr. Miller would not be proud. Why did he waste his wisdom on me? Zona would scold.*

On they rolled through the wind-swept emptiness of South Park. The splendor of the scenery lost to her troubled mind. When they reached Colorado Springs, she took her satchel and prepared to board the connecting train to Denver.

Now's the time to turn around. It's not too late. She showed her ticket and boarded for the trip to Denver. She was so tired. Pulling into Union Station she anxiously looked out the window and saw him. His face, clean shaven, looked tired. It was Andrew, but he was different, taller, maybe, not quite as handsome as she'd drawn him. He looked worried.

Andrew was nervous. *How does she remember me? Has she made me handsome in her mind or does she remember I'm bordering on homely? What will we find to talk about? I'm one dimensional. Wonder what she thinks about vulcanism? Those foreigners at the mine were so dark and interesting looking and I look so...so pale. What if when we're together it doesn't work? What if I can tell she's disappointed in how I look?*

As she picked up her satchel and headed down the aisle, she felt panic rise. The conductor gave her a hand down and she stood on the platform. She saw Andrew coming toward the passenger car. Moving out of the way of others, she waited. He reached her and stopped. He had not remembered her correctly. In his memory, he had tried to rid her of that horrible hat, the pants and shirt and instead to picture her as she was those few minutes they had been together at the school, dressed as she usually would be. But her face had eluded him. A pleasant face greeted him, but it wasn't the lively face he expected.

She smiled tentatively. "Andrew." She held out her hand. *He's not glad to see me. I knew he wouldn't be.*

"Hello, Josie." He took her hand and shook it gently. "Thank you for coming." *She's not glad to see me. I knew she wouldn't be.*

"Thank you for inviting me." *Does he want to escape?* "Thank you for the tickets."

"You're welcome." *This is awful. I should have brought flowers. Other men had flowers. I never thought of flowers.* Their eyes had not left the other's.

"Was it a pleasant trip?" *She's sorry she came.*

"The scenery was beautiful." *Of course, it was beautiful. He knows that.*

"Yup. Beautiful country." *This is painful. It's like a date.*

"Should we go?" *Anywhere?*

"Yes. We're expected for a late supper at Aunt Janet's." *I can't imagine what a horrible weekend this will be for her.*

"How nice." She was almost in tears she was so distraught.

He picked up her satchel and offered his arm. She stared at it then timidly put her hand through the bend. Had a man ever offered his arm before? He led them to the trolley stop and found a bench. She pulled her arm away and sat down. He sat next to her. "Your hands feel cold." Taking her hands, he put them between his two hands and rubbed them gently. "Where are your

new mittens? The star-crossed ones, or were they snowflakes?"
She didn't smile. Fell flat.

"Snowflakes. *Is he making fun of me?* I made left mittens to match and I have them to give to your mother and aunt. As thank you presents, kind of. There's nothing to buy in Meredith except potatoes."

"They'd prefer mittens, I think." They both smiled slightly then fell silent again until the interurban trolley arrived. He helped her up the steps and they found seats together. The trolley made a few stops before it started speeding up, rocking from side to side. Andrew pointed out landmarks that could be seen in the dark. Her senses so dulled by anxiety, she simply thanked him and said nothing. Her nerves were at a breaking point. *I shouldn't have come. I should have listened to myself and stayed home. I'm exactly like those other girls.*

Andrew was struggling as well. *What's wrong with me? It's like I have a curse that repels women. When she was my captive, she seemed to like me. Now she finds me a crashing, unattractive bore.*

After what seemed an eternity, the trolley reached Golden. Josie felt she had swum an ocean since she left Meredith. *This is the longest day of my life. Will it never be over? Can I ask him to take me back to the train tomorrow without offending his parents? Where did the Andrew go who wrote me those letters?*

Where did my sweet, interesting Josie go? How have I managed to kill her spirit?

"Mom wants us to stop by to say hello. Do you mind?"

"Oh, Andrew. I look so awful and feel so tired."

He looked at her. "What do you mean, awful?"

"You know. Worse than usual."

Can she possibly be feeling the same way I am? "I think you look perfect. I can see you'd be tired. They'll understand if we skip it."

She looked at him gratefully. "Thank you. I'd much rather meet them when I'm presentable." *If I have to meet them at all.*

They walked silently to 12th Street to his Aunt Janet's. He twisted the bell and a young girl answered the door. "Come in, Andy, Mrs. McNown is waiting for you in the parlor."

"Thanks, Mary. This is Josie Carter. Josie, this is Mary Algood, she's living with my aunt while she goes to high school."

Trying to be friendly, Josie said. "I'm glad to meet you, Mary. I'd love to talk to you about your arrangement when we can spend some time together." While Mary took their coats, Josie glanced quickly around. It was a large house with beautiful furniture. She'd never been in such a grand home. Andrew led Josie into the parlor where Aunt Janet was standing, waiting for them. With her arms outstretched, she reached for Josie.

"Dear girl, you must be exhausted from that long trip. We're going to have a simple supper, then send Andy on his way. After dinner Mary is going to draw you a hot bath and you're going to get a good night's sleep before you face family." She let Josie go and gave Andrew a pat. "You're going to be with her all weekend. She gets to recoup tonight."

Josie almost whimpered she was so relieved. "Thank you so much. I am tired and not good company at all. You're very thoughtful."

"Mary, please take Josie upstairs so she can wash her hands." Relief. A moment to regain her composure. Instead she reinforced the inappropriateness of being in this fancy house with a man who didn't want to be with her.

A small table, set for four, awaited them. "Josie, please sit here. Andy, you sit across from Josie. Mary and I will serve."

Andrew came behind Josie and pulled out her chair. What was she supposed to do? She'd never been seated before. She looked at him. *Does he understand I don't know the rules for this kind of life?* He nodded, she sat down, and he pushed her in. He did not sit.

When Aunt Janet brought in cornbread, he said, "Oh, Aunt Janet, you're spoiling us." To Josie, "She's famous for her cornbread." She placed it on the table and Andrew pulled her chair out and she sat down. Mary served bowls of split pea soup. "This soup is legendary, Josie."

She looked at it. She could see small bits of carrot, celery, onion, and pieces of ham. It smelled delicious. She hadn't realized she was hungry. What to do next? Aunt Janet asked if Josie would like a prayer before she ate. *It's optional here?* "Only if it's your custom." Aunt Janet said it was not. Josie watched Andrew put his napkin in his lap and she knew to do that; he didn't pick up his spoon, so she didn't. Aunt Janet passed the bread, butter, and honey. Waiting until Aunt Janet picked up her spoon, Andrew picked up his and tasted the soup. Josie did the same.

"Oh. It is delicious. I've never tasted such good split pea soup."

"I'll tell you how I make it. I only tell family." A conspiratorial wink. "Don't forget the bay leaf and thyme."

Josie could feel the instant blush and looked quickly away from Aunt Janet to see if Andrew were watching, which he was. Her cheeks grew hotter. She looked back at Aunt Janet who quickly dropped her eyes. She looked back at Andrew and he arched his eyebrows. He couldn't suppress a grin, she looked so stricken.

"How do you like the cornbread, Josie? It's another secret recipe. She's given it to my mom, but we never see it."

"I'd say it was the most delicious I've ever tasted, but I've never had it before. Is it difficult to make?"

"Not if you don't have to grind corn on a stone. It's very simple. Don't put any flour in it and bake it in a very hot cast iron skillet with a little bacon grease in the bottom. Maggie could do it, she's just too busy saving the world."

"Maggie?" Perplexed, Josie looked at Andrew.

"My mom. Her little sister. Really, they're quite close, but not in priorities. Is that fair, AnJan?"

She laughed. "Fair enough. Maggie has a great heart and wants to make the world better for everyone. She's pretty sure if all women could vote we'd do that. I'm not so sure; sometimes I don't think we could make it any worse, though."

They ate in silence until Aunt Janet asked, "Tell me about yourself, Josie. Andy has been charry with information. Maggie says boys are like that. My girls told me everything, or at least professed they did." Aunt Janet chuckled. Josie nervously nodded, anticipating the questions. "Where are you from?"

"I live in Meredith. It's over the mountains."

"Yes, yes. I mean where were you reared?"

"I spent most of my childhood in Denver."

"Oh. A Colorado girl. How nice. But mostly. Where was the rest?"

"I was born in Goderich, Ontario. We came here when I was five."

"A long trip. What brought you?"

"My father had consumption. I understand many people have come to Colorado for a similar reason."

"Oh my, yes. Our dry, clear air. Your mother didn't come down with it as well?"

"No. She died six years ago of cancer. My father has recovered from consumption."

"I'm sorry to hear about your mother."

"Yes. I miss her terribly." It was almost too much, thinking of her mother, feeling unsure of Andrew, out of place in this beautiful house. She drank her water to keep from choking up.

"I'm sure you do. Now, tell me, how did you and Andy meet?"

She'll think she has to tell the truth. I've got to do this.

As Josie started to open her mouth, Andrew blurted out, "Josie was out wandering around in the woods all by herself and I came upon her. I was all scruffy and bearded, dragging a mule. She pulled out this huge gun and I yelled 'Don't shoot! I'm relatively harmless.' She asked me to define 'relatively' so I launched into its etymology. She rolled her eyes and kindly put the gun in her holster. Seeing she was malleable, I pulled out my harmonica to calm her and began playing 'Red River Valley.'" He watched Josie to see if she understood his message of affection. She dropped her eyes and nodded. "She succumbed to my charms and I convinced her to exchange letters to pass the long winter. What with my elegance of expression and fascinating life, she couldn't resist wanting to know me better and here she is." He had not taken his eyes off Josie since he began. A smile played on his lips the entire telling of the fable. She looked up, smiled at him, grateful for his rescue and humor, seeing in him once again her dear Andrew. He grinned and ducked his head. *There she is. There's my Josie.*

As if they were alone, the joy that had eluded them spread across their faces. They glowed with the pleasure of having found each other. Assured their affection was shared, they relaxed.

Aunt Janet, who watched with interest, broke the spell. "I think, Andy, if Josie had been allowed to answer, I might have gotten a different story."

Without taking her eyes from his, Josie answered, "Not significantly different. It wasn't a great big gun." Together. Laughter. Happiness.

Mary cleared the table and brought cookies and tea. "Mary baked these. Her family understands the benefits of butter, and lots of it. You'll love these." She watched with fascination how the two strangers who had come to her table became completely absorbed in one another. "They're tasty, don't you think?" Aunt Janet asked pointedly.

"I apologize, Mary," Andrew, brought back from his daze, said, "I was eating without tasting. A very bad habit. They are outrageously good. May I have another?"

"No." Aunt Janet scowled, "I want some to take to dinner tomorrow and Mary is leaving first thing in the morning to go back up Golden Gate Canyon to be with her family. You've had enough, Andy; Josie may have another."

"I've already had my share, as well. Mary, they are, as my mother used to say, scrumptious."

"You two are on your own now while Mary and I clean the kitchen. The parlor is yours. I'll knock before I enter, so I won't be embarrassed. Then, Andy, it's off with you."

He rose, pulled out Aunt Janet's chair and gave a slight bow. "Thank you, AnJan, for a special dinner and for inviting Josie to stay with you."

Shooing him away, she and Mary disappeared into the kitchen. He stood behind Josie, "May I help you, Mademoiselle? I know I didn't say that right, but you know what I mean, don't you?"

She turned to face him. "I wouldn't know if you said it right or not. I do know your fiction tonight saved me from a very awkward situation. Thank you."

He nodded, "My pleasure. I mean that. It was fun to watch you squirm. Will you join me in the parlor?"

"I will. You were a naughty boy, I can tell."

He impishly concurred, "Relatively."

"Andrew, did you not tell them how we met?"

"I gave you my word I'd never tell."

172

"You may be naughty; you are certainly honorable. Thank you."

He pointed to a velvet davenport and she sat down. He pulled up a chair so he could face her. "I need to say this. I'm hopelessly happy you're here even though it was strangely uncomfortable at first. Your letters have let me know you better but seeing your beautiful smile and watching you navigate embarrassing situations has reminded me how interesting I found you at Savage Lakes after the great revelation. I know why I want to know you better. I'll be honest with you. I was afraid you'd regret coming to Denver because you'd find me, shall we say, less attractive than your active imagination had made me."

"Oh, Andrew. I almost couldn't get off the train I was so afraid you'd be disappointed because you'd remembered me as someone I am not."

He reached for her hand. "It's true, I miss the hat! Oh, Josie, life was playing tricks on us. Your face had escaped my mind. I've accurately remembered your joyful curiosity and bright smile. I couldn't be anything but thrilled to see you. I was preoccupied with my probable rebuff. It didn't occur to me you might have apprehensions as well. May I be so presumptuous as to hope you've overcome your imagination and accept me as I am?"

"I remembered you fairly well. My imagination didn't betray me. You look as I drew you, as I see you every night, except for the beard."

"You drew me? When?" He couldn't imagine when she had done that.

"At the little lake. You were leaning against an aspen and I was drawing. Remember? You observed the flower I'd drawn wasn't in that location. It's because the picture I showed you wasn't what I'd been sketching."

"You had a picture of me, but I had to rely on my memory of you. How I would like a picture. Will you do a self-portrait for me? Please?"

"Oh, no. No, I couldn't do that. It would be too disappointing. I'd rather imagine I look better than I do," she said without looking at him, enjoying the feeling of her hand in his.

"Does it seem to you we've been silly in wasting our first evening worrying about how we look instead of enjoying being together which is what I've dreamed about for months?"

"Is it too late," she asked, "to say I'm sorry I didn't get off that train full of confidence and joy?"

"I have much the same apology. Can we go forward now as the friends I think we've become through our letters?"

"I'd welcome that. You've made me feel safe in your regard," she offered timidly.

"Safe in more ways than that, I hope. Safe in knowing I want more than friendship from you. I want to court you, whatever that means to each of us. To me it means finding out if there is some special bond between us, which I believe there may be. A kinship of minds that could grow into something lasting and fine. Will you let us find out?"

"I've come here to find out. Your letters let me believe we're on a journey of discovery. I'm excited to see where that takes us."

"I have such an overwhelming need to hold you in my arms. I don't know if asking to do that is appropriate or if one simply grabs hold. I would like your permission, though." He stood.

Standing, nervously nodding her head, Josie said, "I believe if you held me, I would enjoy it."

He put his arms around her and brought her to him. "You may grab hold of me, if you'd like."

She put her arms around him, whispering softly. "I'd like."

"And may I press my luck by asking for a kiss?"

A knock on the door and they sprang apart and sat down. Aunt Janet entered and observed blushes on both their faces. "Did I interrupt something?" Her mirth was not shared. "Okay, Andy, good night. Josie will see you in the morning after ten o'clock. And not a minute before. She's going to help me in the kitchen. Women are busy on Thanksgiving and we don't need a bumbling man underfoot."

"The General made drill sergeants of you and Mom."

"Close. He's referring to our mother, Josie. We called her the General behind her back, which was a shame, because she would have relished being called that. Talk about tough. She came in a covered-wagon and walked beside it most of the trip except when she had me. Then she took a day off, or maybe a couple of hours. She didn't cotton to whiney girls, I assure you, and when she spoke, we listened. Tomorrow, as usual on Thanksgiving, we will be grateful for her courage, industry, and fortitude, qualities our father lacked. We will be grateful for his knowledge and gentle nature, qualities our mother had in short supply. It's been great fun through the years, Josie, to determine which traits went to which child or grandchild. I'm happy to say I got the best of both. Andy is, I fear, a grab bag, fortunately with some offsetting Allan influence. Now, go home."

"I'll see you at ten sharp."

He pecked his Aunt Janet's cheek where she pointed. "You did get the best of both. So did Mom. Good night, Josie."

"Good night, Andrew. Thank you for a delightful evening."

He let himself out the front door and walked dreamily a couple of blocks to his house. *Sleep well, dear Josie. Look at the stars. I forgot to tell you those three in a row are Orion's Belt. I'll have to get you out in the dark tomorrow night to see them.* He happily hummed "You are my Sunshine."

"Now, dear girl, upstairs with you and into that hot bath Mary has drawn for you. We'll see you whenever you awaken. There's really no need for your help in the kitchen. I had to tell Andy that because men understand if they want to eat someone has to fix it. Mary and I have been putting things together all week. I wish you were going to be eating it, but it's all going to Eleanor's, my daughter, who's hosting this year. Trouble is, she thinks turkey is the whole show and her sisters and I have only to fill in the rest. It works, but it takes a lot of co-ordination. Scoot, now. We'll see you when you rise and if Andy has to cool his heels waiting for you it won't hurt him one bit."

Heading upstairs after bidding Aunt Janet good night, Josie took time to observe her surroundings. Her family's lack of funds and the absence of an extended family gave her a narrow view of how people live. Her family did not socialize with other families and her few friends lived in circumstances like her own. Aunt Janet's house felt grand by comparison: beautiful wallpaper, carved furniture, colorful rugs on the floor.

Mary, waiting for her at the bathroom, looked pleased. "I hope you'll enjoy Mrs. McNown's bath crystals. They smell so good."

"I don't know about bath crystals. What does one do with them, Mary?"

"They're in the water. They make your skin soft she says. Mrs. McNown gives me some occasionally. I feel like a lady when I use them."

"I believe a lady is how one behaves, Mary. I think you should always feel like one, you are so well mannered and nice to be around."

"Thank you, Miss Carter. May I tell my mother you said so?"

"Please do. I'm sorry we won't have time together. I'd love to hear about the school where you live, and how it is to come to town for high school."

"We have a good teacher in Golden Gate Canyon, so I didn't feel far behind when I came to town. School there goes only through eighth grade and I want to finish high school so I had no choice but to leave home. It's been a change living with someone other than family, even though Mrs. McNown is kind to me. At home, I feel loved and I miss everyone."

"What is it you want to do?"

"Be a teacher, like you. In a little school where I know everyone. It's where I'm comfortable."

"I hope for some lucky children your dream comes true. Now, I think I'll take that delightful bath you've fixed because I'm tired and sooty."

Had anything ever felt so luxurious? Three months without a real bath and now, feeling the warm, sweet-smelling water surrounding her, she relaxed and reflected. *Andrew. He is the same boy. He wants to be with me. He held me and wanted to kiss me. Mr. Miller was right. We do intend more than friendship.*

As she climbed into the high bed with the down comforter, it suddenly occurred to her Andrew might be looking at stars. She jumped from bed, pulled the curtains back and looked at the sky. Her bedroom faced north and when she got down on her knees to see high up, there were her old acquaintances, Cepheus and Cassiopeia, high above. *Good night, my more-than-friend Andrew.*

She was up, dressed and in the kitchen by seven o'clock. Aunt Janet was rolling out pie dough. Mary was beating dough for rolls. Surprised at such early morning enterprise, Josie exclaimed, "You've gotten an early start."

"We're getting the worms," said Aunt Janet.

"Excuse me?"

"Early birds."

"Oh. You startled me. In Meredith they cook wild mushrooms that have little worms in them and don't think a thing about it. For that matter, neither did Andrew."

Aunt Janet turned to look at her. "He's cooked for you?"

Feeling her face grow red, she stammered, "Not really. We, I mean, he, cooked his own food."

"Ummmm." She kept rolling the pie dough.

"Shall I put the roll dough above the stove to rise?" Mary asked.

"That would be good. You would like coffee and oatmeal, Josie?"

"I would love both, thank you. Then please put me to work. I know how to do dishes, if nothing else."

"That would be helpful because I'm going to lose my Mary here in about half an hour when her father comes to fetch her."

"I understand she's going home for the holiday. I don't know what that means in the way of travel."

"It means a couple of hours by buggy. I'm sure her father left at first light. They're anxious to have Baby Sister home again. Right, Mary?" There was a sweet, joking tone to her voice.

"We'll be glad to be together. We've never been apart before."

Four pie shells, formed, crimped, and filled with pumpkin custard, went into the oven where the coal fire had been banked for a decreasing heat: hot to start, crisping the bottom crust, then a gentler heat for the custard. Josie watched it all in reverie remembering her mother's delicious pies.

"Do you enjoy cooking?" she asked Aunt Janet. "You're so efficient."

"My mother ran a boarding house. I grew up working in the kitchen. Hungry men will eat food a good cook wouldn't be proud to serve, and we did feed them some strange concoctions based on what the General could buy cheap. I did learn a few things, though, and now I enjoy putting a decent meal on the table."

"I'm surprised you're not kneading your bread dough."

"That's because this is for rolls, soft, buttery ones. I'll let you try one when they come out of the oven. Nope. You'll be gone with Andy. I'll leave a few here for you two if you come back and want a bite. There's jam in the larder."

A knock on the back door and Mary ran to it. "Oh, Papa." Josie couldn't believe how teary the two of them were seeing each other. Josie's father had been cordial when she returned last spring after nine months in Meredith. Mary was so excited she hardly remembered to gather the bundles she had ready at the door. Aunt Janet and Mr. Algood exchanged greetings. He asked if Mary had been a good girl. Assured she was a remarkable girl, he agreed.

"Goodbye, Mrs. McNown. I'll be back early Monday morning in time for school."

"I'll look forward to seeing you. Have a wonderful weekend."

Josie watched out the window as Mary and her father got into the buggy, talking, touching, and laughing. *It's so strange to see other families and how they behave. There seem to be endless ways for people to show they love one another.*

"Mary was happy to be going home," Josie observed.

"Oh, she's a cherished child. Her mother lost her first two children, little girls, to whooping cough one winter and she vowed to never have another child, but she was pregnant. It was a boy and she called him Precious. And it stuck. To this day, and he's over 30, he's known as Presh. Then she had five more boys and was through. Ten years later, along came Mary and each of those boys carried her around and played with her as if she were born to amuse him. They call her Baby Sister. Her mother and father dote on her. The amazing thing is she's completely unspoiled and sweet."

"That's a remarkable story, but sad about the first ones who died"

"True. It happens more often than we think. I recently read one in four children dies before the age of five."

"That's terrible. Mother said women who lose a child can almost break under the grief."

Aunt Janet poured herself a cup of coffee and sat down at the table with Josie. "Maggie almost did. Andrew was about two months old and she hadn't coped well after his birth. She was sad, couldn't eat or sleep, was cross with the older boys and her daughter Bessie, and withdrawn from Angus and me. Then Bessie came down with pneumonia and died. I didn't think we were going to keep Maggie. She took to bed and had nothing to do with anyone. She felt her neglect caused Bessie's death. My, she dearly loved that little girl, as she should have. Bessie was a bright light. Angus was desperate and asked me to take over. That's when Andy and I became attached to one another. Poor little guy, I'd take him in to nurse and she wouldn't even look at him. His first word was AnJan, not Momma. Maggie doesn't know that. It took her over a year to come out of it. My girls, who are older than Maggie's boys, and I practically lived at the Allans' house. We'd be there all day, get dinner, and run home to fix dinner for John. I think she threw herself into making the world better after that, to ease her pain. She's good now, but sometimes I see a look come across her face that's the old sadness. I don't think a mother ever stops grieving. She made it up to Andy over time. He was such a sweet boy she took special pains to read to him and encourage his talents. Angus, bless his heart, also took Andy under his wing during the grief. Strangely, Andy's brothers never seemed to resent their attention to him. Little responsible Edward assumed a parent's role for Steve and they became independent, while Andy, being three and seven years younger, tended to find friendship in adults and became a bit of a loner."

Josie watched Aunt Janet's expressive face as she told these family secrets. *Why is she telling me these stories about people she obviously loves and should want to protect? She must think I need to know. Is this a warning? Does Andrew's mother want to keep him safe from me? Does she want to keep him to herself? What am I to do with this information?*

"Thank you for sharing this with me. I'll try to be respectful of what Mrs. Allan has suffered and not say anything that might upset her. Andrew hasn't shared any of this with me, which is appropriate. I imagine he tries to protect his mother from these sad memories."

"If he knows about them. Maggie closed the book after that chapter of her life and asked all of us never to mention it again. I'm not sure if Andy knows he had a sister named Bessie. I've told you because Andy obviously has great affection for you. It wouldn't be fair to him or you to let you ask questions that might cause unhappiness. It's natural when people become acquainted to ask questions about each other's life, as I did with you last evening. You will undoubtedly be asked about your family, your work, and how you met. And, by the by, you would do well to get your story straight with Andy on that last question. He was humorous but not convincing."

"Do you want to know how it really happened?"

"Of course. His crazy story made me more curious. You don't have to share it, if it makes you uncomfortable, which he obviously felt it would."

"It does, but you've been honest with me and maybe you can help me figure out what I can truthfully say." She began at the beginning with Zona and went straight through to Andrew seeking her out in Meredith. Aunt Janet laughed at Josie's attempt to be a boy. When Andrew showed up at the post office she nearly cried. Then she listened quietly when told of their correspondence.

"I think Andy handled it perfectly last night. His parents, though, should have the truth. Warn them Andrew will make it dramatic and ridiculous, as he did last night. Maggie will enjoy it because she's a feminist. Angus will follow her lead. They'll get into the spirit."

"No wonder Andrew loves you. I've dreaded what to say because I try not to lie, but the truth can sometimes serve one badly, even when nothing bad was intended."

"True. Now, let's check the pies, see how the roll dough is progressing, and if the cream is cold enough to whip. I'm always torn on whipped cream: should I pre-whip it and hope it stays up or wait until time to serve it then beat it, or rather let a gentleman there do the honors. I think today, I'll let Harriet's husband whip it. Maybe he won't dominate the conversation if he has a task."

The pies were beautiful, some slight browning on top, the crusts deep brown. She shook them gently to see if they were set and pulled them from the oven.

"Will you help me by rolling out the roll dough while I carry these to the back porch to cool?"

"I'd love to. How thin do you want it?"

"Like this." She held up her thumb and forefinger to show the depth. "We'll butter it, then make two layers of it and cut them with the biscuit cutter. As Mary says, 'More butter never hurts.'"

Aunt Janet handed Josie the apron Mary had worn and left with a pie. The pastry board was still covered with flour from the pie dough, so Josie began her assignment. The doorbell rang and she heard Andrew's voice, "It's ten o'clock, ladies. Anyone home?" She caught her breath.

"We're in the kitchen, Andrew." She wanted to appear calm, but her hands were shaking.

He came in, looked for Aunt Janet who hadn't returned from the porch, and quickly kissed Josie on the cheek. "Good morning, sunshine. Did you sleep well?"

"Good morning, Andrew. I did, thank you. Did you see the stars last night?"

"I did. I wondered if you'd remember. I thought that was too much to hope for."

Aunt Janet came in to get another pie. "Andy. Good morning. Now, make yourself useful and grab some hot pads and carefully carry a pie to the porch for me. Don't put your thumbs through the crust. You'll see where I'm putting them." He left, doing as told.

"The rolls are all I have left to do, so take off that apron, young lady, and go be with that boy who appears to want to be with you in a most determined way." She shook her head. "Don't forget to come home before dinner to change. Do you have a pretty dress?"

"I have a dress. It's my nice dress. I hope it will pass muster."

"Maggie and Angus will care about you. Andrew is oblivious."

He reappeared. "I am not oblivious. I don't care about unimportant details. What are you talking about, anyway?"

"Nothing. Take her by to meet your parents, have lunch with them if that seems to be important, then escape and show her Golden and get her back here in time to dress for dinner."

"I'd salute but you'd whap me."

"Indeed, I would. Give me a peck and leave."

"Indeed, I will." He pecked. They left.

As they walked down the street, Josie said, "You and your Aunt Janet have a comfortable relationship."

"Yes, she's almost as dear to me as my mom is. I'll explain someday how that came about."

"I'd love to hear."

Does he know? "In Canada I have aunts and uncles whom I knew as a child. We wouldn't know each other now. I've always longed for an extended family, people who would love me for no other reason than I belong to their clan, so to speak, especially when I was unlovable to my close family. As isolated as we were in Denver, there was no family to catch us if we tripped. Perhaps that's another reason why losing Mother was so difficult. We girls had no adult female guides for the rough terrain we were going through."

"None of your aunts came down when your mother died?"

"It's not a trip one makes lightly. Mother was dead. Her sisters didn't know us girls. Father's sisters and husbands had supported us, as they could, while Father couldn't work. An expensive trip was out of the question. Besides, Father had three girls to take care of him. But to answer your question, no. No one came to help us. Funny, isn't it? I didn't expect anyone to come."

"Then you weren't disappointed. Something to be said for that."

They quickened their pace as their spirits lightened. "You picked me up last night on the interurban. Does that mean your family doesn't own an auto or," her grin was mischievous, "they won't let you drive it since you've been so 'distracted?'"

He pulled himself up to show dignity, "My family owns Prince. He's been with us fourteen years and Mom says we will get an auto when Prince dies and not before because it would hurt his feelings. Dad doesn't think Prince is that sensitive, so he has a Ford truck he uses for work. I thought it would be better to pick you up on the trolley than to make you ride in the truck and Prince said he'd prefer not to walk all the way to Denver and back at night."

"Thank you for taking care of Prince and me. I know <u>all</u> about donkeys and mules, but I've never met a horse. Will I get to meet him?"

"Sure. After we've spent some time with my folks I'll take you out and introduce you. He's looking forward to meeting you. I've read all your letters to him. He feels as if you're his friend too, although he doesn't want more than friendship. A bunch of hugs and kisses would embarrass him, unlike me." He glanced quickly to see if she smiled. She did. He stopped walking. "We're almost there. Are you nervous? I would be."

"I've been trying not to think about it. You asked if I slept well last night, and I did, after I quit worrying about whether they would approve of me or not. Mr. Miller said worry rarely helps."

"He knew you were worried?"

"He let me unburden my heart to him about whether you would still want to be with me when you saw me again."

"He assured you I would?"

"He said not to worry. If you didn't, I could come home. That seemed so reasonable it calmed me down–for a while."

"He's a good man, Josie. He didn't lie to you and tell you it would be all right when he didn't know if it would be. Here we are. So you know, they're nervous too."

When they reached the door, Andrew said, "Take a deep breath, they don't bite." As they entered, Maggie and Angus rose from their chairs, as if they had been waiting for them, and came forward.

"Mom, Dad, this is Josie Carter. Josie, these are my parents, as you might have surmised."

How could she suppress a genuine, big smile? Andrew looked just like Angus. Maggie took a deep breath and looked quickly at Angus who turned from Josie to look at Maggie. There was fear in his eyes. Maggie's eyes became teary.

What have I done wrong?

Andrew was mystified. Angus quickly took control saying how pleased they were to have her come for a visit. They had been looking forward to meeting the much-discussed Josie. Maggie agreed. It was good of her to come to Golden to spend time with them. She invited them into the parlor. Andrew looked furtively at Josie and she at him and he shrugged his shoulders.

They sat down. Andrew and Josie on the davenport but not near one another, Angus and Maggie on chairs facing them.

"Thank you for inviting me to visit. Your sister is a marvelous hostess, and I appreciate your making the arrangement for me."

"She was delighted to do it. She misses her girls." Maggie seemed to choke up saying that.

Angus picked up the conversation. "I suppose Andy has told you we're having a very quiet Thanksgiving dinner tonight."

"He didn't explain much about the weekend. Perhaps he would have if he hadn't been in Trinidad."

"Yes," agreed Angus, "we were very relieved when he returned."

"I tried to reassure everyone we were safe, because miners didn't want us in their way. We stayed busy; we weren't in danger. It was swell to be home, though, to get a bath and some home cooking." With that he smiled at his mother who slightly nodded. She was obviously disturbed.

"Perhaps you men will excuse Josie and me to check on some preparations for supper and discuss what we'll have for lunch."

"You don't need to feed us lunch, Mom. We can get something at the hotel."

"Nonsense. You'll have a bite of lunch with us. Will you come with me, Josie?"

They left the room. After she closed the kitchen door, Maggie took Josie's hand and carefully studied her face. "I apologize for the way I behaved when we met. You reminded me of a child I once knew whose smile lit up the world, as yours does. For an instant, it brought back memories of her. You have a beautiful smile. I hope to see it often." She dropped Josie's hand.

Be careful. Don't give away Aunt Janet's confidence. "Thank you. It is touching to see a person who reminds us of someone else." *I don't think I should have said that.*

"Yes. Touching." She turned to the cupboards and started to pull down plates, cups, and saucers. "I don't know why I'm doing this. Lunch is a few hours away, isn't it? Let's go back to the men, they'll wonder what happened to us."

Returning, they found Angus and Andrew talking about what would be interesting for Josie to see. "Dad thinks I should take you to Clear Creek. After you meet Prince we could go for a walk along the road. It should be a good autumn hike to build appetite. What do you think?"

"I think I should help your mother with supper preparations and also with lunch."

"Oh, my, no. Please go and have a nice walk. Lunch will be simple because we'll have a big supper. After lunch you and Andy can help in the kitchen."

Josie looked at Andrew for direction. "Okay. You know I always take a suggestion that gets me out of work. Let's go, Josie. We'll be back in time for food." They laughed without joy and Andrew and Josie escaped.

"I'm so sorry, Josie. I don't know what came over them."

"Your mother said my smile brought back memories of a child she once knew." She didn't want to say more because Aunt Janet had indicated Andrew might not know about Bessie.

"Oh."

They walked on silently until Josie started asking questions about Golden. Where was the school he attended as a boy, where was the college, were those the Table Mountains? The mood repaired, they walked arm-in-arm to Clear Creek and along the road next to it. They sat on a large rock to watch the creek flow by.

"You do have a captivating smile. It's as if the sun comes up when you shine it on me. I remember it as being brilliant from our time at Savage Lakes but you only flashed it a couple of times and at the schoolhouse not at all."

"I tried to hide my feelings for you at the lake. Occasionally I forgot. I do enjoy letting you know now, and your shy grin comes back to me. If I remember correctly, most of the time at the schoolhouse I was emotional."

His laugh erupted, "You weren't stoic. We were both afraid we had misread the other's feelings. I trust you understand my intentions now."

"I think this weekend will clarify many things," and she gave his arm a squeeze.

"I can't put my arms around you, or kiss you, but please know it's what I'd like to do."

"That's a nice clarification. Will it clarify my feelings for you that I would like you to?"

"Ever so much."

"Do most people who want more than friendship enjoy being close together?" she asked.

"I believe it's something that comes naturally when friends...become dearer."

They sat quietly for a while, watching water flow past them. Andrew broke the silence, "Josie, I think Mom has always regretted not having a daughter so if you could avoid saying anything about her having three boys and no girl to soften that blow, I think it would be best. Your mother probably was happy not to have boys."

"My mother had three boys. Her sixth child, a boy, died shortly after birth soon after we came here. Losing the baby on top of leaving family and friends and having my father be so sick was almost too much for her, she told me. She really had no choice but to carry on. My twin brothers died three years ago in Panama working on the Isthmian Canal. Francis died of yellow fever and Walker three weeks later in a construction accident. It was to be a great adventure. My father agreed to their going because he thought it would be good work experience. He'd been a sailor as a young man and loved to recall his time on the Great Lakes. It was an important part of his youth and I think he wanted that for them. The three of them would often talk about the canal and what it would be like in a jungle. The boys were alike as peas in a pod. It's difficult to imagine one without the other. I suspect Walker wasn't careful after Frank died. He wrote he wanted to come home. It wasn't fun anymore. Then we got the second telegram. My mother died before they did, thank heaven."

"You've not mentioned your brothers."

"No. My sisters and I talk about the twins, remember tricks they played on us, nice things they did, and how close they were to each other. Although alike, they were different in many ways. I loved my big brothers and thinking of their wasted lives makes me sad."

"Yes. It would."

"I didn't mean to put a damper on our day. At some point I would have told you about them. My father hasn't been the same since. He could understand them better than us girls, especially after Mother died."

"I imagine he could." Andrew sat quietly for a while. "I think you may have reminded my folks of my sister Bessie. I never knew her because she died shortly after I was born. Edward told me never to say the words sister, daughter, or dead in front of Mom. Dad told me about Bessie when I was about ten. I've not heard her name mentioned by anyone since then. I guess Mom had a rough time with it."

He does know. What a strange silence this family keeps. "My mother said losing a baby, even at birth, isn't something you get over. Children are a part of you. You love them more than you love yourself."

"Let's not think about it. Let's think about happy things because we can't change the sad ones from the past." He reached over and put his hand on hers. "I've never lost anyone I love. You've lost three that I know about. I hope you'll not lose another for a long time."

She put her head on his shoulder. "Reading Dickens, I'm struck with how he creates villains to make his story interesting. I think life is villainous enough. Then he comes up with happy endings for his lead character. That doesn't seem honest to me. There are many good, decent people whose lives don't end happily." She took her head from his shoulder and studied his face. "If we should be lucky enough to have happy lives, let's remember to be grateful and realize how much we owe to chance and not take credit for the good we receive."

"If <u>we</u> should have a happy life, I will always be grateful." He pressed her hand to his lips, then tucked it between his hands. "If we should have villainous times, as you call them, I hope we'll be there to help each other. I'll want to help you, I know."

"Thank you. I can't imagine trying to survive another painful time without your help. I did so need solace when Mother died, yet I was the consoling big sister for my little sisters. The boys probably needed comforting as well and would naturally have gone to my father, but grief overcame him. If you ever face sorrow, I trust you'll tell me. I'll want to take care of you."

The melancholy mood they found themselves in matched the skies overhead. "November isn't my favorite month," Josie observed, her nose wrinkled in dislike. "The world, the skies, the moods of people all seem gray." She scowled and said firmly, "We don't have to let November determine the day for us. How about seeing who can find the first bird, first nest, first beautiful leaf on the ground."

Shaking his head in amusement, "I'll be your pupil, Miss Carter. Let's go." They jumped up, started looking in the trees and on the ground.

"Up there," she yelled, "see the bird. What is it?"

He frowned. "A crow. Not an elegant spotting. You win that one."

"A crow's a bird. Who's to decide on elegance? Dressed smartly in black, alert. I like it."

"Don't eat it, though."

"Why would I eat a crow? I'd have to kill him."

"It's an expression: To eat crow means you must admit you were wrong. I guess we can assume they're not very good to eat."

"Oh, I've eaten crow, probably not as often as I should have. You're right, it wasn't tasty."

No other people were wandering around instead of preparing Thanksgiving supper or being with family and friends. Andrew caught Josie by the hand. "You need your mittens. I'll keep you warm."

"What about my other hand?"

"It's next. Are you looking for a nest or leaf?"

"I was distracted, sorry. Now I'm focused on winning. Do you remember you taught me about focusing?"

"I showed you about focusing, so you could appreciate the long view. How do you feel about long views now?"

"I tend to look more closely at what's in front of me. There's so much to see when one opens one's eyes and really looks. Long views can make me dizzy. Are you an up-close person or a long-view person?"

"Right now, I'm an up-close person trying to appreciate the person right in front of me. If I can work out an understanding with that person, then I'd like to focus on the long-view."

"Will you then forget about the up-close?"

"Nope. In the lab when you look at a thin slice of rock under the microscope, you can see the structure of crystals. They're beautiful and surprising because you didn't know they were there. When you look at the rock with your bare eyes, you see what a marvelous thing those tiny crystals created." He turned so he could look at her.

"It's like seeing a field of flowers," she said, "then examining one flower up-close, observing the stamens and petals and how leaves are arranged, then realizing how beautiful the whole is because of all the parts."

Is she reading into this what I intended? I'm being obtuse. I think romance wants a more direct approach.

"Andrew, do you think that wad of sticks in the cottonwood tree is a nest?"

"Definitely not. Why would a magpie want such an ugly house?"

"Then it is a nest!"

"If you insist."

"I do."

"Then you didn't need to ask me and rub it in that you have two wins and I don't have any."

"If you find a truly beautiful leaf, I might make it worth two wins."

"You're going to let me, not win, but tie you. This is the new female plot, I suppose, to humble us."

"Do you need humbling? I hadn't noticed an over-abundance of self-confidence."

"All men need humbling. We're born needing it. At least that's the message I get at home."

"Well, I wouldn't want to let your mother down, would I?"

"She'd prefer her earnest endeavors for twenty-two years were not wasted." They strolled on. "Andrew, what's that noise?"

He looked up. "Those are geese. They honk when they fly."

She looked up, then down. "Oh, no, Andrew, you're almost to step on a really pretty leaf." Her voice lacked innocence.

He looked down on a perfect yellow cottonwood leaf.

"Merciless. You distract me, then say, Ah-ha!"

"You're right, that wasn't fair. I'm not comfortable competing with you. We've had fun sharing with each other because we see things differently and we benefit from that."

"Oh, Josie, how I want us to go forward sharing the world's mysteries. May I say again, completing, not competing? Your little game did conquer the gloom, though. Thank you."

"I like your idea of completing, not competing. I really don't enjoy competition that much, unless I win." She didn't try to suppress her grin.

He held her hand. She was glad he wanted to be close to her. After walking a short distance, he asked if she would like to take Prince for a picnic up Golden Gate Canyon the next day.

"Where Mary lives?"

"Not that far. There's a nice spot to picnic on Cedar Creek. I think you'll like it."

"If you do, I'm sure I will. Can we buy a picnic somewhere? I brought money."

"The day after Thanksgiving we should be able to rummage up something at home."

"If you want to bring a book to read, that's okay," she ventured.

"Why would I do that?" He was confused. Didn't she want to be with him?

"So you won't be bored." She didn't look at him.

"I wasn't bored for three days, why would I be now?"

"Maybe you've discovered all there is to know about me."

"I'll never know you well enough and I can't imagine running out of thoughts to explore with you." He hesitated. His eyes danced with playfulness. "For instance, how do you feel about Tzar Nicholas and Kaiser Wilhelm deciding on spheres of influence in the Middle East?"

"See? I don't know what you're talking about."

"Neither do I. I read the headlines a while ago. I could give you my opinion on foreign governments, ours included, going into other countries, and making decisions for them. Like the way we did in Colombia when they wouldn't work with us on the canal. We got the Panamanians who were part of Columbia to revolt so we could sign a treaty with them instead. Now we're building the Isthmian Canal in Panama and will own it forever. But I'd rather talk about other things I also don't know anything about." His glee in having come up with something so obscure made him duck his head.

"Oh, Andrew, I'm not sure I can keep up with you."

"I'm talking wildly because I'm afraid I can't keep you interested in me. You're so creative and wide-eyed with the world. You make me see things I wouldn't otherwise notice. I need what you bring, Josie, to make me feel whole. I hope I bring you something."

"Oh, you do. I need your knowledge, your–don't laugh– wisdom, your strange sense of humor. I need your steady approach to life, not my impulsive one. You're thoughtful, rational, systematic. I want to borrow those traits. Occasionally."

Her wistfulness touched him. He acknowledged her conditional desire for systems with a nod. "Then let's go tomorrow to see how we do, without distractions, the way we were up the North Fork. Are you game?"

"I'm game."

Walking through November's chill, leaves crunching underfoot, gray skies overhead, they felt complete.

"Andrew?"

"Yes, Josie."

"I'll try to quit worrying you'll change your mind. I know I won't change mine."

"Thank you. I would love for us to feel secure in our...our regard for each other."

Suddenly remembering Mr. Wallace, Josie felt her cheeks grow hot. "I need to tell you something that will make you justifiably cross with me."

"I can't imagine what that would be, but your blush makes me nervous."

"You have good reason. Last year I rode on the train as far as Leadville with a man named Wallace. He teaches science in their schools. He and his wife befriended me, and we went to Aspen together last fall for the weekend. They invited me to Thanksgiving dinner last year and I went. They invited me this year and I wrote them I was coming here to be with you. I foolishly used your name. I'm so sorry."

"It's my name."

"Yes, but Mr. Wallace wrote a friend of his father who teaches at Mines and inquired about you. I don't know how he explained his interest. I'm afraid he may have said you have a girlfriend."

"I hope I do have."

"They may gossip about you."

"They'll be relieved to know I'm normal."

"You're not angry with me?"

"I thought we agreed to feel secure in each other's regard."

"Regard is one thing. Forgiving poor judgment is another."

He laughed. "You're forgiven. What's your friend's name?"

"Charles Wallace. His father taught at Mines."

"Alfred Wallace. He was a legend, Josie. He must have written to Professor Ellis. He's a good old guy. He won't gossip too much. We're safe, but he may eye me in the hall and wink."

She thanked him, squeezed his hand, and surveyed the world with bright eyes.

Andrew congratulated himself. *The Leadville connection. The last piece of the puzzle.*

When they reached home, Mrs. Allan was fixing lunch. "I'm so sorry we didn't get back in time to help," Josie said. "It took longer than I expected to meet Prince. What may I do?"

"You and Andy can set the table in the kitchen, pour that hot water into the teapot, and find Dad and tell him lunch is ready." They quickly went about the tasks. Lunch on the table, everyone relaxed.

"Is the turkey ready to go in, Mother?" asked Angus.

"I put it in a minute ago. Pin feathers out; stuffing in. What a pain those little feathers are."

"Do you buy your turkey or raise it?" Josie asked in innocence.

The men howled. "If she raised it we wouldn't be eating it," Angus answered.

"Mom is something of an animal rights champion which fortunately doesn't extend to eating meat."

"I understand. We raised chickens. When a hen got old and quit laying, my mother would whisper to my father then take to her room. We'd have stewed chicken the next day, but she wouldn't eat it."

"Exactly," said Angus. "Maggie equates it with cannibalism."

"The turkey you don't know is different," Maggie chimed in. "It had no personality for me. If I didn't have men to feed, though, I'd probably be a vegetarian and sleep better."

"Thank you for not making us anemic," Andrew added.

"Oh, you and your chemistry."

Josie changed the subject. "This is delicious. What do you call it?"

"It has a French name; we call it egg pie. They're getting it because you're here and I had some pie dough left over.

Otherwise they'd be hunkered over the ice box searching for something to eat." She cast a knowing eye at the men.

"I've never had it before. Is there cheese in it? I think I can taste some."

"Cheese, milk, a little ham, some mustard. It's basically scrambled eggs baked in a pie."

"And we love it," added Andrew. "Thanks for a nice lunch, Mom."

She gave him a loaded look that said: If this doesn't go well, it's your fault, not mine.

He understood and nodded assent.

Angus broke the uncomfortable silence. "Where did you go for your walk?"

"Along the creek. Josie spied a crow, a magpie's nest, and a leaf." He squinted at Josie.

She smiled sweetly.

It was obviously a private joke and neither Maggie nor Angus responded.

"What fascinating topic did Andy choose to discuss with you, Josie?" Angus asked playfully.

"He mentioned the Kaiser and the Tsar and the Middle East, but I didn't know anything about them."

"And you do?" A surprised Angus asked Andrew.

Josie jumped to Andrew's defense. "He said he didn't know about them either."

Angus and Maggie both raised their eyebrows.

"What those looks mean, Josie," Andrew said, "is Mom is surprised at that rare show of humility and Dad is amazed I would want to discuss something I don't know anything about."

"Well, that," said Angus, "and it's not a proven courtship topic."

"Well, what did you talk about when you were courting Mom?"

"I can answer that," said Maggie impishly. "Your father was rather passionate about the colonization of Africa."

Angus wilted. "You asked good questions."

"I wanted to appear intelligent. I fell in love with you because you had a wide-ranging mind and cared about others." Reconciled, she continued. "And about Nicholas and Wilhelm, did you know they're first cousins, along with King George?"

"I thought those titles were hereditary." Andrew said.

"They are."

"Then how can they be first cousins and all rulers of different countries?"

Maggie was happily imperious. "A very masculine perspective, Andy. They had mothers as well as fathers. All three were Queen Victoria's grandchildren, by a son as well as daughters. Ought to mean peace, don't you think?"

Angus answered. "We won't count on it. Now what are your plans for the weekend?"

"Could Josie and I take Prince to Cedar Creek for a picnic tomorrow?"

"It's okay with me; you better check with Prince."

Lunch cleared, the real work of supper commenced: The turkey needed basting; rolls were shaped to rise; sweet potatoes were peeled, sliced, and put in butter, brown sugar, and molasses to cook; white potatoes peeled and put to boil; canned green beans were brought up from the store room, bacon fried to mix with them; Josie's chokecherry jam put into a dish; butter put on a plate.

Chatter between chores was easy and infrequent as everyone focused on his or her job.

"What time is dinner?" Angus asked.

"When the turkey's done. I'm shooting for around five-thirty. Does it matter?"

"Not at all. I was wondering if you'd have time for a hand of cards before we sat down. You have everything so organized and ready."

She looked at him in amazement. "Oh, no. There's still a lot to do."

"Okay. I was hoping you could get off your feet for a few minutes."

"I don't think so but thank you," she said lovingly.

Work kept apace. The table was set with a lace cloth Maggie had crocheted for her hope chest. Plates were on the warming shelf above the stove.

"Your other sons won't be joining us?"

"No. I told them to go to their wives' families this year. You didn't need the whole clan to contend with. You'll meet them later."

"I'll look forward to that." *Will there be another time?*

Preparations were almost complete when Josie remembered her pretty dress." Oh, I forgot. Aunt Janet said I could change my dress at her house before dinner. Do I have time?"

Maggie looked at her. "Why would you do that? We've all seen you the way you are. We think you look lovely. Save it for your special night."

Josie was perplexed. *Isn't this the special night? What should I do? I want to show Maggie I appreciate her effort.*

Andrew offered, "I thought we could go to the hotel for dinner your last night, Josie."

"Tonight, you might get it dirty doing the dishes," laughed Angus. "Andy knows what rounds off the evening."

"Oh. I'll be delighted to help with dishes. It's my strong suit."

"Are you a bridge player?"

"No. Why?"

"Strong suit. It's a bridge term."

"I didn't know that. No, we didn't play cards at my house though I have no objection to them."

"Your house," said Maggie. "I want to hear about it at supper. So many questions to ask."

"Mom." Andrew had the pleading voice kids get when they want their parent to behave.

"No, I won't ruin the evening with a cross-examination. I have a normal mother's curiosity, is all."

He rolled his eyes and Josie laughed. "I won't mind. It wouldn't be fair to see your family and not to share mine."

Maggie smiled. *A good woman. She understands.*

Turkey and stuffing out, rolls in, beans warmed, potatoes mashed, sweet potatoes caramelized, tomato aspic unmolded, gravy made, rolls out. It was ready. The big meal of the year. When they sat down in their appointed places, they held each other's hands and the family said in unison, "Let us be thankful for the blessings we have received."

Angus raised his water glass, "For those present and for our loved ones not present, we are thankful."

Doing as others did, Josie raised her glass and dropped her head. "For our loved ones not present" struck her. *For my dear mother, for Francis and Walker, who are no longer present, for my father, my sisters, and for Mr. Miller too, who never knew a family supper like this, I am thankful.*

Maggie raised her glass, "To my mother, for her courage, industry and fortitude; to my father for his knowledge and gentle nature; and for their good qualities inherited by my sister, Janet; and for their various qualities inherited by the rest of us, we are thankful." Josie was surprised, then they all laughed. She had been afraid they were making fun of Aunt Janet, but it was apparently a family joke. Maggie turned to her, "Early in our lives, Janet claimed the good qualities and she was such an admirable big sister, none of us disputed it. It has since become a tradition to remember our parents and her goodness, although she would appreciate our forgetting the last part, but it's too much fun to tease her."

A family that laughs and teases each other. What must that have been like growing up? "I think it's marvelous you all enjoy each other so much."

"Most of the time," Angus replied, and they laughed again.

Turkey carved, food passed, conversations quieted as people began to eat.

"Outstanding, Mother," said Angus.

"Terrific, as always," said Andrew.

Josie looked at Maggie. "There is so much experience, effort, and love represented at this table, I don't know how to thank you for including me in your celebration."

"Thank you. May you be at many more celebrations."

Josie thanked her and silently noted she didn't say "of our" celebrations. No one was making commitments for Andrew he might not want to keep.

Andrew whipped cream until his arm gave out, then Angus took a turn at it. When the cream thickened Maggie added sugar and vanilla and beating re-commenced until she deemed it perfect.

"She has very high standards for the beaters," Andrew said." She doesn't care that our arms fall off."

"You always regain your arms when it comes to eating the pies."

"We rally, yes."

They were delicious and cream was abundant. Tea finished the meal. The men pushed back and slouched in their chairs.

Angus patted his stomach. "I've done it again, Mother. You're too good a cook."

Josie observed the love that passed between them. It wasn't a memory she had from her childhood.

"Now," said Maggie "I get to ask some questions."

"Please do." Josie responded as graciously as she could, dreading what might come next.

"Andy says you're a Denver girl, sort of. Canadian, I think. Scottish descent. A schoolteacher. Tell me about the town where you practice your trade."

I can do this. "It's called Meredith, named for a man who started the quarry. It's a railroad stop, post office and general store."

"What do the people there do for a living?"

"The community includes workers at the limestone quarry and kiln, ranchers and loggers. Most are bachelors who tend to leave on the Saturday night train for Basalt and come back Sunday morning."

Angus laughed. "Wonder what they do in Basalt?" No one answered but Maggie glared at him.

Josie innocently continued, "We have six families accounting for the fifteen pupils. Families stay put and have what they call Saturday night supper in the schoolhouse. They sing, tell stories, or children perform. This fall and winter people are telling where they came from and how they got to Meredith."

"We've heard some of their tales. You enjoy this life?"

"It was difficult at first because the cabin for the teacher is by the school and it's a walk from the post office and store. I didn't know anyone but the postmistress whom I met there. I gradually grew accustomed to solitude and found quiet evenings necessary after being with kids all day. I do enjoy the people now. They're from many countries."

"Do the women speak English?"

"Some don't speak it well. They're trying to improve by listening to stories I read the children and since it's the only common language they want to practice. We meet on Friday evenings to knit or quilt together. They've taught me those skills, or rather they're trying to teach me. I will say they tolerate no mistakes. I rip out a great deal."

Maggie smiled, "I believe Andy said you draw."

"I enjoy drawing. I've had no lessons. My mother was artistic, although not trained."

"Tell me about your mother."

"You know she died six years ago?" Her voice caught on the word died, a word this household didn't use.

"Andrew mentioned you had lost your mother."

"She was the most wonderful person I've ever known. She was kind, selfless, and gentle. I'm not much like her. Her families came from Scotland and England before Canada."

"You remember her fondly. She would appreciate that."

"My sisters and I don't want to forget her. We tell each other memories of her so she'll always be in our hearts."

"And your father?" asked Angus quickly.

"A stern, quiet man. His family came from Scotland. He was a carriage-maker in Canada before he came down with consumption. He's well now, but he has never regained his full strength."

"And your brothers and sisters?"

I may not be able to do this. "I have two younger sisters." She looked to Andrew for help. She could feel herself getting emotional, and it also involved death.

"Josie lost her twin brothers in Panama where they went to work on the canal. They were older."

"We share memories of them as well."

Angus spoke up. "I'm sorry about your losses, Josie. I think the time for questions may be up. What do you think, Mother?"

Maggie was thoughtful. "Yes. I feel I know you better. Thank you for being patient with my interview."

She smiled bravely. "You should know who Andrew's friend is."

Amused, Maggie said, "His good friend, I believe."

Andrew and Josie caught each other's eye for a second. Andrew said, "She's more than a good friend."

"One more question, please. Josephine isn't an English nor a Scottish name. How did you come by it?"

"My mother's best friend from childhood was a French Catholic girl named for St. Josephine. Some in the family didn't like my name because it was Papist."

Maggie laughed. "I'm assuming they were Presbyterians."

Josie nodded. "My father's side. Mother was Anglican. They didn't object."

"That's enough, now. You two may begin the dishes while I put food away. Angus, are you going to bone the turkey?"

"Are you going to make turkey soup if I do?"

"Will you still love me if I say no?"

"Most likely, but I hope you won't test me." The teasing banter intrigued Josie.

They left the table, each carrying his or her dessert plate and teacup to the kitchen. Angus began working on the bird, Maggie gathering leftovers and putting them in smaller dishes with plates on top to keep them from drying out. Andrew and Josie began scraping plates and gathering scraps for the neighbor's dog. It was a busy group, not a noisy one, though small laughs occasionally erupted. Josie felt she had been dropped into a foreign country.

Turkey carcass in the soup kettle on the back of the stove to simmer all night, food to the ice box or screened-in back porch, dishes, pots and pans washed, dried and on shelves. It was nine o'clock. All that planning and effort dispensed with in a little over three hours. Josie wondered about it while she dried dishes. Was it worth it? She didn't think she'd ask Maggie tonight.

As they were leaving the kitchen, Andrew reached for Josie's hand. "I enjoyed being with you tonight. I didn't even mind doing dishes."

"It was fun being with you," she paused, "your family isn't like anything I've known. I love how you treat each other,, pitch in to help, and joke about things. It's good to see the background that formed you."

"I'm anxious to peak into your past. I think I'm getting a feeling for it. Now what would you like to do? We have the rest of the evening ahead of us."

"If it's up to me, I want to be alone with you. Every letter, every time we're together, I see a different facet of you that makes me want to see more. We've hardly been able to be ourselves yet and I'm eager to understand what we feel."

Reaching behind her, Andrew clicked off the kitchen light and pulled her to him. "I'm so thankful to hear you say that. I need to understand too. Right now, though, I think it would help if I could collect on that kiss I was cheated out of last night."

"What about your parents?"

"They're in the parlor and won't be patrolling the kitchen, I assure you."

"I've never been kissed. I don't know how."

"We'll figure it out." Bending slightly, his hands on her shoulders, he put his lips gently on hers. He straightened, "I didn't dream it would be so nice."

"Nor did I. You may kiss me again."

He kissed her. "I think we can get very good at this if we practice enough."

"I think so," she agreed.

"We'd better go. I don't want to." Reluctantly leaving the privacy of the kitchen, they drifted to the front room.

Stunned. There was no other word for what Josie felt when they entered the parlor. Maggie was sitting with her back against the davenport arm, legs extended into Angus' lap. He was rubbing her feet. Josie had never seen a display of intimate affection to equal it. Her instinct was to turn away, as if she had caught them doing something shameful, but Andrew barged into the room as if nothing were amiss.

"Thank you for cleaning up the kitchen, kids. I wasn't up to it tonight."

"After preparing that dinner, I don't wonder. We hope the kitchen passes inspection in the light of day. That foot rub feel good?"

"Divine. Your father has such strong hands and knows precisely how to use them."

"I'll walk Josie home and stay until Aunt Janet kicks me out, if that's okay."

"Of course. Tell Janet we blessed her."

"I'll tell her. She'll be thrilled. See you in the morning."

"Good night, Josie, we're so glad you could be with us. We're going to have left-overs tomorrow night and Janet will be joining us. We look forward to you two being with us."

"Thank you. Dinner was perfect. I'll look forward to your left-overs." She wanted to curtsy or bow to indicate she honored them. Instead, she settled on, "I've enjoyed your company so much."

Andrew put his arm behind her back and guided her to the door. Coats and shoes on they entered the darkness of a night waiting for the waning moon to rise.

He was holding her hand again. It seemed natural the way he slipped his hand around hers and the way hers fit into his. It was dark and corner lamplights left deep shadows in the middle of blocks. When they came to a particularly shaded place he stopped. "May I please hold you?"

"I would like that."

He put his arms around her and held her tightly. She could feel the roughness of his tweed jacket, the wool of his sweater. She put her arms around his back and held him close. After the kisses, it was the most satisfying feeling she could remember.

"Your hair smells like lilac. I love lilacs. May I kiss you?"

"What if someone sees us?"

"They'll be jealous."

He kissed her mouth, her cheeks, and buried his face in the warmth of her neck. "I can't get enough of you."

"That's a nice thing to say." *I hope you never will.* "If you look you'll see the stars whose names I don't know."

He held her close and looked up. "They're called Orion's Belt. It's part of the Orion constellation. The Hunter, remember, from the poem?"

"I do remember. Orion was the son of Poseidon, god of the sea, who gave Orion the ability to walk on water. He went to an island and harmed the king's daughter so the king blinded him. Orion made his way to the Sun god who healed him. Then Orion angered the Earth mother and got bitten by a scorpion and died. Then for some reason Zeus put Orion and the scorpion in the heavens."

"Sounds like the Jabberwock to me. You got this from a sister?"

"She was an avid reader and loved mythology. She could give you the story in much greater detail. You studied stars. She studied their stories. You may have a lot to share with each other."

"My folks gave me the star book when I was a kid and I studied it nightly for a while. I mispronounced everything, but I did learn where some stars are. I've since learned how to pronounce them, at least the way a teacher did, but as you know, I can't spell them."

"You've opened up the night sky for me and my pupils. After Saturday night suppers we go look at them. Some of the Scandinavians were fishermen and they know stars by different names, but they do know their stars. It was important to finding their way home, they said."

"I suppose every culture had its own mythology and overlaid it on the stars. If you have a name and a story for something it makes it easier to remember, the way it's easier to remember a poem if it's a song."

They walked on, hand in hand until they could see light in Aunt Janet's house.

"Andrew, why did you and Aunt Janet make fun of your mother's cooking when she's a wonderful cook?"

"Did we make fun of her? We shouldn't have. She can be a great cook, it's just not something she enjoys. We always had good food at our house but not the variety that AnJan cooked. AnJan helped Grandma in the kitchen. Mom cleaned rooms, did laundry, and bookkeeping. She helped in the kitchen at night enough to learn to cook the basics and that's where she's comfortable. AnJan treats it like an art form and keeps giving Mom new recipes which she dutifully files and seldom cooks. It's a way of relating, I guess."

"My mother was a plain cook. As you say, good food, not a great deal of variety. I don't think the British are known as good cooks."

"I wouldn't know. Mom says Grandma got to be a good cook before she sold the boarding house, and no one died in the meantime."

"What did your grandfather do?"

"Do? Grandpa? He visited with boarders, staff, people on the street, whoever would stand still long enough to have a conversation. He came from a wealthy family but an older brother inherited the money. I think he thought Grandma would take care of him which she did."

"Didn't that bother him, not to help?" she asked.

"Didn't seem to. He read a great deal. He wanted to know what people thought and why. In effect, he watched Janet raise the kids, because Grandma was busy running the business."

"Did the kids go to school?"

"When they were too little to help. They got the basics. He read to them and gave them books to read so they educated themselves. He had manners and class. Grandma gave them common sense and math skills so they could check bills."

"She was the practical one, wasn't she? He was the dreamer."

"Yup. You're undoubtedly thinking Grandpa and I have a few things in common. Others have mentioned the similarity. I loved the old guy, but I can see he could drive an energetic person crazy. They seemed to get along, though, since she got to be in charge and heaven knows he didn't want to be. This is a forewarning: You may have to call me Grandpa to get me moving." His tone was apologetic.

"I doubt it," she said gently. "So, what good about him did Aunt Janet inherit?"

"That's a problem. She and Mom are little generals themselves, but nice ones, and I guess that's the Grandpa part. It was the General in Janet to announce she got the good qualities, and no one dreamed of challenging her. She is definitely the big sister of that clan in that kind Grandpa-way. Families are complex little worlds that totally confuse the outsider. Don't worry if you don't get it at first."

"I wonder what our family would have behaved like had we stayed in Canada. Mother always spoke highly of her brothers and sisters, but we didn't have to be around them. People you can avoid are often remembered more favorably than ones you have to live with."

The house reached, they stopped, hugged and kissed again. "I do believe we're getting better at this. You wouldn't believe how often I've dreamed of holding you, Josie."

Snuggling into his arms, she said, "I confess I've wanted you to. It's much nicer in person, though." They went to the door and rang.

Aunt Janet, wearing a comfortable robe, let them in. "Your mother called to say you were on your way an hour ago. Did you have an accident?" she asked satirically, her eyebrows raised.

"It was not an hour ago and we were star gazing."

"That's one of the better ones. Now, I'm going to bed, so let yourself out shortly, and Josie, you know your way around. Please turn out the lights as you come to bed. Good night, you two. I'll see you at breakfast, Josie. Meaning don't show up earlier than that, Andy."

"You were blessed at dinner. I'd think that would make you peaceable."

"Peaceable, yes. Wise, I am, with or without the blessing. You have until ten-thirty."

Glancing at his pocket watch, Andrew protested, "That's half an hour."

"Good night, Andy. Good night, Josie."

"Good night, Mrs. McNown. I'll see you at breakfast."

"Good night, AnJan." He pecked her cheek.

In the parlor Andrew turned off the ceiling light, leaving on table lamps. The beautiful furniture, soft lighting, warmth after the chilly walk, and tender moments with Andrew made Josie feel as if her world had gently turned from harsh reality and fear of rejection into the most romantic, safe cocoon she could imagine. She glowed with happiness.

"Will you sit beside me?" she asked.

"Happily." Sitting as near each other as possible, holding hands, he was pensive. "On our way here I kissed you. It was an amazing experience. Kissing you has been my dream. Earlier, in the kitchen, you let me. Now I kiss you and it seems as if we've always kissed. It's so natural and comfortable and right. I don't want you to think I mean it's become ordinary. It's just the opposite. It's even more wonderful than I could have imagined."

Josie tried to look into his eyes. He was staring straight ahead as if he were trying to figure out something. "It mystifies me, too. How quickly kissing you and holding you became natural. I didn't know how and you haven't said, but I think maybe you aren't used to kissing girls, and yet it's as if we've always known how."

He turned to look at her. "I'd never kissed a girl before tonight. You're like a magnet to me. Do you know about them?"

"My brothers had some little ones. They'd either stick together or push each other away."

"Well, you pull me to you. I love it, Josie, how you attract me. It confuses me a little. I haven't experienced anything quite like it."

"You want to analyze it, don't you? And I'm content with just enjoying it. It's one of our differences. I invite you to join me on this. It's so much fun not thinking about it, letting it sweep you up in the joy of it."

"You're right. I am analyzing it. I will join you. Now before AnJan kicks me out, will you join me tomorrow. May I pick you up around nine o'clock? Wear hiking shoes, if you brought some. There's a sheep trail with a beautiful view from the top."

She was confused. "I have shoes. I'm not sure about hiking a steep trail in a skirt. I'll try and if it doesn't work, I'll wait for you in the buggy." *Doesn't he remember the letter he wrote me about not teasing me about hikes since I can't do them in a skirt?* Her mood was sagging. *Is he really going to abandon me?*

"Maybe a skirt won't bother you."

"I'd like for you to have a nice day, and if hiking is what you'd enjoy, then you should hike even if my skirt keeps me from going." Her voice was failing her. *I sound pouty. Well, how else should I sound?*

He took her hand. "I'm not going without you. I have a plan. My jeans should fit you well enough. I have an old shirt, jacket, and hat you can wear. There's an abandoned sheepherder's cabin at the creek where you can change clothes. Will you do it, Josie? I'd love more than anything for you to be free again, to be able to hike as you did this summer. No one goes there in November. I think I can guarantee you'll be safe. If we should meet someone, you'll be my weird cousin from Kansas."

"I thought you were going to go without me." She leaned into him, "I didn't want you to leave me."

"Oh, Josie. I told you I wouldn't make you sad about hiking with me when you can't do that in a skirt. I wanted the disguise to be a surprise. You may be cross with me."

She sat up straight. "I'm not <u>cross</u>. You'd been talking about being attracted to me like a magnet and I thought you hadn't meant it the way I wanted you to."

He held her hands. "I never want to make you sad. I'm glad you want to be with me, though."

"Without you I would be lonely. I don't want to be and I don't want you to be either."

"That would be nice, not to be lonely." He studied her face. "Lonely, not from want of people, but from missing a person I care about."

She had come to Denver fearing she would be rejected. She had tried to protect her heart from what she feared would be an eventual disappointment. His surprise refreshed those feelings of vulnerability. Contrite, she said. "I fear I care too much."

"Don't be afraid. I'll try to take care of your tender heart."

"I don't want to be taken care of. I don't want pity." *I think I sounded ungrateful.*

There's that independent streak. "I will take care of your heart out of affection, not pity."

"There is a difference," she said, trying to justify her response.

"Indeed." His look was gentle. *I've a lot to learn.*

"I want to earn your affection." She felt further clarification was necessary.

She's going to be a great feminist. "And I yours."

"I do want to hike with you, even as Joe. I'll love being free and taking long strides to keep up. It will feel so good, especially if you'll remember I'm Josie." She looked at him asking for confirmation.

"I could never forget." *Joe may have been less complicated, though.*

"It's probably getting late."

"Yup. I'll go unwillingly. Tomorrow at nine?"

"I'll be ready"

"A good night kiss?"

"Please."

As he walked away, he turned, pointed to the stars, and waved. *It's a little like walking on thin ice. I hope she'll give me time to figure this out before I fall through.*

Up at seven, washed and into the kitchen before Aunt Janet appeared, Josie had a chance to look around unobserved. The kitchen was spotless and a model of efficiency. A large table usually occupied the center of kitchens and was the dominant feature. Not at Aunt Janet's. The round eating table was large enough for her family of five and in a bay window, close enough to be a part of the kitchen but not something to walk around. The cupboards had doors instead of being open to dust, and there were ample flat surfaces close to the stove, ice box, and sink. Aunt Janet had kept her cook stove instead of modernizing to gas. Josie approved of the choice because she loved the constant warmth of one, although they did need tending and ashes and soot were dirty. Gas was easy, clean, and on when one wanted it on. She understood why Maggie had gone to gas.

She was kneeling to build the fire when Aunt Janet came in. "Good morning, Josie. Did you sleep well after that nuisance left?"

Laughing because there was such good will in her voice, Josie said, "Yes, I finally got rid of him about ten-thirty."

"They can be such pests when they're falling in love."

Startled, Josie looked up, blushed, and said, "I don't think he is."

"Is which? A pest or falling in love?"

Completely flustered, her face hot with embarrassment, she answered, "Neither."

Equally surprised, Aunt Janet said, "My dear girl, he's over the moon for you. Open your eyes."

"I guess I don't know what to look for."

"How did your other sweethearts look when they fell in love with you?"

"I've never had a sweetheart."

"Not even a puppy-love?"

"My father wouldn't have allowed it."

"Most fathers aren't consulted."

"I guess no one ever wanted me for a sweetheart before."

"You two are a pair." Aunt Janet picked up Josie's face and looked at it. "I believe you're innocent of how you appear."

"I'm very aware of how I look. I know I'm plain."

"You're judging your appearance by your reflection in the mirror, aren't you?

"How else would one see their reflection?"

"By the way people look back at you."

"I don't understand."

"No, I don't think you do. You have an alive, interested, open face with a smile that melts hearts, and you've surely melted his."

"He hasn't said anything like that."

"Well, he will. I hope you can say the same thing to him. It would mean the world to him that you love him too."

"Oh, Mrs. McNown, we've only spent five days together, counting yesterday. We're still getting to know one another."

"You've been writing for several months, I believe."

"Yes. He's written me wonderful letters. I've seen his sense of humor. He's shared his thoughts about life and the people he's observed."

"And you've shared your thoughts with him?"

"We've tried to be honest."

"And you like how he thinks?"

"I find his mind interesting and unusual and, yes, I like how he thinks ever so much."

"And he wanted you to meet his family and, coincidentally, to spend time with him?"

"Yes. He sent me the tickets. To be honest, I was afraid to meet his family, but I did want to spend time with him. I wanted to know him better than letters let me know. We did have those days camping when he didn't know my name, so I got to know how kind and intelligent he is. He didn't do those manly stunts I've heard men do to impress a girl. I think that's very much in his favor, don't you?"

With that, Aunt Janet laughed heartily. "Very much in his favor. Now, let's have breakfast before he shows up to ruin our little talk."

All this while Aunt Janet had been putting the coffee pot on, stirring oatmeal, handing Josie plates, cups, and spoons for the table.

"Do you eat on this pretty cloth or should I remove it?" Josie asked.

"It washes. We eat on it. It's my token elegance."

"Your whole home is elegant. I've never been in such a beautiful house."

"Thank you. My husband wanted fine things. It mattered to him what people thought of us. The General didn't give a hoot about that. She cared we covered the bills."

"Please tell me about your husband." They sat down to their breakfasts.

"Here. The roll you didn't eat when you didn't come home to change. What happened with that?"

"Mrs. Allan said they'd seen me as I am and Mr. Allan said I didn't need a pretty dress to do the dishes, I should save it for tomorrow night. Andrew's taking us to the hotel for dinner."

"Ah. A romantic evening. I wonder who suggested that to him?"

Josie laughed. "He said he's inexperienced with women."

"A typical male. He underestimates his ignorance. You'll have to help him navigate this, I'm afraid."

"How can I help? I'm more ignorant that he."

"Instinct. They get the mating part, not the courtship part."

Josie's face flamed again. She had no idea what "mating part" meant. She suspected it was something she wasn't supposed to know, let alone talk about.

Aunt Janet read her face. She reached over and patted her hand. "That comes later, don't worry about it now. Maggie and I'll help you when the time comes. We know you don't have a mother to see you through what we call, 'the trials.'" She read the fright in Josie's face. "No, no. Don't let me scare you. That's a family joke. They're trials for some women. If you have a nice man, and Andy is surely a nice man, and his father will insure he's an informed one, then it's nothing to worry about. We'll guide you through it. You can count on us."

"Thank you. I do miss asking my mother questions. I have only Zona now."

"Who's Zona?"

"The postmistress in Meredith. She and her husband are what they call 'Roosians'. They came from Russia but speak German so they're called Volga Germans. I'm not sure about that history. She came over as a child and worked in a factory until she was fourteen, then she came to Colorado to help take care of her aunt's new triplets. She's rough around the edges, as my mother would say. She has a great heart, a big laugh, and has been very kind to me. She and Otto have five kids."

"Her advice will be like ours, more plainly spoken, I imagine. I'm glad you have Zona. Her advice is bound to be down-to-earth."

"She was nervous about Andrew to begin with. Once she saw him and saw how often he writes, I think she understands now how nice he is."

"You do appreciate your camping trip and the letters you've exchanged have let you get to know each other better than almost anyone gets to know someone before they marry them, don't you?"

"No. I didn't know that. How well did you know Mr. McNown before you married him?"

"Mr. McNown was a widower who took his meals at the boarding house. He asked me to go for walks with him after dinner. His talk was frivolous and topical, as it would be, I suppose, with a nineteen-year-old girl. After a few months of this he asked me to marry him and I did. I was desperate to leave the boarding house and get out from under my mother's thumb."

"Did you find him admirable?"

"I had no idea who he was. It turned out he was not unkind, not particularly contemplative, an indifferent father, socially accepted, and he did make money with his general store, so he provided well for us. He was fifteen years older than I, died at sixty, left me with a prosperous business and three nearly grown girls."

"You apparently managed."

She nodded. "With help. The General sold the boarding house, took over the general store, and made it larger and more profitable by the time she died. I worked alongside her, but the business sense was hers. One of my daughter's husbands now runs it. It provides a nice income for the family."

"But you didn't know him?" This troubled Josie, to not know one's husband yet to share a life with him.

"No, never did. He worked hard, came home at night, and read the paper. We didn't argue because there was nothing to argue over. He provided for us, was a respected businessman, and I tried to do my part. But Josie, I was never truly in love with him, nor he with me."

"That seems sad," Josie sad, "not to love each other."

"I'm not saying we didn't love each other in our way. I mourned when he died. We had developed a working relationship and were comfortable with each other, but there was little passion. I hope you'll cherish being loved and loving back and work to keep that part of your relationship alive. It makes life richer. It gives it meaning. I see Maggie and Angus and how they love one another, and I wish I'd known that kind of love."

Josie stared out the window. "I don't know if my mother ever knew my father. When she was dying, he was very kind to her. I believe he loved her and she loved him. I don't know if they ever acknowledged what they felt."

Aunt Janet patted Josie's hand. "Much goes unsaid that should be said. If you and Andy can love joyfully and understand the value of that, you are miles ahead of most."

Nodding in assent, Josie, trying to eat her oatmeal, had too many questions racing through her mind. "I hope I remember everything you've told me. I want so much to give a complete love. Do you know what I mean? Or do I know what I mean?"

Studying her earnest face, Aunt Janet nodded. "I think we understand each other and whether you understand yourself or not, I can't say. You have good instincts and if you get the right man, I believe you'll love him completely."

Watching her carefully, Aunt Janet changed the subject. "So, tell me about Maggie's dinner."

Brought back to the moment, Josie smiled as if to thank Aunt Janet. "It was not only delicious, it was beautiful. She had a lace tablecloth, nice dishes, and the turkey was golden brown. We had green beans with bacon on them, mashed potatoes, dressing, gravy, cranberry sauce, sweet potatoes, tomato aspic, and rolls. Have I forgotten anything?"

"Pumpkin pie with whipped cream?"

"How could I forget that?"

"It was good?"

"Perfect."

"She can be a good cook when she wants to be. She wanted to make a good show for Andy. She was probably worn out when it was over."

"Mr. Allan gave her a foot rub." Josie blushed at the remembrance.

"What a lucky gal she is."

"They seem very considerate of each other."

"Yes. Andy has a good example to follow."

What could she do but nod? "Your daughters. Are they all near?"

"Here in Golden or Denver."

Josie grinned. "And whose traits did they inherit?"

Aunt Janet laughed, "Harriet is like her father in that she is very self-contained and doesn't need anyone else to complete her. Eleanor is a little general who tries to organize us. Imagine. Organizing me! We clash a bit and always have. The little one, Ida Louisa, is sweet and loving like my father. She keeps peace in the family."

"They married good companions?" It was on Josie's mind.

"Their husbands are a mixed bag. The general married my father, so to speak, and drives him like a mule. The closed one, Harriet, has an ambitious husband who runs the store and makes us all happy with his industry. The sweet one has a dear husband, thank heaven, and they're happy together."

"Does it ever amaze you children from the same mother and father can be so different, even opposite, sometimes?"

"Wait until you meet Andy's brothers."

"I've only heard their names."

"Edward and Steven. Edward is rather dull. A lawyer by trade. Steady, reliable, boring, predictable. His wife, May, is a mirror-image. I can't imagine what their life is like, although they have produced several children, perfunctorily, I imagine. He's seven years older than Andy."

"A typical oldest child, wouldn't you say?" Josie smirked.

"Don't forget whom you're talking to," Aunt Janet laughed.

"Oh, you're right. I was truly thinking of myself, though. I've been the bossy big sister to my little sisters. The twins never took on that big brother role. What about Andrew's other brother?"

"Steve. He's three years older, a hellion and hasn't gotten much better as he's aged. He's been in a couple of misadventures, financially. He married a darling girl who truly loved him, and he loved her. Unfortunately, he had a dalliance with a woman who worked in his office. His wife found out and left him, brokenhearted."

"Poor girl. I can't say I blame her."

"I suppose not, but this is something you need to know, Josie. Men have trouble with faithfulness. They do stupid things that can ruin their lives for a little fling with a woman they don't necessarily like. Steve would have gone back to his wife in a heartbeat. She would have none of it. She lives a lonely, sad life now. He married the woman-of-distraction, Bertha, who is a social climber who thought she was marrying money and is bitter to still be common. Steve doesn't enjoy being with her. If his first wife had swallowed her pride, if he'd been sincerely contrite, they may have put it back together. Never wholly. But maybe they'd be happier than they are now. Remember, men are distractible. It may not mean anything more than that."

"Does everyone get along when you're together?"

"It's as you'd imagine. Men in a corner talking business: Steve promoting some hare-brained scheme he wants others to invest in; Edward droning on why it won't work; my sweet son-in-law trying to keep his mouth shut and out of the fray; the other two arguing against Edward and Steve; and Angus and Andy out star-gazing."

"What do the women do?" Josie was curious about her future role.

"The women are in the kitchen working on food: Eleanor ordering everyone around; Edward's wife, May, always doing 'her share'; Bertha, hiding out, hating the kitchen work she'd like to be above; Harriet giving her cousins-in-law the cold shoulder; Ida Louisa smiling and laughing to break the tension; and Maggie and I trying to avoid the scene. But there's no disagreement, only confusion and mild dislike among some of them. It works, the way family gatherings work."

"I've been watching how families get along, or in some cases, don't. Ours was a subdued family when my father was home. We had no relatives in the States. In Meredith, families have come from all over the globe and yet I don't think that determines the way they behave. Some people are loving, others are not. One person can ruin the stew; one person can make it work. It fascinates me."

"You mentioned sisters?"

"Two. Younger than I. We're close, more so since Mother died. I'm the headstrong one, but I think in a different way from the General. I don't want to be in charge, just not bent by other people's will." She dropped her eyes. "I have warned Andrew about this stubborn streak."

Aunt Janet's eyes twinkled. *I think Andy may have his hands full.* "You have brothers?"

"I had older brothers, twins. Very alike and adventuresome. They're not with us anymore. They died two years ago in Panama working on the canal."

"Both of them?"

"Walker died from yellow fever and Frank shortly after in a construction accident. Frank was waiting for passage to come home. Maybe he was lost without Walker."

"How tragic. Your poor father. How has he handled their deaths?"

"With silence. He has begun to build a miniature sailing ship. It is tedious, solitary work and absorbs him. I was glad to escape the house. We living didn't seem to matter, only the dead. The past six years have been terrible for him and I try to remember that when he raises my hackles."

Her eyebrows lifted, Aunt Janet asked, "You have hackles?"

"I try to quell them; sometimes they overwhelm my good judgment."

"Sometimes it's good to let 'em rip. Clears the air."

They laughed together at this, knowing women rarely have the opportunity to let 'em rip.

Her coffee gone, oatmeal eaten, the roll left on her plate, Josie stood. "May I do the dishes before Andrew arrives, please. And may I take this roll with us, so he can have part of it?"

"I didn't realize you were saving it. I wouldn't have eaten mine, but he's had them before. Yes, take it, and we'll do dishes together."

The doorbell rang as they finished. "I don't remember his being so formal before. He always pounded on the back door and came in. Well, this good behavior is an interesting change." She chuckled, "I doubt it will last and I have to say, I hope it doesn't."

She left Josie to finish. "Andrew, how nice to see you. We weren't expecting you." She laughed heartily.

"I've come to fetch a young lady to haul her off into the woods for unseemly purposes."

"Shame on you. The young lady I know, will resist unseemly overtures."

"Okay. Maybe take her for a hike?"

"Better. Do you have a picnic, or do you need one?"

"I foraged in the ice box and came up with delicacies. Mom oversaw the process and says I have a balanced meal. She thought Josie might want more than turkey and dill pickles."

"She has a roll to share. What else do you have?"

"Mom sent a couple of apples, some cheese, two jars of water, and cookies."

"Good girl. I thought you cooked on your excursions. Where did those culinary skills go?"

"I wasn't distracted by unseemly thoughts then."

"Get on with you. Go claim that innocent child and behave yourself. Or have you heard that already today?"

"A version of it."

A heavy sigh. "It is always thus and always ignored."

They went to the kitchen where Josie was hanging up the dishtowel.

"Good morning, Andrew." Her smile delighted him.

"Good morning, sweet Josie. Are you going to tell me to behave myself as well?"

"Why, no. Why wouldn't you behave yourself?"

Aunt Janet answered for him. "Because he's a male and you're not."

Here came the blushes rushing up her neck and onto her cheeks. "I'll be ready in a minute."

As Aunt Janet watched her go, she shook her head. "She's as naive as a newborn. Please, Andy, don't break her heart. She's a lovely girl."

"I know. I won't. It's more likely she'll break mine when she finds how feckless I am."

"Oh, please. You have so much to give, Andy, make sure you give it well."

He nodded. "I'll try."

Josie reappeared in her roughest skirt, carrying boots she had worn on the train.

"You don't have a coat, dear. Remember, it's November."

"She won't need one. I have an old one for her."

"Your mother's?"

Andrew's turn to blush. "No. Mine."

Aunt Janet looked from him to Josie, "Why would she want to wear your old coat?"

"Because," Josie spoke up, "I'm going to hike with him and he's lending me some of his clothes, so I can be free. The way I was this summer. He said no one will see me, or if they do, I can be his cousin from Kansas." She looked at Andrew whose mouth was hanging open. "She knows, Andrew. I couldn't lie to her."

"Have fun. Watch out for that sheepherder's ghost. I hear he's a Peeping Tom."

Completely befuddled, Andrew looked from one woman to the other and back again. He would never understand them.

"Go on. You're wasting time." She turned him around and headed him out the door. Josie grabbed the roll as she and Aunt Janet laughed at him.

Into the buggy, properly separated from each other for the sake of prying eyes, Prince clucked up, they headed out of town. Andrew, quiet, pensive, asked Josie. "Why did you tell her?"

"She commented on your outrageous tale of my threatening to shoot you. It was too confusing so I told the truth. She was delighted and said I should tell your mother because she would love it." She watched his expression. "I didn't tell your mother."

"She wasn't appalled we spent four days together unchaperoned?"

"Didn't seem to be. Because you were a gentleman even when you knew I was a girl."

"Then why are they telling me to be a gentleman now, as if I wouldn't be?"

"They know you will be. I know you will be. You are a gentleman, Andrew."

"They act as if a man can't be a man and a gentleman at the same time."

"I'm confused too. There have been hints that I don't understand all there is to know. I hope you'll explain what they're talking about."

He slipped his arm around her waist and drew her closer. "I'm not sure I'm the one to explain what I don't know. Someday we can discuss it. Today, let's go for a hike, a picnic and enjoy ourselves. I will be a gentleman and you will be my lady. Is that a deal?"

"It's a deal, if a lady can wear a man's pants." The seriousness over, they laughed as they followed the road north out of town and started up Golden Gate Canyon.

They rode in silence for a while until Josie, frowning, said, "Andrew?"

He chuckled nervously, "Yes, Josie."

"When I was in normal school they would occasionally bring in entertainment for us and one night it was a couple who did

216

fancy dancing. When it was over, all I could think was they had practiced a lot. Last night I felt like I was stepping on your toes or not twirling when I was supposed to. After you left I thought, this is going to take some practice and until we get our steps down we're going to stumble over each other. Especially because I've never danced before. What I'm asking for is patience on your part. I've been the bossy big sister for six years and a teacher for one and I'm not used to being a partner. Will you please help me learn?"

He put his arms around her and held her. "We both have to learn. You to guard your toes from my big feet and I to learn to catch you when you twirl. But we can figure it out and someday we'll dance our shoes off. Okay?"

She nodded and snuggled into him.

They reached the turn-off to Cedar Creek sooner than Josie thought they would. "Are you sure people won't be here for an outing?"

"You'd be surprised how few people go outdoors when they don't have to."

"Especially in November, I suppose. It's not like it's a summer day."

"No. But we did get a sunny day. The cool air should make hiking pleasant."

He pulled the buggy under a tree, helped Josie out, put a feed bag on Prince and unloaded the picnic. Pointing to the sheepherder's cabin he handed Josie the change in clothes. "You'll probably have deep cuffs on your pants and need to roll up the sleeves. That'll make you stylish, okay?" He walked with her to the cabin, looked around inside to make sure it was safe. "I'll take Prince for a drink and we'll be off."

When she came out, she was a young boy with worn out, dragging pants, a belt gathering them unnaturally at the waist, a shirt that was too large and a hat. She was delighted. "They work, Andrew. Joe is ready to go."

Josie put on the coat and had to laugh. Although she'd never been to a circus, she knew she looked like a clown. It didn't matter. She was free to hike with her favorite companion.

"You're even more dapper than I remember you from this summer and that's saying a lot."

"Thank you. I'm sorry you can't wear my clothes, so I could laugh at you too."

"I'm not laughing at you. I'm laughing with you. Or don't you think you look comical?"

"I'm glad I don't have a mirror handy."

"I'll be your mirror. You look fetching. You light up my heart." As he kissed her the hat fell off and her hair tumbled out. "The first time I saw your hair I realized you were a girl. A surprise, but I'm glad your braid betrayed you."

"You were different after you knew. You went from mountain man to gentleman. I liked both Andrews. I'm lucky it turned out so well."

She stuffed her hair under the hat, he rolled up her cuffs, and they were off. It wasn't a steep trail; it was rocky, worn by years of sheep's cloven hooves on their way to higher pastures. It was surprising how often they had to stop to talk. Josie was full of questions about rocks, trees, and the few birds that remained for winter. Every answer was punctuated with a kiss.

"Do you mind I kiss you so often? Is that what they were talking about?"

"I'm not sure what they were talking about. It can't be something so pleasant."

"Good," he kissed her again. "Are you game to go to the top of Mount Galbraith, it's a way yet?"

"It feels good to be out in the fresh air hiking with you. I don't care if we never stop."

"You'll probably change your mind after a while. If you're up for it, though, we'll keep climbing."

So much walking tested her legs. Since they were in foothills and not mountains, the altitude was in her favor. It was surprising what a difference three thousand feet made. "Andrew?"

"Yes, Josie?"

"Do you remember?

'How do you like to go up in a swing,
Up in the air so blue?
Oh, I do think it the pleasantest thing
Ever a child can do!'"

He picked it up from her.

"'Up in the air and over the wall,

> *Till I can see so wide,*
> *Rivers and trees and cattle and all*
> *Over the countryside'"*

They finished it together:
> *"'Till I look down on the garden green*
> *Down on the roof so brown*
> *Up in the air I go flying again,*
> *Up in the air and down!'"*

Laughing, they held each other. "Oh, Andrew, don't you feel like we're going up in a swing when we climb like this. That when we reach the top we'll be able to *'see so wide, rivers and trees and cattle and all, over the country side?'"*

"I'd never thought of it that way. You're right. We are on the upswing, so to speak. Josie, Josie, you do make me open my eyes wider."

"And you take me places that let me see." This necessitated another hug and kiss.

Andrew realized he wasn't feeling gentlemanly. All this kissing was giving him thoughts he knew he shouldn't have. Feelings that had come to him in the night, but without a person to focus on, now were coming over him with a very specific person in mind. He looked at Josie and knew they'd better move along.

"Is there something wrong, Andrew?"

"No. Nothing's wrong. I'm thinking we'd better get a move on, that's all."

She was confused. She loved his hugs and kisses and the feelings they gave her were feelings she'd never had before, exciting, but kind of scary. *Is he having these same feelings? Are they frightening to him too?*

They had been hiking as fast as she wanted to go. It had been a pleasant pace and they had taken time to share many things. Now he wanted to hurry. Why?

After striding out, leaving her behind, he stopped, turned, and waited for her to catch up. Taking her in his arms, he held her for a few moments before he said anything. "What I'm running from, Josie, is an overwhelming feeling of love for you. I love you. I want to be with you. I've been acting like I'm falling in love with you when I fell hopelessly in love with you months ago."

The expression on his face was pained, tender, confused. She wanted to cradle him in her arms and tell him it was all right. "I love you too, Andrew. I fell in love with you at Savage Lakes. I didn't dare dream you would love me too."

"You knew so soon?"

"I knew who you really are. I was afraid you'd romanticize me as some daring, courageous woman who flaunted society's rules. I wasn't sure you'd love plain, dull me."

"I suppose for some that was a possibility, but I could see the softness of your heart and the inquisitiveness of your mind, even in that hat. You'll remember I came to find you. I was in love with you by the little lake. You didn't have to convince me who you are. I knew. Every letter and these past two days, you've made me love you more. You've assured me I'm right to love you."

She closed her eyes, expecting a kiss. "I can't kiss and hug you anymore, Josie, and still be a gentleman. Trust me on this. The old gals knew what they were talking about."

She opened her eyes, surprised. "What do you mean?"

"It's complicated. We can discuss it much later."

Shaking her head, "No, Andrew. We can't keep secrets. Everyone is talking around me as if I'm a child and can't understand. I need you to explain this to me. You've got opinions on the Civil War, child labor, religion. You know about stars, rocks, birds, and flowers but your feelings for me are too complicated for me to understand. I have to hear about them much later?"

"Please, Josie, don't do this to me."

"To you?" She folded her arms across her chest. "I'm old enough to know this stuff." He had no choice but to hold her.

"I'll try my best at lunch. I'll have to think what to say. You have no idea what you're asking of me." *No idea. And I have no idea how to get out of this mess.*

She pulled away from him and looked at the frightened expression on his face. "Maybe we can go slowly with the explanation. If you'll begin it, I'll try to grasp what you're saying."

He nodded, looking distressed. "Let's get to the top, have lunch and see what happens." *Being a guy in love is different from being a girl in love, I'm thinking. One step forward, two steps back.*

They climbed on silently, joy gone, curiosity dimmed. *What have I asked that's so terrible? Why are there things he can know, I can't? We're in love. We've said so. Isn't love all we need to solve our problems if we're honest with each other? Am I twirling out of control?*

Reaching the top of Mount Galbraith, Andrew turned to her. "The view is very nice from here, don't you think?" *That was insipid.*

"Yes. It's beautiful." *We're back to where we were when I got off the train. I've ruined our outing.* "Andrew, I don't want to know. It's not worth it if we can't be friends."

He took her hands in his and studied her face. "No. I owe you an explanation. Let's sit down where we can talk."

They found a soft, dried grass knoll and made themselves comfortable. He pulled out the picnic and offered her some turkey, pickles, cheese, the roll, an apple, and a jar of water.

They picked at their food and he began. "I don't know what you know about men, Josie, or for that matter, women, but I assure you, I don't know about women. I don't know if you know how babies are made?" He couldn't look at her.

"I know the rooster gets on top of the hen and after a while there are eggs with chicks in them. I don't know anything about the process."

He sighed. "That's a step forward. Josie, men and women make babies much the same way." His face turned bright red as he said this. "I can't do this, Josie, I really can't. It's all so strange what happens between men and women and it makes no sense when you're trying to explain it so I'm either going to frighten you, make you sick to your stomach or something horrible. I can't go on."

She reached for his hand. "Then don't. Aunt Janet said she and your mother would explain things to me, so I'll wait. I didn't know it would be so awful for you. I'm sorry."

"I want to be truthful; this isn't about truth. I don't know enough myself except what I've heard guys talk about and feelings I've had I'm not proud of. It's hard to explain to someone I want to think fondly of me and not think I'm some kind of pervert." He looked at her solemnly. "I think women think most men are perverts, which probably is true. It's also the nature we're born with and women don't really understand us any more than we understand them."

"I promise I'll leave you alone if you can tell me why you can't hug and kiss me anymore."

"Okay, so now I convince you I'm a pervert." He put his head in his hands and rubbed his hair. He talked very slowly and deliberately. "When I hold you and kiss you, I get feelings inside of me that make me want to touch you," he paused, "in inappropriate places and my body reacts in an embarrassing way." He looked at her, his hands clenched he was so distressed. He blurted out quickly, "I want to make love to you. I want to know you as every man wants to know the woman he loves, which is intimately and as close as they can be." He didn't look up. He started packing the lunch, "Let's go. I'll take you home."

"I don't want to go home unless you want to be rid of me. I've had feelings too, Andrew, that I don't understand. I've wanted you to caress me and hold me very close to your body. I've been ashamed of those feelings. Maybe we shouldn't deny what we feel. Maybe what the old gals were telling us was to be careful we don't get carried away. Can't we figure out when we're getting too close to the edge of that precipice?"

He couldn't believe what he was hearing. "You aren't disgusted with me?"

"Oh, no, Andrew. You were honest with me, so I can be honest with you. I still have many questions, but I see you don't want to answer them. I was wrong to ask you. Had I known a part of what you told me I wouldn't have asked so persistently. But, if you feel what you said, and I feel what I know, don't other people feel the same, and if they do, then why does it embarrass us?"

"I need to hold my Grand Inquisitor. Please sit close beside me. I'll write you a long letter on why people deny themselves what makes them happy. You'll be surprised I have an opinion on that. To be brief, though, it's what the church tells everyone: If it's good; it's bad."

They were able to laugh together and with great affection, gazing lovingly into each other's eyes. "Eat, Miss Carter. I didn't carry this food up here to carry it out."

They began their picnic in earnest, enjoying the view and their surroundings. Josie had completely forgotten her disguise until she looked down at her pants.

"I'm thinking you wouldn't have had trouble explaining things to Joe. I should have asked in my deep voice."

"Oh, I'm not so sure it would have mattered. Unless a man's bragging about his prowess, he really doesn't want to talk about it very much. Everyone wishes someone else would do the explaining so it doesn't get personal. There's a lot of ignorance about all this, is my guess, and I have more than my share, and I'm guessing you have a double load. We'll figure it out, Josie. Let the women help you then you can help me. I'm not sure my dad will be much use to me. As I said, men don't want to talk about it much. We assume everyone knows more than we do."

"I'll look forward to figuring it out with you. I know you'll be kind, gentle and, yes, a man. I wouldn't want you any other way." She put her head in his lap and looked at the sky. "'*Up in the air so blue, I do think it the pleasantest thing ever a child can do.*'"

He bent and kissed her as she wanted him to.

They were silent a while, trying to figure out what had happened, going over what they had said, what they wish they had said instead, what the other one had said and why had they said it that way.

"Andrew?"

"Yes?"

"I know I promised no more questions, but I still have one."

"And you <u>will</u> ask it."

"How do you know you want to make love to me?"

"It's a strong feeling I have."

"Like being hungry?"

"No. Yes. Like being hungry then having an ice cream cone only better. I think it would make me feel very good and maybe it would make you feel good too. I don't know."

"I can't imagine that feeling, can you?"

He stared off into space without answering her. He could feel heat rising in his neck and up his cheeks.

She repeated her question. "Can you imagine that feeling, Andrew?"

"A little. It will be very different if I'm with you and we love each other."

"Different from what?" She frowned.

"You seem determined to make me a pervert."

"How?"

"By making me admit shameful behavior."

"What behavior?" Her eyes danced with mischievousness.

He stared into space. "Okay. Here we go. We used to go to church. I was about fourteen, I suppose, and beginning to be uncomfortable with many of the sermons the minister preached, such as denying evolution and insisting on the creation of the universe in seven days, because I had read about science in books I got for presents. I started asking my folks questions they had no answers for and that made me wonder, because I thought my parents were smart. Then one Sunday the minister asked all of us young boys to go to another room for a lecture and he told us what was sinful and how we should pray to prevent shameful behavior. He told us about the sanctity of marriage and how we had to protect the innocence of women. Most of it was over my head. So later I asked Steve what the minister was talking about. I will say he thought it was funny and did tell me. Of course, I tried it and it was nice and it didn't seem shameful to me. Who cares? was all I could think. Shortly after that, we quit going to church because the church ladies took a strong stand against women's suffrage and my mother was outraged, so I got out of the science confusion. The sinful part has lingered. Now don't ask me what I'm talking about. That's as far as I'm going to go."

"Maybe Mr. Miller will tell me," she said with a twinkle in her eyes.

"Don't you dare do that to that old man."

"I won't. I'll ask Aunt Janet what you're doing that's so shameful."

"Josie, this isn't funny. Well, it is, sort of. The way we let stupid, old messages haunt us."

"Pretend I'm a prodigy boy minister, and I tell you whatever you're doing that you think is naughty is what you're supposed to do. Would you like that?" she grinned.

"I would, because I would want to believe you, but I wouldn't, because you're only a boy and what do you know? You're probably the devil incarnate. It's easy to spot him. He's a woman who dresses as a boy and leads real boys astray."

"I want to lead you astray."

"Don't say that out loud."

"Andrew?"

"No more! You promised."

"Someday, will you tell me?"

"Go away, devil."

"The way to get rid of devils is to kiss them so they can't talk."

He kissed her passionately, then pushed her away. "You really may be the devil."

She smiled impishly, then started to nestle her head back into his lap.

"No," he said sharply and quickly rolled over onto his stomach, perched on his elbows.

Surprised, she said, "No?"

"I mean, let's lie on the grass next to each other and look at the sky."

"I love you, Andrew Allan. I really do. Do you know it was less than twenty-four hours ago we had our first kiss and you're already telling me how to make babies?"

He groaned. "Aunt Janet will find that interesting, I'm sure. She'll call my mom and ask her how I know. Josie?"

"Yes, Andrew?"

"When did you become such a tease? You were a nice girl last summer who asked reasonable questions. You acted as if you enjoyed learning what I know about nature. Now, you get pleasure by making me miserable all the while telling me you love me. Which Josie is the real one?"

"Which Josie do you love?"

"The one who makes me look good and not dumb and bad."

"I'll have to decide which one is more fun, I suppose, and see if you still love me."

He rolled over to look at her. "I'll love all my Josies. Even the one in boy's clothes, but they'll have to know that people who tease usually get teased back."

"Do you know, Andrew, I've never teased before? Why do you make me want to be naughty?"

"It's been bottled up, I guess, but it seems to come naturally, almost joyfully."

"Umm hmm. Very joyfully."

He answered her with:

"*Happy hearts and happy faces,*
Happy play in grassy places'

something, something,

'*But the unkind and the unruly,*'

they don't end so well. Remember? So, Josie, if you insist on being unruly, you must hope, '*not for glory, but a different story.*' That's how it goes. Are you certain you want to take this naughty path?"

"Does one have to choose a path, or can one wander through life, enjoying many different scenes, many places to explore, many ways to behave?"

"If you wander holding my hand, will I ruin it for you?"

"You will make it possible."

"I will relish holding your hand."

"And I, yours."

They were quiet, lying in the sun and crisp air. The love of life, the tranquility they now felt with one another, seemed to cast a blanket of well-being over them. Neither had ever felt the serenity that comes with the assurance of love and acceptance. Andrew broke the spell.

"Josie?"

"Yes, Andrew."

"We probably ought to go. They're expecting us around five-thirty and it's three now."

"Oh. I forgot. I'm so happy here. Can we stay?"

"We don't have to go. We can offend everyone."

"It's that black and white, isn't it?"

"Probably."

"They'll never know what we've given up for them."

"My parents would, I think."

"Okay. Let's go. Back to the world of meeting expectations set by others."

"Maybe we'll be able to set our own expectations soon. Would you like that?"

"I would."

He got up, extended his hand to her and they packed the remnants of the picnic and headed downhill. It was a quick trip out, not so many questions. Andrew put the harness on Prince and put him in the shafts while Josie resumed her feminine identity. It was four o'clock.

"I rather expect you'll behave better, now you're a lady."

"I expect you'll start being a gentleman and quit talking about shameful things you do."

Andrew shook his head. *It's confusing but fun.*

They reached Aunt Janet's in ample time for Josie to wash and change into her good dress. She insisted to Andrew she and Aunt Janet could make the few blocks to his house without an escort and he left. After Aunt Janet was assured that no one saw her in Andrew's clothes and heard a little, but not all, about their day, the two women headed out. Josie was anxious to see how the two strong-willed sisters related to one another, and how the two men fit into the picture when the women were together.

Aunt Janet knocked on the door and walked in. "We're here. Everyone at attention, please."

There was laughter and Angus, Maggie, and Andrew came to the entry to greet them.

"Come in, come in. We've been awaiting your procession." More laughter and surprising good humor, Josie felt. She had expected a certain amount of rivalry from the way Aunt Janet talked about the family, and how Andrew said she'd always been in charge, but the dominance didn't evince itself–at least yet. Maggie said they would have a drink of cider in the parlor before dinner, then it would be a first-come-first-served free-for-all in the kitchen. This news seemed to cheer everyone as they gathered in the parlor for their drink.

"So, Andrew, tell us about your outing."

"Prince agreed to take us out to Cedar Creek, and we hiked to the top of Mount Galbraith and had a picnic. The weather was perfect. Mom made sure we had a nourishing lunch. We had a terrific day, didn't we Josie?"

"A wonderful day. It couldn't have been prettier."

The adults looked at each other. Angus, with a serious look asked, "You took Josie to the top of Mount Galbraith?"

"She's a good hiker."

"Clear to the top?"

"That's where the view is best."

"Josie, did you know you were in for an expedition?"

"I didn't know where we were going, but we had a pleasant walk."

"A walk? Interesting use of the word. I always considered it something of an effort. Maggie, Janet, have you ever <u>walked</u> to the top of Mount Galbraith?"

"I remember your trying to drag me up there once, Angus. Some steep sheep-drive trail or deer path. It was impossible. I kept stepping on the front of my skirt. If I remember correctly, we came down after a short burst of enthusiasm on your part and a long grievance on mine."

"That's how I remember it too, at least the long grievance part." They all enjoyed the jab.

Maggie asked, "Did you have any time to visit or was it all an endurance contest?"

Josie answered to defend Andrew. "We had some very nice talks. Andrew knows so much about this country he makes it fun to explore."

Aunt Janet's turn to interrogate. "What does Andrew explain to you?"

"About trees, for instance. They're not cedars at all, they're junipers. America has no cedars, he said."

"Really?" Angus, smirked. "Then what are those shingles we put on roofs?'

Andrew looked a little pained. "They're red cedar from the West Coast. But they're not really cedars; they're Cyprus like the junipers we have here. Real cedars are in other parts of the world."

Angus shook his head. "Where do you get all this stuff?"

"From the books you gave me when I was a kid. Didn't you want me to read them?"

"Not to use in courtship."

Josie piped in again, "We talked about other things as well." She shot Andrew a look of such mischievousness that no one missed it.

His blush was an intense red and he looked at her imploring pity.

She continued, "We talked about geology and what formed the valleys we were looking into. We talked about some of the rocks we saw. He told me some of the history of the ranchers and farmers in the area. All because I asked. I love to understand where I am and how it all fits together. Don't you?"

She looked at each of them and when she came to Andrew she smiled gently to reassure him she would behave. She could see his shoulders sag in relief.

"Well, I guess if it works for you two, who are we to question it?" Maggie said.

Angus raised his glass of juice and toasted the company gathered. "There's nothing like family to keep a person off balance," he shook his head in confusion.

Supper was delicious the way leftovers can be better than the original meal because no one was frazzled, there were no dreaded pots and pans, and everyone relaxed. They sat around the kitchen table and made light conversation, the family finding reasons to tease Josie and Andrew about the hike, their lengthy journey to Aunt Janet's the night before and the tales Prince had shared with them. It seemed Prince was a dependable resource for gossip in the family.

The group's camaraderie and the lack of mean-spirited humor enchanted Josie. She had imagined Maggie as a dour, do-gooder who ruled the family with a forceful personality when, in fact, she had a dry sense of humor and a loving disposition. Angus, who she had imagined would be meek and subservient to Maggie's will, was instead a steady, reliable source of strength for them, more as she imagined Andrew would be. Aunt Janet didn't come across as domineering as she had been portrayed, instead she was a lively and acerbic character. Andrew was the butt of much of their humor because of his tendency to know facts and they could tease him about Josie. This was a family of love and spirit one would want to belong to.

Time for pie and another round of whipping cream. Andrew and Angus observed that everything else had been easy, why did they have to work? No one sympathized with them and work proceeded.

"I have to say, Maggie, your dinner was exceptional." Aunt Janet was sincere and correct, in Josie's mind. She had enjoyed it more than the night before when she was so nervous, and she had been impressed then.

"My Maggie's an exceptional person, and her cooking's part and parcel of that." Angus raised his glass and everyone joined him.

Aunt Janet looked at Angus with affection. "I told Josie, Maggie's a lucky gal to have you, Angus, because you appreciate her. I'm hopeful Andy will be as smart." She looked at Andrew with a critical eye. "I'm hopeful, Andy."

Josie, again, to his rescue. "Andrew is the most appreciative person I've ever known, as well as the most interesting. So, you know, ladies, I heard all about you this summer and he really values who you are and what you've been to him."

Maggie and Aunt Janet spoke at the same time, "Really?" They looked at him in amazement. His mother said, "I didn't think he'd noticed us."

"Andrew can quote whole poems you read to him as a child. He understands where his curiosity came from. You and Mr. Allan were ideal parents and Aunt Janet was a reliable, marvelous friend."

They looked around the table at each other, surprised. Angus spoke up, "Well, Andy, we didn't think you knew where you were most of the time. Seems maybe you did."

"I knew. I suppose I never mentioned it, which I'm ashamed to admit. You're all terrific. Kids forget to acknowledge that, I suppose, being kids."

Everyone was quiet for a minute, perhaps thinking of their children or their own childhoods. Maggie spoke, "You know, Janet, we always made such fun of Momma and how bossy and busy she was. We valued Daddy because he was so easy on us. It was Momma's industry that got us through, and her skills we still use to make our homes. I don't think I ever thanked her, or really, ever took the time to miss her."

Aunt Janet nodded. "John's store would have fallen by the wayside, I'm afraid, if it had been left up to me. I like the unimportant details of it. Momma saved it and made it better for me and the girls. I think I thanked her for that, but not a lot else, and you're right, we owe her a lot for how we live, and to Daddy, too, because he educated us and was gentle, and heaven knows we needed a little of that in our lives."

"Thank you, Josie, for helping us realize some truths we've chosen to ignore," Maggie added.

"But you do. You toast your parents every Thanksgiving."

"In fun. I think we'll do it differently next year. What say you, Janet?"

"I agree. And maybe you'll be so kind as to leave my boast out of it. I think we all know it's a jest as well, not that I don't deserve it."

"Deserve the jest or deserve the boast?" Maggie asked laughing.

"Now that I think about it with less humility, I suppose I do deserve the boast."

They're jolly people. They enjoy a good joke. Josie joined in the laughter and was surprised to see Andrew watching her and not laughing. She stopped. *What's the matter? Did I say something wrong?* He smiled to reassure her, then stood.

"Josie and I are going to do the dishes now. I have a fierce need to be with her. Please excuse us." He came to her chair and helped her out. "Is this all right with you? You don't mind helping, do you?"

"I'd love to help."

The adults watched this exchange and said nothing for a while after they left the table. Everyone was still in the kitchen and it occurred to Maggie they were in the way.

"Let's go to the parlor and get away from this industry. It's making me tired."

Angus and Aunt Janet quickly agreed, and they left, closing the door behind them.

"I thought they'd never go," Andrew growled, grinning. "May I please hold you?"

"Oh, yes."

He held her, then pushed her away. "I really thought you were going to say something awful. Thank you for not embarrassing me."

"I was tempted, but you looked so pained I couldn't do it. I don't think they would have been surprised, though, if I'd said you told me about making babies. They'd think, there goes Andrew again, explaining things."

"Except they didn't give me a book on that. Had they, I would have memorized it!"

"Andrew?"

"Yes, Josie."

"You didn't tell me about making babies. If I'd said so, it would have been a lie."

"Had you said it, though, they would have laughed, or been horrified then laughed, or been horrified and sent me to my room to repent and they would have apologized to you for my bad behavior. But I assure you no one there would have volunteered to tell you in front of the others. I'm going to go to the library to see what I can learn, then I'll tell you in all the gruesome details, with lots of Latin words and medical terms. You still won't know anything, but I'll feel I've done my job."

"You might want to put it in a letter, for both our sakes."

Dish washing and drying kept apace and they finished quickly.

"Go for a walk, Miss?"

"I'm not Mademoiselle tonight?"

"I can't say it. But if you want to be that word, I'll take you for a walk as that."

"I only want to be your Josie."

"That you may be." He reached for her hand.

When they came into the parlor all eyes were on them. "Thank you, kids. That was very nice of you." Angus, having escaped the dishes, was grateful.

"I'd like an escort home. Could I trouble you kids with a walk?" Aunt Janet asked.

"We were thinking how nice a walk would feel. Do you want to come along, Mom and Dad? We might keep going; you could come home without us."

"What a splendid idea, Andy. How about it, Mother?"

"I'm in."

They put on their coats and headed out the door. It was a chatty group that walked the few blocks to Aunt Janet's house.

"I'll leave the door unlocked for you, Josie. Tonight, Andy, your parents may decide when you must have Josie home. Good night, all, and thank you for a lovely evening."

Andrew looked at his parents, expectantly. "We have only two more nights. May we stay out until eleven o'clock tonight?"

Angus spoke up quickly. "You're both over twenty-one. Seems to me you can stay out as late as you like. Let's go, Mother."

"But, what about Janet?"

"She's over twenty-one too. Let's go."

He turned Maggie around and they left. Andrew looked at Josie grinning. "He's not as old as he looks."

They walked down the block then Andrew had an idea. "It's Friday night. There's a saloon in town that's bound to stay open that long. We can go there, get a beer, and find a quiet table and talk. Will you go with me?"

"To a saloon?"

"Is that improper for a lady?"

"I don't know."

"Does your father drink beer?" he asked.

"He has a beer occasionally. I think he'd like one more often. Why?"

"I thought maybe he goes to a saloon. Mine does occasionally. Mom's tending toward the temperance frame of mind."

"But you drink beer?"

"With the guys."

"You don't get drunk, do you?"

"I did once. It's a horrible feeling. Don't worry, I won't get drunk tonight, or maybe ever again."

"I got drunk one night."

"You got drunk?"

"When I first went to Meredith. The Saturday night suppers. People bring beer and chokecherry wine they make. I didn't know anything about either one of them. I didn't like the taste of beer, so I had a glass of wine. I liked it and had another. I didn't realize people were watching me and smirking. Then I had another because I was thirsty, and it tasted good. By the end of the evening, I was reeling, and Zona had to help me to my cabin. I never want that awful feeling again in my life. The whole cabin whirled around me and I couldn't make it stop. I guess it was a great joke, my getting drunk. Some of them still tease me by offering me a glass of wine."

"You haven't had any since?"

"No, thank you. I may someday have one glass. I liked it."

"I'm not sure you can have wine where we're going."

"That's okay. What kind of beer do you drink?"

"In Golden? There's one kind: Coors. It would be ill-advised to order anything else, if there is anything else available."

"Why's that?"

"They make it here and it's the livelihood of a lot of people."

"In Meredith they bring all sorts of beer up from Basalt on the train. We have Swedes, Germans, Italians, Brits. They all drink beer that tastes like home and they argue over which one is best. Not that they've tasted the other fellow's."

They had made their way downtown and Andrew guided her to the saloon. She hesitated when he opened the door for her. *Is this really where we belong?* He looked in then shut the door.

"I'd forgotten how noisy and rowdy it is in there. It didn't seem so bad when I was with the guys. I don't think it's the place for you."

She was relieved. She'd hate for her father to hear she went to a saloon. The door opened and a man came out with a woman wearing a very revealing dress. She had bright rouge on her cheeks and lips. They were laughing loudly until they saw Josie and Andrew.

"Hey, Sweetie, if you're looking for someone to take you home, you're wearing the wrong get-up," the woman jeered as they went past.

Josie blushed. Andrew blushed and pulled her away from the door. "It's definitely not a place for us. And you look perfect."

"Did you know those kinds of people were in there?"

"I'd forgotten. I'm sorry I brought you. Let's get out of here."

"How often do you come here?"

"Not often. Maybe a couple of times a year."

As they walked toward Aunt Janet's house Josie was pensive. *How well do I really know this man? Was he telling me the truth? Who was that woman? Does he know her?*

Sensing trouble, Andrew began to walk faster to calm his nerves. He could feel questions coming. *I'd better pre-empt them. I'd better be smart about this.*

"Josie, I think you're wondering how much I know about what goes on there, right?"

"It crossed my mind." She was curt.

"I've gone there with other guys. I drank too much one time. I don't know any of the women who hang out there. In fact, I'd forgotten about them or I wouldn't have suggested we go there. I don't want you to think bad thoughts about me," he pleaded.

She was silent. He tried again, "Please talk to me."

"I was wondering how well I know you. We can say anything we like in letters and who's to be the wiser about what happens before and after the letter is written?"

"You do know me. You know me from camping. My letters are honest. I study or go to school before and after I write them. I have thought of you constantly since we met. I've told you how distracted I've been. I love you. I don't want another woman in my life–ever. I want you, Josie. I'm sorry I didn't think. I wanted a place to be with you where my family wasn't watching us. It's hard to find an inside place on a November night in Golden. Please hear me."

They had stopped walking and he bent to look at her face. He felt frantic she was imagining him as a cheating phony who had duped her.

"You don't think I'm that kind of girl, do you? I know I went camping by myself and I let you camp near me for four days and we didn't have a chaperone and I didn't leave, but Andrew, I'm not a wicked woman."

"No one knows that better than I do. That woman who said that to you, is a bad woman, don't let what she said mean anything to you. You are the most innocent woman in the world. I know that."

"Are you innocent too?" It was more an indictment than a question.

They walked on silently as he struggled with how honest he could be and not lose her.

"Not completely. One night, not there, in another saloon, a woman sat on my lap and touched me inappropriately and I let her. I'm very sorry I was weak."

"When?"

"Last year. Long before I knew you."

"Did you go back?" *Please say you didn't.*

He swallowed hard. "I did. She didn't come around and I left. I was embarrassed to be there and ashamed of myself."

"Is this why we call you perverts?" She asked, obviously knowing the answer.

"Yes." *Maybe they're right.* He felt defeated.

She nodded. "I knew this morning there were many things I didn't understand. I hoped you would explain. You couldn't, you said. Now, I realize, there are many more things I don't understand. How could you want a woman you don't even know to touch you inappropriately? I wouldn't want a creepy man doing that to me." Her voice was icy and accusatorial.

"No, no you wouldn't. You'd call the sheriff. A man would pay a woman for it. The difference is part of the problem between men and women, I'm beginning to see."

"This is breaking my heart, Andrew, that you'd seek out an awful woman to do that. Maybe even pay her. How can you say you love me when other women can entice you?"

"No one has enticed me since I met you. No one ever will again."

She looked at him with a hard, hateful look. "How do you know?"

"Because you will be all I need."

"Ha!"

"All I'll need, Josie. The other is empty and cheap and shameful. Love is what makes some of the weird things people do okay. I'm not going to promise you there won't be strange things happen between us as man and woman, but they'll be done with love and gentleness and we'll agree about them. Please trust me. I love you with all my heart and mind."

He put his arms around her and drew her close. She was rigid.

"I've never been jealous before. Never had a need to be. It's an ugly feeling, Andrew. Please spare me from it as well as you can. I can't bear the thought of your loving someone else in such a disgusting way." She relaxed a little and he held her closer. "I want to be the only person you love. Is that selfish?"

"No. No. No. A thousand times no. I want to be the only person you love too. Will you forgive me for ruining our evening? It's the last thing I intended to do." *I think I've fallen through the ice.*

"It's not the evening. It's our life. I hoped I'd found someone I wanted to be with forever."

"That's what I want too. Forever, with my Josie. Please let me kiss you."

Standing on the street, partially hidden by the shadow of a tree, the two hopelessly inexperienced lovers tried to regain what they had lost.

They walked slowly down the street, holding hands, remaining silent.

If he truly loves me, and if he means what he said, then other women will be of no interest to him. I know no man could be of interest to me. If he's like other men, and love is something that comes and goes and comes back again, then he'll break my heart over and over and I'd rather have it broken once and be done with it.

Andrew was having his own thoughts. *How can I make her understand even though I love her, other women are going to distract me for a minute? I'll want to look at them, I like the feeling of excitement seeing women gives me, but I don't want those women. Men seek out things that give them a charge. Don't women do that too?*

Andrew spoke, "Maybe we could find a corner at Aunt Janet's house and be quiet together."

She didn't answer for a while. "This may sound unkind; it's not meant to be. I feel so tired and weary I think I'd like to go home and go to bed to try to make sense out of our day. Please don't think I'm angry with you, because I'm not. I don't think I can be at my best right now."

"I understand, Josie, I really do. I feel the same. If we can get a good night's sleep and be together again in the morning, maybe we'll have more energy to figure out things. I'm talking about life, not my love for you. I know about that."

"We'll go home now, okay?"

"Okay."

They went directly to Aunt Janet's house. When they reached the door, Andrew put his arms around Josie and held her close. "Please don't give up on us. We had a rough patch tonight, but we have so much love between us we'll manage this."

"Thank you, Andrew. Good night." She turned to go inside.

"No kiss?" He was overwhelmed with his failure to make her understand.

She turned around and lifted her face.

237

"You don't want one, do you?" he asked.

"I don't know anymore. My heart is confused, and my mind can't make sense of everything I've heard and seen. One minute I love you as always, and the next minute I remember that awful woman and a woman like her touching you and you wanting her to do it again, and I want to run and hide."

"I'm sorry for being a man. I guess that's what you want me to say. Please know this man loves you and this mind loves you. The man may be weak, but the mind is not."

He started to go then turned around. "May I pick you up tomorrow for another picnic or would you rather not see me?"

"Come, if you want. We can decide tomorrow." She opened the door and went in.

Andrew sat on the steps with his head in his hands. He felt helpless. He wanted to crash through the door and beg her to love him. He wanted to be free of guilt people wanted to put on him he didn't feel he deserved. *Why can't she understand? What do I have to say to make her see it was a stupid mistake, one any man my age would make? Why was I so honest with her? She'd never have known if I hadn't told her. We wanted an honest relationship, but it won't work if she can't deal with honesty and see I'm not trying to hurt her. I'm a man doing what men do. Okay, we're perverts. I get it. Can't I love her and be a pervert too? Can't she love a pervert?* He got up and walked home, as low as he could remember being.

Josie closed the door and started down the hall to the stairway then saw a light had been left on for her. As she went into the parlor, Aunt Janet said, "You're home early."

I can't face her. I'll give it all away if she sees me. I have no choice.

"Yes. We were both tired from a busy day, so we thought we'd turn in and get a good night's sleep." Her voice was flat.

"Would you like a cup of hot chocolate and cookies?"

"No thanks. I think I'll go to bed."

"Josie, you are decidedly unhappy. Would you like someone to talk to, or would you rather be alone?"

She burst into tears. "I'm so unhappy. I want my mother. I don't understand men."

"Come here, dear. Sit down next to me and we can talk about them."

Josie crumpled next to Aunt Janet who put her arm around Josie's shoulders and pulled her to her, stroking her hair and calming her. "Tell me what happened you want to share. I promise not to pry."

"We didn't want to leave each other so early so Andrew suggested we go to the saloon where we could talk."

There was a heavy sigh from Aunt Janet. "I guess we forgot to tell him not to take you to a saloon. Whatever was he thinking?"

"When he opened the door, he realized we shouldn't go there. We were turning around to leave when this awful woman came out and told me I needed a different dress if I wanted him to go home with me. She had rouge on her cheeks and lips and her dress was cut way down here." Josie showed her with her hands. "Andrew said he liked my dress and my innocence, and I asked him if he were innocent as well and he said one of those women had touched him inappropriately once and he'd gone back to see if she would do it again."

At this, Aunt Janet groaned. "He felt compelled to share that?"

"We want an honest relationship. I expected the truth, but not that. I don't know what all this means. I said I wouldn't want a disgusting man touching me. He said a woman would call the sheriff; a man would pay a woman for it. And I said is this why you're called perverts and he said yes. So how can I love a pervert? And, Mrs. McNown, I did love Andrew."

Another deep sigh. "My dear, you should still love Andrew, if for no other reason than he loves you so much. There are things you need to learn about men and since your own mother is not here to tell you, do you want me to?"

"Oh, please. I'm so confused about what we feel and what we want from each other and now all this other-woman stuff. My heart is breaking."

"Indeed. All our hearts break a little every time a man proves to be a man and not a nice lady. Not that we'd want a lady-like man. We don't want a man-man either, but of course, we do want a manly-man. Josie, men have a burden most women don't share. They seem to have an appetite for what I'll call bodily arousal that constantly bothers them. Women can enjoy bodily feelings as well. Anticipating them doesn't dominate our lives the way it seems to for men. You'd think they'd figure out a way to avoid those thoughts, they cause them such grief, but no, they go out of their way to get them. Arousal gnaws at them. It must be satisfied. It's a compulsion. It seems ridiculous to us, because we don't have something gnawing at us. They do, and the sooner we recognize it, and either love them in spite of it, or decide to let them be gnawed by themselves, and do without them, the happier we'll be."

"Did your husband suffer from this?"

"All men suffer. And I do believe some of them suffer a lot. Happily married men suffer because we make them feel unfaithful every time they look at another woman, also because they can't ease their pain by sleeping with us as often as they'd like."

"Why would sleeping with us help?"

"It's an expression, Josie, it means making love, copulating, mating."

Josie stared at her.

"You really don't know anything, do you?"

"I'm learning I'm totally ignorant of an important part of life."

"This is more than I bargained for, but let's go. I'll try to be more delicate than my mother was when she explained it to me. To give her credit, she did get the point across."

"Not if you don't want to. I can learn somewhere else."

"From Andrew?"

"He tried to tell me some things today when I asked, but he said he couldn't do it."

"A stroke of good sense. I wouldn't have expected that."

"He meant well. I shouldn't have asked him."

"True."

"Andrew's been insightful about so many things, I thought he'd know what makes men and women feel the way they do. He said he knows nothing about women and not that much about men, so we sort of quit talking about it."

"Good. It was bound to be misinformed. Let me ask you what you do know. Did your mother explain the monthlies to you?"

"After they came to me. I thought I was dying and she assured me I wasn't, it's something all women do once a month. She gave me some clean rags and told me what to do with them. That's all I know."

"Will you promise me something?"

"Most likely. What?"

"If you have a daughter, you'll tell her she'll have them, before her monthlies start? No child should have to think they're dying, especially in public, and most women let their girls find out that way. It's not fair. Now, do you know why you have monthlies?"

"I'm not sure Mother knew why. She didn't tell me if she did."

"When a woman reaches an age when she can have a baby the body stores blood to nourish it. If the woman doesn't have a baby in her, then the blood comes out and she starts all over again preparing for a child. All female animals do something like this, most not every month. Do you know how a woman gets pregnant?"

"No. That's what I wanted Andrew to explain."

"Poor Andy. Have you ever seen a man without his clothes on?"

"No! Never."

"Have you ever seen dogs mate?"

"I don't think so."

"You'd know if you had. Well, this is more difficult than I thought. It's good if girls have little brothers or farm animals, but you don't, so we'll forge ahead."

"Do you want to postpone this?"

"No. I want to get it over with for both of us. Josie, you know how down where you urinate–pee–whatever your family calls it, you have another opening where the blood comes out. This is a passage in your body that has moist skin on the inside. It's where the baby comes out when it's born. Inside that passage is where men put the fluid that fertilizes your egg. I don't think I've mentioned you make eggs. It's when the egg doesn't get fertilized and leaves the body you begin to bleed. Please understand, Josie, this isn't a topic I know all that much about either, although I've had to explain it to my three girls. The way the man fertilizes the egg is by putting a part of his body into that cavity. His part is called a penis. It's down between his legs too. Surely you've seen male horses with their penises hanging down."

"Oh. I didn't know what those were. Yes, I've seen them. Are men's that big?"

"Only in their minds. Now, let's get back to the topic. When a man is, umm, ready to do that, his penis, which is usually like a short piece of bread dough, becomes larger and firm and he places it in the woman. The first time this happens it can hurt, because there is some skin in the woman's cavity that must be broken. It doesn't hurt for long, but it does bleed a little. The man typically moves back and forth on top of the woman then the liquid that fertilizes the egg comes out of the penis and the man leaves and falls asleep." She stopped and looked at Josie to see if her explanation was getting through to her. Josie's eyes were wide with horror.

Aunt Janet continued despite the look. "Husbands will want to do this regularly, say every few days or so, not to fertilize the egg, but because it feels good to them. It feels good to us, but not like it does to them. We enjoy the closeness of the man we love. It makes us happy that he has pleasure, and we're glad when he goes to sleep. It's a part of life. It's how babies get made, and how we keep the man at home. It doesn't hurt, Josie. It's a natural thing to do and your parents did it, your grandparents did it, and way back to Adam and Eve they did it or we wouldn't be here today."

Aunt Janet took a deep breath and rubbed Josie's back. "Now I think we need a cup of chocolate." She got up and hurried to the kitchen, taking deep breaths, shaking her head, and muttering to herself. *What we do to children. Why can't a doctor come to school and give girls this information? Why do they have to get these half-baked hand-me-down old-wives' tales that may or may not be true? When I asked Dr. Martin to explain this to me, he was as uncomfortable as I was and who knows if I remember it? Something's wrong with us.*

Josie sat on the davenport staring at nothing. *No wonder poor Andrew faltered. It's horrible. My mother and father did this? I can't believe my mother did. Then how did we get here, if Aunt Janet is right? Would Andrew want to do that? Not if it hurts me. Then we couldn't have children. I like for him to kiss and hold me but to put a part of him inside me? How would he even do that? Oh, no. Will we have to take our clothes off?*

One discomforting thought after another ran pell-mell through her brain. She tried to keep coming back to Andrew's goodness, his letters, how kind he had been to Joe. *Maybe it all works out in spite of how awful it sounds.*

Aunt Janet called from the kitchen and Josie joined her. The hot chocolate smelled comforting. "Thank you, Aunt Janet. I think that must have been very difficult, especially with someone you don't know well. I have no one to go to for this sort of instruction except Zona, and her advice might be a great deal like your mother's. You made it not as awful sounding as it might have been from someone else."

"Thank you for calling me Aunt Janet. I hope to be that someday, but you're welcome to call me that now. We women must take care of each other. Men want to and often do a decent job of it, but there are some things they simply can't handle. You may always come to me."

"I do have a question. What happens when you don't want any more babies?"

"When my mother announced she was through breeding, as she put it, she gave my father a dollar and told him to go find another woman to scratch his itch. Weekly, he would ask for his dollar. He always came home after his tryst, nothing was ever said about it, and they stayed together until he died."

She continued. "When I didn't want any more children, I asked my husband if he wanted the same arrangement and he said absolutely not, we could afford skins. I learned there are animal skins men put over their penises to keep the fluid from reaching the woman. He used those until he died. They work. I suppose Angus and Maggie do the same because I can't imagine Angus going to another woman. Every couple works it out their own way."

Josie interjected, "My mother said my father announced, 'No more,' after the child she lost was born. I guess it nearly killed her coming. I know my father wouldn't go to another woman because we couldn't afford it and he loved my mother."

"Stop right there. You need to remember men love to think about mating and they're not always discriminating about who they think about it with. They agree to marry us, but that gnawing never stops. You must remember this, Josie. It's not a personal thing. It's who they are."

Josie sighed. *I'm never going to remember something so foreign and so painful to think about.* She nodded. "I'll work very hard on remembering."

"You'll serve your man well by understanding he's different from you. He's a man."

They rinsed their cups and went to bed.

Andrew, meanwhile, shuffled home, dejected, sad, and worried he had lost Josie. He opened the door and headed up the stairs to his room. Then he heard his father.

"Andy? I thought you were going to be out until all hours."

Andrew didn't turn around. "We're tired. We decided to turn in early." He started up the steps.

"Son?" His dad's voice was from the bottom of the stairs.

Not wanting to face him, knowing he had to, he turned and said, "Yes?"

Seeing the look on Andrew's face, a pain shot through Angus' heart. "Come down, Andy. We need to talk."

"I'm tired, Dad."

"I can see that. Come down anyway."

He couldn't refuse. His hand on the bannister didn't want to let go. He wanted to escape. He went slowly down to meet his father.

"Come to the kitchen. We'll sit at the table."

Andrew sat down, Angus went to the ice box and pulled out two bottles of beer, opened them and set one down in front of Andrew saying, "I told your mother if she insisted we have a talk, then it demanded some beer and she didn't have a lot to say about it."

"Thanks." Andrew took a deep drink.

"There are some things I have failed to talk to you about, Andy, and your mother reminded me tonight. I apologize for not realizing you were ready for this discussion."

Andrew nodded and took another drink.

"What I have to say, Andy, is that men and women regard love differently. They have different expectations from it." He was obviously uncomfortable and started rolling his beer bottle between his hands. "Men get all tangled up in their passion for wanting to touch and fondle and eventually, copulate. Women are much simpler. They want affection and some touching, but they're more interested in bonding with someone than we are. Don't shake your head at me. I know you're interested in bonding as well, but your passions are not what she's feeling. Men love to be excited by mating. You go to a ranch where they're breeding horses and the corral fence is lined with cowboys hanging over it watching. Every one of them will be looking for a woman that night or doing himself. You do know about that, don't you?"

Andrew sighed. "The church told us it was a sin. I didn't know what they were talking about. Steve told me."

"With glee, I'm sure. Men like anything to do with breeding. They collect pictures of naked women. They put names such as male and female on things like the ends of electrical cords because it excites them. They make walking sticks out of dead bulls' penises because it gives them a jolt. Hear me, women don't do these things, Andy. Men do. Have you seen pictures of the male statues primitives carved with the huge, ummmm, erections? I think we can be certain men carved those. We find our women's bodies endlessly fascinating, so we want to explore them. We want women to be amazed at us, to want to fondle us. They find our privates, shall we say, intimidating. They do not need to handle us, much as we'd love them to. We're different and we need to respect that difference. Women enjoy the hugging and kissing, or at least your mother says they do.

"This is what your mother and I want you to know. Men, and women, too, have two levels of attachment. The animal part and the heart and mind part, what we call companionship in this house. I love your mother, as you know, and don't want another female to take her place in my heart. The animal part of me might enjoy knowing some of the other women I meet. I look at them, unless your mom's with me, and I assess them. So you know, I have never been unfaithful to your mother and that's important to me and her. I have, though, as the Bible says, lusted. That, she probably doesn't want to know. Why, when I love your mother, would I lust? Because I'm a man. It's not because I'm weak, or evil,"

Andrew interrupted, "or a pervert."

"No, I'm not a pervert and the people who want to make me one are the people who want me to beg for God's forgiveness for being the animal God made. I'll have none of it, Andy, and you shouldn't either.

"Now, what your mom asked me to tell you is to go slow with Josie on the animal part. She's young and innocent and won't understand a lot of this. She'll come around, because women do, but you need to give her time. Your mother wants to remind you the sleeping together part shouldn't happen until after marriage, and the first time can be scary for her. It should be. It hurts and she'll lose her virginity. What can a man lose? Nothing he doesn't want to lose. Yes. Except his heart. I can read your mind. Okay?" If Andrew had been watching, he would have seen Angus let out a deep breath.

"Okay, Dad. I think I was on my way to figuring out some of this stuff. It's been painful to learn, though. She is, as you guessed, remarkably innocent and since I am too," with the word innocent having recently caused him such grief, he regretted using it, "it didn't go well today, or at least a part of it didn't. I'm hoping she'll want to be with me tomorrow. If she does, do you think Prince would mind another picnic?"

"He was hoping you'd ask."

They heard footsteps on the stairs. "I don't think I can take a lecture from Mom tonight."

"I'll do what I can."

Maggie came into the room in her robe and stood behind Angus with her hands on his shoulders. Angus said, "I think he has all the information he needs for right now, Mother, and we're both ready for bed."

"I know, but I have something I want to say."

"Please, Mom." He didn't want to hear again he was a pervert.

"No. I want to say it. I want you and your father to know that when a woman loves a man, she may not feel all you feel or understand some of what you find fascinating, but it's all right, because your loving us makes it all right. Dad may have something to add to this, but for me, love is two best friends who have a strong physical attraction to each other. And I will say, there's nothing in the world that compares to going to sleep curled around the warm, sweet body you love and waking up to

246

it in the morning, full of love and tenderness. Now come to bed with me, dear heart, I need your warm body. Good night, Andy."

"Good night, son."

"Thanks, Mom and Dad. Good night."

Bottles to be returned were put on the porch. Glad to have it over, the two uncomfortable men parted.

When Andrew knocked on the kitchen door at nine o'clock the next morning Aunt Janet let him in and asked him to sit down. She leaned over to talk to him. "She's upstairs getting ready to go. I think you can expect a rough start but a smooth finish, providing you don't drift into the mating talk, and keep it light-hearted. She's had the same warning, so expect a nothing conversation to begin with. She and I discussed the facts of life last night. She knows more now than she did yesterday and a lot of it was unsettling to her, as it should be. When you think about it, Andy, it's peculiar."

She chose not to mention the woman touching him because she was sure he would never recover from embarrassment and he'd suffered enough for his honesty.

"Aunt Janet, I didn't think I'd done anything wrong yesterday. It's her inquisitive mind, which I love, that got us in over our heads. Thank you for talking to her. I really couldn't tell her about so much of it. It was embarrassing and besides, what do I know?"

"I hope not a lot. I can assure you, you know more than she did. She didn't know what those things were hanging out of a horse."

Andrew blushed. "Oh, no. I hope Prince behaves himself."

"If he doesn't, tell her you're not quite that large, okay?" She laughed heartily. Andrew's blush grew deeper.

"It's not funny, Aunt Janet, she'll look at it and think horrible thoughts."

"May I suggest you spend the day in the buggy? Oh, Andy, it's a painful, confusing time and we who've survived it can but laugh at how ridiculous mankind is. The animals don't blush, or if they do, we can't see it. Be a good boy and she'll love you again. She's predisposed to it."

They heard Josie coming down the stairs without any lightness to her step. Andrew stood and waited to see her face,

247

hoping for a smile. She came into the kitchen and seemed surprised to see him. "I didn't hear your ring." No smile.

"I came in the kids' door. Are you all right?"

"I'm okay."

Aunt Janet wanted them to figure it out, but she couldn't stand the painful silence that followed. Even though she felt like a busybody, she said, "Well, kids, you've got a beautiful day if you want to take advantage of it and I suggest you do because they say there's a storm coming down from the north."

No response. She tried again. "Did your mother pack you a picnic again, Andy?"

"She did. I hoped Josie would join Prince and me on a ride up Clear Creek for a little outing. Will you come, Josie?" He felt hopeless, she was so unresponsive.

Josie felt defenseless. She wanted him to take care of her but she didn't trust those feelings. She didn't know where to turn.

Aunt Janet answered for her. "She'd love to go, Andy. Get your coat, Josie, a little fresh air will do you good. Go on, now."

Josie nodded and went to get her coat. Aunt Janet looked at Andrew and said, "She's a little dazed by this. Her world has been turned upside down with all this talk of copulation and penises and men enjoying other women. It's a big pill to swallow and she's choking on it. She'll get it down with some gentle help."

Josie appeared wearing her coat and Andrew nodded to Aunt Janet and they went out the door. Prince was behaving. They got into the buggy and headed out. Watching from the window as the silent couple left, Aunt Janet whispered, "Talk, Andy, talk. It's what you do best."

He talked. He told her how Ralston Creek got its name from a miner who first discovered gold in Colorado, how Ralston Creek flowed east and joined Clear Creek in Arvada, a community closer to Denver where they grew a lot of celery. Miners had followed the gold up Clear Creek and had found riches. He realized he was babbling out of nervousness but didn't know what else to do.

She gradually started listening and finally asked a question. "Did we go through Arvada on the trolley coming here?"

"No. We were south of it. We went through Lakewood. Did you enjoy the trolley ride?" *She's reverted to Joe; I'm the big boy with answers.*

"I was so nervous you wouldn't like me when you saw me again, I don't really remember it well."

"We were silly about that. I loved you then and I love you now, Josie." *Does she hear me?*

Looking at him, totally confused about who he really was, she felt her heart would break and she wanted him to comfort her. "Thank you for coming to get me this morning. I imagine you were undecided too."

"Not for a minute. I want to be with you more than you could know. I want your friendship and your love. I hope you can find them in your heart again, someday."

"I cried for you last night. I'm so confused about life and love and all that goes with it and you're whom I've come to rely on for wisdom and you weren't there. Aunt Janet tried to help me through it, and I'm grateful to her, truly, but I wanted you to explain everything. I know now, that's impossible. She helped me see that. And I'm not supposed to be talking about it now, but I can't sit here next to you and behave as if I don't love you when my heart is calling for you even though my mind is saying no, don't let him hurt you again."

He secured the reins and put his arms around Josie and held her as she cried. "I'll try to be a better man, I promise."

"Please don't promise. Aunt Janet said you're a man and I need to understand and respect that and love you anyway."

"Dad talked to me last night and said I need to respect our differences and love you every way."

"Can we agree we love each other, Andrew, and try not to judge what we don't understand? I'll try very hard to listen and not be destroyed by what you tell me, if you'll try to tell me in a kind way." Her voice was quivering and her tears were still coming, but she was trying to smile.

"I do agree. Please believe I'll always want to be kind. I do need your love."

He put her face between his hands and held it gently, wiping away the tears with his thumbs and looking into her eyes. "I'm a man and you're a woman and that's what makes it perfect, and complicated. Let's treasure the differences and make them work for us. Okay?"

She nodded and smiled as well as she could.

Prince kept going as if he knew it didn't matter where he went.

Andrew realized Prince had taken a wrong bend in the road and reined him around a block to set them straight. *I wish it were as easy to make things right when I mess up with Josie. Maybe I'll learn. Dad seems to have, at least most of the time.*

He pointed out where the School of Mines was and asked if she had seen the "M" before this trip. She had not, so he explained the "M" on Mount Zion stood for Mines. The senior class a couple of years ahead of him wanted an "M." They designed and laid it out and took a pack train of burros loaded down with rocks and tools to build it. He was proud of his part in it, although he was only a rock carrier.

"Wasn't that hard work?"

"We're young. We had a good time and it was our project, not the school's, or we probably would have complained about the stupidity of carrying all those rocks up a steep hill to make a letter out of them. I've found attitude makes a significant difference in whether something's work or play."

"So true. When I wanted to sew doll clothes, I enjoyed it. I didn't enjoy mending my clothes, even when I was the one who tore them."

He looked at her and smiled. It was becoming easier. He was relieved.

Prince kept going until the road turned rough then he stopped He didn't like rough roads. Andrew pulled him into a turn-around and tucked him into a shaded spot.

"Would you mind hiking up the trail until we find a secluded place where we can sit and look at the creek and have a picnic?"

"I won't mind." He helped her out of the buggy, secured Prince and put on his pack with the picnic and a blanket his mother had suggested he bring.

Walking up the rough trail used mainly by pack animals and horseback riders, the two once again fell into the question and answer mode they found comfortable. Andrew, in his element with geology, was able to explain how gold was in nearly vertical veins in fractured rock from a former geologic time. She asked how the gold got there and he reminded her of their discussion at Savage Lakes.

"I don't remember everything you told me. I do remember wondering if you'd talk to me about interesting things if you knew who I was instead of a stranger you'd never see again."

"Maybe you're right. I couldn't talk to girls, Josie. I tried. I wanted a girlfriend like other guys had, but it didn't work. I can talk to you, though, and I love your questions and I love answers you give when I ask you something, but I know I do most of the talking. Someday, I promise, it will be your turn to talk." He wished he could make it a joke but he was on such thin ice he couldn't.

She turned to look at him. He was serious. "Don't be silly, Andrew, I ask because I want to know, and you usually have the answer. If I ever know anything, I'll share it with you."

"You know about people, teaching and household things. I couldn't survive without the women in my life taking care of me."

She became thoughtful. *I know more today than I did yesterday. I wonder if he wants to ask me about making babies.*

He suspected she was thinking about things he'd rather she didn't. Nervous, he began to natter on again to fill the quiet. "All those cracks in the rocks were filled with hot, mineralized water that cooled in them, we think. Or rather the professors think. I have no theories on this, you'll be glad to learn. Here, in what we call the Mineral Belt, water contained not only gold but also silver, lead, zinc and copper." He glanced over at her. Her eyes were glazed. *I don't think she's with me.* "They've taken a lot of gold out of here, which is why Mr. Loveland built train tracks up to Idaho Springs." *Nothing. What is she thinking about?* "Are you looking for a pretty place for our picnic?"

Aware of a rise in his voice indicating a question, she turned to him. "I'm sorry, Andrew, I wasn't listening. Would you ask again?"

"I asked if you were looking for a pretty place for a picnic."

"I wasn't. Will you please? You always pick nice places."

He nodded. *Have I lost her? Will she ever come back? What am I supposed to do?*

"Andrew?"

"Yes, Josie."

"When that woman touched you, it made you feel good. If I touched you in the same way, what would you feel?"

I knew it. Is honesty best? "It would be heaven. I don't want you to touch me that way until you want to, and Dad says women don't really want to touch men the way we want to touch them."

"Then why did that woman do that?"

"They do it for money. Men will pay for that kind of pleasure. Women won't."

"Do women who love men touch them like that to give them pleasure?"

"I don't know. My dad didn't tell me about that."

"What do suppose?"

"Josie, I'm not supposing anything anymore. I'm as confused as you are."

"Well, if I loved a man and knew he'd like that, I suppose I'd do it. Or at least I'd try to do it. It might frighten me a little."

"Maybe it should. It could make a man have thoughts about more touches."

"Would it make a man want to touch a woman too?"

"My dad says men lust for women and want to touch them but they don't because...well, because women don't lust for men, first off, but also because it wouldn't be proper and women wouldn't enjoy it. Dad says most women want that kind of touch only from men they love. Now please don't ask me any more questions about this, you know I don't know about it." *And every question gets me in deeper trouble.*

"I don't care what you <u>know</u>. I want to know what you <u>feel,</u> and I want you to help me understand what I feel. We promised to discuss this in a kind way and your not answering isn't kind." She glared at him with a stern-teacher-look.

There's that stubborn streak. "I'm sorry, I've forgotten your question."

She restated it: "If a woman touched a man she loved would he want to touch her?" She looked at him squarely.

"If you were to touch me that way, out of love, I would have such feelings of...*what do we call this when we're talking to women?* I would want to sleep with you, Josie." *That ought to put an end to this romance.*

"Thank you. You were honest. Aunt Janet explained that euphemism for mating. I think if you had those feelings and I could tell you had them, I might want to sleep with you too."

He stopped walking and stared at her. "Really?"

"If my mother and father did it, and so did my grandparents, as Aunt Janet said, then why wouldn't I want to? I presume my father didn't force my mother to do something she didn't want to do. Aunt Janet said it could be lovely if you cared for the man, so why would I feel differently toward a man I love?"

He shrugged his shoulders.

"Well, I think I know, and I don't think I would mind if I really loved him. If it's something all animals do, and our parents did, why would we be different? It seems to me we've made it more complicated than it needs to be by being so secretive about it and making it naughty."

He nodded.

"The problem is the making of babies. We can't have people running around doing what feels good to them and having babies without a home to take them to, so that's why people need to get married before they do all these touches and things. Don't you agree?"

"Mmm hmm."

"Still, there is the desire to touch. This must be why they arrange marriages in some places. So they won't have that desire because they don't know the person and therefore they won't do it and make a baby. Here, though, we get to be together and feel these feelings and need to act as if we don't feel them, to keep us from touching even more than we are and we end up sleeping together before we're ready to make a home. Right?"

He nodded. *I think this is called female logic but she's getting there and I'm not going to step in the middle of it.*

"For you and me, Andrew, that means we have to be careful how we behave so we don't tempt ourselves with too much touching."

Stopping in her ramble to look at him, she realized he hadn't been saying anything.

He sensed she wanted a response. "I'm afraid you're right."

"Why are you afraid?"

"Because I love the thought of touching you, Josie."

"It's sad, isn't it, what tricks life plays on us?"

I think she's calmed down. I think she swallowed the pill without anybody's help, certainly not mine, and maybe, just maybe, we can go on. "Yes, life does play tricks on us. I suppose that's why we have brains, to try to rise above the tricks, to make sense of our lives, not that we can ever make sense of <u>life</u>." He reached for her hand as they started walking again.

"I'll help you look for a peaceful place to stop," she offered.

Yes, a little peace would be welcome. "I'd love your help." He squeezed her hand gently and they touched their shoulders together in a mute gesture of companionship.

They selected a spot near the edge of the creek in a grassy hollow hidden from most of the road. Scrambling to it Andrew offered Josie a hand, remembering the first time he touched her. She took it, acknowledged their shared memory with a squeeze and smiled at him. He threw the blanket out and they settled down to watch the creek and flip pebbles into it.

"Make sure you don't throw away a gold nugget," he advised with a grin.

"If I did, and realized it, would you jump in and find it?"

"I'd jump in, depending on its size. I'd probably never find it in all the rocks down there."

"Have you ever panned for gold?"

"We did in one of our classes, to understand what happens. I didn't find anything and neither did anyone else, but it was fun. I could see how men might get addicted to it, the way some men gamble, because every pan has the potential to show color."

"Color?"

"Gold."

"Men like to tease themselves, don't they?"

Oh, no. Here we go again. "I don't think I understand what you mean."

"With gambling, it's a tease: will they win or not. With touching, it's will she let me or not and if she does, how much more will she let me do and so on."

I've got to deflect this. "Don't you think women do the same thing? If they make a dress will it look good on them. If they try a recipe, will it taste good?"

"It doesn't seem quite the same to me, but if it does to you, I'll take your word for it." *I think he missed my point.*

He threw some pebbles before he spoke. "We need to talk about your leaving tomorrow. I think you have a very early departure to Colorado Springs."

"I do. I need to be at Union Station around seven o'clock. I can take the early interurban to the station, so I'll need to leave Golden around six, I think."

"I've asked Steve if I can borrow his car to drive you to town. It'll be faster. We'll still need to leave around six, but we won't need to make all those stops that can make it unnerving."

"I hoped you'd let me do it on my own. There's no need for you to give up your Sunday morning when I'm perfectly capable of getting around Denver by myself."

"I wouldn't dream of letting you go home without taking you to the train. I sent you a round-trip ticket, remember?"

Relieved she wouldn't have to negotiate the trip alone, she smiled at him. "You know, Andrew, I am a grown woman, or at least that's what the law says, but it's awfully nice to have someone who wants to take care of me. Thank you."

He lay back on the blanket and reached for her. "Will you lie beside me, please? I promise I won't do anything inappropriate."

She lay beside him then turned and put her body close to his. "I think I would like to be very close to you someday. I wonder if you and I will ever know what that feels like."

Swallowing hard, he tried to remain in control. "I hope so, because I love you, Josie, and your nearness is everything."

"I'm having feelings for you, Andrew. They're nice, now that I know what to think about them and not to be afraid. Are you having feelings too?"

If you only knew. "Yup. Nice feelings. Feelings I should cool down, if you know what I mean?"

"I do. I hope you enjoy them while you have them, though."

"May I kiss you?"

"Yes. That's probably not going to cool the feelings, though."

"I'm not really anxious for them to cool."

"Me neither."

Horseshoes clicking on the rocks on the road split them apart. Josie set up and pulled her coat around herself. Andrew rolled over on his stomach and rested on his elbows. The rider didn't seem to notice them and rode on.

"We should probably have lunch. Our reservation at the hotel is at five-thirty because I knew you'd want to go to bed early."

"And I need to get home in time to clean up for our party."

"We should eat and head back, I suppose."

"I suppose," she said sadly.

"I enjoyed hugging and kissing you."

"I enjoyed it too."

He spread the picnic on the blanket and they ate in near silence as they regained their composure and recouped their casual sense of fun.

When they were through eating Andrew picked up the napkins and leftovers and packed them away. "It looks like a storm's coming, Josie. We'd better head for home. Prince doesn't like storms." He shook his head, frowning. She was struck again with how Prince was playfully used by the Allans like a hand-puppet.

"Wait," she said softly.

"Yes?" he asked.

"We won't be together like this again. Before we leave, will you lie with me for another moment?"

"Oh, yes." Lying down on the blanket he pulled her close. "I don't know how I'll bear not seeing you until Christmas. It seemed forever for Thanksgiving to come and I had no idea what I was missing. Now I know, and I'll grieve for it."

"I didn't know what a kiss felt like when I came and I've learned what a kiss can mean and what closeness feels like. I've also learned a lot more and it's good I have. What I've learned, Andrew, is I love you and my body loves yours. Does that seem shameful? It doesn't feel that way to me."

"To hear you say that makes me as happy as a man can be. I thought I'd lost you. I didn't know how to bring you back. Last night two lines from Tennyson kept playing in my mind, *'Tis better to have loved and lost, Than never to have loved at all,'* which didn't comfort me. Then I looked up a poem by Robert Burns. Did your parents read him to you too?"

"Doesn't every Scottish parent read Bobby Burns' <u>Wee Mousie</u> to their children?"

"I suppose. Do you know this one?
    'Had we never lov'd sae kindly,
    Had we never lov'd sae blindly!

Never met—or never parted,
We had ne'er been broken-hearted.'"

"I don't know it, but it makes me sad."

"Then you understand how I felt last night."

"I was broken-hearted too and confused. I hope you understand why."

"I do. And I thank you for thinking for yourself and giving us a chance for happiness."

"Oh, my no," she said, "I didn't think for myself. Aunt Janet was a guiding light and I think your father's advice has helped too. My thoughts were muddled. It's been such an awakening. I never dreamed what goes on in private. It was difficult for me to reconcile my parents with sleeping together and why I'd never heard how babies are made and men's lusting for women. It's been overwhelming. You stayed with me through it and I'm not sure many men would have been that kind. Thank you, Andrew, you've proven to be a good friend as well as the man I want to love, in all love's ways." She paused. "Dancing together will be more fun as we learn the steps."

After a few more kisses they reluctantly agreed it was time to go. Back at the tree, Prince seemed anxious.

As they were passing through town Josie remembered she wanted to buy a book for Mr. Miller. "Do we have time to find a bookstore? I'd love to buy *Adventures of Huckleberry Finn.*"

"I think I still have it. You can take it with you."

"Thank you, but I'd like a new book. This is a gift for Mr. Miller. It will be the first book he owns. I thought it might be fun for him to have words he can read. What do you think?"

"I think he'd enjoy it. I'm going to send you some others he can read when he's through with that. *Treasure Island, Kidnapped*, Robinhood, I don't know, I'll have to look on the shelf."

The bookstore was on their way and Josie ran in and bought Twain's book, hoping it wouldn't be too childish for an old man. She asked the owner if he thought a man in his seventies, who was learning to read, could enjoy it. He assured her many adults read and re-read it because they always find something new. She bought it, quickly inscribed the flyleaf, and asked him to wrap it to make it more like a gift.

When they reached Aunt Janet's it was four o'clock. Josie had over an hour to get ready. Andrew rang the doorbell and Aunt Janet called for them to come in. Anxious to see if their day had gone well after such a rocky start, she had to hide a grin when she saw the two of them together, contentedly holding hands. "Do you want to come in, Andy, or give this girl a chance to relax and get pretty for tonight without feeling rushed?"

How could she be prettier than she is right now? "Whatever you tell me to do, AnJan."

"Then leave and go get pretty yourself."

As soon as the door closed behind him Aunt Janet hugged Josie. "You look happy. I was worried about you when you left."

"You had cause. Andrew was patient with me. He talked about the history of the area, geology, the school, I don't know what all because I was so preoccupied. I could tell he couldn't stop talking because I was gloomy and I made him nervous. I couldn't help it. I gradually worked out things in my mind and was able to talk to him and tell him I understand he's a man and what you said about loving him anyway. We became friends again after we talked about it. It all worked because of what you told me last night. I'm still baffled I was so ignorant about what you said, but I was. I still wouldn't know if you hadn't talked to me like a mother. Thank you for telling me the truth about men and women. It's a mystery why we love one another then have those feelings, but we do love and feel, and I guess mankind goes on because we do."

Nodding her head, Aunt Janet agreed. "Mankind goes on. That's the crux of it. Now, dear girl, how about a hot bath? And I have something to show you in your room. I'll come upstairs with you."

On Josie's bed lay two of the most beautiful dresses she'd ever seen. Aunt Janet explained, "I thought you might not have a pretty dress in Meredith and would want something special to wear tonight. Harriet left these. She's tall, as you are. Maybe one of them will suit you."

"I do have my good dress I wore last night because my sisters mailed it to me; it's my church dress and doesn't hold a candle to these. I've never worn such a beautiful dress. Won't Harriet mind?"

"I asked her. She didn't remember they're here. She's a clothes horse and has many pretty things. I'll draw the bath for you. There's a robe on the chair, call me when you're ready to try one on."

When Josie entered the bathroom the steam and delightful smell of bath crystals greeted her. She breathed deeply and sighed. *Such luxury.*

"You have time for a nice soak, enjoy yourself," and Aunt Janet disappeared. When she reluctantly stepped out, warm and pink, Josie wrapped herself in the robe, went to her room and put on her clean underthings.

Aunt Janet came when Josie called. Holding up one beautiful dress, then the other Aunt Janet asked, "Do either of these appeal to you?"

"I've never had anything as gorgeous as these."

"Would you be comfortable in one? It's important to be comfortable in an unfamiliar situation."

"How could one be uncomfortable wearing something beautiful? May I try on the pale blue? I love the color."

Aunt Janet helped her pull on the dress. She buttoned it in back then turned Josie around to look at her. "Stunning. Harriet has a shape like yours, but your coloring brings this to life. Come look." She guided Josie to a long mirror.

"Aunt Janet, this is too good for me. People will think I'm someone I'm not."

"Good. Keep them guessing, not that you're likely to see anyone you know tonight, except a special boy, and we want him to see you in a different light."

Josie turned around and looked at herself in the mirror again. "Andrew won't know who I am. He'll think you swapped me for someone else."

"Keep him off balance. It's good for him. Do you want to try on the other one?"

"I can't imagine it would be prettier. Maybe when I come home I'll try it on for fun. Like playing dress-up when I was a little girl."

"Yes. I hope it's fun for you. Now, let's do something with your hair. You must remember I raised three girls; I know a thing or two about last-minute hair-dos." She sat Josie in a chair and braided the back of her long hair, tying it in a knot. She loosely braided the sides, draped them softly against her face and pinned them under the back braid. "Look."

Josie held up the mirror. "You've almost made me pretty. You're a magician."

"Only a mother."

The doorbell rang. They looked at each other grinning. "He won't believe his eyes, Aunt Janet."

She was right. He simply stared at her. He shook his head. "What did you do? You look...different. I mean, you're always beautiful, but this is a different beautiful."

"Your aunt is a miracle worker."

"Aunt Janet, what makes you think she'll come home with me? All the men there will try to take her away."

"Might make you pay attention, wouldn't you say?"

Realizing she didn't have her shoes, Josie ran upstairs to get her good ones.

He whispered, "Thank you, she's glowing, and she wasn't last night. You've saved me, again, and you've made her see herself as beautiful. She needed that."

As they got into the buggy, Andrew observed, "Prince isn't sure he's anxious to go on a date in the weather he feels is coming on." Looking apologetic, he added, "I know this is an imposition, but Mom would love to see how we look all dressed up. Do you mind?" He kept looking at her and shaking his head. *Where did my Josie go?*

Maggie and Angus were genuinely pleased to see her. Maggie took Josie aside and told her she looked lovely. Josie confessed the source of the loveliness. Maggie chuckled softly. "She didn't want you to face the evening without a winning hand. Well, I think you won this game a while ago, but it's always fun to play an ace."

"We didn't go in for fancy things at our house. I couldn't resist wearing this beautiful dress because I've never worn anything like it before. It's fun to dress up and have my hair done."

"How did he behave when he saw you?"

"Dumbfounded, really. I'm not sure he approves, although he hasn't complained." She laughed softly, thinking she could sense what he was feeling. "I think he may prefer me in camping gear."

"How would he know?"

"Oh, instinct, I suppose."

Maggie nodded her head. "They don't like change, Josie. It takes them a while to adjust. You'll be ahead if you ease into things, like different furniture arrangements and hair-dos."

"I'll try to remember."

"We'd better go, Josie."

"Goodbye, Mr. and Mrs. Allan. You've been so kind to me. Thank you." She pulled from her coat pocket a pair of the mittens she had knitted, wrapped in tissue paper. "I made these for you. I hope they'll fit. In truth, I made a pair and ended up making two right-hand mittens and so I made another pair for the left hands. I'm going to give Mrs. McNown the other pair. You might not want to wear them at the same time. You'd confuse people." They were glad she could laugh at herself.

"Thank you for your beautiful workmanship, Josie. I'll wear them with pride, and so will Janet. We've loved meeting you. Our curiosity has been pleasantly satisfied. We'll look forward to seeing you at Christmas."

Josie and Andrew, walking into chilly night air, noticed a few flakes falling. "Maybe Aunt Janet knew what she was talking about. Weather forecasting is a very inexact science, usually based on someone's rheumatism."

Tying Prince in front of the hotel, they went into the dining room where a table was set for them. Josie, trying to act the lady she was dressed to be confused Andrew who kept looking at her, mystified. How could Joe turn into this lady? He'd never given costumes enough credit for changing the way people behave. His attire was his best, but nothing unfamiliar to him. Eating at the hotel wasn't an unaccustomed event. His family had eaten here on his mother's birthdays. His parents had explained how he should behave as a host and not as a hungry kid. The waiter asked if they had decided on their dinner. Neither had looked at the menu. When he left they grinned, aware they were playing at being grown-up, yet enjoying the game.

"We should look at the menu, Josie."

"How do you know how much something costs?" she asked.

"It says so over on the right."

"Mine doesn't."

He looked at her menu. She was right. Hers had no amount beside the items.

"Andrew, you'll have to help me. I don't want to order something terribly expensive."

"Fairly expensive?" he laughed.

"You know what I mean."

"I do. Thank you. If I tell you what I'm having and other things about the same price, would that help?"

"Ever so much."

"I'm having jellied consommé, oysters on the half-shell, lamb chops with mint sauce and asparagus in buttered breadcrumbs."

"I don't know what you're talking about, but I think you're pulling my leg."

"I am. Those are the most expensive things on the menu. How do you feel about a quarter of roasted chicken, steamed, buttered carrots, and mashed potatoes?"

"Sounds delicious and very romantic."

"I hoped you'd feel that way." They were happy and glad to be past the tension of last night.

After Andrew said they both wanted the chicken, the waiter asked if they cared for a bottle of wine with dinner. Josie, alarmed at the prospect of making a fool of herself again, quickly shook her head. Andrew ducked his head to hide a grin. "No, thank you, just a beer."

Their meals arrived, beautifully served, and delicious. Their talk was light-hearted, gay. Halfway through the meal, Josie stared at the uneaten food on her plate and declared she couldn't eat another bite, would Andrew be interested in helping her? He was, and in typical young, active, hungry male fashion, he cleaned her plate. After the waiter cleared the dishes, Andrew put his hand on the table and asked Josie if he could touch her. She put her hand on the table and he put his on hers. "You've been beautiful tonight. I was shocked when I first saw you because you weren't my Josie, the one I know and love. You've shown me, once again, you are many women, and I love all of them. I feel as if I'm predictably one man, no shifts, no surprises, no variations on a theme. Just me. You, on the other hand, are Joe, a tough little camper, Miss Carter, a comely schoolteacher, and Josie, an elegant lady. You're full of surprises. I hope you won't be bored with me too soon."

"You, Andrew, don't need a fancy dress to make you interesting. You will never bore me. I love the facets of your mind, your challenging perspectives, your sense of humor. I will not tire of you."

He lifted her hand to his lips and kissed it even though his mother had advised him against displaying his affection in public. Who were these noisy people to him? Josie was his world.

Leaving the restaurant, they encountered a snowstorm. Prince, covered with snow, his head hanging down, his mane frozen, looked pitiful. "Prince, poor boy. Let's get you home and into your stable. I'm sorry." Andrew turned to Josie. "We try to be better to Prince than this. He expects kindness." They brushed snow off the buggy seat and headed home.

"I'll drop you off at Aunt Janet's, dry him, get him some oats, and come back to you. We still have an hour or so before we need to turn in."

They rode in silence, happy with the evening, sorry for Prince and dreading the next day. When Andrew arrived back at Aunt Janet's covered with snow himself, Josie let him in and offered to dry him and get him some oats. "Nay, nay," he said, laughing, then ducked his head. He shook his coat outside, took off his snow-covered boots and set them on the rug put out for that purpose. From the parlor, Aunt Janet listened to the playful talk and laughter of two young people exploring the humor, the sensitivities, the depths of each other: an age-old journey from the unknown into the delightful regions of friendship, love, and companionship. Her thoughts turned to seedlings, sprouts vulnerable to exposure, drought, insects, animals. Those that make it through that stage having the chance to grow. Could this romance survive? She hoped so. She loved Andrew as a son. Josie felt right for him. With her hand on her heart, she silently wished them well.

"I was on my way to bed. I'm reading a gripping book and I want to be covered up until they solve the mystery." She rose, smiled at them both with a tenderness Andrew couldn't remember seeing before, and started to leave.

"Aunt Janet," Josie reached for her, "I won't see you in the morning. We're leaving early for the train. Thank you from the bottom of my heart for everything you did for me, from showing me the most elegant hospitality, to educating me about life, and letting me feel beautiful for a night. Your kindness saved Andrew and me from heartache today and probably in the future. I hope I will see you again."

"I believe I'll see you often. I enjoyed our visit and you're always welcome to stay with me. I've packed the other dress in a travel bag. Please put the one you're wearing with it. Who knows, maybe you'll receive an invitation to go out again some time, eh, Andy?"

"If I can afford consommé, oysters, what were they, Josie?"

"He's teasing, Aunt Janet, we had chicken with mashed potatoes and carrots."

"You'll be pleased to know I managed to eat most of Josie's dinner as well as mine."

"Very pleased you didn't explode. Have a nice evening and I'll look forward to hearing you arrived home safely. Good night, you two."

They settled on the couch, as close to each other as they could, Andrew holding Josie's hand, not knowing what to say nor how to say it, to make it last until Christmas. "Telling you I love you isn't original, but it's true. Saying I'll miss you is hopelessly weak when I'll long for you every minute. Wishing you won't leave is foolish. I know you'll leave because you're responsible and have a duty. How can I make you know my days will be longer than winter days have any right to be? My nights will seem endless without your laugh, your tender kiss, your delightful smile to make the dark not matter?" He put his arms around her, pulling her to him, kissing her hair, her cheeks, her lips. "I want to know every part of you I can know. I want to keep your sweet smell, feel your hair on my face, know the softness of your cheek. Oh, Josie, how can I let you leave?"

How can I go? What will happen in Meredith if I don't return? How can I possibly be having these thoughts? "I don't want to go. I can't bear leaving you. I must, you know that. Christmas is only four weeks away. We'll write to each other. We'll learn more about one another with our letters. My heart is aching. I can't be brave anymore." She tucked her head into his chest so he couldn't see her sad face.

They held each other wordlessly for a long time. "I have to go, Josie. We need to leave at five o'clock to catch the trolley.

I'm not going to borrow Steve's car because I would worry about driving on slick roads. Prince doesn't do slick roads, either. Do you have boots so you can walk to the station? I'll break trail."

Life! It always comes back to make us face reality. "I have what I wore on the train and to hike in but I wish I had my overshoes. I'll be ready. Knock softly, please. There's no reason to disturb Aunt Janet."

"How will you wake up?"

"I don't think I'll sleep."

"I'll come at four-thirty to get you. I'll tap on your door. I have an alarm clock. Please sleep."

"I'll leave my shoes outside my door so you'll know which room. I won't lock the front door."

"Lock it. I'll come in the kids' door. Please check to make sure it's unlocked."

Problems, ideas, solutions. The romance gone, not the loving kindness.

"Kiss me, please, and I'll go. You know I don't want to."

She nodded, kissed him, let him out the door and locked it. She hurried to the kitchen, unlocked the back door, and looked around for a piece of paper. Finding one and a pencil, she went to bed.

It was still dark when she heard the tap, the door open and his whisper, "Josie, wake up."

"I'm awake, Andrew. I'll be right down." She washed her face, dressed, gathered her bags, and went downstairs. Andrew had lit a fire in the stove and put on the tea kettle.

"Will a cup of tea and a piece of toast last you until you get something on the train?" He had a slice of bread on the toaster. "Now, don't distract me or I'll forget to flip it and burn it. I'm an expert on scraping toast but I'd rather not have to scrape yours."

She put her arms around his waist and nestled into his back. "Good morning, Andrew. Flip it, please."

He did." Thank you."

She hugged him again. "Better take it off. I'm sure it's enough and we don't want to leave Aunt Janet with smoke in her kitchen."

He lifted the toaster off the stove with a long fork and handed her the toast.

"What are you going to eat?"

"I'll eat at home when I get back if I have any appetite for it."

"Because of your big dinner?"

"Because I'll be so sad."

"Please don't. I'm trying to be cheerful."

She put the other pair of mittens on the table for Aunt Janet.

"What mittens will you wear? Your hands were cold when you got here. I was sorry they were but glad for the excuse to touch you."

"I didn't have time to make myself new ones and my old ones were too awful to wear. I shovel snow in them, you know, so the kids and I can get to the outhouse."

"Then you're not leaving these. I'll explain to Aunt Janet you'll be bringing her some at Christmas. She would not want your hiking through the snow and going on that train without mittens. Trust me." He put the mittens in his pocket. "Mom sent along the blanket we had for the picnic. She thinks you'll need something to wrap up in on the train in this weather. It's in my pack. Don't let me forget to give it to you."

Such loving concern made her feel pampered. *I've forgotten what it's like to have people care for me. Mother cared for us like this. I've been caring for the family since she died. I didn't realize how much I've missed it.* He poured a cup of hot water and looked around for tea. "It's okay, Andrew. I like hot water." He sat down to be with her.

She touched his hand. Toast gone, hot water drunk, it was time to leave. They tidied the kitchen, put on their coats, and headed out the door. Tapping on the window upstairs drew their attention. Aunt Janet was waving goodbye through the frost coated window. Josie, warm in Aunt Janet's mittens, waved back.

The walk to the interurban trolley seemed long on a dark morning in late November. Andrew, kicking snow out of the way, made a minimal path for Josie to walk. Streetlights cast a soft glow on the fresh snow.

"It really is beautiful, Andrew. I wish we had time to enjoy it."

"I'd make an angel for you."

"You are my angel, with or without snow. May I be your cherub?"

"I'm visualizing cherubs. You're a little old for one, otherwise I like the image."

"I think you were just naughty."

"Probably, is that bad?"

"Aunt Janet was right. You men like to tease yourselves."

Laughing at the truth, they trudged on, reaching the shelter of the trolley stop. "I suppose it can make it through this. I doubt if there's been enough snow since the last run to keep it from coming. If it doesn't come, I'll be happy," he said gloomily.

"So will a bunch of kids."

The trolley was late but not late enough to inspire hope. They got in, snuggled together for warmth, and pounded their feet on the floor trying to rid their shoes of snow, Josie's promising cold, damp feet all the way home. Before it melted and soaked in, they brushed off Josie's skirt that carried a deep hem of snow. They didn't talk much on the trip. They'd said it all the night before. Andrew held her hands between his in a pretense to warm them when in truth he wanted to hold on to her. The trolley rocked as it had coming to Golden and before they were ready they were at Union Station. Andrew looked like Santa Claus with his pack, carrying her two travel bags, snow falling on his cap and shoulders.

Trying to put a happy face on the situation she said, "The next time I see you, it will be Santa time. Seeing you will be the best present I've ever received."

"And you, dear Josie, will be mine."

Making their way through the station, they found the train, steam making a cloud in the cold weather. "Please don't get on until the last minute. You have a reserved seat. I don't want to lose a minute when we can be together."

Shaking her head, "Nor do I."

The All Aboard call, then the Last Call made it final. Josie reached into her pocked and handed him a folded piece of paper: "To remember me by." Miserable, they parted. He watched till he could see her seated and waited until the train pulled out, walking beside it until he ran out of platform. *Can men weep? How can I not?* He left and headed home.

On the trolley he pulled the paper from his pocket, unfolded it, and saw a rose drawn at the top of the page and below a beloved poem, altered.

With apologies to Robert Burns:

My love is like a piece of gold
That sparkles in the sun
My love is like the mountain springs
That make the rivers run

My love is like the twinkling stars
That overcome the dark
Cassiopeia, Cepheus,
The Dipper's gentle arc.

So strong art thou, my handsome lad
So deep in luve am I;
And I will luve thee still, my dear,
Till a' the seas gang dry.

Till a' the seas gang dry, my dear,
And the rocks melt wi' the sun;
I will love thee still, my dear,
While the sands o' life shall run.

And fare thee weel, my only luve!
And fare thee weel awhile!
And I will come again, my luve,
Though it were two hundred mile.

Andrew leaned his face against the cold window and closed his eyes. He couldn't see her face, nor hear her voice; he could only hope what she might say if she were to slip into the seat beside him and reach for his hand. "I need to be with you."

The train to Colorado Springs sped through the storm, nothing but darkness and the blur of snow out the window. A small stove in the passenger car intended to heat the space, had more work to do than it could accomplish. It was cold. Josie gladly pulled the blanket from Maggie around herself and wrapped her wet ankles in it. The mittens had not come off. She longed for Andrew's warmth, his hands rubbing hers to take away the chill. She wanted to lean against him instead of trying not to touch shoulders with the older lady next to her.

To the east the sun made a feeble attempt to light the sky through dense clouds, making the storm seem even more intense. The farther south they travelled, the lighter the snow fell, the brighter the sun. Relieved, Josie relaxed. She dreaded a trip over the mountains in a blinding storm. She turned her head from the window to look about her. Surprised to see many other young people on the train, she remembered it was the end of the Thanksgiving holiday. They were returning to Colorado College in Colorado Springs. These young people were Andrew's and her age, but she felt years apart from them. She was employed, in love with the man she wanted to spend her life with. The students seemed young to her, immature, and silly. A wistful feeling came over her: Had she ever been young and silly? She couldn't remember it, couldn't think of a time when she had been carefree with boys. Yes, she and her sisters had giggled in the privacy of their rooms, and her older brothers had teased them when their parents weren't around, but the easy, lightheartedness of the students made her feel as if she had missed a part of her life. *I want to be more playful with Andrew and if he and I end up together and have children I want them to know this ease with all kinds of other kids. The way kids in Meredith who've grown up together treat each other. A familiarity that's comfortable, where they know each other's vulnerabilities and, if they're kind, work around them. Oh, Andrew, I miss you. I need to be with you.*

She became aware of the woman next to her who had been reading the morning paper. She folded it neatly and looked at Josie. "Would you care to read the news?"

"I would, thank you. Is there any good news?"

"There's an ad in here for a new Victor phonograph, also an electric washing machine. Isn't it something that we can now bring music into our lives without having to learn how to play the piano? And science is surely doing its part to make our lives better. Most of the news, though, seems to dwell on the dark side. There was a fire in a factory in New Jersey that killed twenty-four women and girls. We have a new lightweight boxing champion who was able to hit the other man harder, but I doubt that seems like good news to you either."

"The women and girls interest me, especially the girls. They shouldn't have been in a factory, but we haven't decided to make child labor illegal. Not that I think it's right for the women to die," Josie added.

"It sounds as if they were trapped in the building without proper exits. I imagine that would have been a desperate feeling, knowing you were going to be burned alive."

Josie shuddered at the frankness of her remark. "Yes, I would think so."

They rode on for a while, Josie glancing at the paper's ads and news. "Papers, while necessary for information, can make a person sad."

"Indeed. Do you have good papers where you live?"

"I'm lucky to get this one occasionally."

"It's biased. I suppose they all are."

Again, they were silent. Josie wondered if Andrew could find things in common with this woman and start a fascinating conversation. How would he do it? She could learn something from this person. Her experience with Mr. Wallace had been so fortunate she thought she'd try it to take her mind off Andrew. "You're going beyond Colorado Springs?"

"No, it's my home. I'm a sociology professor at CC. I study and teach social issues."

"Therefore, your interest in the fire."

"Yes, workers' rights are one of my specialties. I regret to say I've made pitiful progress talking to Colorado's legislators about the subject."

"I'm a teacher too, not on your level, though."

"Where do you teach?"

"In a tiny community over the mountains called Meredith. It's on the rail line. It's a community of immigrants, fairly representative of the western world. I've enjoyed learning about their lives."

"Your students speak enough English they're educable?"

"Oh, yes. By the time they leave eighth grade they've studied math, reading, composition, rhetoric, history, basic science, spelling, and some music and drawing. Their parents are anxious for them to learn, but not concerned about their going on to high school which would be expensive. The children would have to live with a host in a distant community where there's a high school."

"And college is an impossibility."

"Unthinkable. The families are all struggling to feed themselves."

"What's to become of these children?"

"I often ask myself that."

The woman nodded. "I saw a young man put you on the train. He seemed to care for your well-being. Tell me about him. Is he a fellow teacher?"

Josie felt her face grow hot. *Does it show I'm in love?* "No. He's in his final year at the School of Mines in Golden."

"I know the school. It has a fine reputation. He wants a career in mining?"

"His mother says he likes pretty rocks."

This tickled the lady. "His mother has a sense of humor every serious young man needs. He is serious?"

"He is thoughtful. He also has a sense of humor and is very kind."

"Admirable qualities."

They looked out the window for miles, the sun gaining in the sky, the snow almost over. "There's the Black Forest looking like the White Forest, very beautiful in this light, wouldn't you say?" the woman asked her.

"The long shadows, the darks under the bows, it's like a charcoal drawing, isn't it?"

"Yes, much like that." *That's why they've had some drawing.*

They were nearing "the Springs" when the woman opened her purse and took out a card and wrote on it: Alna Baker, PhD. "If you should find you have an especially talented student, write to me at the college. I could send you tests your pupil could take. If he or she scores well, we could see if we could find him or her a home to live in to complete high school. If the child proves to be exceptional, we could see where we could place him or her. I have friends in most state schools and it's our job to help the state's students. Scholarships are available at most universities."

Josie looked at her in awe. "Really?"

Smiling, she said, "Really."

"I do have a special boy and a remarkable girl. I may be in touch with you. My name is Josephine Carter."

"I'm pleased to meet you, Miss Carter."

The window no longer held interest for her. Could she possibly help Lars and Anna go to college? Her mind raced on the obstacles ahead of her.

The train pulled into the station and Josie struggled with the blanket and two bags. The woman offered to help with a bag and said she hoped to hear from her. *See? Trying to do what Andrew would do may have made a difference in the life of a child. I have so much to learn from him.*

Her connection to the Colorado Midland was seamless and she was soon on her way to the Continental Divide. Surprisingly, they met the storm again as they headed northwest and climbed in elevation. This time she had no seat partner and was glad of it. Making friends with a stranger had been taxing for her even though it turned out well. Now she was ready to sit back, watch the beautiful world pass by and relive the past three days.

They stopped briefly at Manitou, went through two tunnels, and quickly were rolling across the top of the high trestle. The feelings of enclosure in the tunnels contrasted sharply with the exposure on the trestle. She reflected on how loving Andrew made her feel sheltered and being without him left her vulnerable to the world. Again, she curled into the blanket. Andrew had lain on it during their picnic and it made her feel close to him. Snug and comfortable, she slept. When she awoke, it startled her to see a driving blizzard outside the window. She looked around and other passengers were closely watching their progress. The conductor came by and she asked him where they were. "Approaching Buena Vista, Miss." She had slept through South Park! She asked if there would be a problem for the train to make it to the Continental Divide. "We expect no problems. Some years ago we might have had difficulties but now we use the lower tunnel and there should be no trouble."

What else could he say? Start to panic, ladies and gentlemen, we may be stranded at 11,000 feet for the duration of winter?

A sudden break in weather. The scenery had a cold, severe beauty: bare, dark, aspen branches like filigree against the pewter sky; snow-covered evergreen boughs sagging beneath the weight of a foot of snow; soot-covered snowbanks along the tracks; bleak, wind-swept country beyond. The storm engulfed them again. She closed her eyes and tried to sleep, but she was wide awake. She went to the dining car and ordered coffee and a sandwich, realizing she hadn't eaten since five o'clock that morning. The crew seemed concerned, looking out the windows and whispering to one another. *Maybe we'll lay-over in Buena Vista and wait out the storm. Wouldn't that be the reasonable thing to do?* As she ate, she heard them announce Buena Vista and realized they were going on. *The workers on this train don't want to be stuck up there either. They must know what they're doing. I need to trust their good judgment.* She laughed at herself. *What option do I have?* Headlong, the train glided, iron wheels on iron rails covered in ice. She started to think about that reality and wondered how that could work. The conductor came through again, apparently to preserve an aura of competence and calm. She stopped him and in a low voice asked, "How do engines go uphill when rails are icy?"

Bending over to honor her whisper, he answered, "There is a device that puts sand on the tracks before the wheels get there, Miss. It assures traction." He bowed as if that solved the weather problem and walked away.

A little sand is not going to get us over these mountains, I don't care what he says. How much sand do they have? She was watching the storm swirling past them and consoled herself the snow seemed to be going fast because the train was moving in the opposite direction. Still, she thought it might be wise to wait this one out. *I know. We'll lay-over in Leadville. Yes. That's what we'll do. That's better than Buena Vista since we don't go into that town.* Having rationalized the situation, she pulled out the interminable *Oliver Twist* and began reading. She put it down, weary with Dickens' grim outlook on life. Soon needing a distraction, she began reading again.

When they reached Leadville, the conductor announced there would be a thirty-minute lay-over. Passengers were welcome to disembark for that duration. *That means they're going for the top. I'd better stock up with food so I can last a week up there.* As she stepped off the train, a blast of frigid air hit her face. *Of course, we're at 10,000'. What did I expect?* She had completely forgotten the Wallaces might be there to greet her and sure enough, she heard their cheerful call. Hugs all around, seats found in the station so they could visit. The questions began. Had she had a good time? Yes, an exceptional time. Did she like Golden? Very much.

She remembered the Mines connection. "Andrew said your father is a legend at school."

"How nice. He was at Mines for years. A knowledgeable man who explained things well."

Mrs. Wallace asked, "How was your trip here? The weather is so dreadful."

"An interesting trip to Colorado Springs. I sat next to a professor from CC who said if I have exceptional students she would send me tests they could take and she would help find homes for them so they could go to high school and if they were quite good they could get scholarships to college."

"Interesting the professor would offer to help. You must take her up on it, Josie, then let me know what you've found out."

She could tell Mr. Wallace was thinking of his own special students who would benefit from a college scholarship.

Josie added, "I'm excited because I have a boy who's advanced in science. His father expects him to go to the lumber mill. A girl is a whizz at math and poetry. Her parents understand she's special."

Mr. Wallace nodded. "Follow up, Josie. It could change their lives." He then wanted to know what they had done in Golden. She told about climbing Mt. Galbraith, walking along Clear Creek, and going to dinner at the hotel.

"Sounds as if you did about all there is to do there this time of year."

"We had a splendid Thanksgiving dinner at Andrew's. It made me think of your delicious dinner last year. Did you have a table full of strays again?"

"We had a somber dinner this year." Mrs. Wallace explained. "One of our little friends was taken from us by a father who has not proved to be a good man. We're all very concerned for little Walter. Children are so vulnerable in this world. It's hard to bear when the people who should protect them are the very people who harm them."

Josie sensed the frustration at her inability to help the child. "Is there any way you could get him back?"

"If we prove negligence or maltreatment. I regret to say those will be easy to prove. The father has a bad record. If he leaves with Walter, we'll have no recourse."

"I'm sorry that cast a shadow on your holiday. Did it ruin it for the other kids?"

"They all live with a memory of abandonment or fear of being sent back to a bad situation. It was felt."

"Let's talk of happy things," Mr. Wallace interjected. "We have a young woman here who has found a nice friend. We should rejoice in that."

"Indeed, we should."

The conductor announced the final call. They said their farewells and she was off to climb slippery tracks with dribbles of sand in a snowstorm.

At the train's concession counter she bought several boxes of Cracker Jacks, five pretzels, and a small bag of candy. *This should keep me for about five hours unless there's a need to share.* Carrying her meager supplies, she found her seat.

On they went, wending their way up the valley, the storm blowing drifts along the tracks. *I'll be happier if I close my eyes and have loving thoughts about Andrew.* She shut her eyes, tried to remember his face, his touch, his words. No. She had to watch. The long valley ascending into the mountains would have been peaceful this late afternoon had it been August. Except this wasn't peaceful and it wasn't August. The conductor calmly walked the aisle again, bowing as if there were nothing to worry about. The train climbed on its gritty tracks. Having successfully attained nearly 11,000', they entered the tunnel, dark as a moonless, starless night. Who knew what awaited them at the other end of the nearly two-mile bore? Could they get out, even with the sprinkles of sand? What becomes of a train stuck in a tight tunnel?

A clear, winter twilight of lavenders, blues, and faint pinks greeted them, the storm magically gone. What happened? The conductor walked the aisle smiling. He stopped, "You see, Miss, the East Slope can have different weather from the West Slope. It can be the opposite some days."

Down the mountain they coasted, darkness coming quickly. She didn't mind not seeing the edge of Hell Gate. She wouldn't know when they were about to fall off, so it couldn't frighten her.

The trip to Meredith was uneventful. When they stopped for her to jump off the train with her bags and blanket, it was moonless. Zona was there to give them her sack and fetch the mail. She dropped it as soon as she could and greeted Josie with a firm pat on the back. "Glad to have you home. It was good?"

"It was very good, Zona. We had a wonderful time."

Catching Josie's eyes in the light of the kerosene lamp hanging from the roof beam, Zona could see: Josie was in love.

Zona summoned Willy who was instructed to help Miss Carter get to her cabin. *It's good to be home.* "Thanks, Zona. I'll see you after school tomorrow."

"Have anything to eat down there?"

"I have pretzels, Cracker Jacks and candy I didn't eat on the train."

"Wait here. I'll get you something more substantial. You can share those with the kids tomorrow." She returned with a small pail of goulash that smelled delicious.

Josie fished out the snacks. "Give these to your family. The kids won't miss them."

Zona laughed. "They won't last long here."

Following Willy, Josie headed for the cabin, walking the trough of a path through the snow. She was so intent on staying on the path, she hadn't noticed the cabin. She was surprised to see a light on in it. "Is someone there, Willy?"

"No, Miss Carter, Ma had me bring you a bucket of water and light a fire, so it wouldn't seem so cold coming home."

This act of neighborliness when she was feeling so forlorn about leaving Andrew, touched her. As he turned to leave, she said. "Wait, Willy. I want you to know how your mother's and your thoughtfulness has made me feel. It makes me want to be kind to someone in return."

"I hope you'll be kind too, Miss Carter, because I haven't done my homework."

"Oh, Willy, you are a rascal. You have an extra day."

"Thanks, Miss Carter. See you tomorrow." He was out the door and up the path.

Was Andrew like this when he was a boy? Probably. That's why Aunt Janet bosses him around the way she does.

Unlatching the bag with the beautiful dresses, she held them next to herself to appreciate their luxury. In the bottom of the bag was a jar. The bath crystals' perfume filled the air. She sat on the bed and wondered at the generosity she had experienced that night. Hot goulash for supper, a warm cabin to come home to, fresh water, two beautiful dresses, and bath crystals. *I must remember how much these affected me. I must pass them on.* She started to put the bag away when she saw a folded piece of paper in the bottom.

It was a letter Andrew had slipped in as he carried her bags.

My Darling,

When you find this, you will be a long way from me and I will be as lonesome as a man can be. I will also still be glowing from the love you and I shared and feeling you will love me when you are away from me as I will love you.

Thank you for coming to Golden. I knew I loved you, but I wasn't confident you loved me. You have been most generous in assuring me you do. In four weeks you will be in my arms again. Until then, in my imagination I will kiss your soft lips, and hold your dear hands.

Yours alone,
Andrew

Holding the note to her heart, she stepped outside to look up to the stars. *I will hold you in my imagination too, Dear Andrew. I send you a Dipper full of kisses.*

The night air was cold. The goulash beckoned. She sat and ate her lonely supper in a dream.

Greeting Miss Carter as if she had been gone for a long time, the little ones' welcome was especially rewarding. Older kids were more casual in acknowledging her return, yet they seemed glad to see her. She was especially happy to see Mr. Miller coming down the path, the book he was reading carried carefully in his mittened hands. *Huckleberry Finn* was in her drawer, waiting for the end of day when she would give it to him. The hours passed quickly. They shared stories about what they had done in her absence. Willy, smug he didn't have homework to turn in, amused her and she said nothing about it

When she dismissed the children, she asked Mr. Miller if they could visit. He seemed glad for the opportunity to talk. She asked about the book he was reading, and he proudly said it was the fourth-grade reader. Delighted he was making such progress, she opened her drawer, pulled out his present, and handed it to him.

He seemed confused, then took it from her outstretched hand. "You may open it, Mr. Miller, it's a gift for you."

Shaking his head, holding the package, he said, "I've never had a gift I can remember."

How can it be? Never to have had a present?

His hands were shaking as he carefully untied the string and unfolded the brown paper. He held the book gingerly, looking up at her with questions in his eyes.

"I think you may be able to read this book. It's about a boy, so it's not really a man's book, though a famous man wrote it. Many have enjoyed reading about Huck. I hope you will. I wrote a message to you on the inside."

He slowly opened the new cover and saw written: To my dear friend, Mr. Miller, who has made my life richer, Josephine Carter. He read it to himself and looked up at her with questions in his eyes.

"Do you understand what I have written?"

"I don't think so."

"I mean having you as a student has made my life more pleasant and I feel grateful to you for being my friend."

He visibly sighed. "Oh. I didn't know exactly what you meant."

"I hope you'll like it."

He looked at it carefully, touched the cover, opened it to the title page.

"Can you sound it out?"

"*The Ad-ven-tures of Huck-le-ber-ry Finn.*" He raised his eyes.

"You know an adventure is something you do that's out of the ordinary and you don't know what to expect."

"Like coming to school when I'm an old man?"

She chuckled. "Exactly. In this case, it's boys doing things that are risky."

Staring at the page, "I don't know what this sound is." He pointed to the parenthesis.

"That isn't a sound. It tells you what's between it and the one at the end, aren't that important. It's called a parenthesis. You don't need to remember that for now."

"So, I say, 'Tom Saw-yer's com-rad-e.'"

"Yes. Comrade means friend."

He nodded. "'By Mark Twain.'" He looked away, puzzled.

"Would you read the first line of the book to me?"

"I'll try." He stopped to look at the picture of the little boy holding a rifle in one hand and a dead rabbit in the other. "He's a better shot than most soldiers." He turned to the opening page of the story and read, "You don't know about me, without you have read *The Adventures of Tom Sawyer,* but that ain't no matter." Mr. Miller frowned. "Should he say it that way?"

"Mark Twain was a master at writing the way people really speak. He explains up front they will all speak differently, according to where they come from and what race they are. It may make it difficult for you to read, but I imagine in your travels you've heard people use English many ways."

"Yes'm. Folks in Wales don't sound much like the English, and Scots a body can hardly understand. Then I come to America and everyone talked funny, especially Southern folks, it seemed to me."

"Then maybe you'll feel right at home with Mark Twain. But I don't want you talking like Huckleberry Finn to the children and giving them bad grammar," Josie laughed.

He nodded, "I wouldn't be a worse example than I am already."

"You're the very best example. You want to learn. They can see it's important. Now, when you get home, see if you can make sense of it, and if you can't, we'll meet after school and you can read to me and I'll help you. That's part of the present."

He still seemed a bit befuddled. "Thank you for a present." He bundled up, hugging the book to his chest, and left.

She tidied the room, banked the fire in the stove for the night, went to her cabin to put coal in the stove and the tea kettle on to heat, then went up the path to see Zona with her pot of tea.

"I want to hear all about it. Sit down." Josie got their cups from under the counter and poured tea.

"His mother and father are very nice. She cooked a delicious Thanksgiving dinner. After dinner, Andrew's father boned the turkey and Andrew and I did dishes. The men at their house know how to help in the kitchen. It was marvelous to see. I stayed at Aunt Janet's house. She's a no-nonsense lady. You'd like her, Zona. She explained a lot about men and women and how babies are made. I didn't know."

"You didn't know how babies are made! Why didn't you ask me?"

"I would have if I'd realized it was something I should know."

"Holy Mother. Yes, you should know. Did he try something?"

"No, not at all. Some woman in an awful dress said something to me and he confessed one of those women had touched him once and he liked it, but he felt guilty about it later. It upset me, and Aunt Janet helped me understand about men."

"Of course, he liked it. They like anything that jangles them."

"That's what Aunt Janet said too. She made them sound kind of pitiful, how easily they're jangled yet how they seek it out."

"Pitiful and a pain in the neck. Well, I'm glad she set you straight. She didn't give you any of that religion stuff, did she?"

"No. The family isn't religious. At my house we were, but since we didn't talk about anything like this, I don't know what our religion wanted us to do."

"Feel guilty about it."

"Do you feel guilty?"

"Used to when we went to church. Up here, there's no church to keep reminding us we're bad. A breath of fresh air, I call it. What else happened?"

"You'll love this. We went for a hike on Friday, out to a remote place and when we got there he handed me a pair of his pants, a shirt, jacket, and hat and showed me an old cabin where I could change. We went hiking like we did last summer."

Zona frowned. "Does he like to fancy you're a boy?"

"I don't think so. What do you mean?"

"Nothing. Just curious."

"He says he likes for me to be free, not to have to worry about my skirt and acting like a lady all the time. When his Aunt Janet asked how we met he made up this ridiculous story about coming across me in the woods and I pulled a gun on him and he had to ask me not to shoot him. She knew he was kidding and later, I told her the truth. She thought it was fine, what I did."

"It was fine. We should all be in pants given the work we do. Did he like you in your Sunday dress?"

"That's another story. After a hike the next day, when I went to Aunt Janet's to get ready for dinner at the hotel she had laid out two beautiful dresses her daughter didn't want. She let me wear one for the evening. Yesterday, when I got ready to come home, she gave me both. I'll show them to you."

"He thought you looked pretty?"

"I think it shocked him. Aunt Janet had also done my hair up in this fancy do, and he didn't know what to make of it. His mother told me men don't like change, so to head into something like that slowly."

"They don't like change; she's right about that. This school he goes to, there are a lot of women there?"

"No, it's almost all men. He's studying mining and geology. His mother says he likes pretty rocks."

Zona suppressed a groan. "He likes you as a woman?"

Confused about her questions, Josie didn't know how to answer. "If you mean did he kiss me, yes, we figured out how to do that. We neither one had experience with that sort of behavior. He's gone places with other girls, but he didn't know how to talk to them, so he didn't go out with them again. He's not as innocent as I am, but nearly so."

"How old is he?"

"Twenty-two."

"And he's inexperienced?"

"He says so. I believe him. His parents and aunt tease him about finally falling in love." She blushed saying this.

"He says he loves you, does he?"

"He does. And I love him, Zona. He's so kind and thoughtful and he talks to me about interesting things."

Nodding, Zona changed the subject. "Were the kids glad to see you? I don't think they got much done with the mothers."

"They're good kids. I had something sort of sad, though. I bought a book for Mr. Miller and gave it to him after school and he didn't know what to do with it. He said he'd never had a present he could remember. Can you imagine that? Never to have had a present?"

"No. Even when my family was at its poorest my mother managed to make us some little thing out of scraps for Christmas and we cherished her gifts. He's had the roughest life I've ever heard of. Nobody ever to take care of him. I think that's why he's so fond of you, Josie. You treat him well."

"I do care about him. He's like a grandfather to me but better because he's my friend too."

"I'm glad you feel that way. It wouldn't hurt if you told him so."

"I did, in a way. I put in the book that he made my life richer. He didn't understand what I meant so I explained it meant my life is better because he's my friend."

Zona sighed. "I'm glad you explained that to him."

Josie stood, "I'd better get down to the cabin. I need to get ready for class tomorrow. It was fun talking to you."

"Sure. Be careful on the ice."

Watching Josie go, Zona shook her head, "Dear God, prove me wrong."

Tuesday dawned cold and clear. It hadn't seemed that cold the night before when she went outside to look at stars, but the temperature had dropped dramatically making snow sparkle with frost crystals. She went to the schoolhouse to build the fire so it would be warm for the children then returned to eat her oatmeal. *Thank heavens for these warm mittens I can wear inside my old, frayed ones. I must remember to make Aunt Janet a pretty pair.* She had written her bread-and-butter thank you letters to the Allans and Aunt Janet and she hurried up the path to get them in the east-bound mail before school started. She met Willy coming down the path.

"Ma found out I'd bargained with you about my homework, so I have to give it to you before school to make up."

"I didn't tell her, Willy."

"No. I bragged to some kids and they told on me."

"You probably learned more from that lesson than you did from the homework, eh?"

"I suppose." He handed her the homework. "Can I take those up to Ma for you?"

"That would be nice. Thanks, Willy. Tell your mother hello, please." Walking back to her cabin she began to wonder why Zona hadn't seemed happier for her since her weekend had gone so well. *Who knows? Maybe she's never been in love with a man who loved her the way Andrew loves me. It may make her a little sad.*

Mr. Miller was the first pupil to show up and his face was bright with happiness. "I could read it, Josie. I read a whole chapter last night before I fell asleep."

"You enjoyed how he tells his story?"

"When I got around the way they talk, I sort of recognize them from people I've known, and it made me happy to understand why he makes them talk that way."

"He was a remarkable story-teller. He died this spring. I think the whole country mourned him because he brought so many people pleasure. I'm glad you like him."

"I see what I've missed all my life because I couldn't read and how I can now because you were willing to teach me. If I keep practicing, I'll be able to read all sorts of books, besides children's."

"That's true, but children's books may be the most fun. I'll keep thinking about what you might enjoy and what will help you improve your reading."

He nodded and took his seat at the side of the room. His arithmetic skills were improving and his personal knowledge of geography had helped them all.

After class Mr. Miller asked if he could talk to her about Mark Twain.

"What is it you want to know, Mr. Miller?"

"His name seems weird. When I was down South near the Mississippi you could hear people on the river boats. They'd yell quarter twain, half twain or mark twain. It all meant something to them like depths of the water someone told me."

"You're right about his name. His real name is Samuel Clemmons. He took the name Mark Twain when he became a writer. Were you ever on a river boat on the Mississippi, Mr. Miller?"

"No'm. I was close by it in the battle of Vicksburg."

"Oh, my. You've experienced so much in your life. My dream is for you to become such a good reader you could write your stories so others would understand the past better."

"Would I have to use another name?"

She laughed. "No. That's something silly some authors do. Everyone knew Mark Twain's real name."

"Makes a body wonder, doesn't it?"

"It does."

Wednesday came and went in the classroom and after Josie heard the train go through, she hurried to see if by any chance she had a letter. It was strange. Zona almost didn't want to give her the letter, or did she imagine it?

November 27, 1910

Precious Love,

Your dear poem touched my heart. Bobby Burns would regret he hadn't thought of those words.

I have been beyond lonely here without you. The trolley ride home was endless. The walk from the stop to the house seemed like miles. Breakfast was tasteless and boring. Mom and Dad seemed to natter on about nothing, constantly expecting an answer to a question I hadn't heard, then snickering because I was so absent-minded. It didn't seem fair for them to pick on a wounded person. I left, grumpy and disconsolate, and went to my room to study, I think. I can't remember what I did. I missed you. I miss you. I will miss you until you are in my arms again.

I'm anxious to hear if your connections were smooth, if you made it home safely through the storm, although it did seem to be dwindling here after a while, so I hope it did the same for you. I wanted to walk beside your train all the way to Meredith to make certain you were safe but my legs and stamina wouldn't be a match for those pistons and steam even to get you out of Denver. I had to trust your safety to other men and that didn't make me happy. I want to be your protector, your hero, your everything, because you are my gentle comfort, my softness in a harsh world, my everything.

There is no news here that I have paid any attention to except Mom did say Queen, the circus elephant, was put down at eighty-six years old after killing her trainer. Wouldn't you imagine after all those years there would be a bond of affection between them. Or had the trainer been a mean person? Maybe after eighty-six we can all get cranky. I don't ever want to be grumpy with you. If I get that way, you should leave. Leaving me would be the worst punishment.

I shoveled Aunt Janet's walk after ours and she told me how much she enjoyed visiting with you. She thinks you're a lovely girl and right for me because you seem to have a tolerance for monologues. I think that was a pointed comment on my need to let you talk occasionally. I said I'd give it a try sometime. Aunt Janet is not hesitant to point out my faults which is her singular fault. Do I need to say she never runs out of topics?

Prince has forgiven us for his frosty evening. He said to tell you hello and he's looking forward to a letter from you. Mom reminded me mail doesn't go out on Sunday when I said I had to hurry to get a letter to you. Then she started humming "Always." It's true, Dear Josie. Always.

I think you receive mail after school. If it's not too cold tonight, will you look at the stars with me? I feel they reach down and touch us at the same time and bring us together and nothing makes me happier.

All my love,
Andrew

P. S. The books are in the mail for Mr. Miller.

It was late before she quit reading it over and over. She fixed a meager supper, tried to concentrate on lesson plans then let herself answer him. She drew a pair of pinecones on a branch for him.

Hello, My Love,

I want to come home to you.

Your heart is my home now. It's where I belong. Always. All ways. When I unpacked and found the tender note you tucked in the bag, I almost packed again to come back to you. Thank you for sharing such loving thoughts, they made me feel close to you and warm inside. Your letter today filled me with such happiness, longing, and loneliness I could hardly bear to quit reading it. There would be no words left on the page if eyes wore out ink.

My trip home was uneventful. The storm raged until north of Colorado Springs then it calmed down only to pick up as we neared the Divide. Once through the tunnel, it was clear skies. The conductor said weather like that happens often: storm on one side, clear on the other. Maybe you'll explain how that happens. I will confess to being uncomfortable about the train's ability to climb those slick rails in icy conditions, but the conductor explained they sprinkle sand on the tracks before the wheels get there. It sounded like hocus-pocus to me except we did climb the mountain and here I am, so what do I know?

The older lady I sat next to on the first leg of the trip is a professor at CC. (Imagine that. A woman professor!) She gave me her card and said if I ever have an exceptional student I should let her know and she will try to find a way to help the student get more education. With this woman's kind offer, and if Lars is as smart as I think he is, and Anna is as quick at math as she seems, something good may come of it.

All my life I've heard "Don't talk to strangers," and I'm sure that's good advice, but not always. The lady did notice you were "concerned for my well-being." She asked about you and said Mines is an excellent school.

Please tell your mother I wore the blanket all the way home. It was cold in those cars much of the time. Please tell Aunt Janet I appreciated her mittens. I'll make her a pair that don't match her sister's.

About Queen, I'm sorry she turned violent. I'm glad I don't know why. Perhaps she never wanted to be in a circus doing things completely against her nature. I wish people treated all animals with the care Prince receives. When you read him this letter, he'll know I'm thinking of him.

Andrew? Now you say, "Yes, Josie." If we always look at the North Star, because I can find it, because the Big Dipper's pointer stars show me, then I'd know we connect. I like the North Star because it's reliably constant, the way my love will be for you.

When I came home, I was in a daze of loving you and couldn't help but think of how miserable we both had made ourselves before we got back together. What a difference seeing you, talking to you, laughing with you, kissing you! made. I'm so comfortable with you, again, and I cherish this feeling.

I almost forgot to tell you: Mr. Miller likes the book. He's read four chapters. Andrew, he'd never had a present before. Isn't that sad? We've talked about the Civil War because Twain was his age and decided he couldn't fight for the South. I asked Mr. Miller if he could talk to the older boys about the war when we get to it. He thought he could, but he couldn't encourage them to ever go to war. It's not the adventure young boys think it will be. I must go now, it's star time.

Yours alone,
Josie

P. S. I don't believe Aunt Janet said that about monologues. At your house, horses say things and now I know aunts do too.

Glad her pupils' various lessons required her to be attentive, Josie's days passed quickly. It was after school she felt lonesome and couldn't keep herself from thinking of Andrew. *I wonder if he's home from school. Is it his responsibility to feed Prince? When does he do the estimating for his father and is he thinking of me and making mistakes? I wonder how often he goes out with his friends for a beer.* She stopped. *That woman!* Her heart pounded. *Don't think about that. He's a man.* New curiosity about this man she was in love with swirled in her mind. *How long will it take to know him, to understand what being a man really means? Do I know what being a woman means? Examine thyself, Josie.* That was too complicated, she went back to Andrew. *What does it take to make him angry or does he get angry? I do. Will it shock him when I lose my temper? How will he feel when I get stubborn about something? I'd better work on those faults.*

Mr. Miller was staying after school every day to talk about his book. If he had a passage he couldn't understand he would read it to her and they would discuss it. Sometimes it was one word he was misreading that would change the meaning of a sentence. For a man who had been so quiet when she first met him, he had become talkative. Curious about what Twain was trying to accomplish with his story, he was anxious to discuss what he was reading. Josie was pleased. Mr. Miller's excitement with learning was infectious and kids noticed what a difference going to school had made in him. He had received the books from Andrew and was happy to think he might be able to read them. He asked to write a note to Andrew, with her help, to thank him. Thrilled to think he had made such progress, she gave him good paper for his note, so he would know she took his work seriously. He did not miss the gesture.

The week ended. She could be alone with her thoughts of Andrew and not have to try to pay attention to anything else. She did her weekend chores, cooked some soup that would last a few days because she could put it outside during the day in the cooler attached to the north side of her cabin, a luxury she didn't have as weather warmed. It was not warm now. Snow was two feet deep along paths, the temperature was dropping nightly to around ten degrees and barely above freezing in the daytime. December would bring shorter days, more snow, colder weather, perfect days for staying inside and copying wildflowers and birds for display in the classroom.

Saturday night supper seemed to drag. Kids recited their poems, Mr. Miller and the boys played their instruments, everyone sang, the food was good, but it went on and on. She wanted to go home to be with her thoughts.

The weekend over, she was back in class again, juggling lessons, trying to keep pent-up kids quiet and seated. Once, when the older boys were being particularly rambunctious, Mr. Miller told them to sit down and behave. The boys looked shocked, sat down, and behaved. Josie was surprised. When she looked at Mr. Miller, he looked surprised as well. She smiled slightly so he'd know it was all right. After class he started to apologize for interfering with her teaching. She shook her head. "There wasn't a lot of teaching going on since they were so disruptive. You did me a favor and them one too. They respect you and if you said they weren't behaving they realized they'd better shape up. Thank you for helping me."

She was now watching Lars closely to see if she had assessed his intelligence correctly. He grasped mathematical concepts more quickly than she could explain them, and he'd come to her aid on several occasions when pupils asked questions about why some mathematical solution worked logically. He was an analytical thinker, grasped the science she could teach and asked her to get him books on chemistry and physics from the library, which she did, which he read and seemed to understand. She asked Mr. Miller one afternoon if she were overestimating his intelligence. "I don't think so. He's smart as a whip and needs to go on to school."

"What about Anna?"

"She makes me sad."

"Why, Mr. Miller?"

"What will the world do with a woman that smart?"

"It is a worry. Do you know she also writes poetry? They're almost mathematical in their forms. Do you think her parents know how clever she is?"

"I believe they do. They would like her to be educated, more than Lars' folks want for him."

"His father wants him to go to the mill next year. I met a woman who might help him go on. How can I talk to his father? I don't think he'd believe me and besides the family wants his wages."

"Will you let me talk to him? I know what it's like to be uneducated. I spent my life wondering about many things and not able to get answers because I couldn't read. Lars is curious and smart. If he's able to learn more, he'll be a happier man. Anders has opinions, but maybe he'll come around. He can't read English; he should understand." They agreed he would try. If he were successful, she would write to Alna Baker at Colorado College.

She was perplexed. "Do you think any of this matters to them?"

"It matters more than you will ever know."

Wednesday afternoon she went to the post office with expectations of a letter. She was not disappointed.

December 4, 1910

Winsome Lass,

How I love you. Thank you for your letter, except for the P.S. I don't think I understand what you mean by "At your house, horses say things." Don't they at everyone's house? I asked Edward if his horse Molly talks to their family, and he assured me she does, and she was jealous of Prince getting to go on all the picnics with you. Molly was glad not to go to the hotel; she doesn't like ice in her mane either.

I'm glad Mr. Miller is enjoying Huck. He must understand what it was like for a child to be worried about where he was going to sleep and when he'd have another meal. Twain makes those troubles not as fearsome as they must have been for Mr. Miller. Huck had a dreadful father and was escaping. You haven't made me feel Mr. Miller's family life was bad. It was his luck that was bad. Maybe he can forget how wearying survival was for a child and get into the spirit of adventure instead. I'm happy he received a present—especially from you because I think he must love you. How could he know you and not love you?

What is there about cold December days? I long to curl up with you under a blanket. Since we were together my heart aches for you as always, but now that I know you love me and want to be with me, it feels more intense. I always want to miss you when you're gone from me. I want to feel the longing if I can't hold you in my arms. It will make me appreciate you more, if that's possible, when I can hold you.

Mom is out marching today despite cold weather. They're afraid the legislators will escape to their districts for a month and the women won't have an audience for their vehemence.

You do know, I suppose, there are three women in our state legislature, a triumph for vehemence, and Denver has, I'm told, (repeatedly), the first woman county commissioner in the country. See what you women can accomplish if you stick together and don't let your husbands vote your ballots? If you're wondering, Mom doesn't have political ambitions. She just wants to bend the country to her will.

I can't blather on anymore. I'm trying to be newsy and interesting, but do you really care that some Brits and some Japanese are separately sailing for Antarctica? No. I would care, normally, but I don't feel normal anymore. I miss you, terribly. I would talk to you about these things. We would find them interesting if we could be together, but apart, they seem sort of boring. When are you coming home? I need to know when I can count on seeing you again. Can you leave school early and let those mothers take care of their own kids for a change? I know you'll do whatever is right, but I can dream, can't I?

Please write to me. Your letters ease the ache in my heart a little then it's worse when I come to the end, so please make them long. It's okay if all you say is the same thing over and over if it's "I love you." I'm finding that's all that matters now.

With a heart filled with love,
Your Andrew

She read his letter, smiling, and feeling very tender toward him. Disciplining herself, she fixed dinner, made lesson plans. Then she was free to be with her Andrew.

December 7, 1910
My Sweet, Fanciful Friend,

You tickle my fancy.

If your horse talks to you, he's a friend who helps you through your loneliness. I'd much prefer him to some young, pretty thing offering you comfort. Oh, Andrew, the very thought of your being with another woman hurts me. I don't want to be a jealous, possessive type who won't allow you to have a variety of friends, but I do hope you'll choose wisely, meaning young men and old, ugly, disagreeable women. I'll promise to choose wisely too. Old, ugly, disagreeable women and young men. Oh, I can't even tease you about that.

Last night I went out to see the North Star and it was a horizontal blizzard. I apologize for a very quick good night. It snowed all day. We must have nearly three feet of snow on the ground. Zona sent Willy down to shovel out the outhouse and stoop so the kids could get in—and out. It was terrific help. He's such a likeable boy I hope you get to meet him someday. (Yes, I gave him a nickel.) He's not as bright as Lars but he's quick and has a nice sense of humor which Lars lacks. It would be fun to see where life takes them. I never talk to you about Anna. She pushes Lars sometimes on math though she's a year behind him. I'm not sure I want to see where life takes her because I'm afraid I'd be disappointed. Mr. Miller expressed the same concern. Your mother's efforts may prove a good thing for the Annas of the world, but not for a long time, I fear.

Mr. Miller is on Chapter X and he didn't understand "ha'nt." We had a nice talk about how some people believe in ghosts and being haunted. You probably don't remember Chapter X, as such. I'm smiling, but knowing you, you might! They have found a dead man and Jim is very concerned he hasn't been "planted and comfortable." Mr. Miller told me about burying his mother and little sisters. It was in paupers' graves, he thinks, without tombstones and it cost him all the money he could find at home. He reckons now, they took advantage of him. He wishes they had a marker on their graves. He's never been back to Wales, though, so he realizes it's not important, simply a feeling he has.

He talked to Anders last night about how smart Lars is. He said he didn't go any further than that. Thought he'd plant the seed how Lars would benefit from more schooling. I found his approach subtle. I hope it works.

Otto has been talking about Robert Scott going to the South Pole. It must be in all the papers because we're aware of it up here. We've talked about it in class and how it would be summer down there. I get a little dreamy when I think of summer and what a good hike I had up the North Fork. I must tell you about it sometime. I met the nicest man. I fell in love with him and I was able to convince him to love me too. It's a long story. You'd enjoy it, though. Now he kisses me if I behave and don't tease him too much.

I have started Aunt Janet's mittens. They're going to be a wine color because her coat has flecks of wine wool in it. I intend to make a right hand one and a left hand one. I hope it turns out that way. Why do I have the feeling your projects always turn out as intended? Is it because you think them through before you begin? Make certain you have enough yarn of the right color, understand the pattern, ask for help when needed, do a test pattern, check your gauge, then proceed with caution? I'll drive you crazy!!

But stay. I can learn. Maybe. If not, will you give me a system?

I'm sorry your heart aches. Please take care of it. It's a gentle, sensitive heart. If you let me put a warm covering of love on it to protect it from loneliness, will it be better?

Hold me tight, keep me safe from this storm. I'll peek for the North Star but I won't see it.

Your distant love,
Josie

When she awoke the storm still raged. Willy came to shovel snow again and when she offered him another nickel he shook his head, reached in his pocket and handed back the nickel she'd given him the day before. "Ma said I couldn't keep it. Helping you is my job."

Josie wanted to give it to him and tell him not to tell, but couldn't undermine Zona. She'd give him a gift later. She said she understood, was sorry and thanked him. He took her letter for the mail and went home. Snow-covered kids arrived, chilling the small room with the open door. Mr. Miller, usually the first one there to help little ones with boots and coats, didn't come. Josie wondered if the storm had him housebound. At noon when the kids went home for lunch, she asked Willy to check on Mr. Miller to see if he were working that day, and if not, to go to his cabin to check on him.

Zona came through the door and quietly shut it behind her. "Josie, Mr. Miller is dead. He shoveled snow then went inside to lie down. He didn't get up."

Josie couldn't understand the words that came after "is dead." Her mind shut down. She shook her head. How could he be dead? He was with her yesterday. Looking at Zona, she said, "I love Mr. Miller. He's my friend."

Zona put her arm around Josie's shoulder. "He loved you too."

"We talked about death yesterday. He was reading about a dead man. He said he hadn't been able to put a marker on his mother's grave. That bothered him." Her mind was a jumble with what they had talked about, none of it making sense with what Zona said. "May I go to him? I need to talk to him. I need to thank him for being my friend."

"Yes. Come with me."

They trudged up the narrow path to the store where town folks had gathered. Everyone was watching Josie, but she didn't see them. Otto came out, and he and Zona led her up the narrow trough of a path to Mr. Miller's cabin. She had never been inside. It was small and cold. Mr. Miller's body lay on the bed, fully clothed with his coat and boots on. Josie went to him and touched his cold hand, knelt on the floor beside him and whispered, "I will miss you, dear friend. I will remember you." She put her hand on his chest and bent her head over it. Tears started to come, then sobs overcame her. Zona picked her up and said they should go to the store. There was nothing Josie could do there. She obeyed and followed them to the store.

Once inside, Zona said that since everyone was there she would open her safe and read a message from Mr. Miller. He had given it to her a few months before. She took out a small box, opened an envelope and read, "I leave all I own to Josephine Carter who changed my life. Signed, Llewellyn Miller, October 26, 1910." Zona added, "Olaf and I witnessed his signature that day. You'll see them here." She held up the paper to show everyone. "He gave me this box for Josie and he gave the key to Olaf. Do you have the key, Olaf?" He took a small key from his pocket. "Do you want to open this now, Josie, or later?"

She didn't know what was happening. It was confusing to her. Why were they dealing with this now? She nodded because she didn't know what else to do. Zona gave her the key and she opened the box. There was money inside. She looked at it and shook her head.

Zona took the box from her, locked it, gave her the key, and put the box in the safe. "It will be here when you're ready, Josie."

Everyone began to shuffle about and whisper, leaving without saying anything to her. Josie went to the window where she sat and stared at snow coming down. Barely audible, she said, "I need to send a telegram. How do I do that?"

"You tell me what to say and where to send it."

"It's to Andrew. Say: Mr. Miller is dead." She gave Zona the address, said goodbye and went to her cabin.

What was she to do? She climbed into her cold bed with her clothes on and cried herself to sleep.

When Andrew came home from school, he saw the envelope lying on the kitchen table. He'd never seen a telegram before, but his name was on it, so he opened it. The message was brief. He knew what to do. He went to his room, put clean clothes in a travel valise, found his warmest coat and boots, gathered his toiletries, texts, and bed roll, and called to reserve a ticket on the next train to Meredith. When his mother came in, he explained what had happened and she agreed it was what he needed to do. She gave him money and put her arms around him. "When people we love hurt, Andrew, we hurt too. She needs you and I'm glad you understand that."

At supper he tried to tell them what Mr. Miller had found in Josie, though he could see the relationship only through her eyes. He felt he knew what that lonely old man came to feel with her: acceptance, friendship and love, the crucial bonds to others he had missed most of his life. For Josie, he had been the kind, caring, extended family she didn't have. Andrew knew she would be devastated by his death.

"They don't lay over here, mister, you'd better get right back on," Zona yelled at Andrew when he got off the train in Meredith. The train gave one short whistle and pulled out.

He came to her, "You must be Zona. I'm Andrew Allan."

"Well, I'll be. Grab some of this, will ya' and help me get it into the store out of the weather."

When they had the lumber inside, he asked, "Is Josie all right?"

"She's holed up in her cabin. I sent some soup down to her, but I haven't seen her. It's been hard on her. You can go on down," she hesitated, "but you can't sleep there."

"I was hoping I could sleep on the floor of the school."

"Ummm. Better if you sleep on the floor of the store. You won't bother none."

He nodded. She was right. The school was too close for curious eyes. "Thank you. I appreciate that. What's the fire on the hill? They're not cremating him, are they?"

"Oh, no. They're trying to thaw a patch of ground they've shoveled off so they can dig a grave."

"I can help with that. I'll do whatever I can."

She looked at him closely. Maybe he was okay. "I'll tell Otto. Go. It's getting late."

He put his bed roll and valise on the floor of the store and headed down the snowy path. He climbed the stoop, knocked softly on the door.

"Come in." She was sitting at the table, a bowl of uneaten soup, a cup of cold tea and a piece of bread on a plate in front of her.

He opened the door. She turned listlessly toward him. "Josie, it's me."

She wiped her eyes and looked at him. His hat, pulled down over his ears, obscured his face, his heavy coat hid the rest of him. "It's me, Josie, Andrew."

She shook her head in disbelief, "Andrew?"

"Yes. I've come to be with you." He kicked off his boots, shed his coat and hat, and walked toward her. She fell into his arms.

Her sobs broke his heart. He cradled her, smoothed her hair, took her to her bed and laid her down, then he lay beside her, holding her as close as he could. Spent with crying, she lay silent. When he raised his head and kissed her wet cheeks, she choked up again. Sympathy was too much to bear.

Gaining her composure, she reached up and touched his cheek. "I didn't mean for you to come. I needed you to know. I wanted you to hold me in your heart."

"I had to come. I needed to be with you."

She nestled into his arms and was quiet. "I'm tired of death taking people I love."

"You've known too much sorrow."

"I want my heart to harden."

"You would miss loving people."

"I wouldn't miss the pain of losing them."

"No. I hope you won't know any more loss for a long while."

"I love you, Andrew. Thank you for coming to me."

"I love you too, Josie. We need to be together, especially now."

"Yes. Together. In your arms."

She sounded sleepy. "Do you want me to leave so you can get some sleep?"

"No. I want you to stay here tonight, holding me."

"I would love to do that, but I can't. Zona said I may sleep on the floor of the store."

"On the floor?"

"I'll be okay. It won't be as bumpy as mountains."

"I have some soup. Will you share it with me?"

"Let's get up and put some food in you, then I'll leave."

He found a pan, poured the soup in to heat, put the tea kettle on and set the table. She watched him from the bed. When he had her dinner ready, he helped her get up.

"I want you to have half of it."

"I ate on the train. I'm not hungry."

It was all he could do not to spoon the soup into her mouth. He sat patiently watching her decide whether she would eat or not. She took a bite then continued. They drank their tea in silence.

"Something happened I don't understand, Andrew."

"What's that?"

"Zona opened the safe, I think, then she read this note from Mr. Miller saying he gave me everything. Then she handed me a box with money in it. I have a key to it. She put the box in the safe, I think. I didn't know what was happening."

"Do you know how much money is there?"

"No. I didn't touch it."

"We can talk about it tomorrow. It's probably not much. Don't worry about it."

"I won't worry. It doesn't feel right."

"You gave him friendship, Josie, I doubt if he'd had much of that in his life. He wanted to give you whatever he had in return. He doesn't need it now."

She shook her head sadly.

"Is the soup good?" he asked.

"Taste it. Zona makes good soup." She held the spoon to his lips and he took it.

"Yes. She makes a good soup. I'm glad you've enjoyed it."

"I didn't enjoy it. I ate it. Nothing tastes good."

"It will again."

"What's that light on the hill. It's making the whole valley glow."

"It's a fire so they can dig his grave."

She nodded. "We read in his book about a dead man that Jim wanted 'planted and comfortable'. Mr. Miller liked that thought."

"It's a peaceful way of thinking about it."

"Umm hmm. Is your little sister's grave someplace you go to visit?"

"You know about her?"

"Aunt Janet told me. You mentioned her. Do you go?"

"I don't know where it is."

"I go visit my mother, sometimes, when I have something to think over. I wish I could go to my brothers' graves. I'm not sure anyone ever loved them as I love you. I'd like to tell them what it's like, tell them about you."

He was uncomfortable with this conversation. "I think it would be good for you to go to bed now. Is it all right if I leave?"

"I never want you to leave. I know you have to go. Will you kiss me and tuck me in? I'll get into my nightgown if you'll turn your back."

He nodded and added coal to the fire in the stove. Keeping his back to her, he put the dirty dishes in the dishpan and poured hot water over them. He rinsed them, took the water to the door, and threw it out. It was difficult to keep his back to her in the small space, but he kept his head down in a good faith effort.

"I'm in bed now. You're safe."

"Yes. You're safe too." *But someday*.... He sat on the side of the bed. "I don't know how to 'tuck in' a person. You'll have to help me with that."

"You pull the blankets up around their chin then you kiss them."

He did as instructed, touched her cheek, and smoothed her hair. "I'll see you in the morning. Sleep well."

He put on his boots, coat, and hat, blew out the kerosene lamp and slipped out the door.

As he walked up the path it occurred to him he needed to talk to Zona. Reaching the store, he followed a path around to the house and knocked on the door. A sturdy boy answered, studied him, then extended his hand when Andrew introduced himself. The boy answered, "I'm Henry." A voice from behind him yelled to bring him in and shut the damn door. "Come on in."

Andrew entered, took off his boots, and walked in. Zona appeared, told him to take off his coat and hat, she needed to talk to him.

"How's she doing?"

"She's going to sleep, I think. She's worn out with crying."

"Poor baby. I'm surprised she took it so hard."

"She's tired of losing people she loves, she said. You know her mother died when she was fifteen and she lost her twin brothers a couple of years ago?"

"I didn't know about the brothers. That's a shame."

"Yes. In Panama."

A voice in the background asked what the hell were they were doing in Panama? He answered, "Working on the Isthmian canal. One died of the fever, the other in an accident. She didn't get to say goodbye to them. It bothers her."

"Of course," Zona concurred. "Sit down. There are some things I need to talk to you about. Kids, leave. This is stuff I don't want you to hear." Reluctant to miss what they shouldn't hear, they left slowly. Henry, feeling he was old enough, was especially slow to leave. "You, too, Henry. This isn't about us, it's about Josie." He grumbled and left. Zona got up, closed the door, looking to see who was hiding where.

She motioned for Andrew to sit at the table and she and Otto joined him. "Do you know Mr. Miller left everything to her?"

"She mentioned it. She doesn't know what it means."

"Right. What it means is she owns the cabin and all his stuff. She also got all his money. Olaf and I counted it one day, to make sure we knew what we were dealing with and I wanted us to be a check on each other. We promised not to tell anyone else. I haven't even told Otto. Right, Ott?"

"I don't know what's there."

"Olaf swears he didn't tell his wife. Anyway, there's over $1,800[1] in that box. I know it was a bad time to tell her about his will, but everyone was there, and I didn't want them sneaking around last night, tearing the place apart looking for hidden money. I wanted them to know it's all hers and the money isn't there. You'll have to help her understand what she's got."

"I had no idea. I told her it probably wasn't much. I'm afraid that amount will confuse her."

"I'd think so. Most of us have never seen an amount like that and it could be a temptation to some of the drifters working here. My safe could be carted off without too much effort. The sooner she decides what to do with it, the better."

"I understand. I'll try to talk to her about it."

"We also need to talk about the funeral. The foreman will say a few words. Do you think she would like to say anything?"

"Do you think anyone else will speak?"

Turning to Otto, "Ott, will you ask if anyone else wants to speak?"

"Nobody will. Makes a body nervous."

"I'll leave it up to her to do what she wants." Turning to Otto she asked, "When do you think they'll have the grave dug and the box finished."

"The box's no problem; it's a box. I'm guessing the ground'll be warm by late morning. The men have all offered to help dig. We should have it done by two."

"I'm willing to help dig, if you can use a city-boy."

"All hands are the same. Come on up when you're through with Josie."

Zona stood, quickly opened the door and bodies tumbled over each other in the hall. "Come back here this instant." Four kids

---

[1] $1,800 in 1910 was worth approximately $47,000 in 2019.

came slowly into the room. "If even one of you breathes a word of what you've heard, you're all going to catch it. Understand? All. And I mean catch it." They nodded with wide eyes, looked at each other, nodded again, and filed out.

Andrew easily picked Willy out from the pack. "Josie's very fond of your kids, Zona. I'm guessing you and Otto have done a good job raising them."

Otto beamed. Zona nodded almost begrudgingly, "They'll do."

Andrew stood, shook hands with Otto, nodded to Zona and thanked them for taking care of Josie and left.

When he was out the door, Zona looked at Otto and said, "What do you think? Is he an okay man?"

"What d'you mean, an okay man?"

"I mean, is he a man?"

Otto shook his head, "Sometimes you women are plumb crazy. He seems like a good man. What else would he be?"

Zona turned her back on him and shrugged.

Josie slept fitfully, tossing and turning all night. Andrew, trying to find a place his body could get comfortable on the floor, tossed and turned. When the bell rang for the miners, both were glad to hear it. Rising in the dark, Josie lit her lamp, built a fire in the stove, made her bed and dressed. Stepping outside into a cold, clear night, she hung a lantern from the nail over her stoop to let Andrew know she was up.

When Willy came into the store to see if Andrew wanted breakfast, he said he'd go make Josie some oatmeal to make sure she ate. He'd eat with her, but please thank his mother. As soon as he saw the smoke, he left, then saw a lantern's light in the breaking dawn.

He tapped softly and called her name. She opened the door quickly. "I put out a signal for you."

"I saw it, thank you. Did you sleep well?"

"Not so well. Were you able to sleep?"

"Not so well. I'm kind of boney for a floor."

She smiled and touched his shoulder. "Not too boney. Perfect."

He smiled. She seemed tranquil. "I've come to make oatmeal. You may remember, I know how. I also make coffee if there's any here."

"It's a luxury I don't afford. I do have tea. No raisins. A teacher lives a frugal life, you know."

"I don't know. I'm still a dependent. I'm given luxuries I don't earn."

"Andrew?"

A smile flickered across his face. "And now I say, 'Yes, Josie?'"

She nodded. "When are they going to bury Mr. Miller?"

"This afternoon, if the digging goes well."

"Will they have a casket?"

"They're building a box. It's what they do. The wood for it came on the train from the mill up the river at Norrie last night. I helped Zona put it in the store. It didn't occur to me what it was."

"I want him to have a marker for his grave. You said there's a marble quarry in Marble. Would they make a marker?"

"I suppose. It's not as hard as granite. You have lots of it up here and I'll bet one of your quarrymen could make you a marker with Mr. Miller's name on it."

"I want words too."

"We'll get a large stone."

"You'll help me with it?"

"I'll help you. I always want to help you, Josie."

She looked into his loving eyes. "I'll always want your help. I'll always need it."

He served the oatmeal and tea. She sat on the chair and he perched on the bed. Reaching across the table he put his hand on hers, picked up his spoon and began to eat. She was puzzled. "I never noticed you're left-handed."

"I'm either. I throw with my left and write with my right–because they made me. I'm not as one-handed as my father."

"I couldn't hit my mouth with a spoon using my left hand."

"Josie?" She nodded. "Do you want to say anything at the funeral?"

"I do. I thought about it after you left last night. I want the children to speak and sing. I want to read a poem and if I can, say a few words about friendship and education. Do you think that would be enough?"

"I think it's whatever you want to do."

"Will you see if the children will come to school for a little while? I want to talk to them."

"Are you sure?"

"Quite."

"After breakfast I'll talk to Zona about the funeral. You and I need to talk about something else as well."

"What's that?"

"I go home tomorrow morning. I have some important tests Monday."

Her eyes filled with tears. "Tomorrow?"

"I'm sorry." He wanted to go to her, but he knew if he did they wouldn't talk about the money. "Zona told me how much money Mr. Miller left you. It's a large amount, Josie. Zona isn't comfortable with it here in her little safe. If you trust me, I can take it to Denver and put it in a proper bank for you."

"Then what would happen to it?"

"It would earn interest and be safe."

"I want to give it to the kids, so they can go on to high school if they want. He thought education was important."

"Education is important. I'm sure he thought so too. If that's what he'd wanted to do, he would have left it to the school. I think you need to think about it when you're not upset."

"I want to write my words down, now. Money will have to come later. Unless you want the money, Andrew. Do you want it?"

"No, Josie. It's yours. He could have given it to anyone. He gave it to you."

"I don't feel right accepting it."

"Everyone you know will have a better use for the money than you have, in their minds. I don't think you should tell anyone what you received."

"Why not?"

"People here will ask you to lend them money for what they consider urgent. You'd have no resistance to the sad stories. Mr. Miller might have been able to say no. If they'd known he had that kind of a stash they'd have driven him crazy with 'needs'. My recommendation is for me to take it to Denver, put it in a bank in your name, let you think about it for a while, and if you decide, when you're not feeling sad, you want to do something with it other than keep it, then it will be there for you to use."

"When I asked if you wanted it, what I meant was," she hesitated, "for us?" She blushed and looked down. *Have I trapped him? He's never said 'marry'.*

A pained look crossed his face. He put both hands on the table and asked for hers. "My love, I've tried hard not to talk about a future with you because I want to do it properly, to give you something pleasant to remember. I have to say it now: Josie, will you consider marrying me?" He stood next to her, bent down on one knee, and smiled at her.

"I've been considering it for months. If that was an earnest proposal, yes, a million times over." She stood so he could rise and kiss her.

"I'll try to do it right later, I promise."

"It couldn't be righter, ever."

"Now, will you sit back down and talk to me about this money, please? I need to go help dig the grave."

"Do you want the money for us?"

"No. I hope I'll earn money for us. Not much, but enough. It would ease the first painfully frugal years for you. Other young couples have survived them; I think we could. It would be nice, though, for you to have a little money to make your life easier. Mr. Miller would like that too."

"You're right. I need to think. You may go. Please don't forget the children."

He bundled up and left.

Everyone from the small community gathered around the minimal grave. The pine box, lowered in, was not that far beneath the surface of the surrounding rocky ground. The foreman stepped forward and said Mr. Miller had been a steady and loyal worker at the kiln for fifteen years. He did his job, never complained, and the men would miss his thorough workmanship because he was always careful to do his job right. He stepped back.

To Josie's surprise, Tony stepped forward. "When our Matteo needed to go to the doctor and we had no money, I found a package made of newspaper tucked under our door with enough money to pay the bill. I hadn't told many people about our plight but I suspected he had overheard. I don't know for sure who left that money, but he was the only one who could have."

Another man came forward. "Five years ago when I got hurt and couldn't work for a month, Miller did my shifts as well as his. He insisted the paycheck go to my family. Later when I offered to repay him he just said no, I'd do the same for him, and that was the end of it."

The group was hushed except for people who were mumbling to each other and nodding their heads. It was as if there were more stories that could be shared if people were willing to talk. A silence fell.

Josie looked around, stepped forward, turned to the children who were standing in a group, and blew a note on the pitch pipe. She raised her hand and the children began singing along with the banjo and guitar players who added their chords to "Red River Valley." They replaced 'the man who loved you so true' with 'the children who loved you so true.' Josie stepped back. One of the children came forward and told how Mr. Miller always helped her with her boots. A little one said when they were reading she would look at him if she didn't know the word and he would whisper it to her. One of the older boys said he talked to them about how important it was for them to learn all they could now because it was easier to learn when you're young. The last boy told how Mr. Miller had helped him learn to play the guitar, how much he enjoyed it and couldn't have learned without his help. Henry stepped forward, to her amazement. He told how Mr. Miller had taught him to use carpentry tools.

Josie then read her tribute: "Mr. Miller was my friend, as he was yours. Meredith became his home. He said he had not known a home since he was a wee child and it was here, on Miller Creek, he felt close to the family he lost when he was such a young boy. It was also here in Meredith, where he found words to express himself and friends who listened to his words and helped him to see that his life had not been shameful, but instead a life of persistence and accomplishment. What he had lost by not having a loving family as your children have, he tried to regain by seeking an education. Your understanding let him

305

attend school, where he learned to read, write, and do numbers. He loved your children and I believe they loved him. You accepted him into your community. He would thank you for your kind, open hearts.

"Now I would like to read a poem by Robert Louis Stevenson who wrote this for his own tombstone. It seems appropriate for Mr. Miller too. The first part of the poem explains that he is dying. The last three lines tell what he wants engraved on his tombstone. It's called 'Requiem'.

> *'Under the wide and starry sky*
> *Dig the grave and...'"*

her voice crumbled. She couldn't go on. Andrew stepped from behind her, took the paper from her hand and with his arm supporting her, began.

> *"'Under the wide and starry sky,*
> *Dig the grave and let me lie.*
> *Glad did I live and gladly die,*
> *And I laid me down with a will.*
>
> *This be the verse you grave for me:*
> *Here he lies where he longed to be;*
> *Home is the sailor, home from sea,*
> *And the hunter home from the hill.'"*

With his arm around Josie's waist he led her to the edge of the grave, where she pulled from her coat pocket a drawing of Spring Beauty and placed it on the box. Each child followed her, putting his or her own flower drawing with hers. People whispered among themselves then began to leave. Some came by Josie to thank her, and to thank Andrew as well. Had it been a different occasion, Josie would have observed to Andrew they were checking him out, which is what many were doing.

When most of the people were gone, Zona came up. "I wasn't sure you could do it, but you managed."

"We managed. Now, I need to go home and be with my Andrew before he leaves tomorrow. You'll excuse us?"

"Go," she said kindly.

Andrew took her home and lay on the bed with her. There was no place for them to be near except on the bed. "Without you, there would have been no poem and I wanted that one because he was a sailor and a hunter. It felt right for him. Thank you for reading it. I couldn't."

"It's a soothing poem. I was glad to do it." They were quiet. "I thought the flowers were a creative idea since there couldn't be real ones."

She nodded. "I chose Spring Beauty because it's from the Miner's lettuce family. That seemed appropriate for him. I knew about that because of the book you gave me." It was peaceful next to him.

"Will you come to live with me wherever I land after we're married?" he asked.

"You don't want to come to Meredith to work the limestone quarry? It's mining."

"Not after today. Did you ever get blisters?"

She picked up his hands and there were puffy, watery blisters across his palms beneath his fingers. "Oh, Andrew. Those are terrible."

"Let's you know what a real man I am, doesn't it?"

"I didn't know that's how one could tell."

"In Meredith it is. If we're going to live here, I'm going to have to work up to it."

"I don't want you to live here. I want you to live where you'll feel best about yourself and when we're married I'll be there with you. Doesn't that married word sound beautiful?"

"Unbelievably. Now, let's get down to basics. What's to eat, woman?"

"You can't last for a day on a bowl of porridge?"

"Back to my question." His tender look softened his tease.

"I have food. Let's feed a real man."

She found enough food to satisfy him and they began to talk. "If Zona's concerned Mr. Miller's cabin could be robbed," she said, "do you think we should see what's in there and get what's valuable to either keep or give away?"

"I suppose. I'd like to help you with it. You shouldn't have to deal with a man's old stuff but it's not how I'd like to spend the rest of the day with you."

"I hope I know how you'd like to spend it."

"You do. Let's go. We can have a nice evening together, alone."

When they reached Mr. Miller's cabin, Andrew built a fire and lit a lamp to make it less gloomy. Although the cabin was made of stone, the walls were lined with pine. Mr. Miller was a tidy man. His few possessions were carefully stored and protected. *Huckleberry Finn* lay on a small, elegantly simple table at his bedside, his slate and chalk were close beside it. He obviously practiced his writing at night. She opened the cover of the book, saw her inscription, and read it with horror. "Andrew, look what I wrote to him. He said he didn't understand it and now I know why. When I told Zona what I'd written, she seemed shocked too. Oh, I hope he realized I didn't know."

She handed the book to Andrew. He read, "To my dear friend, Mr. Miller, who has made my life richer, Josephine Carter." Andrew understood her anguish. "He wouldn't have thought you'd say that, if you knew. It startled him for a minute. Did you explain what you meant?"

"I did. Zona asked me the same thing. I assured her I told him it was because he had been a good student and I was glad he was my friend. Really, Andrew, I had no idea."

"Of course, you didn't. You didn't say, 'Thanks for the money.'"

"No. I didn't know he had any money. So, what am I to do, for us, Andrew, not for me, because I do remember you sort of asked me to marry you this morning?"

"It was a 'sort-of' ask. It wasn't a 'sort-of' intention and I will ask you properly, I promise."

"No need. I do feel asked. Will we have children, Andrew? I'd love a little Andrew."

"I'd love a little Josie, but may they please have their own names?"

"Yes. Their own names, their own minds."

Getting back to work they uncovered his treasures and his necessities. Resting on a shelf were the books Andrew had sent. A beautifully made table and two chairs mystified them. Why two chairs? Why and where had he purchased such remarkable, spare furniture? On a nail hung a rope full of knots and under it a cord with a beautiful, complex knot. Andrew inspected the small pistol he'd lent Josie for her hike. A Winchester 94 rifle was hung on the wall. His kitchen contained a cast-iron skillet, a few pots and pans, a tea pot, dishes for a single person. A rough blanket, a heavy quilt, much used, and a thin mattress made his bed. Two extra shirts, an extra pair of pants and not much else.

They found a set of doll furniture, beautifully crafted, in a box under the bed. "Oh, Andrew, look at these." She picked them up, turning them over gently in her hands. "Do you think we may someday have a little girl? She'd love these and I would love her to have them. I always wanted doll furniture."

"I think I already know a little girl who would love them. Yes, you'd better keep those."

They discovered a toolbox with hammer, planes, chisels, saws, and a steel square, also under the bed. "Curious," Andrew mused. "Not a house carpenter's kit, more like a finish carpenter's tools. I wonder if that explains the table and chairs?"

"Did I ever tell you he gave me a letter opener of the most beautiful wood? It's so smooth and elegant, I love to simply feel it. He made it for me when I left last spring."

"Will you remember to show it to me? It's part of the puzzle of who he was."

She turned the tools over in her hand, observing how well cared for they were. "Would you like any of these, Andrew?"

"Please don't give away tools. I've never had my own because Dad has so many." He smiled, "If we're going to set up house one of these days though, dear Josie, you might need these so you can repair things."

"It would only be fair for me to have something to do while you're doing the washing and ironing. Do you want anything else to help you provide for us?"

"The guns. We may need to hunt to feed ourselves if I you decide you don't want to run a boarding house while I'm busy talking."

"You would never be content just talking. You'd want to play with your rock collection too."

"How do you know about my rock collection?" He couldn't remember ever mentioning it.

She rolled her eyes. Even in the solemnity of the project, they couldn't suppress their youthful joy in each other, this gradual discovery of the other's playful side.

Back to reality, he added, "I'd like you to have the pistol hidden somewhere. You're down in that cabin all alone and it would make me feel better if I knew you could defend yourself."

"Shoot somebody? Andrew, I couldn't."

"You could make a noise, wound them. You were going to shoot me, remember?"

"I was not going to shoot you. Well, maybe if you'd climbed into my tent without knocking first."

"I'll see if Otto will teach you how to use it since I don't have time. In the meantime, I'm going to remove the bullets so you won't have a second chance to shoot me." He opened the gun, removed the cartridges, and closed it. "There. You're harmless." He tucked it into a coat pocket along with a box of shells.

"I love this cast-iron skillet, Andrew. It's a treasure, the way he's kept it. They work so well; you'll love using it."

"I'm sure. Please don't ask me to pack it on our camping trips though."

"What are children for?"

They touched and continued to poke around, and found a drawer in the nightstand. In it, carefully kept, were the letters Josie had written to him that summer. She picked them up and held them to her heart. "I did love him, Andrew, like the grandfather I never had."

"We know he loved you too."

She sat on the bed, pensive, sad. She nodded. "I do believe he did."

At the back of the drawer they found a canvas snap purse with additional money.

Andrew quickly counted it. "I hope you'll take the money in the purse and spend it on something that will make you happy and will remind you of Mr. Miller. He'd like that."

"I can't think what that would be."

"I'm thinking of something enduring."

Her mind went to the intricate knot on the wall. She took it off the nail. "Look at this, Andrew. I would like a necklace with this knot as a pendant. Do you think someone could make it out of silver?"

"I think it would be an elegant reminder of him and something you'd wear close to your heart. He would love that.

When you come to Denver for Christmas, bring the knot and we'll find a silversmith."

She held the knot in her hand next to her heart. "Yes, it will remind me of him."

Struggling to rid herself of the melancholy mood, she changed the subject. "Would it be all right with you if we give the cabin to the community for a meeting room or library or whatever. If the quilters had a room, it would be so nice because no one's house is big enough for all the women and a quilt frame. I think they could fit in here."

"You don't want it when we visit?"

"I hadn't thought of that."

"So, you're not going to give it away right now?"

"Not yet. I think I'll make it available when we don't want it. No. I think I'll wait to decide with you. There's no hurry. Andrew?"

"Yes, Josie."

"If you come to see me, it would give you some place to sleep instead of on the floor."

"That would be nice." He looked around. "Do you think you've seen enough? I'll carry the tools, skillet, and rifle for you."

She took the guitar and banjo for the school room and the knot for herself.

They closed the door. There was no lock.

They put the guns, ammunition and keep-sakes in her cabin or in the school then went back to the store to get groceries for dinner. "There's isn't a great deal of variety, but we can get something to fill you up. Remember corned beef hash? I won't add any more potatoes this time and I'll serve it with poached eggs on top."

"I don't have mushrooms to offer, with or without worms."

"And none of that delicious bread with deviled ham, which I prefer to think about."

They were happy to be together and at ease. Josie was still subdued and Andrew tried to remember he was here to comfort, not court her. They bought supplies, eggs, bacon, and bread for breakfast and a sack of cookies for dessert.

They told Zona the plan for Andrew to take the money to Denver in the morning and she agreed to have it ready when the train came through. She also agreed to tell a few people it had gone to Denver, knowing it would spread like wildfire, so they wouldn't think it was either in the safe or with Josie.

Warming two cans of hash with eggs on top, opening a can of green peas, they moved around each other as if in a dance, touching, laughing about bumps, spills, unimportant things. *What a difference it makes to have someone I love here beside me. How empty it will feel without him, now I've had him with me.*

After they were seated, a candle on the table she hadn't used on the pack trip and had saved for some special occasion she didn't expect to happen, he raised his cup of tea to her. "To my precious love who said she'll be my wife."

Josie raised her cup. "To my best friend who asked me to spend my life with him. Or at least that's what I have in mind."

"It's part of the plan. We'll settle the details when Edward gets the contract ready."

They grinned, touched, grinned some more. Their conversation dipped into what life means. What did Mr. Miller find that made life worth living? Do we live because we can't contemplate not living? Why would a child struggle and suffer as he did instead of throwing himself overboard, which he said he'd considered? Why is death so fearful? Questions they acknowledged with a touch of humor were larger than they had time to address adequately that night.

The dishes washed and dried, they lay on the bed again for a final goodbye. The morning would allow for no affection. Before he left, she gave him the key to the box. "Andrew, please put it in the bank under both our names. I know no matter what happens, you will never take it from me. I also know death can strike anyone and I would want you to have it. Will you please do that for me?"

Everything in him said that was wrong. He told her so. She seemed determined. As a final argument he said his mother would disown him if he did what she asked. It was her safety net and every woman needed one in case her husband left her for one reason or another.

"Are you planning to abandon me?"

"Never. It's not always voluntary. You're making this more difficult than it needs to be. Do we agree it's going in your name?"

She nodded. "It's all so new to me. You first told me you love me a couple of weeks ago; now we're planning to get married someday. Suddenly I have more money than I ever dreamed of, a gun I'm supposed to shoot someone with, I'll need a safety net in case you leave me, you're going in the morning, and I'll have no one to talk to about these things."

"Yes, you will," he said gently, reaching for her hand. "You'll write to me and I'll write to you. We can talk as we always have. It will take a little longer, but we'll be together in our minds. That's what's so important: We have each other's thoughts to help us."

She leaned into him for comfort. He held her and stroked her hair. "Come outside, Josie. I want to kiss my future wife under the North Star."

The light was still burning in Zona's house, so Andrew knocked on her door. Henry answered. "Hi, Henry. Is your dad still up?"

"Yeah. Pa," he yelled as if it were a large house. "Andrew wants to talk to you."

Andrew could hear Otto grunt and mutter under his breath. "What can I do for you?"

"It's not me, Otto. It's Josie. She's taken Mr. Miller's pistol to her cabin at my request, but she has no idea what to do with it. I was wondering if you would show her how to shoot it?"

"I'll show her, Dad." Henry, who had drifted away, but not far, was quickly back at the door.

"He likes guns. He's a good shot. He knows the rules."

Animated now, Henry asked Andrew what kind of a gun she had. "I looked at it briefly. It says Harrington & Richardson on it. I've never had much to do with pistols so she'll have to teach me when you're through teaching her."

"Do you think she'd let me see it tomorrow?"

"I reckon she would, but make sure you don't surprise her. Who knows who she'll shoot?" He laughed. Otto and Henry stared at him. "I mean, she's afraid of it. She's not going to shoot anybody. I took the bullets out. You're safe."

They didn't smile. Realizing they found him dangerous, he made a quick thank you and said good night. *I've never met such humorless people.*

Otto looked at Henry, "We don't joke about killing people in this house, Henry." They nodded as they headed back inside.

The box with the money tucked under the clothes in his valise, the key in his pocket, Andrew was ready to go. With Josie at his side, crying because he was leaving, Andrew hesitated. When asked if he were going to get on or not, he boarded the train. He watched Josie from the window as long as he could, then settled down for a long trip to Golden, giving him lots of time to study for his tests, if he could focus.

"I'm glad he came for you, Josie. You needed him. Otto said yesterday he knew what the business end of a shovel was all about."

"He's worked construction for his father. I did need him."

"He's a good man." Zona nodded, convinced now he is a real man.

"He helps with the dishes."

"A very good man."

When Zona mentioned to Otto that Andrew helps with the dishes, he commented he knew there was something fishy about him.

Josie spent Sunday cleaning Mr. Miller's cabin, putting things out for others to take, and carrying some things to her own cabin. She took his pans, utensils and dishes to her place and carried the ones the ladies had donated to her cabin up to the store, asking Zona if she thought they would like them back. Zona thought they would.

She asked Zona to come look at things she couldn't imagine ever wanting, like his clothes, the worn quilt and blanket, to see if they should simply burn them instead of giving them away. "There's almost always a use for something here, Josie. A dog would love a warm bed to sleep on. They cover a dynamite blast with old blankets to keep fragments from flying. I'll tell people you have some things here you don't want, and we'll see if anyone shows up. You and I better be on hand, though, or they'll haul the walls away, so make sure you've gone through everything and can defend what you want to keep."

The table, chairs, and bedside table she thought might represent his handiwork so she wouldn't part with those. She wanted the cook stove to stay so if she and Andrew did come to visit they could prepare their food. She wanted the bedstead. It was narrow and they would need something larger after they were married, but it would do for Andrew. She'd use some of the money in the purse to buy a new mattress and bedding. The shelves were to stay, the firewood, lamps, lanterns, and basins would stay for Andrew. She shook her head at what seemed the emptiness of Mr. Miller's life. *All that money. I suppose he felt he had to have a reserve on hand. How many hours of labor did it take to save that amount? And what kind of labor? Was he a little hungry all his life so he could save for a time when he didn't have a job or he got too old to work?* The sadness of his lonely, spare life and how her life would now have a safety net made her pensive.

Cleaning and sorting finished, she found Zona and said she was ready for people to come look. Zona told two kids to spread the word and she and Josie returned to the cabin to defend what she wanted to keep. People started arriving almost immediately, looking, picking up small items like a razor, towels, the quilt, and blankets. Neighbors looked around for treasures and were disappointed to find so few. Zona explained about the dishes and many went home by way of the store to pick up items they'd donated. It wasn't the free-for-all Zona predicted and most were respectful of Mr. Miller's possessions. Josie was glad for this. She hadn't wanted them to scorn what he owned. She did notice a reticence in people, as if she were somehow different. Because of the inheritance? Zona and Olaf had agreed never to tell what was in that box.

The evening seemed long, as indeed, it was, with the sun setting so early. She ate her meager meal, not tasting it, wishing Andrew were there in the absence of busy-work and people. She usually replied to Andrew's letters, letting him be the first to write. Tonight, she needed to write, she didn't think he would mind.

December 11, 1910

My Source of Strength,

How I wish you were still with me. Not only to help make sense of this peculiar position I'm in, but to have you here to comfort me. I feel so strangely alone, as if I've arrived in some foreign place with no friends, family, or anyone to turn to. Please don't misunderstand. Zona is there when I need her. People who came to pick up things I didn't think we'd ever want, were courteous but different, somehow. I can't quite figure it out. I suppose after a while we'll settle into a new relationship or go back to the old one. Mostly, they're not you and it's you I need.

I brought all of Mr. Miller's kitchen equipment down here and gave the ladies back things they lent the "new schoolteacher." I gave away his personal items you didn't want. I guarded the stove, furniture, and shelves but no one seemed inclined to take them. I cleaned his cabin thoroughly before anyone came because that's the way he kept it. Our rummaging made it messy.

I went to Mr. Miller's grave today for a few quiet words with him. I think of how much he denied himself to save money and I wanted to tell him I will honor his sacrifices, although I have no idea what that means. How many years did it take him to save that amount?

I don't know if the poem was truly appropriate for him because I don't know that he would say: "glad did I live" or "gladly died" or "laid me down with a will." I think he survived most of his life and it was only in the last year or so he gladly lived. Maybe that's why he left the money to me, because after so many disappointing days he looked forward to one instead of dreading what it might bring and remembering what days had brought in the past.

Thank you for letting me talk to you tonight. You make me feel comfortable telling you my thoughts, even when they're poorly formed. What I most want to thank you for, though, is coming to Meredith: to stand beside me; to take care of me; to remind me that your love will sustain and protect me. The memorial would have been impossible without your being there to support me. I do love you,

Andrew. I earnestly believe I always will. I'm going outside now.

Yours forever and ever,
Josie

Having arrived safely in Golden, his mind as ready as it was going to be for tests the next day, he wrote to Josie.

Both were weary after an emotion-packed weekend. Writing to a person they believed cared about their thoughts was a sedative and both easily fell asleep.

The quarry bell seemed to be ringing earlier every day. Josie didn't like rising in dark, lighting her lamp to find her way around the cabin. It felt like a violation of nature to rise before the sun. She wondered if animals, not ones that ran around all night, ones she saw during the day, got up before sunrise. *Wouldn't they want to stay in their little beds keeping warm until the sun comes up? I do. I wonder if Andrew likes to wake up in the dark of night.* She remembered his rising at four-thirty to help her make her train. *I don't think he does that regularly. I hope not.*

She had barely dressed when there was a knock on the door. Surprised, she opened it tentatively. It was Henry. "Hi, Miss Carter. Andrew said you have a gun and I'm going to help you learn to shoot it. Do you suppose I could see it and take it home, so I can make sure it works okay before you try it?"

She had to suppress a laugh. "I agree, that would be the thing to do. In fact, I have a half-box of bullets so why don't you take some of those with you, so you can make sure it works."

"Really? Okay. I'll try it out for you."

"Come on in. It's cold out there." She went to her dresser and fished out the gun and box of ammunition and handed them to him. He handled the gun as if it were a new baby, awe and mystery wrapped in a small bundle. "Be careful, Henry. I'd hate to think you got hurt trying to help me."

"I'm always careful. I've been taught the rules."

"There are rules?"

"Oh, yeah. I'll teach them to you before you shoot. I've gotta' go to work now." He put the pistol in one pocket, the cartridges

317

in the other. He saw her genial look. "Thanks, Miss Carter." She nodded as he turned to run up the trail.

I thought he might be mechanical or is that "boy" writ large? I hope he doesn't hurt himself or somebody else. I guess he knows the rules, whatever they may be. Andrew seemed okay with his teaching me.

Expecting the pupils to feel toward her the way their parents did, she went to school with a feeling of dread. The children entered, somewhat solemn, as if they had been told she would be sad and they should behave. Or was it that they were sad? They, too, had lost a friend. She wanted them to tell her what they were thinking.

When they were all seated, she asked if anyone wanted to talk about Mr. Miller, his funeral, or how they felt now. All were silent until a second-grader raised her hand and said, "I liked Mr. Miller coming to school with us. Reading is hard at first and it made me feel better to know it was hard for him too, even though he was old."

"The knots he showed us how to tie have sometimes come in handy," one of the older boys offered.

"I didn't know he taught you how to tie knots." Puzzled, Josie asked, "When did he do that?"

"Last summer, when you were gone. We met at school after supper and he taught us knots, guitar and how to make cuts in wood. That's how Henry knew how to make his box."

"Henry made his box?"

"He was his best pupil. He loved making things. He and Mr. Miller put the window in the door. See?"

"I had no idea. I thanked the school board but no one said how it happened. I should have thanked him. *For so much.* How many of you did he teach?"

"Us big kids, mostly. Sometimes our dads would come along. He made us do everything perfect. Made us clean up our messes too. He was really fussy about that."

"Where did he learn to make things?"

"A factory. They made furniture. He liked it but not the way they treated children, he said. He left for the country because he was tired of people."

"I see. So, some of you have good memories of Mr. Miller?"

318

There was a chorus of yesses. "How did you feel about what I said at his funeral?"

"It was okay," said a fifth-grade girl, "but I wished you'd said a prayer for him. My mother said she'd never been to a funeral where they never prayed someone's soul would go to heaven."

Her heart sank. "Oh, my. You're right." She shook her head. "How could we forget? We should have asked someone to say one for him since we didn't have a minister or priest." *This explains it. We didn't send him off properly.* "Let's all close our eyes and be quiet for a minute and if you pray at your house, please say a prayer for Mr. Miller, and if you don't pray, please think some kind thought for him." They all closed their eyes and after a minute, Josie said with a catch in her voice, "Goodbye, Mr. Miller. Thank you for being our friend." The children raised their heads and smiled. "Will you all please tell your parents I'm sorry we forgot the prayer and ask them to say a prayer for him?" She could feel a sigh of relief in the children, as if they had taken care of some unfinished business. The mood changed. In their minds Mr. Miller was now on his way to heaven.

To break the somber mood, she told them of her plans for Saturday night supper to celebrate Christmas: they would learn new songs; guitar and banjo players would have solos; they would make holiday decorations; each child who wanted to would tell a story or memorize a poem. It would be a big night. The kids who liked to perform were excited. The shy ones not so.

After class Willy lingered awkwardly by the door. "Do you want to ask me something, Willy?"

"Henry won't let me touch the gun because he said you gave it to him."

"And you want to look at it too?"

"Well, you know, to see how it works."

"Have you ever shot a gun, Willy?"

"A rifle."

"Has Henry ever shot a little gun like Mr. Miller's?"

"No. But he thinks he knows everything and he doesn't."

"I know you want to look at it too. Why don't I talk to your mother to see if you can handle it?"

"Would you? I really want to."

"I'll come by later. She'll decide who can touch it."

"Okay." Gone, like a leaf in wind.

Thursday, she hoped for a letter and wasn't disappointed. She had two letters. She read the first one he had written the evening he got home and the second he wrote after he received her letter mailed the morning Mr. Miller died.

December 11, 1910

My Tender, Gentle Love,

All the way home I thought of you. I kept trying to study. I hope some of those things my eyes read sank into some crevice in my brain. I'll find out tomorrow; tonight I don't care.

Leaving you this morning, crying, was one of the hardest things I've ever done. A man watching us part said to me, "You'll never see her again?" I was embarrassed because I'll see you in less than two weeks. I said, "We've been to a funeral." "Oh," he said as if that explained everything. It explained nothing. I wanted to cry because the thought of being without you for almost two weeks is unbearable and seeing you cry makes me want to cry. I didn't think he would understand.

I thought a great deal about your inheritance. You'll be relieved to know it made it safely home and tomorrow I'll put it in the bank in your name.

I told you briefly Henry is willing to teach you to shoot. I imagine he was there at the crack of dawn to look at the gun. He seems to love them. My guess is he's a particularly mechanical boy. I wish we could get him somewhere those talents would bring him the most satisfaction. It's when I thought of Henry and the absence of opportunities in Meredith to learn what would benefit him most, I began to understand what you were saying about helping kids there go on to high school, or as in Henry's case, to an apprenticeship, if they want to. We need to talk or write more about the money. You have generous instincts the Scot in me wants to squelch. I'll try to be a supportive partner in this.

My parents said to tell you hello. I don't know why they said that because I didn't tell them I was going to write to you. I suppose it seemed logical I would. Or is logic something one can apply to love?

My dear heart, I wish I could havé stayed with you longer. I know you could have used my help finishing up the cabin, cooking dinner and doing dishes. We'll have a long week over Christmas, but we won't ever be alone together, I'm guessing. How (where) could we be? Anyway, we'll be together even if we must share our time with others.

Good night, my precious one. I hope you get some rest after a very tiring week. Hold me in your arms. I'll go look at the North Star now.

Your companion for life,
Andrew

And his second letter.

December 12, 1910
Early afternoon

Springtime in Winter,

The letter you wrote and mailed before Mr. Miller died came this morning. It all seems a long time ago you wrote so charmingly of "ha'nt" and ghosts and being "planted and comfortable." I hope the trials of the past week have gone and you're back with kids you love, doing what you love.

I have no news since last night except the tests went all right this morning. I pictured myself on the train reading and hoped whatever was put in my brain then would come out on the paper. I'll let you know if it worked. If it didn't, I hope you'll like being married to a student who has to repeat a few classes.

Let me know how the shooting lessons go. I'm anxious to know if I'm safe when I'm within range. I've sent you a box of cartridges. Yes, Henry can have some of them. (I'm assuming you won't have that many intruders.)

I love you, my darling.

Your lonely boy,
Andrew

He was right. It seemed a long time ago she'd written about those things. Some weeks sail by, others mark a change in one's life. That week marked a change. She realized they had not made plans for the holidays and she didn't want him to wonder when she was coming home.

December 15, 1910

My Winter Warmth,

I have reservations to come home on Thursday, the twenty-second with great expectations, not Dickens' style! to be with you. Will you come to our house for Christmas dinner? We usually eat around noon. When my father is home, we eat at exactly twelve o'clock. I'm anxious to introduce you to my family. Be aware, though, it's not the same atmosphere as at your welcoming home now that Mother has gone. Honestly, it never was.

I realized last night I know so little about you. Does it make you more attractive to me if you're mysterious? You couldn't be more so, attractive, that is. Still, if I'm to explain you to my family, they will have basic questions I can't answer.

When is your birthday? How can we do a horoscope to see if we're compatible if we don't know?

What is your middle name?

What do you plan to do with your life? I'm anxious to hear.

What per cent Scot are you and where did they come from and when? I hope not Dundonald. We could be related.

Do you like haggis? Why not?

I'm being silly, but there are many factual questions I've never asked you.

As you predicted, Henry showed up at sunrise Monday to see if he could see the gun. He quivered to touch it. I let him take it and gave him the bullets so he could practice before teaching me. He agreed to take them! Willy stayed after school to complain Henry won't let him handle it. I talked to Zona who said Willy could touch it the next day. She also said Henry couldn't waste the bullets until I was with him. I doubt that made Henry happy. What is it about this gun?

I had a real awakening in class on Monday and found out one reason why people were so different with me: No one had prayed for Mr. Miller at the funeral. It wasn't omitted on purpose. I asked the kids to pray for him and people seem to have moved on.

I also learned Mr. Miller had instructed kids and some fathers during the summer: knot-tying, carpentry, the banjo and guitar. Henry made his coffin. This explains Mr. Miller's tools. He worked in a furniture factory once, which I suppose inspired the doll furniture. It also explains why the boys were so quick to learn the guitar and banjo. In my mind they were musically gifted. They were gifted, by Mr. Miller.

The hidden lives of others. What we don't see to appreciate or, I suppose, to not admire. I said you are mysterious. Do you have a secret life you would like to tell me about? Or hide? I guess you wouldn't tell me about that because then it wouldn't be hidden. I'm not mysterious or enigmatic. Is that another way to say boring? I hope not.

We're getting ready for the Christmas program: songs, poems, decorations.

Have you thought any more about the money? I'm glad you thought about Henry doing something mechanical because he obviously has an aptitude. I would love for him to go to high school and learn more math and science. Your thought of an apprenticeship is also attractive. It's kids like him I want to help.

I love you more than you can know.

Yours eternally, whatever that might mean,
Josie

She sealed her letter and realized she had not told her family she was coming home.

It's more difficult to write this simple note than a whole page to Andrew. What if Father won't let him come? What if Andrew won't come? He'll come. He loves me. Oh, Father, please be nice to him. Don't ruin this for us. I do love him.

December 15, 1910

Dear Father, Margie, and Dot,

I will be coming home December 22. There is no need to meet the train as I will be travelling lightly and can make it home alone.

I have taken the liberty to invite a special friend to Christmas dinner. His name is Andrew Allan and we have been friends since August. He is in his senior year at School of Mines and he lives in Golden. I hope you will find him interesting. I'm anxious for you to meet him.

Sending you Christmas greetings, I look forward to seeing you.

Love,
Josie

She had to write to Andrew out of sequence. They were running out of time to exchange letters.

December 17, 1910
A cold Saturday

My Protector,

It was shooting lesson day. We started as soon as the sun had any warmth. Henry had made a target, a box with a circle painted on it. He shot the gun twice to show me what happens when you pull the trigger. He took out all the bullets, so I could feel the gun in my hand. Next came the rules. #1. Always assume a gun is loaded. #2. Never point a gun at anything you don't intend to shoot. I know you two are trying to make me comfortable enough with it so that if I should ever need to defend myself I could. I thank you both for wanting to take care of me. I'm trying to learn how to do it correctly, but I don't really want to shoot a gun as I think men do. You see it as a marvelous mechanical invention, something that has evolved from canons to this compact device that shoots bullets instead of balls and caps or whatever else poor soldiers used to kill each other. Henry showed me if I want to scare something or if something is close, I should just point it and pull the trigger. I will have five shots. If I want to hit something at a distance, I should cock it first, aim it, then squeeze the trigger. He spent time showing me how to aim. When it was my turn to open the gun, load it, cock it, and point it at the target I was so nervous I could hardly pull the trigger which, he told me, I should do slowly and not with a jerk. He said I should be surprised when the gun goes off because I squeezed it so slowly. Need I say I was surprised even though I squeezed fast?

Andrew, you would have been so disappointed in me. I missed the box completely four times. Finally, on the fifth shot, I hit the box. Not the circle, mind you, the box. We will practice again tomorrow to make sure I remember what I was supposed to learn today.

I wrote to my family saying I want to bring you home for Christmas dinner. My sisters will be all a-twitter with what that means. My father won't understand how I could know a man well enough to invite him home without his having met and approved of him. He will know I've become a fallen woman, as expected.

Six days until I am in the same city as you. I can hardly breathe I'm so excited.

Your love,
Josie

P. S. The box of cartridges/bullets/shells/ammunition came. Has any single item ever had so many names? The boys are beside themselves with envy. I shared some with them. I have not confessed to owning the rifle as well. I'm afraid they'd have a shoot-out or whatever old-timers called them.

Saturday supper was the last before her trip home, so the children performed their skits, songs, poems, and recitations on the seventeenth. The parents all agreed they would welcome repeat performances on Christmas eve which delighted most of the kids.

As she feared, Sunday proved to be clear weather and Henry was at her door again.

"Ready to go, Miss Carter?"

He was never this eager for school, I'd like to remind him.

It didn't go much better. Having written the rules to Andrew she had a slightly better grip on them. Her grip on the gun, however, had not improved and she still jerked it when she shot, meaning she regularly missed the box until her fourth shot when she inexplicably hit the circle. She didn't know if she were more amazed or Henry was, but they agreed they had used enough bullets.

"I'll clean the gun for you, Miss Carter, so it's ready when you come home."

"That is so kind of you, Henry. In the meantime, maybe you'll let Willy come out and shoot it. You can each have five bullets."

He hesitated, not sure he wanted to share the gun then decided it might be more fun with Willy. "He's been wanting to shoot it."

"I thought so. I know you'll be careful since you know the rules. Now, I'm cold and I think I've had all the lesson I can benefit from today. Thank you, so much Henry. You've been a patient teacher."

"Can my dad shoot it too? He's been wanting to."

"Of course, he can. Do we have fifteen bullets left?"

He nodded, looking a little sorry about sharing with others. "I think so."

Monday, she mailed her letters and that evening received one from Andrew.

December 14, 1910

My Radiance,

When you said you could tell me your thoughts, I was so happy. Once a friend said he didn't know who he was, which made me wonder who any of us is and at the time I decided: We are what we think and do. You and I will want to discuss that resolution. Thoughts tell us a great deal about a person. How better to know you than for you to share your thoughts with me? What a person gets around to doing tells us a lot too, although my grandpa didn't seem to think so.

I believe Mr. Miller wanted his gift to bring you happiness. You will have to decide what that means. I will listen and try not to influence you unduly. I may ask questions, though, if I think you haven't thought of something. I hope that will be all right.

Aunt Janet asked if you are coming for Christmas. She invited you to stay with her, if you'd like. You and I were recently together and yet we didn't talk about when you're coming for Christmas. Please let me know your plans as soon as possible. My family celebrates Christmas at noon with a big meal and you are cordially invited to attend. My brothers and their families will be here. Everyone brings something. They have this disgusting term for it: potluck. Like we're all eating out of a pot and we're lucky if we get any. It turns out to be quite a nice feast and not too much work for any one person—meaning any woman. I've noticed the men stand around and feel grand about themselves and the women tolerate it. This is so you can prepare yourself!

I would like to reserve Christmas eve with you. May I escort you to the Brown Palace for dinner? I've made reservations for seven o'clock.

Please hurry to me. I find I miss you more every day.

Yours always,
Andrew

P. S. I passed the tests.

Excited children had difficulty focusing on their work. The decorations in the room reminded them Christmas was coming and for the little ones, that meant Santa Claus, no matter in which language they chose to say it. Older kids were aware they were to keep the secret, even though the ones who had figured it out a year or so before were the ones most likely to want to spoil it for the younger ones. Josie pondered this strange tradition of deliberately telling children a lie. It did create a magic in their lives they didn't otherwise have, but Santa Claus wasn't a uniformly generous elf and she found that difficult to explain.

Like trying to justify "all men are created equal" when they studied the Constitution, which was obviously not true.

On the twentieth she received a telegram. "Will meet train. Andrew." By the time he knew her travel plans, he didn't have time to get her a letter. She began to pack: two new dresses; good shoes; Sunday dress; practical clothes; bath crystals to share with her sisters; the purse with the extra money from Mr. Miller; the money she'd saved from her salary so she could buy her sisters something special and something nice for Andrew. But what would that be? She packed the blanket to return to Mrs. Allan in the travel bag Aunt Janet lent her, the sketchbook he'd given her, mittens, yarn and needles to finish the sox for Andrew she started a month ago. She'd have hours on the train.

The morning of the twenty-second she was on her way.

WINTER, 1910

The train out of Colorado Springs was half an hour late leaving and it upset her because Andrew would have to wait. What a relief to pull into Union Station. She couldn't tell if it were Andrew with another man bent down looking at the wheels of the train as it pulled in. When they stood, she was horrified. The men were Andrew and her father and the two women at the side were her sisters. She couldn't move. How was she to greet them? What would Andrew think when she wasn't glad to see him, and she wasn't now. The train stopped. People began moving toward the door. She looked out her window and Andrew had spotted her and was smiling at her. She waved timidly. He looked confused, then noticed the girls with the man were waving to her. He tried to understand what was going on. The man stepped forward. Andrew stepped back. Josie came down the stairs almost white with panic. Her sisters ran forward and hugged her. Her father nodded. Josie excused herself and went to Andrew who was standing back, not knowing what he should do. She took his arm and led him forward.

"Father, Margie, Dot, this is my friend, Andrew Allan."

Andrew extended his hand to her father; her father seemed stunned. "I was just talking to you."

"Yes, sir."

"I didn't know."

"Neither did I, sir."

"We wanted to surprise you, Josie," said Margie. "Father wouldn't let us come in the dark alone."

"Well, let's go home. You'll join us, Andrew?" Father surprised them.

"I'd be pleased to join you."

On the streetcar Father asked Andrew to sit with him. Josie and the girls sat behind them. They could hear Father asking him questions about the sand on the train tracks. The girls didn't talk. They were too astonished.

When they reached the house, Father took Andrew into the room where he was building his ship. The girls could hear Andrew asking questions, Father answering, at length. They couldn't remember his talking this way since the boys left. Suddenly, here was a stranger and he was sociable. Josie was as uncomfortable as she could ever remember being. What if Andrew said the wrong thing to Father and he got angry? She'd wanted them to meet so Father could see he was a responsible young man and would consent to her marrying him. She did not anticipate they would become friendly. How could she? She had never known her father to be friendly to anyone outside the family. Was there a side to him she didn't know? She longed to be with Andrew. If she couldn't be with him, she would like to be with her sisters, yet she wasn't with anyone. The girls were silent trying to hear what was going on. It was maddening, yet she couldn't change it. She also didn't know if she should rescue Andrew from her father. Then she heard him pose another question about sailing. *If he wants to be rescued, why does he keep the conversation going? Doesn't he want to be with me as much as I want to be with him?*

Taking her travel bag upstairs to her room, she was filled with frustration and disappointment. The girls followed so they could ask about her "friend." Known each other over four months. Met him when she was out hiking. Were together over Thanksgiving. In Golden. Stayed with his aunt. A nice family. Didn't want Father to know she was in town. Yes, they have kissed.

She told them she would be going to Andrew's house for Christmas dinner and hoped they'd understand. She would explain to Father how important it was to her. She would bring Andrew home for a light supper with them.

Opening her bag, she pulled out the two dresses for them to see. They were, as she had been, dazzled. Margie, the seamstress, examined the workmanship in them. Dot held them up to see what they would look like on her. "You know, Josie," observed Margie, "I think the coral one could be made more flattering for you. Will you let me work on it?"

"I don't think we have time before Christmas eve. That's when I want to wear it."

Margie's eyes danced. "Oh, yes, we do. Look what I have!" She pointed to a large object Josie hadn't noticed. "My new sewing machine. I bought it with money from my seamstress jobs. Oh, Josie, it's such a miracle. Come watch what it does."

It was a marvel. "Of course, you can fix the dress. What do you want to do?"

"This empire cut isn't right for you. You don't have enough bust to carry it off. You do have a nice waist, though. If I can find the right fabric, we can make it show off what you have instead of emphasizing what you don't."

Josie threw her arms around Margie. "You have the best eye in the west. If you can make it right for me by tomorrow night, I will love you forever."

"Otherwise, you won't?" she laughed.

"I will always love you. You, too, Dot. It's so good to be with you again."

"Josie?" It was Father at the bottom of the stairs. "You have deserted your guest."

I've deserted my guest? You kidnapped him. "I'll be right down."

Andrew was grinning at her when she entered the room. Father went to sit in his chair, leaving them nowhere to be alone. "Let's sit at the dining table where we can talk, shall we?"

Aching to touch each other, they sat at the corner of the table. "I was wondering if we could meet tomorrow. I thought you might like to go downtown to shop for some presents since you can't do that in Meredith. I will accompany you."

"What a great idea, thank you. We can meet in front of the May Company. You do know Mr. May got his start in Leadville, don't you?"

"I didn't. Will he mind our using his place for our meeting?"

"I think he'll approve. Will ten-thirty be too early for you?" *Please say you'll be there.*

"I'll be there." *I would follow you to the ends of the earth.*

They longed to touch. She felt his hand under the table on her arm. She held it in her hand.

They smiled. It was better than nothing.

Father stood. They quickly retrieved their hands. He came to the table, sat, and said he had a few questions. Josie looked at him panic-stricken. *Is he going to drive Andrew away?*

He directed a question to Andrew. "If you live in Golden and Josie's been in Meredith, how did you two meet?"

Josie answered, fearful Andrew would give his fanciful story. "I was out hiking, Father, up to a lake. Andrew came up the same trail after I did, and we struck up a conversation, then wrote letters."

"Were you alone, Josie?"

"I was."

"You started talking to a man when you were out in the woods, alone?"

"He was polite."

"Weren't you afraid of him?"

Andrew answered with a wicked grin. "Not terribly afraid because she had a gun."

"You had a gun?"

She wanted to kick Andrew under the table. "A friend lent me his."

"A man friend lent you a gun?"

"He was an old man, Father, much older than you. He was my good friend."

"He isn't still?"

Her voice trembled, "He died two weeks ago."

"Oh. I'm sorry." He paused. "You knew how to shoot it?"

"He told me to point it and pull the trigger. It would make enough noise to frighten most things."

Andrew joined in. "She's since learned to shoot it and can hit a target."

Josie coughed to hide her grin.

Father looked at Andrew then at Josie. "I don't think I understand you anymore, Josie. Off hiking alone, talking to strangers, shooting a gun, an old man for a friend. Is this what they mean by a modern woman?"

"I don't know what they mean. I know I'm trying to live my life." Josie was irritated. *He never talks; why does he have to talk tonight?*

"Then you wrote letters to this stranger who was polite?"

"I was interested in the wildflowers and birds and he kindly sent me some beautiful books so I could identify them."

Father looked at Andrew. "That was generous to do for a stranger."

Andrew answered, "She wasn't an ordinary stranger."

Father looked at Josie as if he hadn't seen her before. "Oh."

Father stood, somewhat perplexed, said it was time for them all to turn in and waited for Andrew to rise. Then he extended his hand to him, shook it, and said he hoped he would come for supper tomorrow night. Andrew accepted.

Father waited until Josie had seen Andrew to the door. *Not even a good night kiss.*

"Ten-thirty, right?" he confirmed.

"Yes. I'll see you then." She could hardly be nice to Andrew she was so annoyed with her father.

Father was standing at the foot of the stairs waiting for her. "I approve of your friend. I'm not sure I approve of you, but I'll try to understand. I hope you can keep him interested. He'd make a good catch someday."

That does it! "I don't intend to catch anyone, Father. I hope someone will love me in return. And I hope that someone is Andrew." She wanted to stomp up the stairs as she had done when she'd been sent to her room as a child. She tried to remember she was a woman and women don't stomp. It would have been very satisfying though.

Father watched her go, mystified why she was so peevish. He'd asked the young man to come to supper to help her out.

Upstairs Margie had disassembled the coral dress. Pieces lay on the floor. Josie felt overwhelmed. It was too much, this coming home to family.

"Look, Josie, if I can find a piece of fabric to go with it I can make a high-neck top with a dropped waist and gathered skirt like this, and the sleeves will be perfect as they are, and it will be really beautiful."

Those sewing puzzles were Margie's strength. They weren't Josie's. "I don't quite get what you're doing, but I trust you. I have some money you can spend on fabric if you really want to take this on."

"I'll have to. You can't wear it the way it is." Josie tried to see the humor and felt thankful she had a back-up dress.

"Can you go to bed or should I stay up to help you sew?"

"I'll probably stay up because I'm having such fun. And don't forget, the machine will do the sewing!"

It had been a long day. She excused herself from her sisters to go to bed. She needed to escape and besides, she was meeting Andrew in the morning.

Denver was so much easier to get around than Meredith. There were no piles of snow everywhere. She took the trolley to Sixteenth and got off at Champa. It was ten-fifteen. Andrew was waiting for her.

"I don't suppose we could find a place where I could steal a hug?"

Christmas shoppers crowded the streets. "Let's go into the store and find a corner where clothes are hanging and we can be alone for a few minutes. I'm desperate to be with you. I couldn't believe my father last night. It was perverse how he occupied your time."

"It was okay. I want to get to know him. He needs to know me so he'll let me marry you."

"He couldn't stop me."

"You've warned me about that stubborn streak."

"I truly wanted to stomp up the stairs last night, so he'd know I was mad at him."

Andrew raised his eyebrows. "Is stomping how I'll know when you're mad?"

"I can't imagine I ever will be with you. If you're naughty I'll probably let you know my displeasure. I don't hide it well. You won't ever be naughty, will you?"

"I don't think men are typically called naughty. I think they're called men." He enjoyed his joke.

She grimaced. "I about kicked you under the table when you brought up the gun."

"Solving your problems with violence, Josie? How manly of you," he smirked.

"I would have thought you'd say childish."

"If I'd thought of it, I might have."

"Somehow, you always pull off your naughtiness."

"We're back to manly, aren't we?"

"Andrew?"

"Yes, Josie."

"Will you tease me all my life?"

"I hope so. I love to watch you squirm."

"I hope so too. I love to give you pleasure."

She wanted to put her arms around him. She wanted to be alone with him. Looking around the store, it was as if they had planned it to give no one a place to hide. She shook her head sadly. "I guess the hug will have to wait unless you have an idea."

"I do. They've completed Daniels and Fisher tower but it's not open yet. Maybe somewhere around there we can find a corner. Can you walk a few blocks?"

"I could walk miles for this."

She took his arm, they headed out. They were crossing the alley when Andrew said, "Let's slip down here a little way. There are doorways where we could hide."

She loved it. She would be an alley cat. They found a doorway and held each other for a few minutes. Her mood so improved by his closeness, she felt ready to take on shopping for her sisters, her father, Aunt Janet, Andrew's parents, and something for Zona.

"I have nothing thrilling for you, Andrew. I haven't an idea what would make you happy."

"You. Having you beside me makes me happy. Do you hate to shop for presents as much as I do?"

"I've never shopped for presents before. We always made something for each other. I knew it would be the wrong thing and they'd have to live with it to please me, and they'd make me something I'd have to live with. It makes no sense to me, this compulsory gift-giving."

"Can we agree not to do this after we're married?"

"Can we start right now?"

"No. I already have something for you you'll have to live with. You don't have to get anything for me, though. I'm a big boy; I can handle it." His hangdog look begged pity. "Don't worry about me."

"Ahhh. If you'll tell me something you'd like, I'll get it for you. Do you want a necktie or a walking stick? I've seen gentlemen with walking sticks."

"They look completely pretentious. I can't imagine what they do with them. Can't they walk without help? No, thank you, for one of those or a necktie. You forget I play in dirt."

"Maybe some soap, then?"

They laughed, touched, shopped, had lunch, shopped more.

"You're coming to our house for dinner tonight. I hope my father behaves himself and hasn't come up with more interrogation for you."

"He wants to know whom you've gotten tangled up with. He loves you or he wouldn't care."

"I suppose. He said last night you'd be a good catch. It made me angry with him."

"Must make him glad you're home. You don't think I'd be a good catch?"

"I don't like to think of catching you, like a fish flopping on a hook." She looked impish. "I prefer to think of trapping you." It was easy with him. He made shopping bearable.

Josie had explained to her sisters about Christmas dinner and the importance of her going to the Allans' instead of being home. The girls agreed she should go there and Josie and Andrew would come for a light Christmas Day supper.

They arrived at Josie's house where Dot had made a delicious pork roast with potatoes, gravy, and canned beets. For dessert she had made butterscotch pudding. Andrew said all the right things about the supper. Josie was proud of him.

Father had been relatively silent during the meal, the girls asking Andrew questions instead. Two older brothers, no sisters, older girl cousins. Always lived in Golden. A home builder. A suffragist and feminist. A horse and buggy. A truck. Liked to read and explore.

He had been patient with their questions, even trying to introduce humor when he could, especially about his mother's feminism and what it meant relative to the men's doing housework. They were amazed a woman could make men do that.

So was Father. "Do you mean to tell me your father helps in the kitchen?"

"We all do. We don't know any other way and I think we enjoy it. It's a time we're all together doing something. It's why I can go camping and do my own cooking."

"Your father's been working all day. Isn't he tired when he comes home?"

"Yes. Mom's tired too. She's been cleaning, washing, ironing, tending her garden, and raising us boys. She's also been Dad's bookkeeper all these years. He says the difference between a man's successful small business and failure is frequently having a wife who works alongside him. Now that she has time, she marches and talks to politicians. I think that would be the hardest work. She wants to change the world by getting rid of child labor and cruelty to animals."

Father thought about this a while. "What do you plan to do for a living?"

"When I graduate I'll have a degree in engineering. I could be an assayer, a land surveyor, a geologist, or a mining engineer."

"What do you intend to <u>do</u>?"

Josie blushed for Andrew. *I was afraid we'd get here. He won't know what to say.*

"I'm not sure. They've offered me a job teaching freshman chemistry. I haven't accepted. My dad says I can help run his company."

"Did you need an education to do that?"

"Not the education I got, I suppose. I studied a lot of math and science. I'd use some of that on the job. I know you can find out a lot in books. If I do go to work for Dad, I'll have to study about carpentry and masonry and whatever else we'd be doing. I can learn."

Josie added, "You worked summers for him for years, and you've been doing estimating for him."

"I've learned a lot doing that. Essentially building a building in my head."

Father looked at him as if he were judging the suitability of a piece of wood. *An interesting boy. Yes, he'd be a good catch.*

Nice. Smart. "And you boys turned out all right, doing dishes and mopping floors?" he asked with barely concealed humor.

Andrew responded with gleeful mirth. "Oh, we turned out splendidly, sir. <u>All</u> the girls say we're the best catches in town." The table erupted in laughter. It was like a pine bough springing up when it sheds its burden of snow.

Father stood up from the table, gathered his dirty dishes and headed to the kitchen. The girls were speechless. They'd never seen him touch a dirty dish before.

Margie and Dot reluctantly left the table and Josie said she had to help with dishes and so excused herself, leaving Andrew alone. He followed Father into the living room and pulled up a chair beside him. "I know you don't know me well, but I would like your permission to ask your daughter to marry me. I have reason to believe she will accept."

"Marry her? Already? You don't know her well enough."

"I believe I do."

"Does she know you well enough?"

"I believe she does. We've corresponded regularly for four months and I love your daughter, sir. I will try to be a good and faithful husband."

"I wasn't prepared for this. I told her last night she should try to keep you interested and I guess I didn't need to."

"No, sir, I'm interested. I think I always will be."

"Well, I'll be switched. Josie. I wasn't sure anyone would want her."

"I assure you I do."

It took a moment for Father to gather his thoughts. "I like you. I don't know you well. If you love her and she loves you, then I'm not going to stand in your way. But know this, if I ever hear of your mistreating her, I'll come down on you. I won't allow any of that."

"I'll never do that. If I did my folks would come down on me as well."

"She can be willful, you know."

"My mother, sir, is willful. I know how to live with a determined woman. I admire a certain amount of it."

"I hope she won't give you too much to admire." He shook his head. "She's a good girl, hard-working, honest, sometimes too honest, and she's kind. Her mother was partial to her."

"She loved her mother dearly."

"We all did." He looked away lest Andrew could read the sorrow in his eyes.

The girls burst into the room, laughing, until they saw the serious looks on the men's faces. Andrew stood up, put his chair back, and asked if Josie would join him at the table. She would. The girls and Father faded into the background.

Their hands slipped below the table and found each other. They were content.

"Mom says I need to leave you alone tomorrow so you can spend time with your family, wrap your packages and get ready for our Christmas Eve supper. It's not supposed to snow so Steve is letting me borrow his car so we can go in style. Is it all right if I pick you up around six-thirty?"

I wonder if his mother will always be there to protect me. "I don't want a day away from you, but your mom is right. I need to do all those things. I'll be ready at six-thirty, anxiously waiting to be with you."

Their hands tightened, they looked at each other in understanding.

Father stood, announced it was time to turn in and waited for Andrew to depart. They shook hands, nodded silently to one another. Josie showed Andrew to the door. "Until tomorrow."

"Until tomorrow." He touched her cheek with his hand.

Upstairs Margie was on her knees cutting fabric she had found for the dress. It was a cream silk with coral-colored flowers embroidered on it. It was perfect with the material in the dress.

Josie was amazed. "How did you ever find fabric that matches so well?"

"I'd seen it last week when I was at the store. It's what gave me the courage to take this on. I was pretty sure it would match. You're going to be so beautiful he won't be able to help falling in love with you."

Josie smiled. "That would be so nice, Margie. Do you like him?"

"Ever so much. I'm sorry he doesn't have a little brother."

"I'm sorry for you too, but I understand his brothers are very different from him. Now, may I help you?"

"This is play for me. Please get your beauty rest."

Josie gave her a hug. She was a very special, talented girl and she did love her and Dot. They were trying to make this a happy time for her.

Christmas eve day and there was excitement in the house. Josie had bought real wrapping paper and ribbons for them. The dress, stunning in its new form, had to be tried on, fitted, and tried on again. Father had been unlike himself at breakfast. He had asked the girls their plans for the day, had offered to help them in any way he could, and had taken his dishes to the kitchen. The girls caught each other's eye.

Around five o'clock, the dress, finished and pressed, awaited a freshly bathed Josie. The girls, fussing over what to do with Josie's hair, were like schoolgirls getting ready for their first party. "I know," a delighted Dot cried, "let's braid it with some of those pretty ribbons she bought for the packages. It will be so festive." Josie showed them what Aunt Janet had done. She wasn't sure Andrew needed another hairdo to get used to. But the ribbons, yes.

They chose the green– and cream–colored ribbons and the braiding began, ending with the braids wrapped softly around her head like a Christmas wreath. Josie agreed. It was pretty. At six-fifteen she dressed and went downstairs. Father was waiting. He didn't say anything. He turned and left so they couldn't see his tears. Shortly, he returned. He handed Josie her mother's cameo brooch, a perfect color for the dress.

"She'd be so proud. You are radiant, the way she was." He turned and left again, this time they knew why. Margie pinned it at Josie's throat under the high collar. It was perfect.

The doorbell, a hush fell on the girls. Father reappeared, in control, answered the door and led Andrew in. The two girls, side by side, watching expectantly how he would regard Josie, held their breaths.

He came to her, took her hands in his, "You are beautiful beyond words. Will you go to dinner with me?"

Everyone in the Carter household sighed in relief.

"I would love to go to dinner with someone as handsome as you." He was handsome, dressed in a suit and tie, a gentleman to escort his beautiful lady.

Josie kissed her sisters and father goodbye, thanking each for making this such a special night and they departed. Three pairs of eyes watched the couple get into the car; none of them had been in one. Neither had Josie. She wasn't sure what she should do until Andrew opened the door and helped her in. Andrew had left the car running so he wouldn't have to go through the ordeal of starting it again. She told him this was her first ride. He admitted it was his first time driving a car although he'd driven his father's truck. It was cold inside. He put a lap robe over her to keep her warm.

At the Brown Palace restaurant a man in formal wear greeted them and took them to their table where Andrew had requested they be seated at adjacent sides so they could be close. People nodded as they walked by, a young couple, well dressed, obviously out for a special evening. Only the tattered book bag Andrew carried marred the look of elegance.

Menus delivered, offers of aperitifs declined, they opened the menus to select their dinners. Josie, looking around, asked, "Are you sure we can afford this?"

He reached for her hand. "My folks are giving us this for our Christmas presents. They hope we'll enjoy ourselves. I'm to order for you. They were afraid you'd not do it well." This assumed gallantry amused him. She found him delightful.

"Do they come here often?"

"I don't know if they've ever been here. Prince wouldn't like the trip, you know."

"Is that why you borrowed your brother's car?"

"It is. And why Mom borrowed Edward's suit for me. I hope you understand you're really going out with the whole family tonight."

"And you're going out with your cousin. This is a dress Aunt Janet gave me, except Margie made it over so it would look better on me."

"Beautiful on you."

"Thank you. Here we are, all dolled up, pretending to be people we aren't. It's fun."

"So, at midnight, will we turn back into our peasant selves?" he joked.

"I won't mind. I feel so rich with your love I couldn't ask for more."

The waiter came, asked if they were ready to order. Andrew said, "We're unfamiliar with these items. We want nice dinners. Will you please help us?"

"I'd be honored, sir."

He looked over the menu and suggested some options that weren't the most expensive. Andrew chose what he suggested for Josie and himself.

"You should have delicious dinners with those selections." He left, they grinned at each other. It was like a fairy tale.

They talked easily. Soon the food began to arrive.

Andrew received pickled herring, Josie a lettuce salad with fresh vegetable garnishes, something she hadn't had all winter. "How do they have lettuce, tomatoes and cucumbers now?" she asked Andrew.

"I think they have access to hothouses. It's what money buys."

Small cups of lobster bisque followed for both. Josie had never tasted anything so rich and creamy. She didn't know what a lobster was. Andrew explained.

Tournedos of beef with sauce béarnaise for her, rack of lamb for him. Celery braised with cream and blue cheese, butter-basted stuffed mushroom caps—worms not included.

They ate with relish, sharing bites, excited by the luxury and delicious flavors.

"Do you think he chose the most expensive dinners for us? I hoped he was taking care of you, or rather, your parents." Josie asked.

"I think there were more expensive things on the menu. I can't imagine they would taste any better. Please don't expect this after we're married."

"Please don't expect me to cook like this."

"I'll love whatever you cook."

"It's not my strength; I'm not sure I have one. I can clean. I know how to do that. Maybe you should do the cooking."

"Maybe you'll develop a knack for it." They laughed. It was an enchanting night.

The waiter cleared the table and asked if they would like dessert. They looked at each other. Andrew spoke, "Will you help us again. You've done wonders so far."

"Certainly. I would suggest the strawberry Bavarian for mademoiselle, the crème brûlée for monsieur. And coffee?"

"Please." They waited to see what in the world they had ordered. It was like opening presents.

Yes, the desserts pleased them. Yes, the coffee was like nothing they had tasted before.

Yes, that was all. Except it wasn't.

Andrew reached into his book bag and handed Josie a medium-sized white box. It was heavy and there was a pile of cotton on top tied down in a most peculiar fashion with red twine. She looked at it, then at Andrew with a question. He smiled but didn't say anything. She stared at the package, then at him. He was quiet, his eyes twinkling. She knew there was a riddle. She studied it, then squealed. "It's a diamond hitch. You threw a diamond hitch." They reached out to touch each other.

The three tables adjacent to theirs quit talking and started watching the proceedings.

"May I untie it?"

"Please."

"Did I ever tell you I untied your beautiful diamond hitch before I got to the train? Willy would know I hadn't done it and I wasn't ready to acknowledge you."

She studied the box and untied the twine, removed the cotton. Underneath was a folded piece of paper. "I hope you like pretty rocks too. With all my love, Andrew."

"I love pretty rocks, Andrew. They remind me of you."

She lifted the lid. Resting on cotton was a round, gray rock. She was confused. She looked at him.

"May I help you with it?"

She handed the box back to him.

He lifted the top of the split geode and showed it to her. It was full of crystals.

"True beauty, Josie, is often hidden. You are beautiful to me tonight, but your true beauty is inside. That beauty is why I love you."

He handed the box back to her. She looked at the rock then up at him.

Resting on the crystals inside the bottom of the geode was an engagement ring. "Will you please marry me, Josephine Carter?" She couldn't speak. She nodded. Andrew removed the ring, lifted her hand, kissed it, and put the ring on her finger.

"Well done, lad. Well done." Clapping came from the three tables surrounding them. Josie and Andrew, surprised, looked at the people congratulating them.

"Waiter. We need a couple of glasses of champagne," an older gentleman called.

Andrew thanked them, Josie thanked them, and the noise level picked up. People seemed to share the excitement.

The champagne arrived. Andrew thanked the gentleman and toasted Josie. "May we always love as we love tonight." He was full of good spirits. His surprise had worked.

"May I always remember to remember what a special, kind, loving man you are."

He turned wistful. "But a man."

"I should have said person."

"No. I am a man. We both need to remember that. You are a woman. We'll need to remember that as well. I think we can work around those obstacles, though, if we keep a sense of humor."

How could I love him more? Will I ever deserve such love?

"I believe we'll keep this happiness. I believe in us, Andrew." She reached out to hold his hand. "Thank you for the most extraordinary proposal. It was like opening one magic box after another, and coming at last to the perfect gift." She held her hand out in front of her to examine the diamond on her hand. "It's a very pretty rock, Andrew, about the prettiest rock I've ever seen. I will love growing old with it and you."

The waiter brought the check and Andrew quickly checked the addition and put a $10 bill on the tray.

"Oh, Andrew. Were we that expensive?"

"We'll get change. My father said to leave a ten percent tip. It should be easy to figure, even your fourth-graders should be able to do that."

"Some of them." It made her a little sad. Dinner cost more than her week's salary. She looked around the room at the elegantly dressed women, the suited men smoking their after-dinner cigars and drinking cognac from crystal snifters, not that she knew what she was seeing. Thinking of the workers in Meredith struggling to feed their families, the opulence didn't seem right. "I don't mean to cast a shadow on this precious evening, Andrew. So you know, I don't aspire to this lifestyle. I would like a fairer world than this represents. I will always treasure the memory of feeling so extravagant, but I don't need to repeat it. Well, maybe for our fiftieth?"

"We have a deal. If the Brown Palace is still here, we'll return to do it again."

After showing the nearby tables the geode and ring, they left the sumptuous surroundings of the hotel. At the cold car Andrew helped Josie in, covered her, got in, pulled the choke, primed the engine, set the magneto, and got out to crank it. The engine didn't want to fire. He cranked repeatedly and she was surprised to hear him say a bad word. Finally, the engine sputtered to life and while it warmed, he lit the headlamps. As they drove, Andrew asked Josie if she would please use his comb to scrape the frost from the windshield. "You may prefer a car, but there's something awfully nice about heading Prince home and tucking hands and feet under a blanket."

"Andrew?"

"Yes, Josie."

"Where did you find the rock?"

"They're called geodes. They're found all over the world. Yours came from Utah. A professor collects them."

"It's very interesting, all those crystals poking up, makes you wonder how they got in there."

"Josie, Mom made me promise I wouldn't go into the science of how they're formed. You're tempting me and that's wicked, because she will certainly ask you." They laughed, snuggled closer, and she scraped frost.

They drove almost to her house. He stopped, not letting the engine die, "I would love to hold you here in private before I take you home. I suspect your father is waiting up for you and you know what that means."

"My father! I'd completely forgotten about him." She held her hand out to look at the ring. "Oh, Andrew, how can I tell him? He'll be so certain I'm doing something foolish again."

"You don't have to tell him. Last night he gave me permission to ask you to marry me."

Astounded, "You asked him?"

"Dad said I had to. Your father said if we love each other he won't stand in our way."

Josie sighed. "That must be why he let me wear the brooch. It's what he gave my mother the night he asked her to marry him. He was crying tonight, Andrew. I didn't know why. And he's been so different since you came. He's talking to us."

"Maybe the ice dam broke and the river behind it can flow again. He's a nice man, Josie. Think about his life. After he got sick he had burdens too heavy to carry. To live, he moved his family to another country where he knew no one. He was dependent on his sisters–humiliating for a man, his wife died, then his boys. He lost more than his health. He lost his sense of being able to protect and provide for you. That's almost too much to bear."

"And trying to raise three girls by himself. That alone would make some men cranky."

"And make them stricter than they'd be otherwise, I suppose. Then to have a strong-willed daughter who wouldn't mind." He took her cold hands in his, "I think he was happy to give you away. I didn't have to convince him." He found this funny. She couldn't switch from feeling sorry for her father to finding it amusing she'd been difficult for him.

"I was rebellious. I didn't want to be protected. Poor Father. You've saved him a certain amount of grief, you know. I'm afraid you didn't make the most of the dowry tradition. You were in a good bargaining position." She could be lighthearted again.

He folded her cold body into his arms. The frost on the windshield deepened as they spent precious time together, alone, until the cold drove them home.

When they pulled up to the house, they saw the curtains pull back then close. They opened the door to a family standing, waiting. Josie and Andrew were amused.

"Yes," she said and held out her hand for them to see the ring. The girls circled her with hugs. Father shook Andrew's hand and congratulated him then put his arms around Josie and held her silently, tears running down his face.

"I hope you'll be the wife your mother was."

It was bittersweet for her and her father. "I'll try to be as loving as she was, Father. Mother was special, though." He nodded.

"Come in, we have a surprise for you." The happy girls had put up a Christmas tree, the first since Mother died. Father had brought one home, telling the girls they needed some cheer in the house.

When Andrew left, he told Josie he would come to get her in the morning and they would ride the trolley to Golden. She would have none of it. "If you'll meet me at the station in Golden, I'll be okay. You'll have to come back with me for supper here, that's enough trolley rides for one day." He reluctantly agreed. She gave him packages to take home with him in the car. They said good night at the door, everyone watching.

Christmas morning, Sunday, church bells rang throughout Denver. The Carter family rose early, as usual, and gathered around the Christmas tree. The girls exchanged presents and for the first time in years, Father received a gift. His slippers were worn through, the new ones had fleece lining. He seemed pleased.

Wearing her altered dress, boots, an engagement ring, and carrying her good shoes, Josie caught the streetcar, transferred to the interurban trolley, and went to Golden to meet the family. Andrew was at the stop waiting for her.

"Hello, my beloved. Have you changed your mind?"

"Never. My family is delighted for me. They admire the ring you chose. They're planning the wedding which we're all assuming you intend."

"It did cross my mind."

Walking to the Allans' house they bantered cheerfully. Reaching it Maggie and Angus greeted them with great affection. "We're so thrilled for Andrew," Maggie said.

"Very pleased to welcome you to the clan," Angus added.

Josie described again the elegant evening and thanked them for the beautiful memories they had given them. After coffee and conversation Josie asked Andrew if she could give them their presents. He brought them and handed them around. Angus received beautiful leather gloves, Maggie, a warm scarf to match her mittens, Andrew a pair of socks with a piece of yarn going through the stitches where toes should be.

"Won't my toes get cold?"

"I don't know how long your feet are. I'll put in toes after you try them on." He pulled his socks off and she was surprised to see his pale skin. It felt intimate. She blushed. He looked at her, confused.

"I've never seen your bare feet," she whispered.

"No. I've never seen yours, either." They looked at each other with new wonder. There was so much to learn besides what was in letters.

Maggie and Angus witnessed this brief encounter with fascination, each recalling those moments in their relationship when it had been fresh and confounding.

"Excuse us, please. I need to look at how long I need to make them." She couldn't do it. She couldn't pick up his foot with those naked toes to see how much farther she needed to go. She turned to Maggie, "What would you guess?"

Maggie picked up Andrew's foot and said, "I think you need about what it'll take to make the toe." She patted his foot and put it down. "Don't worry, Andrew, someday she'll love your piggies." Everyone laughed except Josie who felt she had let him down, somehow, by not being willing to touch him. Andrew saw her distress and reached to take her hand.

"When you're good and ready you may send my piggy to market," and he squeezed her hand.

348

She tried to change the embarrassing subject, "I have another gift for you." The note on it said, "For my Savage Friend." He frowned and looked at her. "Have I been a savage to you?"

His parents raised their eyebrows. What had he done? Josie was silent.

Andrew turned the package over and looked at it for a further clue, looked at Josie for an answer. She said, "Maybe you should open it if you don't understand."

He unwrapped it. "Is this the sketchbook I gave you?"

"It is."

"You don't want it?"

"No. It's yours now. Maybe you'll open it."

The first page said, "To Savage Lakes memories. Thank you for your kindness, for teaching me, for sharing your thoughts. From your friend, Joe"

"Oh. I didn't understand. Of course, Savage Lakes."

The first page was a child-like drawing of the topography of the North Fork and the Savage Lakes area. The following pages included drawings of a donkey, a sagging tent, a coffee pot and skillet, a mushroom, the night sky. The next page said, "Thank you for finding me and letting me know you and helping me know myself. Your devoted friend, Josie."

"You've cut a page out of the book here. You changed your mind?"

"It was out of sequence."

The pages that followed included a buck at the lake, a braid poking out of a tent, a harmonica, a mountain range partially seen through binoculars, a columbine, a coney, an engineer's hat, a tent strung tightly, pine and spruce needle cross-sections and descriptions, Andrew sitting at a lake, a gun, the school house, a bouquet of wild flowers, branches covered with birds, two overlapping envelopes with each of their names on them, a steam locomotive, a swing on top of a mountain, Prince, Mr. Miller's grave, an elegant dress. Tucked into the back was the missing sheet: it was a drawing of the diamond hitch. Under it she had written, "You've thrown a diamond hitch on me."

He closed the book gently, "I'll treasure it forever."

"I hope you'll treasure the memories."

His parents were watching, waiting to see the book. "May we see it, Andy?" Maggie asked.

"It will require some explanation," Josie offered. Then she told them the truth about their meeting, showing them the drawings and telling them how kind Andrew had been to her strange boy, how honest he'd been when he found out she was a girl, then his promise to keep their trip secret.

"I'm proud of you for your kindness and honesty, Andy," Angus said, "but a little amazed you had to see her braid to figure it out."

"She had on pants."

Angus rolled his eyes. Maggie came to Andrew's recue. "She has an honest face, Angus. You doubt so much, Andy. You question everything. It's good to know you accepted someone for who they said they were. And Josie, I admire your determination to think for yourself. It's always risky to step outside the boundaries, but important to think about who made the boundaries and why and if one agrees."

Much discussion followed about her adventure and what it had been like to be a boy. Maggie expressed jealousy for her hiking in pants. Josie confessed Andrew had supplied her with a similar disguise to climb Mount Galbraith, which explained why she had been able to get to the top. His parents looked at him as if he were a stranger. Where had their loner boy gone? Love had transformed him.

Before the full family arrived, Aunt Janet showed up.

She pulled Josie aside, "I'm so happy for Andy. You suit him perfectly."

She thanked Aunt Janet then twirled around. "Do you like it?"

"You look lovely. Is that one of the dresses? I don't remember its being so pretty."

"It is, sort of. My sister said the empire look didn't flatter me and I needed flattering, so she found this material and altered it. I hope you don't mind."

"Mind! You look elegant. Your sister's a gem. Speaking of gems, may I see the ring?" She took Josie's offered hand, admired Andrew's taste, and kissed Josie on the cheek. "May you have long, happy lives together. I believe you will."

Soon the brothers, spouses and children arrived and gathered in the parlor. Andrew took Josie around the room, introducing her. Edward didn't seem to be the prig Aunt Janet had painted him, yet when she playfully thanked him for letting Andrew look so elegant the night before he merely nodded. His wife was genuinely nice and pregnant. Steve was cheerful, and when she thanked him for letting them travel in style, he elaborated on the refinements of his car and how much it had cost. His wife, reserved and cold, gave Josie a finger-tip handshake. Edward's two kids were dear. She wanted to play with them to avoid the grown-ups. Questions asked, answers given, details about their meeting obscured.

Breaking into the conversations, Maggie asked them all to listen to her. Angus stood beside her, his arm around her waist. Aunt Janet was at her other side.

"Today, I would like to invite back into our family our dear little Bessie." She had to pause to finish what she had practiced. "Twenty-two years ago, she passed from our lives and the pain of losing her was too much for me to bear. She deserves to be a part of this family. We deserve to have her bright spirit among us. She was a delightful little girl. Her brothers loved her, Angus and I loved her, her aunts and cousins loved her." She turned to Janet who held her hand. "I long ago asked you to keep memories of Bessie to yourselves. Now I ask you to share them so she will live in our hearts as she should." She turned to Angus who held her, then to Janet who held her.

Janet responded, "What I frequently remember about Bessie is her infectious laugh. One couldn't hear it and not join her."

"I remember putting her to bed at night. Instead of asking me for a bedtime story, she would tell me one," Angus said.

There was silence. Maggie said, "I remember her smile. It was Josie's smile that broke open my heart and unlocked precious memories. Bessie lit up the world with her smile."

Edward offered a sweet memory of Bessie sharing her beloved doll with him when he got hurt. Steve remembered hearing she covered him with her blanket when he was sick. The floodgates opened; the memories flowed. At first so painful for

Maggie to hear, she soon found the stories healing. The group broke up and started talking about childhood memories that didn't necessarily include Bessie, but the feeling was freedom.

Maggie sought Josie. "When you told me how you and your sisters tried to keep your mother and brothers alive in your hearts, I realized how I had denied all of us the joy of remembering our little Bessie. Thank you for this precious gift."

The dinner was noisy. Personalities emerged letting Josie see Aunt Janet's perspectives, though not agreeing whole-heartedly with some. It was late afternoon before Josie and Andrew left to join her family for Christmas supper. She asked him if he would spend the night at their house. They needed time to discuss what to do with Mr. Miller's gift. He could sleep in her brothers' room. She didn't think her father would mind. He agreed on the condition if it displeased her father, she would let him come home.

Dot prepared a vegetable soup for supper, knowing they had feasted at noon. Father was in good spirits and engaged Andrew in conversations about geology that had intrigued him for years. It was a cheerful dinner, so different from what Josie had dreaded of Christmas that she had trouble reconciling it with reality.

Father was pleased to have Andrew spend the night. Breakfast saw Father off to work, Josie and Andrew meeting to talk about the inheritance. By the end of morning they agreed half the money should go into a fund managed by the Meredith school board to lend tuition, and as much room and board as needed by a student who wanted to go on to high school. College tuition, room and board would also be lent as the fund allowed, priority going to students to finish high school. The students would be responsible for repaying the fund so pupils following them could have the same opportunities.

Most of the remaining money they would invest as a safety net for themselves and future children. Andrew was adamant Josie should have a small fund for things she couldn't justify buying with their money.

This serious thinking demanded relief so they went for a walk. Coal smoke filled the air. After a few blocks, Josie surprised Andrew, telling him she found the city confining and unpleasant. She hoped they would be able to live in the clear, fresh air of the mountains someday. He had always dreamed of living there but couldn't imagine finding a girl who felt likewise. This opened possibilities for work outside a city. They walked together comfortably, their minds independent and yet remarkably in accord.

Tuesday, they met Edward at his law office to draw up the agreement for the school board. He advised them on safe investments, never expressing curiosity about why Mr. Miller had loved Josie enough to leave her such a nice fund. She marveled at an attorney's discretion and felt no one else in the family would ever know of the gift.

The next day they went to a silversmith's and she showed him the knot. He turned it over in his hands and said, "Are you Celtic?"

"Why do you ask?"

"My mother was Welsh. She called this a St. Justin Knox knot. Celtic knots are used for decorations. I'd love to make you a pendant. Show me how large you want it."

She used some of the money in the purse for this.

The remaining two days of her visit they spent talking of their future and enjoying learning about one another. They were able to quickly pick a date for the wedding because they wanted it to be as soon as possible. Josie's last day of school was June 2, Andrew graduated on June 4, the wedding would be the following Saturday, June 10. A small wedding with family and a few friends, some punch and cake, and they would begin marriage's great adventure.

It was difficult beyond her imagination to board the train, leaving him there that cold, early Saturday morning. It would be two months before he would come to stay in Mr. Miller's cabin for a weekend. It seemed an eternity. There was a difference though from previous departures. They had a plan for their future and, as painful as parting was, their love felt secure.

ABOUT THE AUTHORS

Judy and Lynn met in 1957 while working summer jobs in the Frying Pan River valley. They started writing letters after Lynn had to put down Judy's horse on a pack trip in the remote mountains surrounding the North Fork. Married in 1960, they moved in 1961 into a one-room log cabin where they lived while building their own log home in the North Fork valley. At the time, theirs was the only residence in that valley, their nearest neighbor living three miles downstream. Winter access to their home four months of the year was by snowshoes. When their two sons reached school age they moved to the Snowmass Creek valley where they have lived for over fifty years.

Made in the USA
Coppell, TX
08 August 2020